Changing
Seasons

Other books by Betty Palmer Nelson

From the series Honest Women

Private Knowledge
The Weight of Light
Pursuit of Bliss
Uncertain April

Changing
Seasons

1954–1980

Betty Palmer Nelson

St. Martin's Press ✖ New York

Illustration by Nancy Resnick

Acknowledgments appear on pages 367–369, which constitute a continuation of this copyright page.

Library of Congress Cataloging-in-Publication Data

Nelson, Betty Palmer.
    Changing seasons   /   by Betty Palmer Nelson.—1st ed.
    p. cm.
    ISBN 0-312-13942-X
    1. Women—Tennessee—Fiction.   I. Title.
    PS3564.E429C48   1996
    813'.54—dc20   95-40953
                                                                                    CIP

First Edition: February 1996
10 9 8 7 6 5 4 3 2 1

In memory of my grandparents:

Nannie Mai Scott Proctor, 1898–1990
Lillian Russell Burnett Palmer, 1899–1983
Luther McDowell Proctor, 1890–1988
George Taylor Palmer, 1894–1960

Now the unsatisfied psyche in her emotional aspect wants . . . to love more; her curious intellect wants to know more. The awakened human creature suspects that both appetites are being kept on a low diet; that there really is more to love, and more to know. . . . Art and life, the accidents of our humanity, may foster an emotional outlook; till the moment in which the neglected intellect arises and pronounces such an outlook to have no validity. Metaphysics and science seem to offer to the intellect an open window towards truth; till the heart looks out and declares this landscape to be a chill desert in which she can find no nourishment. These diverse aspects of things must be either fused or transcended if the whole self is to be satisfied; for the reality which she seeks has got to meet both claims and pay in full.

—Evelyn Underhill, *Mysticism*

Gabriel Axel's *Babette's Feast*

What can be made is made,
What given, given;
And if we do not taste,
No fault of wine or leaven.

Afraid to take, we fail
By fixing on the rare
To recognize the bounty
Everywhere.

–BPN

Contents

Principal Families

This is the fifth and last novel in the Honest Women series. The Hendersons have appeared in all the novels; the Laniers appeared first in the fourth, *Uncertain April*. This genealogy presents characters as they first appear in *Changing Seasons* and omits all characters except direct ancestors from the earlier novels.

Hendersons

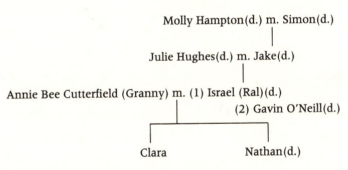

Molly Hampton(d.) m. Simon(d.)
|
Julie Hughes(d.) m. Jake(d.)
|
Annie Bee Cutterfield (Granny) m. (1) Israel (Ral)(d.)
(2) Gavin O'Neill(d.)

Clara   Nathan(d.)

Laniers

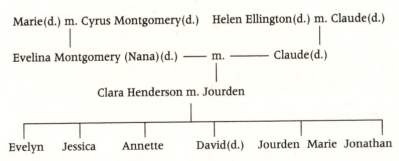

Marie(d.) m. Cyrus Montgomery(d.)   Helen Ellington(d.) m. Claude(d.)
| |
Evelina Montgomery (Nana)(d.) —— m. —— Claude(d.)
|
Clara Henderson m. Jourden

Evelyn   Jessica   Annette   David(d.)   Jourden   Marie   Jonathan

Book One

Winter

And I awoke and found me here
On the cold hill side.

—John Keats, *"La Belle Dame Sans Merci"*

I. Greg
Setting Out

*T*here was no fanfare, no warning, certainly no thunder or lightning. The girl just came into the Laundromat when Greg had half finished his wash. She answered his greeting, filled three washers, and sat down on one of the tables with a paperback.

Nobody else was around, and he had already counted all the rose-embossed squares of the high ceiling in the old building. He was glad to see anyone else still up and moving. He speculated about her. It was already ten o'clock, so she didn't live in the freshman girls' dorm. She acted like an upperclassman, too: no silly giggles or coy glances. Besides, she wasn't with a bunch of other whispering girls. She looked like a lot of other people with her black hair and blue eyes. Like himself, for instance.

Greg had put everything all together into only one washer, and when he took his clothes out, all the whites were pink from his new Harper College red T-shirt. He put them in the dryer and started it.

"You're supposed to separate colors, you know," the girl said. "You must be a freshman."

He grinned. "You got that right. My name's Greg Beall, B-e-a-l-l, not B-e-l-l."

3

"Mine's Evelyn Lanier. Next time, put your reds and blacks by themselves, even if they aren't a whole tub; they're the worst to fade. And make your whites another tub. Everything else can pretty much go together."

"Thanks for the lesson. What are you reading?"

"*Emma*, by Jane Austen. I'm an English major."

Her tubs stopped spinning then, so she went to move the clothes to a dryer. He watched her sort her clothes for drying. She had lace underwear. He wondered if his mother wore things like that; he didn't think so. "Why did you become an English major?"

"Mainly just because I've always enjoyed reading. What's your major?"

"I don't know; I haven't decided yet." Greg's dryer stopped, and he felt the clothes. Most of them were dry, but he left them all in, set the dryer on the lowest heat, and said, "Here goes another dime. Do you know Winston Beall?"

"Is he a junior?"

"Yeah. Business major."

"I think I know him. Is he your brother?"

"Yeah."

She looked at him. "You don't look alike."

"No. We don't think alike, either."

She smiled. "You make it sound like a decision."

"It probably was, sometime. Now it's just the way I am."

"I have a sister here too: Jessica Lanier. She's a freshman."

That certainly rang a bell. Jessica had caught his classmates' eyes right away. Someone in his hall had dubbed her "the Goddess." She looked like a cross between Marilyn Monroe and Liz Taylor, and all the freshmen figured she'd be picked up by an upperclassman right away. But so far, she had snubbed everybody, freshman or not.

He looked at her sister. She wasn't built like Jessica, and a fellow wouldn't spot her in a crowd. But nothing was wrong with the way she looked.

She raised her eyebrows. "I see you've seen Jessica. We aren't much alike either."

"No; when I say something to you, you don't look off into the air somewhere."

She smiled. "I guess I should say thanks."

He acted on impulse. "Would you go out with me this weekend? We'll do whatever you want to."

4

She looked down then. "I didn't mean to lead you on. I'm engaged." She held out her left hand, and he saw the ring.

He didn't like whoever she had gotten it from. "Is he here at school?"

"No; he's already gotten his degree and is in grad school at Tulane. He's a biology research assistant." She said it like a royal title.

"Since he's not here, maybe you'd let me take you places anyhow."

"Why? Are you looking for a status symbol?"

"What do you mean?"

"Somebody to take around just to show that you have a date?"

He grinned. "I can get a date if I want one. But I want you."

She shook her head. "I . . . couldn't do that to Ward. His fraternity brothers here would tell him if I went with anybody. I wasn't brought up to hurt other people."

"Would you go out with me if it weren't for him?"

It was her turn to look at him. She grinned on just one side. "You're good-looking and brash. I'd probably go out with you."

"Is 'brash' an asset?"

"Probably. You're probably smart too. But I don't know you well enough to be sure."

"Then I guess you'll have to see me more to find out."

She shook her head, but she was smiling. "Those clothes will probably dry too much if you don't take them out. Mine have had almost enough time to dry, and they went in a long time after yours."

He laughed. "You don't miss much, either. But I wouldn't want a pretty girl like you to have to walk back to the dorm at night all by herself."

"Then I guess I'm stuck with you for now."

"Girls have met worse fates."

"We'll see."

❧

On the way to her sorority house, he found out about the rest of her numerous family and told her about his successful father and his brother who aimed to be just as successful and his nervous mother. He also found out what classes she was taking. When he got back to his room, he looked them up in the course schedule. Most of them were English courses with only one section, so it was easy. Evelyn was evidently a senior: she had a Hawthorne seminar "for seniors only."

The next day, he just happened to be outside her nine-o'clock History of the English Language class when it ended, and he asked her to go to the Center for a Coke.

"I can't; I have another class."

"Not till eleven. And I can walk you back to Will Hall for that." He smiled.

She looked at him with surprise. "Maybe I'd better add *nosy* and *persistent* to that list of adjectives for you."

He made a face. "I'd prefer *clever* and *loyal,* but who am I to argue with a lady? Will you come?"

She shrugged and gave him the one-sided smile again. "I'm supposed to meet Jessie in the Center now anyhow. You didn't know that somehow and just ask me as a sneaky way of meeting her?"

He gave her a straight look. "No. I've seen her, and I'd rather be with you."

She looked straight back, then said, "Thank you," and lowered her eyes.

Jessica's short greeting and suspicious glance when they were introduced signaled that she evidently questioned his motives too. But he ignored her while he held Evelyn's chair and sat beside her. So Jessica ignored him too and turned to what was evidently uppermost in her mind. "Evie, may I have the car this weekend?"

"Marshall's coming?"

Jessica nodded. "He has a three-day pass."

Evelyn paused, then said, "You know Mother and Father wouldn't approve."

"Father anyhow. I know; that's why he's never let me have a car of my own, though you got one in high school. We've been over all this a hundred times."

"And I always give in to you."

"Well, it's not fair. Why can't I go with anybody I want to? You always could."

Evelyn turned to Greg. "Please excuse us for airing family problems in front of you like this."

"That's okay; everybody has them."

"All right, Jessie. Take the car this weekend. I won't need it anyhow."

"Thanks, Evie; it isn't as if I couldn't get into trouble without a car." She grinned on one side too; it was evidently a family thing.

Evelyn shook her head and sighed. "You make me feel like your mother instead of your sister."

They talked for a while about Sputnik, then the continuing Little Rock disputes over integration. When Evelyn announced that she had to go to class, Greg got up and prepared to walk with her. He was a little surprised that Jessica said she would go with them on her way back to the dorm. Since he was in the men's dorm next to hers, they walked together after Evelyn said good-bye at the entrance to Will Hall.

For a minute they walked in silence. Then she said, "What's with you and Evelyn, anyhow?"

He said, "I like her. Any crime in that?"

"She's already engaged."

"She told me. What's he like?"

"Sizing up the competition, huh?"

"Sure. Even you must have had some competition sometime."

She gave him a wry look again. "But you're not after me."

"No."

"Why not?"

"You're just not my type, I guess."

She laughed. "I like you—I like you a whole lot better than Ward."

"*Ward,* I take it, is the lucky fiancé in grad school."

"Yes—Ward Knight. A stuffed shirt if ever there was one."

"Why does Evelyn like him?"

"Who knows? She's got her own crazy world where everything is logical, and she decided that Ward is the kind of fellow she ought to marry. Besides, she never let any boy in high school get close to her, so Ward's the first real boyfriend she's had."

"Are they in love?"

She shrugged. "Not the way I think of love." Jessica's eyes were gray, and they turned into smoky screens as she looked somewhere he couldn't see.

They didn't talk for the rest of the walk. At her dorm, he said, "Good-bye."

She said, "See you later."

He felt pretty good. He wasn't sure why.

At lunch, Chad Minor poked him in the ribs. "You sly devil you."

"What're you talking about?"

"Don't act so innocent. We know you've got the Goddess on the hook."

Greg grinned at the mistake. "What makes you say that?"

"Now, don't try to wiggle out of it. I saw you with her and some chick today in the Center, and Wes Jones saw you walking across the bridge with her just now."

Greg grinned again. "The chick was her sister; she's a senior."

There wasn't any harm in such a rumor. If everybody thought he was chasing Jessica, he could see Evelyn without hurting her and her precious Ward. Jessica was evidently mixed up with some fellow in the service and didn't want local attention anyhow; he could keep other flies away from that honey. And it couldn't hurt his reputation any for girls or fellows either to think he was succeeding where others had failed. Talk about status symbols! This threesome had decided possibilities.

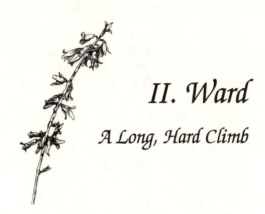

II. Ward

A Long, Hard Climb

SEPTEMBER 1954–JUNE 1957

*W*ard was glad to be back at Harper College, glad to be a sophomore. Most of all, he was glad to get away from Chestnut Grove, especially after the fit Momma had thrown the day before when Dad had said they didn't have the money to buy something she wanted. She had thrown up to him for the millionth time everything she'd lost by marrying him instead of Delbert Gibson. Long before, Ward had learned a fervent hatred of Mr. Gibson without ever meeting him; evidently he combined the charm of David Niven and the money of all the Rockefellers, and Dad ranked somewhere just above the drunken janitor at school. When Ward had studied genetics in high-school biology, he had realized that if his mother had married the marvelous Mr. Gibson, he himself, Edward Austin Knight, would simply not exist. He wondered if that mattered to his mother.

Dad had listened to Momma's complaining all through supper, then gone back to the store, though Ward knew there was nothing to do there. Until he finished packing and told her he was going to bed, Momma had hung over him telling him that he was her only reason to go on living and she hoped he wouldn't grow up to be like his father.

9

Right after unpacking, he went to the college grill. He hoped Rose Muir would come in, and she did. He wouldn't mind going out with her. Her saddle shoes were always bright white and shiny dark, and she looked like a girl in a magazine with her short brown hair high over her forehead and curled over her ears. She had a heart-shaped face and a little rosebud mouth that made her look like she knew what she wanted. Stanley Kerr, his roommate, called her a living doll, though he'd gone steady with Dixie Ann Watts since the second semester of the year before. Stanley had said he thought she was flirting with Ward.

Ward hadn't dated anyone at Harper his freshman year; he had kept Kathy's picture on his desk and intimated that she was still his girl back home. Before his pledge dance, he had pretended to break up with her and accepted a date of convenience with the freshman sister of a junior fraternity brother.

Rose waved at him but didn't come over to his table. Instead, she headed toward someone he hadn't noticed, a thin girl with old-fashioned long dark hair sitting in one of the booths. Rose called, "Evelyn! Evelyn Lanier!" and the girl looked up.

The name startled him. It was almost like the name of his scholarship, the Evelina Montgomery Lanier Scholarship. But the girl wasn't old enough for it to be named for her. She scarcely looked old enough to be in college. And *Evelyn* wasn't *Evelina*. That was such a fancy name he was sure he remembered it right.

He looked at the girl again. She was still talking to—at least listening to—Rose. She nodded in answer to some question and got up, and the pair started out. Then he could see the white monogram on the pocket of her navy Shetland cardigan—like his new one, only his wasn't monogrammed. Hers read *EML*.

He frowned at the flimsiest chance that this girl or her relatives might have given the money to pay his way to Harper. He didn't like her, from her smooth dark hair to her cordovan penny loafers.

The next time he saw her, she was wearing a dink beanie like the other freshmen. He probably wouldn't have to see her often; she wouldn't likely have any sophomore classes. But seeing her again reminded him to look up his scholarship in the catalog: it was "donated by the generosity of Evelina Montgomery Lanier, Class of 1909." That couldn't be this girl or even her mother, but it was probably her grandmother. He tried to remember if any of his friends knew that he had received the scholarship. But he had been pretty careful not to let anybody know his parents didn't have the money to send him on their own.

Ward's mother had handed him the letter telling of the scholarship award one day when he came in from school. She watched while he got a table knife and opened it. As soon as he started reading, she asked, "Well, Eddie? How much is it for?"

"How do you know I got anything?"

"Oh, I know. Good as you've done, they've got to give you something. Someday you'll be president of a college as good as theirs."

"It's a full scholarship—tuition, room, board, books, and some money for other expenses. The only hitch is that I'm 'morally obligated' to help some other student after I start earning money myself."

"Do you have to sign something that says so?"

"I don't know, Momma. The letter doesn't say."

"Well, it don't seem like much of a gift if you have to give it back."

He hadn't said so, but he felt willing to promise anything in the future so he could really go to college, really have a chance to get out of Chestnut Grove and make something of himself. And if he paid it back by helping somebody else later, that just meant that he wouldn't owe anybody anything.

When Dad came home for supper, Ward told him.

Dad straightened his shoulders and actually smiled. "Well, that's great, Eddie. I'll tell Willadette Chappell, and she'll write it up for the county paper."

His mother said, "For once in your life, you've got a good idea, Webb Knight. Then let all those highfalutin women in the United Daughters of the Confederacy read about whose son's smarter than any of theirs."

Ward thought, *Then everybody'll know we don't have enough money ourselves for me to go.* He said, "I don't think so, Dad. It'd look like bragging."

His father nodded. "That's right, son. Glad to see you're not going to get the bighead over this."

The vulgar phrase rasped across Ward's nerves like a file. He finished his supper and left the table as soon as he could.

All that summer, he carried the letter in his pocket until Dad drove him to Harper. Ward made sure they arrived on campus before most of the other students. He didn't want anybody to see him riding in the old Plymouth or carrying his clothes into the dorm in boxes.

Though his scholarship covered all his expenses, he worked in his father's store all summer to pay for his clothes and fraternity. He had deliberately pledged the most expensive one on campus, Kappa, and was careful not to let any brothers know how different his home life was from what he imagined theirs must be. They elected him chaplain for the sophomore year, and he planned to be president his senior year. Being an officer gave him a little income as well as status. But keeping up appearances still required careful planning.

His greatest rival in the brotherhood was Reaves Thompson, whose father was a wholesale grocery distributor in Nashville. That evidently paid a lot more than owning a grocery store in Chestnut Grove. Reaves wore Harris tweed sports coats and oxford-cloth dress shirts every day and sent his shirts to the laundry. Except for the few commuters from the small town of Meadorsville, Harper students were not supposed to have cars. But Reaves did, a Jaguar. Like other rich students, he rented a garage off-campus and rarely drove on campus. The car was mainly for rum runs to Nashville, necessary since Meadorsville was dry. Reaves had been nominated for chaplain too, and Stanley told Ward that he had won only by a narrow margin in spite of Reaves's obvious unsuitability for the office. Ward consoled himself that Reaves was no academic rival at least. He'd see whether money or brains won in the long run.

Rose Muir accepted Ward's invitation to the first football game. Harper's team had a really good new quarterback, Mike Claimer, a freshman from Soddy Daisy, who could pass better than any Harper player in memory, and high hopes for a winning season made everybody go. Taking Rose was not expensive, either. Their tickets to home games were paid for in activity fees, and he brought her back to the Kappa house for refreshments and dancing to records afterward.

As they walked along the lake from the stadium to the house, they talked about Claimer's forty-yard pass to Joe Erwin in the last quarter, which made the Harper Highlanders win eighteen to fourteen. Inspired by Claimer's success, the defense had done an outstanding job too. The season the year before had been mediocre, and Rose voiced the common opinion that better days were beginning.

Entering the Kappa house, Rose exclaimed, "Oh, look, there's Evelyn Lanier; she's with Reaves Thompson."

"How come you know her? She's a freshman, isn't she?"

"Yes, but she's from my hometown, Cedar Springs. Her family's got beaucoodles of money; everybody in high school wondered why she didn't go away to boarding school."

"Why'd she come to Harper?"

"It's a family thing, I think; her father came here or something."

"Well, she looks like a snob."

"I don't think she is. She's really kind of shy. She never had much to say in high school. Except in class. She was a brain. The boys didn't like that." Rose's tone made him think the boys *had* liked *her*.

They bopped together a little, though he felt awkward dancing. But he had practiced hard the year before, dancing in his room with Stanley coaching, even once acting as a partner when he couldn't explain any other way. Stanley was a good roommate, a little heavy, and he had bad skin, but he was friendly and easy to be around. He never had trouble getting a date. Ward helped Stanley with algebra and compositions.

Bruce Gordon, a brother from Illinois, had introduced sloppy joes to the fraternity cook, and that was the dish of the day. The joke of the day became Unsloppy Joe Erwin, who had caught two of Claimer's passes. Like all the upperclass football players, Joe was a Pike, of course, not a Kappa, but for the moment school pride overcame fraternity rivalry.

Stanley and Dixie Ann, Thad West and his date, and Reaves and Evelyn wound up at Ward and Rose's table. Rose and Evelyn started talking about football at their high school, which had been a powerhouse for a small town because of a couple of tricky runners and a lot of muscular farmboy linemen.

"You all won two bowl games in the last few years, didn't you?" Thad asked.

"Yes," Rose said, "and winning's the name of the game."

Reaves grinned smugly. "Well, it's what I'm after in life."

"Actually," Ward said, nettled by the smugness, "the purpose of life is to perpetuate life."

Evelyn said, "That's a bleak outlook. Just existing without any meaning is worth nothing."

"Survival is the most basic need. There can be no meaning without existence." Ward was rather proud of thinking of that.

"Maybe not, but I'd rather die tomorrow than live a hundred years without a purpose other than just existing." She looked downright indignant.

Ward shrugged. "Any biologist would tell you that the first law governing behavior is the survival of the species, and the second is the survival of the individual."

Rose attempted to make peace. "Ward's a biologist, Evelyn, and Evelyn's an English major, Ward."

" 'And never the twain should meet,' " Evelyn snapped.

Ward said nothing but could agree with that at least. He and she were two different life-forms, mutually antagonistic. He tried to think of a biological analogy, but the relationship wasn't parasitic or saprophytic or predatory or competitive. They simply had no relation to each other at all.

The two of them did keep meeting, however, because Ward still dated Rose and Reaves dated Evelyn. Reaves and Evelyn didn't agree on much more than Ward and Evelyn had, and even though she was Reaves's date, Evelyn was outspoken about such opinions as her dislike of the Internal Security Act and McCarthyism in general. Once she called Reaves a bigot in front of half the brothers and their dates just because he said the Supreme Court had no business telling the states to desegregate their schools. Her eyes shot sparks, and Reaves sputtered and sulked.

Later, Ward asked Stanley, who knew everything about everybody, why Reaves kept going out with her.

"Well, *I* think it's so he can say he's dating the richest girl in school. But he *says* that after some petting, she's hot." Stanley grinned. "He seems pretty gung ho about her."

"Does she go all the way?"

Stanley shrugged. "All I know is what the man says. He keeps taking her out. 'Course, I keep going with Dixie Ann too." Ward knew from Stanley's complaints that Dixie Ann drew very strict lines.

Stanley had had a lot of experience with girls. Until his senior year, Ward hadn't really dated. He had necked on Beta Club hayrides or bus trips back from ball games with whatever girls he happened to be paired with. Not that he couldn't have dated; he'd been voted best looking in his class twice, and he got messages through girlfriends that so-and-so liked him. But it was easier to stay cool and let them think he wasn't interested. That even seemed to make them like him more.

Then when he was a senior, he'd picked out Kathy. She was popular, a cheerleader, and her father was a dentist. He waited a long time before asking her out. But she was just a sophomore and had never gone with anyone as old as he was, and he was pretty well known at school as a brain, so she was flattered by his attention at first, and he was proud to go places with her. She was so cute, little and cuddly like a kitten, with curly brown hair.

Then she started complaining. He was saving his lunch money to pay for taking her to Senior Banquet, and she expected him to pay for gas and movies and supper or at least snacks every week and buy her cards and gifts all the time. She nagged about something every time they went out, and finally once as he tried to kiss her good night, she turned her head away and said, "You can't even kiss good." And she had slammed the door. The next week she'd gone out with a football player. Ward decided then never to let a girl treat him like that again.

Right after the football team won the conference championship, Reaves stopped taking Evelyn out, or according to other reports, she stopped going with him. Stanley reported that Reaves said she was an egghead and a square.

Ward commented, "Doesn't sound much like what he said before, that she was putting out."

Rose was indignant at Reaves's story. She insisted on Evelyn's version, that he had roving hands, so she had told him she didn't want to date him anymore. Rose also insisted that Ward and she should include Evelyn in their plans for a while "to help the poor girl through."

Ward assented glumly. He and Rose had gotten into pretty heavy necking, and he was expecting more. He didn't want to make any commitment, but going steady with a sharp girl like Rose was important. And she'd been around. She had already taught him some things. A fifth wheel could really cramp his style.

Evelyn didn't really seem eager to be included either. She turned down invitations to go with them to the Film Series and basketball games. And whenever Ward and Rose saw her and joined her, she excused herself after a few minutes.

One day Ward was looking up sources for his World Civ research paper on the Greeks and found her in the stacks. He greeted her, and she nodded, and he had turned to look for his books when she lightly touched his hand to get his attention.

"Ward, I don't want to intrude on you and Rose. I know she's trying to be nice, but I've told her not to bother." She was looking down, but she was almost as tall as he was. He hadn't realized that she was so tall. She had seemed like a little girl.

"That's all right."

"Thank you." She raised her eyes then. He had thought they were brown, but they were dark blue. Like Kathy's.

That night Rose said Evelyn had told her about their meeting. She ended, "I guess we can't help her. She'll have to get along by herself."

That suited him just fine.

The Monday night after Christmas vacation when Ward called Rose and asked her out, she interrupted him: "I'm sorry, but I already have plans for Friday."

"Oh. Well. See you around."

He was angry. Sure, he hadn't asked her to go steady, but everybody knew they had been dating since the beginning of the school year almost. They'd think she had dumped him for somebody else the way Kathy had. Maybe she had.

Why? He thought about their last date. Nothing had happened to justify this.

Either she was just trying to get rid of him, or there really was somebody else. He didn't know which would be worse. At any rate, he'd find out. Everybody would be at the basketball game against Wilts-Conroy. Even though the basketball team wasn't shaping up as champions, there wasn't much else to do. Stanley would report on Rose for him; Dixie Ann was in Rose's sorority.

When Stanley came in Friday after the women's curfew, his face told Ward he didn't want to hear the news. But he asked anyhow. "Well? Who was she with?"

"Our esteemed brother Thompson."

Part of the fraternity code was that no brother should date another brother's former girl until at least a month after a breakup. Much less cut in on a brother. "The cheating little bitch. The son of a bitch."

"Watch it there, or you'll get into some pretty complicated incest. Like 'I'm My Own Grandpa.' "

"Damn!"

"Look, friend, you've got two roads you can take: you can act like it don't matter and forget women awhile, or you can call Reaves out and slay him in a duel."

"Or I can show up tomorrow night with another girl."

"Attaboy! Into the saddle again! Figuratively speaking, of course. Who you going to ask?"

"Evelina Lanier. I'll call her first thing in the morning."

"You mean Evelyn?"

"Yeah. Sure. Whatever. One woman's good as another anyhow."

"Way to go, daddy-o."

When Ward asked Evelyn to the all-college film Saturday night, there was a silence on the telephone. Finally she said, "All right. What time shall I be ready?"

"I'll come over right after dinner."

"Fine."

It was the first time he had been to the freshman women's dorm all year. At the desk, he said, "Please call Evelyn Lanier," and the desk girl called up to the floor to announce over the loudspeaker that he was waiting.

He didn't sit down but paced back and forth. The date hadn't seemed like such a good idea after she had accepted. Maybe people would just think she was Reaves's castoff and he was Rose's.

He looked her up and down when she got to the foot of the stairs, and he felt a little better. She looked good: cool, not overdressed, in a pleated plaid wool skirt and deep-red short-sleeved sweater with a white embroidered collar. He helped her put on her coat. It felt so soft he thought it must be real camel's hair, and her sweater was probably cashmere, not Orlon. He offered his arm.

There had been a little snow, and it crunched under their feet as they walked down the hill from the dorms and started over the bridge.

She said, "I know you just asked me out because Rose went out with Reaves."

He stopped.

She took her leather-gloved hand off his arm and looked at him and went on. "It's all right. I don't mind. What she did was wrong. She should have told you first, at least."

"So is that why you're going out with me, because you feel sorry for me because of what she did?" He felt hot.

She smiled. "Partly. But mostly because I wanted to. I think she made a poor choice. You're twice as smart as Reaves and three times more a gentleman."

He felt better. "Thanks." He thought he should return the compliment but couldn't honestly value her higher than Rose. "You look great yourself."

"Thanks." She replaced her hand inside the curve of his elbow. "Now we'd better go on, or we'll be late for the movie."

They talked about classes the rest of the way. He knew most of her professors and was surprised at her funny descriptions of them. She called Psych 101 "Dishes and Diapers" because the professor spent class time telling about his quarrels with his wife about helping around the house, and she mimicked the algebra teacher, who always hummed "The Skater's Waltz" as he wrote problems on the blackboard to its rhythm.

Ward didn't see Rose or Reaves at the movie. He made sure lots of people saw Evelyn with him, especially the brothers. During the movie he put his arm around her shoulders and held her hand; she returned his clasp but didn't grip hard or stroke his hand.

On the way back to the dorm, he debated whether she would think he was fresh if he tried to kiss her or think he was square if he didn't. He decided she was more like what Rose said than like Reaves's bragging, so he ignored the couples standing near the dorm doors wound around each other; when he left, he just pressed her hand and said, "I really enjoyed tonight. Will you go with me to the basketball game Tuesday night?"

She smiled. "Next weekend would be soon enough to make us an item. You know one date's enough for the gossips to brand us as practically going steady."

"Gossip isn't why I asked you."

"Then I'm glad to accept."

By the end of two weeks, the desk girl just said, "The usual?" when she saw him. Evelyn's roommate, Marian, warned him about Evelyn's birthday the next week, so he asked Marian what to get. She suggested poetry, and he bought a book by Wallace Stevens. Evelyn seemed really happy about it. She didn't have it, she said, and asked him to write in it. He thought as long as he could. He didn't want to rush things, and they hadn't gone together very long. But she was waiting. Finally, he wrote, "Happy birthday to Evelyn. Always,

19

Ward." She looked at it and sort of smiled and kissed him, so it must have been all right.

During first semester finals, Ward and Evelyn spent every night studying together in the library. She was as serious about studies as he was. He realized that for the life he planned, she was exactly what he wanted: smart, pretty in a cool, polished way, really very feminine except for her outspoken political views. By comparison, Rose was a little common. Evelyn wasn't as peppy as Kathy, not the cheerleader type, but he wasn't afraid she'd treat him like Kathy either.

He felt good when Rose called him the first week of second semester to say she missed him. He responded politely but didn't pick up the clear hint to ask her out again. Later he learned through Stanley that Reaves had tried to date Evelyn again, but she had turned him down. Ward felt great.

He didn't push the relationship with Evelyn. When he put his arm around her shoulders as they walked, she put hers around his waist. But she made it seem asexual somehow, as if they were just friends, not boyfriend and girlfriend. He had always kissed her good night at the dorm after that first date, and sometimes he kissed her before good nights. She always returned his kiss. But she did it coolly—no long, deep kisses like some with Rose or other girls.

But that was all right too. He didn't want to get married until he went to grad school at least—her senior year. She could transfer or just not finish her degree. And it might better to wait until he had finished his master's degree anyhow. Or maybe his doctorate.

Whatever they did, he wouldn't take money from her family. Ever.

He worried continually about her reaction when she found out what his family was like—no money, no education, nothing to be proud of.

In Botany I, he'd forced some narcissus bulbs for an experiment, and after the class presentation, he'd given them to her. She made over them like they were really something. He decided it was a good time and asked her to go steady.

She smiled. "I thought that's what we've been doing."

Near the end of the second term, Evelyn invited him to spend a weekend visiting her family, and he couldn't say no. Reaves Thompson would know then for sure that Ward rated and he was nowhere. But Ward wasn't sure what kind of clothes he would need, much less whether he had them or not. He would have to borrow a suitcase. Even getting there would be embarrassing; he would have to depend on Evelyn for a car. He knew she had one, though she kept it garaged while on campus.

Seeing the car when she drove to his dorm embarrassed him even more. It was a new white Corvette. He had seen pictures of them, of course, but he had seen only a couple of other real ones since they had come out.

She got out, said "Hi," and unlocked the trunk. He was pleased that her luggage, marbled beige, was solid Samsonite like his—well, Stanley's—saddle tan. After he had put his suitcase in beside hers and her laundry cases and closed the trunk cautiously—he didn't know how fragile fiberglass bodies were—he said casually, "Neat car."

"My father's a General Motors dealer. Want to drive?" She held out the keys.

"Sure." He took them and stood looking at the fins on the car's back fenders before he remembered to go to the right side to open her door.

He wondered if driving the car would be different, but he had driven a few cars besides the Plymouth, and everything looked pretty normal. It felt strange to ride so close to the road, but he liked the tilt of the seats. He'd have to watch his speed; six cylinders with a body that light could really move, he bet.

He asked for directions and was glad he didn't have to drive through Nashville. He had been there a few times, but always riding with someone.

Concentration on the route and driving occupied his attention awhile. He kept thinking about people saying that if a Corvette hit anything, its body would just shatter like a water glass into a million pieces.

Evelyn commented on the scenery a few times, and he responded, but couldn't think of much to say. The silences began to weigh heavy until he thought to ask her about her family. "I know you have three sisters and one brother, but that's all I know."

"Well, Jessica's a sophomore in high school. She's the beauty in the family. Annette's in seventh grade, and Jourden Marie's in third. Jonathan's only four."

"He's the only boy?"

"Yes. Another brother died when he was born. Do you have any brothers or sisters?"

"No, I'm an only child."

"I've wondered what it would be like to be an only child. It must be lonesome."

Ward wondered what it would be like to have brothers. He decided that he wouldn't have liked it.

Their route followed the Cumberland River much of the way. It was still light enough when they approached Cedar Springs that Evelyn pointed out her house across the river. It was humongous, as Stanley would have said, an old brick mansion with six white columns on top of a bluff.

The back was almost as imposing. They drove up to it on a long circular brick driveway and unloaded the luggage onto a huge porch with a brick-arched one-story roof.

Her parents were imposing too: both tall people who looked younger than his own parents. Dr. Reddick, his Art History teacher, would have called Mrs. Lanier Junoesque. She was wearing a fitted dress with a fancy collar and high-heeled shoes. She probably always wore high heels. Mr. Lanier was wearing charcoal suit pants and a pink dress shirt and tie; he probably always wore a tie too.

After welcoming Ward, Mrs. Lanier told Evelyn to take him to the guest house. Evelyn apologized on the way. "I'm sorry there's no guest room in the house, but we're such a big family, and there aren't many rooms. . . ."

"That's all right."

The guest house was as big as his parents' home, out of sight of the house but within easy walking distance. "This is also my father's studio; he paints as a hobby," Evelyn explained. "It used to be a stable. But there's a bedroom and bath here. I hope you'll be comfortable."

The bedroom was more luxurious than any Ward had ever slept in in his life. "It's great. I'll be fine."

"There's time to unpack and freshen up before dinner if you want. Come back to the house whenever you're ready."

"Thank you."

She still stood, waiting for something. He didn't know what, and finally she said, "I need the keys to put the car up."

"Oh—sure. Sorry." He had put them into his pocket.

Ward was glad that at Harper his dorm director, Mrs. Willoughby, had taught the freshmen to wear coat and tie for dining with ladies. And he was grateful for her instructions in which silverware to use for what. Indeed, the Laniers' dining room reminded him of college: it was as large as the Kappa house dining room.

He began sorting out the stair-stepped children. They looked very different from each other. Jessica and Jonathan looked like their father and the sterner, older man in one of the two portraits on the wall. Annette looked like the other portrait, a woman who looked proud. He wondered if she was Evelina. Jourden Marie, who chattered all the time, was red-haired like her mother but had Evelyn's slighter frame. They all behaved themselves, even the boy, who wore a coat and tie like his father but kept a Davy Crockett coonskin hat on his lap. He petted it as if it were alive.

A black woman called Dona waited on them. She evidently had cooked the meal too, from their compliments and her thanks. Evelyn asked her about various relatives, and she asked Evelyn about college.

The Laniers asked about Ward's interests and family. He said as little as possible about his parents. Her father complimented Evelyn on her grades, and her mother asked about a classmate who had been sick.

Then talk turned to the children at home. A boy had asked Jessica to go to a movie, and Mr. Lanier withheld permission. "Now, Jessica, you know that sixteen is the limit for anything but parlor dating. If you want to invite what's-his-name to come here and sit in the living room with you, that's all right. Otherwise, you can wait till November."

"His name is Marshall Wade, and he's a senior and has been dating for years, and he won't want to come here and 'sit in the living room'!"

"That's all the more reason for you not to go out with him. And you just watch your tone, little lady."

Jessica looked at her plate. "Mother, may I please be excused?"

"Yes, dear." Mrs. Lanier was looking at her husband.

He wrinkled his nose, then smiled and shrugged his shoulders.

Jessica had already gone out the door in a swirl of crinolines.

The Laniers had a huge Zenith television set in their living room. Ward's mother had nagged his father into buying a small set his senior year, and he sometimes watched the set in the fraternity house. But the Laniers didn't turn theirs on.

There were also paintings all over the room, probably by Mr. Lanier. Most showed Mrs. Lanier or the children. There was even one of Mrs. Lanier pregnant.

Mr. Lanier suggested that they play a game, and a noisy debate began about what to play. They finally settled on some kind of rummy. Mrs. Lanier didn't play. She said it wasn't a real card game like bridge or canasta and they had enough players already. Jessica hadn't reappeared after the argument at dinner.

On the card table they spread a cloth with various sections marked on it, and Annette, acting as banker, began distributing chips. Evelyn began shuffling. Jonathan, who sat on his father's lap and would play his hand, began dealing under direction. He sometimes flipped cards upside down so the faces showed, but no one seemed upset. Ward straightened his as each new card was dealt.

Every player had to ante an inordinate number of chips in the sections labeled all over the cloth. They decided not to play the poker hand first, so at least Ward didn't have to ante for that.

All the cards were dealt out, with some players getting more than others, an inherent unfairness, Ward thought. Jonathan had dealt an extra hand that they called the dummy that the dealer could take instead of his own hand or sell. Annette bought it for a single chip and discarded her original hand.

The chips would be won, Evelyn told him, by whoever played the cards shown on the table cover: the ace, ten, and face cards of hearts or the six, seven, and eight of any single suit. Having both king and queen of hearts won an additional pile.

Ward reassessed his hand. He was pleased to see that he had two counting hearts, the ten and the king. That meant he would probably get two pots, ten chips. But that would just repay his ante plus one chip. He could obviously go broke fast in this game. No wonder Annette had dealt so many chips.

He asked, "So if I have, say, the ace of hearts, I get the pot on that spot?"

Annette laughed. "No, sometimes you have the card and don't get to play it."

"How does the play go?"

Evelyn explained that they played cards in sequence, alternating colors when sequence in a color ran out. She started play with the deuce of clubs, and the sequence piled on fast. The players were vocal in their enthusiasm, gloating when the six and seven were split from the eight. Mr. Lanier seemed to enjoy the game the most. Mrs. Lanier commented that the clubs always ran together. Ward made no response about probability theory, which he had been studying in genetics. But the clubs stopped running at the ten. It must have been in Annette's discarded hand. Ward had played the nine, so he played his low heart, a seven, anticipating being able to collect on his ten of hearts.

But Annette said, "Do you have any diamonds? You have to play low number *and* suit in red."

He took back his seven and played the eight of diamonds. Of course, the game would make hearts the last suit played. Why hadn't they told him before he misplayed?

Finally someone played a black that had no sequel and then played the nine of hearts. Ward played his ten and scooped up the corresponding pot. They congratulated him, but no one had the jack, so play on black began again, and he had to wait to play his king.

Mrs. Lanier asked Annette, "You discarded the jack?"

"Yes."

"I would probably keep a hand with a card I might score on."

Annette smiled. "I'll do all right."

"Yes, she will," her father said. "You know she's the lucky one, Clara; whatever she does always works out for her."

Mrs. Lanier only shook her head. Ward doubted the concept of luck too.

After a few spades, diamonds began again. Then, finally, Annette played the queen of hearts. Ward was already laying the king on the table as she proclaimed, "And I'm out."

Ward took back the king. He had gotten five chips for the ten of hearts in return for his ante of nine.

Annette said, "And you all owe me a chip for each card left in your hand." She had said "you all," but she was looking at him to be sure ·
he understood.

He had four cards left, including the king. That meant he had lost eight chips, counting his ante, on the round. And no one had told him that a pot went to the one who went out. There might not be such a thing as luck, but Annette was doing all right.

Some of the next hands went better. Ward realized that in addition to going out, getting the sequences—six through eight or king and queen of hearts—paid off big, for those pots were usually left uncollected. There were cheers and taunts when they were won. He got the three-card run once, in clubs, and got nineteen chips; someone must have failed to ante in that pot once. That was the trouble with letting children play. And he went out a couple of times. Annette never had to pay him much, though.

The game seemingly had no end until all but one went broke, so they set a deadline of the ten-o'clock news. The winner would be the one with the most chips then. In the last round that they would have time to play, Ward drew both the king and queen of hearts. He counted the chips in that pile; there were many reds and blues, and the points totaled forty-five. That would make him winner, he was virtually sure. He looked at his cards and tried to keep a poker face.

But Annette went out again before he got to play his pair. He put his cards facedown and paid her the three chips he owed, but Mrs.

Lanier turned his cards up and gave him a sympathetic look. "It's all just luck, you know," she said. "There's no way to show skill except in bidding for the dummy, and even that's unpredictable."

Evelyn saw his cards too. She said, "It doesn't matter whether you win. It's just the playing that's the fun."

He nodded. But he'd never play that stupid game again.

The younger children went off to bed as the news began, Jonathan in the care of his sisters. A newscaster talked about the censorship of movies and television by blacklisting reputed Communists, and Mrs. Lanier commented that censorship was good, but Evelyn said it violated the principle of free speech.

Ward said, "You mean you think people ought to be able to say or print any kind of Communist propaganda here?"

Evelyn said, "Yes. Even if I don't like what's printed, I think the author has a right to say what he thinks. Many of the best works of literature ever written were banned just because someone disagreed with them. How can anybody learn anything if he never reads or hears anything different from what he's always been taught?"

Ward thought that was really wrong but didn't argue. He would change her views gradually.

After the weather forecast, Mr. Lanier suggested that the four of them play another game—"Some real game," he said, looking at his wife.

But she and Evelyn both said no at the same time, and then Mrs. Lanier went on: "Remember, Jourden, you have to get up early in the morning to talk to Jasper about the tobacco."

"I get your point," he said, grinning on one side again. "I'll go to bed like a good boy."

Evelyn waited until their voices diminished as they went up the stairs. Then she said, "I'll walk you to your room." She took his hand, then let it go.

She took it again as they walked through the May night. And her good-night kiss seemed longer than usual. But when it ended, she said, "Good night. Sleep well." She didn't hurry away, but she didn't linger.

The next morning when he arrived at the house, Evelyn was doing her laundry in an automatic washer in the kitchen. He had never seen one, and he watched the sudsy clothes tumble past the little glass door on the front like a television screen. Dona was cooking, and Evelyn helped carry things into the dining room.

After breakfast, she took him on a tour of the house. She told him that the portraits in the dining room were of Claude and Evelina Lanier, her father's parents, who were dead. So he had been right about Evelina being her grandmother. There were a big library and a small office on the first floor that he hadn't seen before, and upstairs there were only four huge bedrooms and some bathrooms. The girls evidently shared bedrooms, two girls each in two rooms, and Jonathan had a bedroom of his own across from his parents' on the front. Mr. Lanier must have finished his early meeting, for he was sitting on the floor with Jonathan running an electric train.

"Would you like to visit my mother's mother this morning?" Evelyn asked. "There's not much to do till lunchtime."

"Sure," he said. He wondered if that grandmother was like the other.

He knew when he saw her house that she wouldn't be. She lived on a farm like those of his own grandparents on both sides, a white frame house with a porch across the front and two square dormers upstairs and lots of big trees and a rock fence around it.

Evelyn had explained along the way that her grandfather had died and her grandmother had remarried several years before, so he met Grandad Gavin as well as Granny, who asked them to stay for dinner. But Evelyn said that her parents were expecting them back. Then Granny said she didn't want to spoil their dinner, but she brought out iced tea and pound cake with strawberries on top. They sat on the porch and talked about the weather and school and the farm and garden until Evelyn said they had to go home. She hugged and kissed her grandmother and step-grandfather, and Granny hugged and kissed Ward too and Grandad Gavin shook his hand, and they left.

The visit eased something in Ward. Yes, Evelyn belonged at Lanier Bluffs, the big house over the river. But she belonged here too, in this house like his own grandparents'. And she belonged at Harper, and she would belong in whatever house they had someday, maybe a modern ranch house with a two-car garage. She could belong wherever he belonged.

That night they went to the drive-in north of Nashville to see *The Rose Tattoo*. Evelyn said the movie had been a play by Tennessee Williams, but she hadn't read it.

It was a sexy movie; it was about nothing but sex, a bunch of Italian women wanting men. Ward thought the author must really have been hot for some woman. He felt embarrassed seeing it with Evelyn. They didn't hold hands or talk about anything on the screen. He was glad when it was over.

They went to an ice-cream place afterward, a sort of truck stop on the edge of Cedar Springs where Evelyn said everybody hung out after the drugstore closed. They had malts, and Evelyn introduced him to some high-school friends.

When he was parking the car at Lanier Bluffs, she suggested that they go sit in the studio in the guest house. He took her hand on the walk there, but let go to open the door for her. The studio was like a living room except for the unfinished paintings and supplies all around. Mr. Lanier still did mostly portraits of his family, evidently, but some landscapes were in-process too. Ward and Evelyn sat on a couch, and he asked her about some of the paintings.

After a few minutes, he reached for her hand and played with it. She stroked the back of his hand with her thumb, then raised her other hand to run her fingers through his hair and said, "I'm really glad you let your flattop grow out. I like your hair this way." Her voice sounded husky.

He put his arms around her and kissed her.

She returned his kiss, but then she stopped and pulled loose.

He said, "I'm sorry."

"It's not you—it's me."

"What's wrong?"

"I—my parents weren't married nine months before I was born."

"Well, I'm not going to attack you."

She laughed. "I know it. I—it's myself I don't trust."

When she raised her eyes, he knew he wanted her. It wasn't like just wanting something, the vague desire he had known before he had a name for it, or wanting a lay—any lay—to relieve his urges, as he had wanted her before or Rose or other girls. But now he wanted her particular body, bony and willful, to cling to him and open to him.

But he knew they couldn't do it. It would wreck all his plans. And they weren't supposed to. Her mother had trusted him, whether her father had or not, the night before.

"You can trust me," he said. He put his arms around her again and kissed the top of her head.

She raised her face to his.

While they kissed, he began reciting the periodic table to himself. When he got to polonium, he couldn't remember what came next. He broke away then and said, "You'd better go to the house now."

She nodded and left.

On the way back to Harper, Ward felt that he controlled the Corvette. He tried its power out on some of the straight stretches.

Evelyn asked, "Will you be able to visit me any this summer?"

"I don't see how I can," he said. "I have to work, and I can't afford to come."

"I'd pay for your gas."

"I wouldn't take your money." He didn't say that he didn't have a car, any car, that he could take away for even a weekend. But he knew Dad had to have the Plymouth to deliver groceries.

He could, of course, ask her to come visit him. She had the Corvette and probably all the free time in the world. But he didn't want her to meet his parents and see how they lived—not till he was surer of her.

Her head was turned toward the side window as she talked. "Will you write me at least?"

"Well, of course." He realized she was crying and reached for her hand, but it was too far away, so he clasped her arm instead. "It's not like I don't want to see you."

30

She slid over against him and put her face against his shoulder then, and he put his right arm around her.

He drove that way awhile, then said, "My folks don't have money like yours, you know."

"That doesn't matter." Her voice was muffled against him.

"Maybe not to you."

"Well, it doesn't." After a silence, she raised her head and went on. "May I call you sometime?"

"Sure. You call me any night you want to, and I'll be home thinking about you." He looked at her, and the black stuff all the girls drew around their lashes into cat's-eye points at the corners had run down her cheeks and she looked a mess. But she was smiling. He felt happy.

That fall he was elected treasurer of Kappa. But Reaves Thompson was elected secretary. Stanley assured him that the brothers just trusted him with their money more than Reaves, but he wasn't sure. Reaves had been nominated first and elected by acclamation.

At the Kappa Fall Formal, Ward asked Evelyn if she would wear his pin, and she accepted. Without talking about it, they had made their own rules about necking. Petting was out; it was too risky. Ward had almost two more years to get through college and planned graduate school after that. His professors urged him to get a doctorate and come back to Harper to teach. Dr. Chandler called it academic incest, but he smiled, so it must have been a joke.

Ward suggested to Evelyn that they marry after she finished her bachelor's degree. "Then you could get a job while I finish my graduate work."

She looked up, startled. "I plan to get at least a master's degree myself."

"It's not necessary for a woman to get advanced degrees."

"Maybe not, but it's important for me. My parents would pay for my study."

"Not if you're my wife."

"But you think it would be all right for me to stay out of school and work so you could go to grad school."

"That's different. Lots of wives do that so their husbands can get an education to take care of them."

"Later."

"What?"

"The husbands take care of the wives later, after the wives have supported the husbands. Wouldn't it make just as much sense for the wives and husbands each to support themselves? Then later each can take care of himself or herself."

"That's not the way it's done."

"Why couldn't it be? Do we have to do something just because everyone else does? Why can't we both work and both go to school?"

"It just doesn't make sense. There's no reason you should get a master's degree. You won't ever have to work after I finish my degrees and start teaching."

"Maybe I want to work."

"And maybe I don't want you to."

She gave him a look then as if he were some kind of new specimen under the microscope, and he turned away and said, "Let's talk about this some other time. We have over a year to decide."

They didn't announce an engagement, but everyone they knew talked about their marriage as a foregone conclusion. Knowing he had to do it sooner or later, Ward asked her to visit his parents for a weekend that fall. He had thought about asking her for Thanksgiving break but decided that would be too long; the less time there the better.

The drive took longer from Meadorsville than the two hours north to Cedar Springs, and the roads were poorer. Chestnut Grove was in the backwater middle of the triangle formed by Nashville, Knoxville, and Chattanooga. They went in her Corvette, of course, and he was sharply aware all during the trip of the contrast it would make with his parents' '48 Plymouth in the driveway of their little house. But most of all he dreaded the time they would have to spend with his parents. He could have slept on the couch and given her his room, but instead he had asked his grandmother Knight if Evelyn could sleep at her house; that would keep her away from his house more.

Maybe it would remind her of her grandmother's house instead of her parents'.

His mother and father had dressed up to meet her, but he knew that the Laniers never wore clothes like theirs. The travelers arrived just in time for dinner, which was all right—Ward had dictated the menu, saying he was hungry for those things and never got them at school. He had also asked his father not to pour his coffee into the saucer to drink it. Other infractions of etiquette he had resigned himself to.

Evelyn seemed to take things all right. He reminded himself that she knew country people—probably had country relatives besides her grandmother, and she had gone to Cedar Springs' small schools. But she did seem to draw in when his mother started asking her about her clothes—where she got them, how much they cost. Ward was surprised to learn that she had sewn the skirt herself. Then his father asked how much her car cost, and Ward could have sunk through the floor.

Evelyn said that she didn't know and added, as she had told Ward, that her father owned a car dealership.

"That how he makes his living?" his father asked.

"Partly, sir."

"What else does he do?"

"He has land—raises tobacco and corn and wheat. And some cattle."

His father went on, "How much land does he have?"

"I don't really know, sir."

"Probably a lot."

Evelyn didn't say anything, but Ward's mother said, "More'n you'll ever own, Webb Knight."

His father said, "Well, some people can throw more out the window with a spoon than others can bring in the door with a shovel."

"Ain't been much of a shovel you've ever had."

Ward ate as fast as he could. He didn't look at Evelyn.

Right after supper he drove Evelyn to Momma Knight's. He hadn't noticed before how many things about her house needed paint and repair, from the front gate to a cracked windowpane in the room Evelyn would sleep in. As long as Ward could remember, Poppa Knight had said he was ailing. But Evelyn went on about how pretty the quilt on her bed was and seemed interested as his grandmother rambled on about what Ward had done when he was little.

They went to the high-school football game and saw some of his friends, who of course called him Eddie, as his relatives had done. Afterward Ward didn't take her to any of the parking spots he knew but drove her back to Momma Knight's. The house was dark; Momma and Poppa Knight went to bed with the chickens. It was too cold to sit on the porch, so he turned off the motor and reached for Evelyn in the car.

She returned his kiss, but then she said, "I'm really tired. Maybe I'd better go in and go to bed."

"Yeah. Sure."

He opened the car door for her. She didn't take his arm or hand, and he didn't kiss her again at the door. She didn't seem to expect it.

Luckily, the next day was beautiful. Before he drove to get Evelyn, he called Tom Edmondson, one of the friends they had run into at the game, and asked him about the way to Fall Creek Falls. He couldn't imagine spending all day with his parents and Evelyn together. He told his mother they were going and wouldn't be back till late that night, so she didn't need to prepare dinner or supper for them.

She crossed her arms and frowned. "Reckon we're not good enough for your rich girlfriend, huh?"

He didn't answer.

"Just see that you don't get above your raising, boy."

At the moment he could think of nothing he wanted more.

He took the car to the service station and had the gas tank filled and the tires and oil checked; the dirt roads around Fall Creek Falls were no place to have car trouble. The car would get filthy, but he would wash it for her before they went back to school. He got the makings of a picnic at the Dairy Bar.

Evelyn didn't comment about his sudden plan to spend the day driving again, although she did say she hadn't brought any slacks to wear for hiking. He wore good slacks rather than let her see him in his old blue jeans, and he assured her that they wouldn't be going anywhere rough. He noticed her flimsy flat shoes and hoped he was right. It had been a long time since he had been to the falls, but talking with Tom had sharpened his memories, and he was pleased that when they got to Spencer, the little town closest to the falls, it looked as he remembered.

Just a small sign at the pull-off showed where the path to the falls began, and he worried about leaving the fragile, expensive car unprotected beside the lonely road. A pickup truck was already parked there with a couple of ladderback chairs in the bed.

Evelyn had exclaimed about the leaf color along the way, especially the sumacs and maples, and she seemed more like the girl he knew at Harper than she had the night before. She recited some poem about two roads in a yellow woods as they walked through the trees.

The path led them to the creek and then followed it. The water was scanty but enough to make some noise. They met a family of five who Ward guessed went with the pickup. The lean, tanned man just nodded, but the woman said howdy and smiled.

Ward said, "Hello. How far from here to the falls?"

"Take you 'bout five minutes to get there. Sure is pretty."

The rest of the group, near-grown children, watched the path.

After they were around a bend, Ward warned Evelyn, "This isn't the prettiest side, you know. We'll have to walk around to the other side to see the falls itself. All we see here is the rim it falls over."

But the rim was worth seeing. The creek, small now after summer's dryness, was a torrent in the spring, and it had worn the gray limestone smooth for a wide expanse on each side of its thin yellowish stream. Drying but still colorful, the fallen leaves stirred in the breeze and skittered over the rocks when it gusted.

Evelyn reached for Ward's hand, and he set down the food and drinks. They walked to the rim and looked over a wide expanse of woods toward lower hills. The air was hazy with moisture, but the breeze and the paleness of the sun made it comfortable.

Evelyn said, "Thank you for bringing me here." She raised her arms to his neck and gave him a long kiss.

He held her tightly a moment and ran his hand down her back and over her hips, then quickly let go and stepped back.

She stepped back too and looked out over the valley again. "I wish I'd brought a camera. But I'll just have to hold on to it without. Maybe we can come back here after we're married; then everything will be different." She walked to the food and began arranging it on napkins on the rock.

"This isn't the best part," he insisted as he joined her.

"Oh, yes, it is." She brushed his cheek with her fingertip.

He didn't want to look away from her eyes, but he forced himself to choose a chicken salad sandwich and begin eating.

After lunch they walked around the rim and down the hill until they could see the falls from below, a thin veil of water coming straight down a long way over the lip of the ledge and disappearing among the treetops. They held hands but didn't kiss anymore.

It was late when they got back to Chestnut Grove. They ate supper at the café, and then Ward drove Evelyn to Momma Knight's. When he turned off the motor, he didn't know whether he was going to try to kiss her or not.

But she reached her arms up to his neck and began kissing him. "My love, my love," she whispered.

He felt that they were floating on the tenderness of her kisses, her lips so smooth and soft on his that there was nothing else in the world. Their kisses were a red bloom that flowered between them and grew, sending out petals like flames that engulfed them and the whole world.

He took his arms from around her and put his hands on her shoulders and held her back from him. "Evelyn, sweet, no. No. We mustn't."

She nodded and opened the car door. "Don't come with me. I'll let myself in."

The next summer she wrote him every day. He wrote her only twice a week, but he was holding down two jobs; he worked on a construction crew all day, and he cleaned up at the store and stocked shelves at night. He was saving money to buy her a ring for Christmas. He wished he could get her a really big diamond; she had several rings with other large stones already. But it had to be at least a quarter of a carat, he told himself. She didn't know that he was saving for it; she never asked him about his finances. He had never told her about his scholarship, and he didn't intend to. Somehow he'd pay it back without her ever knowing.

Both he and Reaves were nominated that fall for president of the fraternity. After the voting, Stanley's face told him first that he had lost. Being vice president was no compensation. He knew that if he'd had Reaves's money, he'd have won. Reaves's father was a wholesale grocery distributor, so Reaves must have found out that Ward's father was only a grocer and told the brothers. Evelyn didn't think that would make any difference, but she had money.

After that, the only thing he wanted was to win the Senior Biology Award for his independent research project. He was studying the distribution of cedar trees—junipers—in Cedars of Lebanon State Park. Dr. Chandler lent him a car sometimes, and sometimes Evelyn rode with him in the Corvette and helped him chart the location of the trees, which were monoecious. He was studying the effects of topology, soil, water, and wind direction on the distribution of the pollens and the seeds. The only project approaching his in complexity was Barth Johnson's work with fruit flies, and Ward thought his own more impressive. But Barth was a good student too, his biggest rival in science classes.

At the conclusion of the projects, all the seniors presented their findings to the underclassmen and the faculty. It was the project judges, Dr. Weiss, Dr. Chandler, and Dr. Mosby, who made him nervous. Since he hoped to come back to Harper to teach, the presentation was also like a job interview.

Joe Tucker, who was a nice guy but no powerhouse, presented first, with Barth right after him. Barth had hired an art major to draw charts for him, and they were better than Ward's. But Ward had practiced his presentation and felt good about it. No one asked him a question that he hadn't prepared for. Afterward, the professors shook his hand and complimented him, especially Dr. Chandler. But he wouldn't know until the department banquet whether he had won. And the majors all brought their dates to the banquet, so Evelyn would know if he lost. He couldn't think of any way to live with that. Not after the fraternity election.

He got ready for the banquet with eagerness and dread. What if somehow Barth Johnson had beat him? Or even one of the others? As he and Evelyn walked to the dining hall, he tried to listen to her plans for her parents' trip to his graduation, but he couldn't pay attention. He couldn't even eat much; he was waiting for the announcement of the awards.

When Dr. Weiss called his name as winner of the Senior Biology Award, he got to his feet too fast, and then he couldn't remember what he'd planned to say; all he could think of was just "Thank you." He held one corner of the walnut plaque with his name engraved even when Evelyn was reading it. As they were walking back to her dorm, he said, "Did you think I'd win?"

Her eyes were bright. "I've known for a long time that you're the best there is. When we're married, everything will be perfect."

III. Greg

A Detour

*O*n the Friday after he met her, Greg called Evelyn to ask her and Jessica to go bowling with him the next week, and he listened to her silence as she tried to figure out his angles.

Finally she said, "Why don't you just ask Jessie?"

"Because I don't want to go out with her."

"Then why ask her at all?"

"Because you won't go out with me without her." There was silence again, so much that he said, "Right?"

"Ri-i-i-ght. . . ."

He knew from the way she drew it out that she was considering. She'd have to decide whether she wanted to see him or not. His throat felt dry. It was like a poker hand, and he didn't dare call; he didn't know yet how she felt about him. So he waited. "No" would build a wall hard to blow up. "Yes" would be . . . sweet.

After an eternity, she said, "I . . . guess it's all right."

"Great. I'll meet you at the Center after dinner."

"Now, wait. If Jessie doesn't want to go, I won't either. I don't want anyone getting the wrong idea. Especially you."

"I know. Do you want to ask Jessica, or do you want me to?" That gave her another out if she changed her mind right away.

She said, "It'd look better if you call her."
"Great. I can't wait till Tuesday."

The Center was newly opened that year, and the only bowling alley before had been upstairs over the defunct theater downtown. There the students had had to sit behind the pits and reset pins after each frame, sometimes a risky as well as tedious task. So the new alley with its automatic pinsetters was a popular spot. But Tuesday was not a crowded night, and Evelyn, Jessica, and he talked without disturbance except for the clatter of the pins and the jukebox's renditions of "All Shook Up" and "Banana Boat Song." All three had bowled before, but not much, and they spent most of the time coaching each other and laughing at the results.

After two lines, they turned in their smelly shoes, and Greg got them big glasses of cold orange juice and some chips. They sat at a table and watched other couples and groups come and go while they talked.

Evelyn was wearing a turquoise blouse and dyed-to-match slacks, and he noticed that the top blouse button was undone. He leaned over and whispered a warning.

She blushed a little as she fastened it, then grinned and said, "It's not as if I stretched the cloth there."

He and Jessica both laughed, and Jessica commented, "You never would have said that to Ward."

Evelyn turned deep red then but said nothing. The conversation never really recovered, and they left soon afterward.

Greg was sorry, but he was glad to know more about Evelyn and Ward. They went to Evelyn's house first again, and on the walk to the freshman dorms, he pumped Jessica for all she could tell him about Edward Austin Knight, whom he had already looked up in last year's annual. Ward looked like Frederic March in a glum plot.

The three became a regular group, Greg usually sandwiched between the sisters. Jessica enjoyed playing up her supposed relation to Greg and took his arm and held his hand in public. In the Center she would bop with him; he tried to get Evelyn to dance, but she never would. They went bowling every Tuesday and got pretty good.

He took endless ribbing from his floormates about having to go out with a chaperon all the time. He just gave his teasers a worldly-wise look and asked if they would swap places with him. So far, they hadn't come up with convincing denials.

The three often studied together in the library. Evelyn was serious about her classes, and Jessica had nothing better to do in school, which she viewed basically as a prison. In high school Greg had been part of a winning debate team, defeated only by the Castle Heights Military Academy team in the state finals, and he had joined the college team too. The question for the year was "Resolved, that the electoral college should be abolished and the President of the United States should be elected by a direct popular vote." Greg preferred debating on the positive side of any issue but according to the rules had to be prepared to argue either. He tried his points out on the sisters.

After a few weeks, Evelyn revealed another of her interests to him. For a couple of years, she had been writing an irregular satiric column for the newspaper. She submitted it under the pen name Vivian Bond, and even the editor didn't know the author. Greg asked Jessica if Ward had known, but she wasn't sure; she thought he probably had.

Harper had an honor code, so news that twelve calculus students had been caught cheating ran quickly through the community. Greg told Evelyn about it as he walked with her to the Center; he asked if she knew of other cheating at Harper.

She didn't say anything at first. Finally, she said, "No. But I cheated once. That was in high school; I would never break the honor code." She looked at the sidewalk, and he knew she was upset.

"What'd you do? Use crib notes?"

"Oh, no! I didn't do it for myself." She looked up, shocked. "I just let somebody else see my answers on a test when he'd asked me to."

"How come?"

She smiled the one-sided smile. "I liked him. A lot. Not that it helped."

"I guess we've all done funny things for love."

"The real irony was that he told my girlfriend later that although he liked me, he wouldn't ask me out because I was too smart. Maybe if I hadn't been smart enough to copy from, he'd have dated me."

"I'm glad you're smart."

"Most boys don't like smart girls. And I usually didn't like the ones that did."

"Maybe that's why you don't like me."

"Oh, no. You're different. And I do like you. . . . I mean . . . it's just that Ward . . ."

While prizing her unintended admission, he wanted to avoid any reminders of Ward. "Didn't you ever go out with anybody you liked except Ward?"

"Yes. There were a couple in high school. But as soon as they got . . . physical, I froze." She paused, and he didn't say anything; if she wanted to go on, she would. Finally she did. "I—was afraid I'd go too far."

"We've all been there." He had never wanted so much to touch her, but he thought that'd really scare her. Then he reached out anyhow, squeezed her hand, and let go. And it was all right; she looked at him and smiled.

Later he wondered what made her the way she was. What made anybody the way they were? Why out of all the girls he knew did he have to want her?

Homecoming attendants were usually elected as girlfriends of football players, but the freshmen had disregarded tradition and chosen Jessica as undisputed beauty queen; her victory also owed something to a rivalry between two other freshmen girls, both dating players, who had split the football vote. Evelyn asked Ward to fly to Nashville for Homecoming, where she would meet him and drive back to Meadorsville, and he agreed.

Greg had mixed feelings about meeting his rival. It would be good to size up the competition in person. But after they had met, he could no longer pretend Ward Knight didn't exist. He also had no date for the game: Jessica would be escorted by a member of the team, of course. He couldn't with good grace ask another girl or go with Evelyn and Ward or stay away from the game. The senior Laniers and at least some of the other children were driving to Meadorsville for the event, so he would meet Evelyn's parents. The pleasure of that was balanced by his false position as Jessica's, not Evelyn's, boyfriend. But of course he had no true position.

Then two days before the game, Jessica called Greg to tell him that Evelyn was all torn up over a letter from Ward. He was not leaving New Orleans after all; he needed to stay there because of his research project, he said.

Jessica said, "I know it's a lousy thing to ask, Greg, but I have to go to rehearsal for the ceremonies tonight, and Evelyn shouldn't have to be alone. Will you call and ask her to see you? Make up some desperate need."

"I can't use the real one?"

"Not with Evelyn. You know that as well as I."

So he called Evelyn and finally persuaded her to meet him at the library to talk about a paper he was working on.

She looked as if she had been crying, and he hated Ward as much as he envied him. He asked her if they could go for a walk so he could tell her about his problem, and she nodded. But as soon as they were outside, he said, "What's bothering you? Something's wrong."

She burst into tears. "Ward can't come."

He put his arms around her, and she cried on his shoulder. The irony of their first embrace didn't escape him, but she felt good in his arms. He stroked her back and mumbled meaningless comfort.

He gave her his handkerchief. They sat on a bench outside Meadors Hall, and he stroked her hand while she calmed herself. She didn't seem to notice his arm around her shoulder.

She finally stopped crying, blew her nose, and moved out from under his arm. "I'm sorry, Greg. I shouldn't use you this way. I wasn't brought up to do that."

"I asked for it. And I'll tell you when I want to quit letting you."

"You ought to quit right now. Get some other girl and go to the game; forget me."

"You're the one I want to take. And now I could—if you'll let me."

"It's not fair to you."

"Let me be the judge of that."

"It makes me so selfish to use you this way."

He wondered just what she meant: was she using him as a status symbol? Or did she want to be with him for his own self? At least if she couldn't be with Ward. Was it better to be second choice than none?

Evidently so. He heard himself saying, "I'll be by to get you tomorrow for the pep rally. What colors are you wearing?"

She wore Harper red all weekend—for the pep rally a red sweater and for the game a red wool dress that skimmed her slight curves without hiding them. The day was beautiful, and the sun gleamed on her black hair. He gave her a white pompon mum corsage and wore his gray plaid sportscoat with red and blue and met her parents and two more sisters and the little brother. And Jessica pecked him on the cheek in front of her parents, mischief shining out of her eyes, but he sat beside Evelyn during the game and didn't envy the guard escorting Jessica. Greg wanted to take Evelyn's hand, but every time he looked at it, he saw Ward Knight's ring.

He met Marshall Wade, Jessica's boyfriend, just before Christmas recess. Marshall had bought a car, a five-year-old Ford sedan, and arranged to meet Jessica, Evelyn, and Greg in Nashville at a party at a friend's house. Greg drove there Saturday afternoon while the sisters shared the other seat in the Corvette, their usual places when riding. The girls had signed out from their dorm and house for the night for a trip home; after the party, they would drive to Cedar Springs with Greg. They ate barbecue plates with pickled green tomatoes at Charlie Nickens's by the bridge and drove to the nativity scene in Centennial Park. Every year Harvey's Department Store added some white figures, concrete or plaster, to the illuminated display in front of the replica of the Parthenon; Evelyn and Jessica told him they had seen it every year since the first. The tiny lights were white, and they made a starry cloud. Finally, after some winding around, they found the address Marshall had given Jessica.

Marshall looked like the football linebacker he had been. The only detraction from his dark good looks was a crooked nose; Greg guessed that it had been poorly set after a break in some pileup. Marshall was a year younger than Evelyn and two years older than Jessica and Greg. Jessica plastered herself to his side when they met and obviously intended to stay there. He seemed to take her very matter-of-factly.

The host was a fellow Marshall's age who had just gotten out of the army, gotten married, and set up housekeeping. The couple had rented an old house and owned little to fill it. Someone had given them a sumptuous Oriental rug, which furnished the living room. Otherwise they subsisted with mattress and box spring in a bedroom and a table and two chairs in the kitchen. But the house was not empty; there were at least ten other army buddies with their assorted companions and friends. Everywhere, people were doing the dirty bop. Beer and cheap wine and loud music abounded. There wasn't much food, just some chips and pretzels, but no one seemed to mind.

To Greg's surprise, Evelyn tried some of the beer. She didn't like it, but she liked the wine. She finished two glasses while they talked to various people they didn't know. He got her another.

When a slow song started, he asked her to dance, and she accepted. She was stiff in his arms, and when he tried to dip, she almost threw him off balance.

"You know, you could break my back that way," he complained.

"I'm sorry; I never really learned slow dancing. Some of the churches in Cedar Springs didn't approve of it. And as I told you, I didn't date that much in high school anyhow."

"I could teach you. The main thing is to relax and feel how I'm moving. I'll guide you; close your eyes and just feel."

She did. He felt her give up her will and yield in his arms, and it was almost as good as he had imagined sex would be. The churches were right about dancing. They moved alone in the crowd together, their heads and bodies against each other. They danced first to "Unchained Melody," and its words kept going through his mind.

When the tempo changed to calypso, he let her go except for one hand and led her to the improvised bar in the kitchen and got them each another glass of wine. He saw Jessica and Marshall kissing, oblivious to everyone else.

He set down his wine and stood behind Evelyn and put his arms around her, holding her, the swell of her breasts resting on his forearms. She leaned against him and put her empty hand over his. The wine made every nerve in his body alive to the feel of her. "My little sweetheart," he whispered into her ear.

She didn't pull away, but she didn't answer.

Her silence was a weapon, he realized; he wasn't sure whether it was offensive or defensive. But it was against him.

When she had finished her wine, they worked their way back into the living room, and she sat on the floor against the wall and stretched her legs out in front of her. He lay down beside her and laid his head on her long thighs and looked at her. She looked back at him and curved one hand around his face and ran the fingers of the other through his hair. He didn't close his eyes; he wanted to see her. They gazed at each other, time frozen. In the crowded room he felt alone with her, more private than he had ever felt before.

"What's your whole name?" she said after a while.

"What?" He felt as though her voice came from some great distance.

"I want your whole name. I don't even have your whole name."

"Gregory Douglass Beall. With two s's." He could see her write it in her mind.

"Greg. Greg. Greg Beall. Gregory Douglass Beall. Gregory Douglass Beall." She looked at him, the hollow at the base of her throat going in and out with her breaths, her veins swelling and contracting. She bent and kissed him, long, searching.

When they stopped for breath, he sat up and took her in his arms and began kissing her again.

Finally she broke away from his lips, but she was still holding him. "Greg Beall. Gregory Douglass Beall. I want you, Gregory Douglass Beall." She moved her hand up his thigh.

He closed his eyes then. "I can't, Evelyn. You don't know what you're saying. Tomorrow you might hate me."

She moaned then, not a short sound, but a low cry lengthening into a wail, lost in the noise of the room but piercing him like a bullet. He held her and wanted to cry out with her. Or to tilt up her face and cover it with kisses, tear off her clothes and take her there in the middle of the chaos, crazy as it was. He could lead her outside, take her to some motel or just to the Corvette, where they could contort their bodies to fit each other in the cramped car.

But he wouldn't. Not while she was drunk.

He pulled loose and went to the kitchen and looked for coffee. There wasn't any. He didn't know if water would help or not; he had

46

heard that it made a wine drunk worse. But he found a cup towel and wet it in cold water and wrung it out.

When he got back to her, she had passed out or gone to sleep. He mopped her face, and she opened her eyes. Then she closed them again.

He sat on the floor and held her head on his lap while she slept. He leaned his head against the wall and slept too.

Jessica shook him awake; Evelyn was already standing up, holding her head with one hand and Marshall's arm with the other, threatening to teeter down at any moment. The party seemed to have died. It was nearly two o'clock in the morning.

Jessica was laughing. Her eyes were bright, and she danced as she moved. "What am I going to tell Mother and Father, bringing in the two of you like this? Good thing I'm around to get you out of trouble!"

Marshall laughed too and put his arms around Jessica.

Greg didn't laugh. He just looked at Evelyn to see what she remembered and how she felt. She leaned against the wall; she wouldn't look at him. She must remember. And regret.

He drove; he felt sober enough by then. He also knew that Evelyn would not want to share the passenger seat with him if Jessica drove. Except for Jessica's directions and her songs hummed to herself, the trip was a silent one. When they reached Cedar Springs, Jessica took Greg to a guest house; Evelyn had disappeared as soon as the car had stopped.

At ten on Sunday morning, Jessica knocked on his door. When he let her in, she said, "Everybody's gone to church but Evie and us, and she's still sleeping it off. You don't look so chipper yourself."

"You don't look as if you spent your time drinking."

"No, I had better things to do. But I want to know what happened between you and Evie."

"Nothing."

"You can't tell me that. I know her too well; you too by now. Did you—make passes at her?"

He shook his head. "More—the other way around."

"I thought so! That's why she's all shook up! What did you do then?"

"Nothing."

"Well, more's the pity. Don't you want her?"

"Of course. You know I do."

"And she wants you. But she has to get drunk to do anything about it. What did she do, anyhow?"

He shook his head. He could feel his face grow hot just thinking about telling her sister.

"That bad, huh?" She grinned. "Well, you should have taken her up on it. Then she'd be morally obligated to break with Ward and take you."

He felt really confused; things were all topsy-turvy. "You should be the one going out for debate."

"I wouldn't waste my time. But you'd better figure out your rebuttal now, Mr. Debater. Because she won't ever want to see you again, whether she feels guilty or just rejected."

"I didn't want to give her up."

"I know that. But she may not."

"Well, I have till after dinner to prepare my rebuttal and two hours' drive to Meadorsville to deliver it."

"You need all the time you can get."

He tried to use his time the best possible way. He avoided Evelyn as long as they were at her parents'; he was supposed to be Jessica's boyfriend anyhow. Her parents made the role comfortable; probably they would have welcomed anyone instead of Marshall.

Jessica made sure that Evelyn sat next to him on the way back, and then she pretended to go to sleep. He waited for Evelyn to open the subject, but it soon became obvious that she was not going to say anything at all to him if she could avoid it.

He cleared his throat. "I want to take you to the Freshman Christmas Dance next week, Evelyn. Without Jessica."

"You know that's impossible."

"I don't know what's impossible anymore."

"Everything's just the way it was before, except that I can't see you again. If you and Jessie want to go on with your little game, that's fine."

"And what game are you playing?"

She was quiet. "Last night I didn't know what I was doing."

"I think you knew. I think you remember." He looked at her, but she had her head down.

"I wouldn't have done it if I hadn't been drunk."

"Was what you said true?"

She didn't answer.

He went on. "Because if it was, you're not doing Ward Knight any favors marrying him."

"I'd hurt him too much if I didn't. And I've wanted him too."

"As much as me?" His mouth was dry.

She didn't answer for a while. "I—haven't seen him in a long time. Not since before I met you. I don't know."

It wasn't like a debate. He knew he had made his points and his opponent hadn't refuted them. But his opponent and his judge were the same. He felt that he was losing even while he was winning. He tried another tack, just to hold on to the chance of keeping on seeing her. "It's not fair of you to punish me for not taking advantage of you."

"What do you mean?"

"Last night, if I'd done what you wanted me to, you'd be mine now more than you're Ward's."

She twisted her ring. "How do you know that?"

He knew that she was testing him, stalling for time. "I know. You aren't even sure you want him as much as me."

She avoided that. "It's not fair to you, either, to lead you on, go on seeing you, and then leave you."

"I'll take my chances. I'd rather see you and not have you than have nothing." *If she says it's not fair to her for me to go on seeing her, I'll have to yield,* he thought.

But she didn't say that. She didn't say anything, and he thought, *She's trying to decide. I'd better leave her alone.* He wanted to ask more about Ward, but this was certainly not the time to remind her of his rival.

They didn't say anything for a while, so Jessica "woke up" and began talking about the couple who had given the party. They all moved on to other safe subjects, and by the time they reached Evelyn's sorority house, Greg had formulated his plans. As he got Evelyn's overnight case out, he said, "I'll see you after your nine-o'clock class tomorrow. I'll give you the car keys then."

She turned to protest, and he knew he had lost. But she didn't say anything. His heart lifted.

He explained his strategy to Jessica as he drove to her dorm before returning the Corvette to its garage: he would try to restore the threesome to its old relationship. If Evelyn would still see him, that was better than his never seeing her. And there was always hope.

The next day, Evelyn permitted him to walk with her to the Center for their usual meeting with Jessica, and little by little, she relaxed enough to talk with him in the old way. Jessica had become his true ally, and he thought ironically how thrilled he would be at their closeness if she were the genuine object of his interest. She went with him to the freshman dance, without Evelyn, and campus opinion linked them firmly together. They had fun. That was all.

He had Jessie take Evelyn a Christmas gift, a silver pin; she sent it back unopened.

Not long before spring break, Greg saw in the paper that *The Three Faces of Eve* would be at a Nashville drive-in, and when he saw Evelyn and suggested going there, she obviously wanted to see the movie. But she refused, saying that she had already promised the Corvette to Jessica, who was driving to Fort Campbell, Marshall's base. Greg said that he could ask for Winston's car.

"That's not the only problem," she said.

"What else?"

"Jessie wouldn't be with us."

"I've never asked you anywhere for the sake of being with Jessica."

"That's precisely the problem."

"Can't you handle me without your little sister?" He would have taken the words back, but they were out.

And it worked out all right; she seemed stung. "Yes. I can handle myself."

"Then I'll get you about four Saturday afternoon if I can get the car. I'll call if I can't."

He walked away before she could explain her answer.

Greg avoided his older brother whenever possible. Before coming to Harper, he had wanted to go to almost any other college, but his family had always gone there, and his father had been upset when he had even mentioned another school. It was bad enough that he didn't want to major in business.

But Winston was capable of admiring success in any field, and Greg knew that his apparently dating the freshman who would have been named Most Stacked whether her body or her bankroll was being measured hadn't hurt Winston any. So he readily agreed to let his little brother take his car for a weekend. "I guess Evelyn won't let Jessica use her Corvette," he said.

"Sometimes," Greg evaded.

Greg thought how surprised Winston would have been to see him pull into the drive-in with Evelyn, not Jessica. They had stopped to eat on the way. He tried to avoid all the stereotypes about drive-in dates. He knew the movie wasn't steamy, and he didn't touch Evelyn. He got them popcorn and because the early March evening was cold, coffee.

Evelyn had read the book, and she told him what the movie was about. "When I was in high school, I thought I would have schizophrenia. I wrote a term paper on it, and I even used to wonder if I already was schizophrenic and no one had noticed yet."

He laughed, but she said, "No, I really thought so."

"Why?"

"Oh, I guess now, looking back on it, it was silly. But Mother used to tell me all the time that I was too sensitive; things bothered me too much. And I felt withdrawn. I know now that the way I felt wasn't what psychologists mean when they talk about withdrawal, but I didn't then.''

"How did you feel?''

"Like a spectator. I felt that everything in life happened to someone else, that nothing was ever going to happen to me. Sometimes I felt that no one even noticed me, that I was invisible. Or that what they saw wasn't me.''

"I've felt like that.''

"Have you? Really?''

"I've waked up in the morning and heard the birds call and thought that it was going to be a wonderful day, that something marvelous was going to happen. Then I'd realize that it would be just another day to have to get through. And I didn't even know what there was to get through for.''

"Yes. It's just like that.'' She looked at him, then dropped her eyes.

He said, "But I don't feel that way anymore.''

"No? Why not?''

He just looked at her. Then he reached out one finger and ran it down her hair from her temple.

She shivered.

"Evelyn—'' he started, knowing he had already gone too far.

"I'm cold.'' She had turned her face away.

He realized that neither the car's heater nor the one supplied by the drive-in had reduced the spring chill enough to matter. She had worn only a topper over her blouse and skirt, hose, and flats, and she pulled her legs under her. He took off his jacket and said, "Put this over your legs.''

She shook her head. "No. Put it back on.'' She turned toward him and started pulling the sleeve back over his hand, so he complied. He realized the movie dialogue was still droning on, unheeded, over the speaker on his door. He looked at her, questioning.

She ran her palm over the back of his hand on the seat between them. Then, staring at him as if she were memorizing his face, she slid across to sit against him. He felt her leg alongside his own, and he put his arm around her shoulder and took her left hand in his. She reached up and caught his right hand and leaned her head on his shoulder, her eyes closed.

"You won't see much of the movie that way,'' he said.

She opened her eyes to look at him, and he kissed her. He knew

52

she wanted him to, and she responded: her lips parted, and her tongue met his.

Finally they stopped. She put her head on his shoulder again. "This is crazy," she said, her eyes closed.

He turned down the volume on the car speaker as far as it would go, then squeezed her shoulder. "I know. I've wanted you since that first night in the Laundromat, before I even knew your name."

"Me too."

He closed his eyes and leaned his head against hers. "I don't ever want to let you go."

She didn't say anything, and when he looked, he saw that she was crying.

"What's the matter, sweet?"

"I can't hurt Ward that way."

"Can you hurt me?"

She kissed him again then, slow, deep, long.

Just when he knew he couldn't stand for her to stop, she did, and pulled away from him.

He folded his arms across the steering wheel and put his head on his arms and didn't move. She laid her hand on his arm, and he took his right hand off the wheel and held it out for her. He didn't raise his head. She took his hand in both hers and gripped it.

They stayed that way until the sound of the cars around told him that the movie was over. He rolled down the glass, returned the speaker and heater to their rack, rolled up the glass, and pulled the car into the line leaving. They were the last out of the lot.

Neither said anything on the drive back to Harper. Evelyn sat over against her door. She opened it to get out as soon as they pulled into the drive at her sorority house.

He didn't try to get out and walk her to the door, but before she closed the car door, he said, "I love you, Evelyn."

She didn't say anything; she was crying again. She closed the door.

After that, she wouldn't take his calls. When he showed up next outside her classroom, she ignored his words and walked beside him as if he didn't exist. He still saw Jessica and begged her for advice, even telling her everything that had happened to try to get her help. And she was willing, but she told him she thought his case was hopeless; Evelyn had given her word to marry Ward, and she would do it, come hell or high water, Jessica said. She was working on plans for her wedding right after graduation.

One afternoon in early May, Greg was called to the floor phone. Evelyn's voice said, "Greg?"

His heart jumped. "Evelyn?"

"Yes. I've called because . . . because I didn't know what else to do. Jessie's run off with Marshall."

"How do you know?"

"Her roommate called me. She's packed all her clothes and left."

"Do you know where they're headed?"

"No. Probably across the state line. If they plan to get married."

"How do you know she's with Marshall?"

"Somebody saw her get into a car like his."

"Have you called your parents?"

"No. It'd break Father's heart. He can't stand Marshall; they've gone together since Jessie was fifteen, and he still can't bear to say Marshall's name."

"He'll have to learn if they get married."

"They can't, Greg. She ought not marry him. She's never even gone with anyone else."

Except me. "Isn't that for her to decide?"

There was silence a moment. Then she said, "I want to talk with her at least. And I'd like you to. She thinks a lot of you."

"Thanks."

"No, really. And I . . . I'd like you to come with me too."

He didn't know how to meet that, so he didn't try. "How do you know we can even find her?"

"There's a justice of the peace down at Florence that marries lots of Tennessee couples. The place is pretty well known—like the places to buy liquor."

"Do you want to get the car, or should I come get the keys?"

"No, I will. I'll pick you up in fifteen minutes."

54

He watched for the car, and she was already in the passenger's seat by the time he got outside. On the drive to Alabama, he asked why her father objected so much to Marshall.

"He's older than Jessie."

"Lots of men are older than their wives." He didn't say, *Ward's older than you.*

"He's a lot more experienced."

"Not much by now. She's gone with him four years."

"Father just doesn't like him."

"Is that reason to stop them?"

"She's too young; she hasn't finished school."

"Most girls don't go to college."

"He joined the army instead of going to college."

"Could he afford to go?"

"No-o-o-o, but he didn't want to either."

"And people who don't want to go to college aren't worthy of being married. At least, not to a Lanier. Is that where all your liberal ideas lead?"

"Jessie's never really dated anybody else."

"Have you ever seriously dated anybody except Ward Knight?"

"Ward has nothing to do with this."

"What if your father opposed your marriage to Ward?"

"He hasn't."

"But what if he did?"

"I don't know."

"Might you run away with him?"

"I don't know. It's not fair to—to debate with me about this. Jessie hasn't finished her degree."

"Does Jessica care anything about college? She doesn't have a major, doesn't want to do anything particularly. I've never seen that she cares about much of anything except Marshall. And you."

"She cares about you too. She's always telling me—well, she cares about you."

"That's one of you."

She wouldn't rise to the bait. "I have to try to keep her from ruining her life."

"Isn't it hers to ruin?"

"You just don't understand."

"No, I guess I don't."

Evelyn decided that Marshall and Jessica would stop for dinner, so they checked out the parking lots of every restaurant along the highway to Florence. They found Marshall's Ford at a diner just over the Alabama line. Evelyn didn't want to confront them inside, so she and Greg waited in the car till they came out.

Jessica was looking at Marshall, so he saw the Corvette near his Ford before she did. He called her attention to it, and they stopped.

Greg wanted to tell them, *Run! Get away while you can!*

But Marshall headed toward them, Jessica on his arm.

That's the way you charge the other team when they've got the ball. But you've got the ball, man; you ought to go for the goal. Greg wondered if Marshall had been a very good football player.

Either he wasn't, or he was so sure of Jessica that he wasn't afraid of anything Evelyn could do.

And Jessica was a pretty clever player herself. She came up to Evelyn and hugged her. "Oh, Evie, I'm so glad you're here. You and Greg can stand up with us."

Evelyn disentangled herself. "That's not really what I have in mind." Her expression accused Jessica.

Jessica looked at Greg.

He said, "I'm not telling anybody what to do. Count me out."

"Thanks, Greg. At least you understand. Evie, I'm going to marry Marshall, and you can't stop me. I love him, and I don't want anything on earth except to be with him."

"Even if it breaks Father's heart?"

"What about my heart?"

Evelyn pressed for delay; she begged Jessica to give their parents time to get used to Marshall.

"After four years they're not used to him?"

"How much has he been with them? You've always been slipping around to see him."

"And whose fault is that?" Jessica exploded for the first time since Greg had met her. But at the same time she was crying.

"You just ought not do it this way, behind their backs. You weren't brought up to do that."

"I've done a lot of things I wasn't brought up to do. I'd have a pretty dull life if all I ever did was what I'd been brought up to do."

"Like mine." Evelyn started crying too.

Jessica hugged her, and they cried together. And Jessica began to wear down. Evelyn pictured what her parents would have to face, what Jessica would be doing to them.

Finally Jessica asked Marshall, "Couldn't we wait? Maybe they'll come around if they know for sure I'll never give you up."

Greg willed the right arguments into Marshall. *Tell her you love her. Tell her her parents love her and will accept you if she marries you. It's the fourth down, man, and goal to go.*

But instead of advancing the ball, Marshall just stood his ground. "You got to choose, Jess. You come with me now, or you go back with her. I can find somebody else that knows she wants me if you don't."

Evelyn held her, and Jessica cried harder. Then Evelyn began propelling Jessica toward the Corvette, and she went.

Marshall just stood there. He was still standing there when Greg drove out of the lot.

Greg didn't try to see either sister for the rest of the term. He and Jessica greeted each other when they met on the sidewalks and in the halls. But they never mentioned Evelyn or Marshall.

After exams, Greg stayed on campus for Evelyn's graduation, arranging to sleep on a couch in Winston's fraternity house after the freshman dorm was closed.

All graduation day, it rained off and on with the spitefulness of weather in haying season. He watched Evelyn graduate *summa cum laude*, and after the ceremony, he went to the reception in the Center. He spotted her across the crowded main room with her family and an old couple and a blond fellow that he took to be Ward, but he didn't approach them. Ward Knight was the last man on earth he ever wanted to meet.

He watched the group, and when she and Jessica separated from the rest, he hurried to the hallway they were headed toward and waited by the outside door, his hands in his pockets.

The rain was pelting the skylights again. She came into the hallway first and stopped in mid-sentence when she saw him.

Heart pounding, he held out his arms, and she walked into them like a sleepwalker and kissed him. Then she pulled back.

"I love you, Gregory Douglass Beall," she said. "Good-bye." She pushed open the Center door and ran out, dropped her mortarboard, and stooped to pick it up. Then she ran on toward Will Hall with her black hair and her black robe streaming behind her in the pouring rain.

"She's a fool," Jessica said, laying her hand on his arm. "And you're another. And I'm the biggest fool of all."

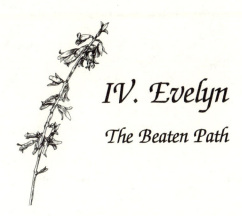

IV. Evelyn

The Beaten Path

*E*velyn married Ward in the garden at Lanier Bluffs the weekend after her graduation. Jessie was her maid of honor, and Annette and Jourden Marie were attendants. Stanley Kerr was Ward's best man, and groomsmen were two other Kappa friends. One was supposed to have been Marshall Wade, but the breakup made that unnecessary. Jonathan was ring-bearer.

At the reception her father joked that it would be easier to support them both when they were together than it had been to pay her telephone bills to Tulane the year before while they were apart.

Ward turned red and clenched his fists. "I'll support my wife myself, thank you. She'll take no money from you."

Father nodded and said, "Whatever you want, Ward. I just know sometimes money problems make it hard for a young couple. We want what's best for you."

Not many people had seen the incident, and Ward's mother had gotten through the whole day without attacking her husband in public (an achievement indeed), so Evelyn was relieved. Now that they were married, she would make up to Ward for his mother, who had never loved anyone but herself. Evelyn was grateful for her own mother. And she'd had Father and Granny and Nana and Grandad and Grandad Gavin too. How lucky she'd been!

She and Ward planned to leave right away for New Orleans; Ward's research assistantship continued through the summer, and she would get whatever job she could. For the fall she had a teaching assistantship and would begin work toward her master's. And now she and Ward could be different with each other because they were married.

She wore cornflower-blue silk for her travel outfit; a French silk jacquard ribbon with cornflowers encircled its navy straw hat. While Jessie and Mother were helping her change, Mother handed her an envelope. It contained money—quite a bit of money.

"What's this for?" Evelyn asked.

"Your father and I want you to have a little cash in case you need it. You don't have to let Ward know."

"I can't do that, Mother; you heard what he said."

Mother hesitated, then took it back and hugged her. She was crying. "Just remember that if you ever need anything, you're still our little girl."

Evelyn hugged back. But she really wanted to go. "Don't worry, Mother. We'll be fine."

When Father kissed her, he called her by his old nickname, Li'lun. She almost cried then.

Ward had made reservations for a room at the Maxwell House in Nashville, so they didn't have to drive far. He made her leave her hat in the car; he said everyone would know they were newlyweds if she was all dressed up. They didn't talk much as they ate dinner in the hotel. Evelyn couldn't think of anything to say, and she wasn't very hungry.

Ward asked her not to look at him while he ate.

Everything—the meal, the trip upstairs to their room, their unpacking nightclothes—seemed to take forever. She changed first in the bathroom and came out with her white peignoir over her gown. While he changed, she took the peignoir off and got into bed and pulled up the covers; she wasn't used to air-conditioning, and it seemed cold.

He came out of the bathroom in his pajamas and turned off the light, but they could still see, both from the summer twilight and from the city lights. He closed the Venetian blinds and the drapes and got into bed.

He leaned over and began kissing her. She felt that every cell of her body was straining toward him. She turned her body against his and began caressing his face and head and the back of his neck as they kissed. She moved her hand down under his pajama collar, then to his chest, and began unbuttoning the top.

He lay back on his side of the bed. "I don't think I can do this tonight. I'm too tired."

She lay on her back again, not touching him. "It's all right; we can wait." But she was thinking, *What's the matter? What did I do wrong?*

They lay still, so still, as still as death. But she felt as if she were trembling inside, shaking until she would fall apart. Finally she could bear it no longer. She turned toward him and propped herself on one elbow and began drawing slow circles around his face, down his arms, down his chest. Then she kissed his face, his neck, little short kisses. Her eyes had accustomed themselves to the dim light, and she could see his closed lids.

They didn't open, but he reached out for her, caught her head, and pulled it down until her mouth was on his. Her tongue explored his mouth, and they both moaned. He pushed her down on the bed and pulled up her gown.

Their life in New Orleans was fine. The nights were hot, but she and Ward made love anyhow. They learned to sleep naked, and she liked feeling his skin against hers when she awoke. Besides the pleasure, there was the deep satisfaction that he needed her love.

They lived in the attic apartment that Ward had shared with another student the year before; a mockingbird sang in the cedar tree outside their bedroom window every night. They pushed the twin beds together, and Ward preferred the arrangement to a double bed; he pointed out that when one of them turned, the separate mattresses kept the other's sleep from being disturbed.

His roommate had been gone awhile before she moved in, and

when Ward showed her the few empty drawers she could use, she asked if that was all the roommate had used.

Ward said, "No, but I needed more room for my things." He had the grace to blush, but he didn't empty any more drawers.

She said, "I need more room too. But I guess I'll have to make do." She left some of her clothes in her suitcases and slid them under the bed like drawers, banging them into the wall.

She became a waitress, short-order cook, and scullion at the lunch counter of the neighborhood drugstore. She could have made more working at a tourist restaurant, but that would have meant going to the French Quarter and working late; at the drugstore, she worked breakfast and lunch and was home by five minutes after three to tidy up their small apartment and get Ward's dinner ready. The same neighborhood people came in every day, and she came to know and like them. Ward was so busy with his studies and research that she was lonesome, and the customers became almost like her family and the people from Harper that she missed. Sometimes she caught herself missing Greg, but she tried not to think about him.

She got a card for the public library, a lovely old house on St. Charles Boulevard surrounded by the ubiquitous live oaks draped in Spanish moss. She enjoyed going there even after she enrolled in Tulane and could use the university library.

Ward got a weekend job at a pizza parlor in addition to his research fellowship. She thought pizza tasted strange when she first tried it but got to like it.

She enjoyed teaching from the beginning. Her first students seemed very young, although really they were only four years younger than she. Their faces and names and even the papers they wrote stuck in her mind more vividly than those of any students she had afterward.

Living in New Orleans could be cheap. A streetcar ride cost seven cents, a hamburger a quarter, coffee a nickel. She could buy green shrimp for less than hamburger, and she learned to cook shrimp and oysters many ways. She could buy French bread, *pain ordinaire* or baguettes, about as cheaply as she could make it, but she did learn to make it just so she knew how. Gasoline was nineteen cents a gallon.

They had no telephone, but her parents used her system for calling Ward: they called her at the pay phone on the corner every Thursday at six-thirty. Occasionally Ward and she treated themselves to a night out at Tony's, a cheap spaghetti house, or the Steak Pit, a basement restaurant where the place mats, age-bitten rectangles of linoleum, curled up at the corners.

Ward didn't want children until he finished his doctorate. He told her about a recently developed pill containing synthetic hormones to suppress ovulation, but it was not yet approved for human use. They tried to be careful. He charted her cycle, and they practiced the rhythm method (which Evelyn thought appropriate in Catholic Louisiana, although she knew its popular local nickname, papal roulette). They also used more than one kind of prophylactic.

Despite their care, her period in November was delayed. Ward kept track of her cycle as carefully as she did and obviously was worried even when she was only one day late. The second night he tossed and turned and finally got up and switched on the light in the living room/dining room/kitchen. She listened to him moving around, mumbling to himself, until she fell asleep.

By the time she was three days late, he was frantic. She decided to use some of their scarce reserve and had a rabbit test done; anything was better than the uncertainty. But she didn't tell him about the test.

The results were positive. She didn't know how to tell him; maybe it would be better after all not to. But he'd have to know sometime.

As she walked home from the clinic, she kept remembering her father when he had told her Jonathan was going to be born. On a hot July day he had asked her to go to Nashville with him. She hadn't particularly wanted to but became curious when he wouldn't tell her why they were going or why Mother and the other girls weren't. He just said, "You'll see," and grinned.

They drove all the way with the car windows down, and her skin

63

felt sweaty and gritty. Finally he parked at a jeweler's shop on West End and told her they had come to pick out a special gift for her mother. "I thought you could help me find something she'd especially like," he said, playing up the appeal in his look.

"What's it for?"

"It's sort of a return for a gift for you and me. Next January about the time of our birthdays, she's going to give us another baby like you, Li'lun. You see why this has to be something very special." His eyes had shone.

Surely Ward would be happy about this baby too.

But he wasn't. He wasn't angry; he was just depressed. When he had read the report, he laid it facedown on the table and rested his forehead on his hand. "Well, we'll manage somehow," he said, his muffled voice grim.

She was hurt. But she controlled herself. "Having a baby while we're still young might be good."

"It'll mess up all our plans. A life ought to be planned; things ought not just happen any old way."

"You said yourself that the purpose of life is to perpetuate life. Well, we're perpetuating life."

He raised up. "That's not what I meant. When did I say that, anyhow?"

"The first time we met, when I was with Reaves and you were with Rose Muir."

"Holy shit, I'd've been more careful what I said if I'd known you were going to remember it to use against me years later."

"I'm not using anything against you. I'm just trying to . . . to . . ." She couldn't finish; she burst into tears, ran into the bathroom, and slammed the door.

That night he purported to sleep on the couch and she in the bedroom. Actually she lay awake all night and heard him tossing and turning, getting up and down. She had never felt so alone in her whole life.

At dawn, he opened the bedroom door. "You awake?"

She sat up and nodded, then held out her arms to him. He came to her and sat down on the bed and held her while she cried. Then they made love.

She wished that she were a snail, that she could draw back and protect herself. She imagined building a shell, growing it out of herself.

One of Ward's classmates, Fred Haskins, would stop at the apartment and talk with Ward about classes. Ward said Fred had a fine mind but spent too much time talking with people and amusing himself. Fred lived with his girl, Marge Plott, a history major from South Carolina, just as though they were married. That shocked Evelyn. But eventually, he and Marge and Ward and Evelyn started getting together in the evenings. Most often they would share a meal and then sit around and talk; occasionally they would splurge on a movie or even eat out together. Evelyn liked Marge; she had a raucous sense of humor and a horse laugh, and Ward said she wasn't ladylike, but she was very sensitive to people's feelings, and Evelyn insisted on keeping up the friendship. Not long after Evelyn found out about her pregnancy, Marge asked if something was wrong, and Evelyn told her. Marge comforted her, and Evelyn felt a little less alone.

Ward and she didn't talk about the pregnancy; it was a wall between them. She wrote her parents to tell them and then wrote his. Hers sent flowers—pink roses, blue irises, and lots of baby's breath—and a letter with a check. The letter made no reference to the check, which was made out to her. She didn't tell Ward about it but cashed it and hid the money. Mrs. Knight wrote that she hoped the baby wouldn't keep Ward from getting his degree. Evelyn vowed to herself that it wouldn't; she wouldn't be guilty of that.

Her parents sent a large check for Christmas too, saying she and Ward should use what they needed for expenses for the baby and requesting that they use the rest to fly home for Christmas if they could. But Evelyn's doctor advised against her traveling during the first three months. Her parents were disappointed; they themselves would have flown to New Orleans for the holidays except that Jessica was bringing a friend home from college. Her mother was relieved. This was the only boy Jessica had dated except Marshall Wade, barring Greg Beall, and even Mother and Father had recognized that Jessica and Greg were not romantically attached, though they had never guessed the true relation. So Mother and Father were eager to welcome anyone Jessica was interested in instead of Marshall.

It would be Evelyn's first Christmas away from her parents.

They told Evelyn to use the travel money to replace what she would lose by not being able to work the next summer; the baby was due in July. So she suggested this to Ward.

He said, "I won't take your father's money to support us."

"Ward, it's a Christmas gift. Surely it's all right if they give us a Christmas gift."

He finally said, "All right." But he was angry, and she felt disloyal to him for insisting on keeping it.

One evening before Christmas she draped Mardi Gras beads on the split-leaved philodendron and fashioned a wreath out of red bell peppers and magnolia leaves on a bent coat hanger. When it got dark, she cut deep-red camellias from a bush on the university campus and brought them home to float in a glass salad bowl on the table. She waited for Ward to come home from the library.

When he came in, he looked at her decorations and smiled. Then he examined the leaves on the wreath. She had used both green and bronze-gold dried ones.

"Aren't they beautiful?" she asked.

"You're beautiful," he said. Then he kissed her.

On Christmas Eve she gave him a dusty-blue pullover that she had knitted, and he gave her Chanel No. 5, her perfume, which she had run out of. She also gave him a poem she had written about him. He read it and said, "Thank you. I'm flattered that you wrote a poem for me, but I don't understand it."

She shrugged. "That's all right." She felt alone again.

In January, Marge Plott caught the flu and was sick for over a week. Evelyn took her and Fred soup a couple of times despite Ward's concern about contagion, and Marge looked awful, really thin and worn out. Fred stayed home to tend her and asked Ward to borrow his notes for two classes they had together. Ward let him have them. Then Fred got sick himself and missed several more days right before finals.

Ward grumbled for two days that Fred had notes he needed to study himself. Finally he told Evelyn he was going to Fred and Marge's apartment and get his notes.

"Has Fred had time to copy them?"

"I don't know; that's his problem. He shouldn't have missed just because Marge was sick anyhow."

"But he's your friend. And what about the notes for the classes Fred's missed since he got sick himself? Won't he need yours?"

"That's not my problem either. It's every man for himself in grad school, Evelyn. You don't seem to realize that."

Evelyn was still working at the drugstore on weekends and didn't have time to sew, but she needed maternity clothes for teaching, so she bought them with part of the secret check from her parents. She let Ward think they cost less than they had. Another English major lent her some tops and two skirts also.

She first noticed the baby moving one night when she had gone to bed. Ward was still up studying, so she called him. "Ward! Come here!"

"I'm busy."

"Please—come."

He appeared in the door. "Are you all right?"

She nodded and beckoned to him. When he was close enough, she caught his hand and pulled it down and put it on the spot where the baby had been kicking. Of course then the baby was still, but in a minute it moved again.

She looked at him, and he smiled. Then he leaned down and kissed her, slowly, gently.

Ward received his master's degree that June. He already knew that he wanted to study diseases affecting conifers for his dissertation and had begun his bibliography. He didn't rent the academic regalia for graduation but got excused because of Evelyn's pregnancy, and as soon as exams were over, they drove to Cedar Springs. Her doctor had said it would be all right to travel if they stopped every hour so she could walk to keep her legs from swelling. Ward had protested her going home to have the baby, but she had cried, and he had given in.

He always drove fast, and on the trip north he drove faster than usual to make up for the time they lost while she walked. He didn't want to have to pay for a motel.

At Lanier Bluffs they stayed in the guesthouse, and Jessica had company too, the same boy who had come home with her for Christmas, Bradley Cunningham. He seemed nice enough, certainly more suitable than Marshall Wade. Bradley stayed with Granny and Grandad Gavin.

In July, Elaine was born in the Cedar Springs Hospital. Ward seemed pleased; he called his parents, who drove to see their grand-child. Mrs. Knight said Elaine looked just like Ward as a baby. Evelyn wanted to name her Elaine Annie for Granny, but Ward said Elaine Annette would sound better, and Mother agreed, so they named her that. Evelyn's parents showered new clothes and keepsakes on her as well as giving her some special things Evelyn had worn, like a pink sweater set Granny had made. At the christening they also gave the new parents a check with instructions to buy a bed, high chair, play-pen, and buggy. Ward frowned, and Evelyn wished they hadn't given so much. But he took the check.

Ward and Evelyn had agreed that it would be best for her to nurse the baby for at least six months, and although the little thing didn't seem hungry at first, she soon was thriving. She slept most of the time.

Ward wanted to get back to Tulane as soon as possible; the Biology Department would pay him for the rest of the summer. So they left two weeks after Elaine's birth.

Again, Evelyn was supposed to take frequent stops for exercise, and again, Ward chafed at the delays. They had taken Highway 43 south from Nashville, and near Florence, Alabama, they were caught behind two semis in a long, slow caravan of cars. Ward cursed under his breath. Evelyn tried to concentrate on the scenery.

A Cadillac pulled out two cars behind them to pass.

"Damn fool!" Ward said, and he speeded up till he was riding the bumper of the pickup ahead of them.

The Cadillac was beside their car when he said, "There's a truck coming."

"Oh, Ward, let him in!"

"Be damned if I do." His teeth were clenched.

The Cadillac blew its horn, but Ward looked straight ahead and kept on the pickup's tail. The car behind them braked, the Cadillac fell into line, and the truck coming the other way passed them, a string of cars following it.

Evelyn was limp. The baby, riding on her lap, had awakened and began to fret; it was not long till time for her to nurse. After a moment, Evelyn unbuttoned her blouse, undid her nursing bra, and tried to nurse the baby. But she couldn't let down her milk. She fastened her front up again and put the baby on her shoulder and tried to soothe her. She didn't know whether her shaking came from fear or anger.

Evelyn finished her master's degree the next year, and Ward had done all but the dissertation for his Ph.D. by August 1960. By then she had thirty hours beyond the master's, and the two of them had arranged to go back to Harper to teach, she as an English instructor and he as an assistant professor of biology. She was pregnant again.

That spring, Jessica graduated from Harper and married Brad Cunningham, and Evelyn's parents decided to sell the buggy and implement company and the mill. Father would take over the management of the farms from Jasper Stone, who had been there as long as Evelyn could remember and wanted to retire. Father would spend his spare time painting, and he and Mother planned to do some traveling too. As Mother explained, they wanted a simpler life. They had calculated their assets, including Lanier Bluffs and the farms, and worked out a division of property. Jonathan, past ten, who had been Jasper's shadow, was to have Lanier Bluffs eventually and a share of the farm profits; until he was grown, Father and Mother, Annette, Jourden Marie, and he would live on those profits. The rest of the assets were divided among the parents and the four sisters, given at once to Evelyn and Jessica and put into trusts for the two younger. There were some tax advantages in not leaving the money as inheritance.

Ward said he would have nothing to do with her parents' money. Evelyn wanted to use the money to buy a house, and he said she could do what she wanted, but it was her house. She said that was all right as long as he would live there, and he didn't say anything, so she started looking.

She favored a brick house on six acres next to the Meadorsville Presbyterian Cemetery. The real estate agent, who remembered when the house was built just before World War II, told them he wouldn't mind living next to a cemetery himself unless he had to use well water. Ward complained that the floors weren't level, but she argued that the structure was sound, and a new house would not be level either after it settled. She liked its spaciousness after their cramped New Orleans quarters and decided to buy it despite some drawbacks.

Two days after they moved in, Evelyn took some clothes to the dry cleaner and told the woman at the desk her address.

"Oh, you're Mrs. Knight then," she responded.

New Orleans seemed a long way away.

The house was matronly, though sturdy and ample. Designed and built by a former Harper mathematics professor, it was a perfect square, divided on the two main floors into perfect thirds from front to back. The exposed basement violated the neatness of this geometry; Evelyn was sure that Professor Garrett regretted the need for a garage underneath that caused the violation. A later owner who collected antique cars had built a four-car detached garage across the driveway from the two-car basement garage.

In other choices, Professor Garrett had also sacrificed convenience to geometry. The staircase to the basement didn't connect with the staircase upstairs. There were strange, narrow, scarcely accessible closets—part of the house's total of twenty-three; some had windows in concession to the house's exterior symmetry, and some opened off other closets. And the central third of the main floor, the living room, was fifty feet long by sixteen and two-thirds feet wide, scarcely pleasing proportions. Evelyn wondered if the good geometer had never heard of the golden rectangle.

He had attempted to break up the space. Across the front he had defined a foyer by a stub partition coming out from each side below a partition descending two feet from the ceiling across the whole span, with square posts between the upper and lower partitions. The back of the area was glassed in; this sunroom overlooked a wide sweep of lawn to the ravine and trees at the back.

The sunroom at least had been a happy idea. She and Ward put a table in front of the windows and made it their most frequent dining area. And he could grow orchids there; it could be closed off at night to lower the temperature for cattleyas so that they would come into bloom. But since there were no windows except at the ends, the living room itself was dark: the foyer and beyond it the screened-in front porch shaded the east, and the sunroom, despite its glass, kept out some of the afternoon sun.

Her father said that the living room should be a parlor in a funeral home, and her mother, called in for decorating advice, suggested knocking out the wall between the living room and the dining room to improve their long, narrow proportions and brighten the dark living room. Evelyn was excited about the idea, but Ward just said he'd think about it.

She bought decorating and remodeling magazines and picked up samples of paint chips, wallpaper, and floor coverings. But whenever she showed him something, he said it cost too much or would take too much time. Finally she asked him if he'd thought more about knocking out the wall, and he told her he didn't want the house all torn up; it would interfere with his dissertation. "Besides, I like the wall; it keeps things separate and straight."

"But it makes the room dark and gloomy. And straight lines aren't always interesting."

"That's your view, anyhow. I like things more orderly, like poems that rhyme."

"You mean you don't like my poems because they're free verse or slant-rhymed."

"I didn't say that."

"But that's what you meant."

He gathered up his papers and stomped out. She simmered; what irritated her the most was that she let his judgments hurt her, even though she thought them based in ignorance. And she acted by his preference; they didn't knock out the wall.

Ted—Edward Austin Knight, Jr.—was born that Christmas Eve. Right after Ward knew the baby was a boy, he scheduled a vasectomy.

After Ted's birth, Evelyn felt strange. She fell into tears over nothing, over spilled food (and she dropped everything, it seemed) or a stained bib. She had taken a leave of absence from teaching, and the days at home with the two babies were endless with boredom and hectic with washing and feeding, playing and tending. She felt that she was living with a doppelgänger: she watched herself with amazement and dismay. Everything she did seemed wrong, and Ward criticized her for it all.

She felt cut off from him. He had never been demonstrative; he never held her hand in public or kissed her hello and good-bye as her parents had always done with each other. She knew that this was partly because of his own parents' continual battles, and she had tried at first to warm him by showing him affection. But gradually her tenderness itself had shriveled, like a plant without water. She had withdrawn into herself. The only times they caressed each other were when they made love. And they couldn't make love until after her six-week checkup after Ted's birth.

Ward considered it important for his career to keep up their social life. He expected to be made chair of the Biology Department when he received the Ph.D., and he selected the people they should entertain and court invitations from. Because of her semester's leave of absence to recover from the delivery and be with the children, he assumed that she had ample time to entertain. He combed the *Sunday New York Times Magazine* and *Life* magazine's "Great Dinners" series for the most impressive menus and dishes for her to prepare, just as later he mined *Southern Living* and *Bon Appétit* to know when paella replaced quiche.

She came to dread each social occasion. She was afraid that she would break down over some trifle, that her misery would spill out and embarrass him and make him hate her.

She began to think that already he didn't love her. He gave her no tenderness; he seemed cold and distant, a stranger. A rank stranger, Granny would have said.

She longed to be with Granny or her mother. But they had their own lives. The two-hour drive to Cedar Springs was not all that separated them; she was a woman grown and should be able to handle her own problems herself. But she didn't know how.

A tall blond student named Diane Skinner baby-sat for Elaine and later Ted. She reflected for Evelyn the changes in dorm life and campus fashion since Evelyn's own undergraduate days, although her upbringing in Cincinnati had made her more urbane than most of Harper's current students. Certainly her skirts were shorter than the Tennessee and Alabama girls had adopted yet, although they knew about the mini. She came to baby-sit the first time looking like an alien with her short skirt and her long hair rolled on beer cans. She told Evelyn that it was set with beer too; the object was to give body without curl, to get hair as sleek and straight as little Caroline Kennedy's. Later Diane said she had learned that just ironing her hair made it as straight as possible. Evelyn tried to envision the contortions necessary to iron one's own hair; it must be like that mixed metaphor about keeping one's nose to the grindstone, ear to the ground, shoulder to the wheel, and so on.

Diane made Evelyn aware of the changes in herself too. She had been as slim as Diane when she was in college, and she had immediately lost the weight she had gained when she carried Elaine. But she had gained more with Ted, and nothing she owned fit her right. She felt bloated and ugly all the time. Without her teaching salary, she didn't have the money for a new wardrobe, either.

About a month after Ted's birth, Ward brought Diane to the house to baby-sit while he and Evelyn went to a party at his division chair's house. Evelyn was looking out the kitchen window when they pulled up, and she saw Diane lay her hand on Ward's arm as he opened the car door for her. They were laughing at something. Then Diane came into the house and told her that Mr. Knight was waiting in the car.

As she and Ward drove to the Chandlers', she said nothing. What was there to say? Nothing to talk about had happened. Ward had done nothing wrong. The girl had touched him, an innocent touch, in all likelihood. And couldn't he laugh with someone besides his wife?

But she felt betrayed. She sat beside Ward in the car and imagined questioning him: What were you laughing at with Diane? Why did you let her touch you? And she knew how absurd the questions were, but it took all her control to keep from asking them. When Ward did say something to her, she had to ask him to repeat it; she was scarcely able to pull her concentration from her imagined world to the real one.

When they returned home, she didn't go to the bedroom right away as usual. She watched Ward pay Diane, then hold her coat for her. When they left, she went into the kitchen, turned out the light, and watched Ward turn the car around and drive down the driveway and out of sight.

She calculated how long it should take him to drive Diane to her dorm and come back. And he was back a few minutes after the time she had estimated. But she still lay rigid in the darkness beside him long after he was asleep, reviewing everything she could remember about seeing Ward and Diane together.

And the whole time, she knew that her thinking was totally insane.

The next week, Ward planned a dinner party for them to give that Friday. She preferred to have no more than six at the table because that permitted one general conversation instead of several smaller ones, but he insisted on repaying several of their social debts at once, so she invited the four other couples he designated, the Chandlers, the Wiltons, the Adivinos, and the Mosbys. She knew that partly he wanted to show off the rosewood table they had gotten for Christmas.

She planned a New Orleans menu. None of the dishes had to be prepared at the last minute; they could all be assembled earlier except the bread, which she could bake Friday morning, and she could put the chicken and the bread pudding in the oven at the same time and temperature.

She cleaned the living room, dining room, sunroom, and downstairs bathroom on Wednesday and kept the children upstairs or in the nursery for the rest of the week. They ate in the kitchen, and she even set the table a day early.

Thursday night, Ward said, "I asked Diane Skinner to sit for us tomorrow night."

She controlled her voice. "Why did you do that? I can put the children to bed before the guests come and check on them right after dinner. We can't afford it."

"I just thought it'd be easier on you. You've seemed tired lately."

She knew he was being considerate. But she said it anyhow. "Not having the whole damn party would be easier on me. And not having that trollop in my house."

He looked astonished. "What's wrong with Diane? She's as nice a girl as I know."

She burst into tears and left the room.

At five o'clock Friday, Evelyn started the oven for the chicken and dessert. The crabmeat was in cocktail dishes in the refrigerator. The marinated okra and tomatoes and the bread were ready to serve. The wine was chilled, and the dripolator was loaded with water and chicory coffee. The table looked elegant with lace place mats that had been Nana's, the English bone china and silverplated flatware they had gotten as wedding gifts, and the Waterford crystal her parents had given them.

After nursing Ted, she went to the bedroom and found Ward there dressing. They had scarcely spoken since her outburst the night before, and they didn't speak as she began dressing.

When he had finished, he said, "I'll go get Diane now."

"Isn't it early?"

He didn't answer but slammed both the bedroom and back doors as he went out.

She heard them come back, but she was putting the seafood cocktail at the place settings in the dining room and didn't see them. Ward must have led Diane through the kitchen to the nursery. The route was out of the way; he must have done it to avoid seeing her.

Why did he go with Diane to the nursery anyhow? It wasn't as if she'd never been there.

Evelyn listened to hear him come back from the nursery. She cut the bread and put it in the linen-lined silver trays and put butter at each end of the table. She got ice and put it in the goblets and poured water. Still she heard nothing.

Finally she went toward the bedrooms. He was coming out of the hall into the living room. She asked, "Where have you been?"

"Combing my hair," he said. "Is that a crime? What's wrong with you, Evelyn? If I'd known you were going to be like this, I never would have married you."

She burst into tears and ran toward the bedroom. She saw Diane standing in the nursery doorway. Just then the doorbell announced their first guests.

Evelyn repaired her makeup as fast as she could and mustered her manners. At her end of the table were Kip Chandler, Anna Adivino, Lloyd Mosby, and Nina Wilton. Nina and Anna were two of Evelyn's favorite women. Anna had been a warm, helpful neighbor. Nina, about ten years older than Evelyn, had been her Art History teacher, but she had never treated her with the condescension of some of the faculty at the college who had taught her.

The marriages of the Adivinos and the Wiltons interested her too. Judd and Anna were always connected to each other, even when they were talking with other people. Judd particularly seemed always conscious of Anna, so whenever she said it was time to leave, he was already getting her coat. The Wiltons played their wit off each other; they had certain stories that they performed like a well-rehearsed play.

The guests praised the food, and everything went smoothly. They talked of the inauguration and Kennedy's address. His style was universally admired, and they judged his speech as having substance too. Evelyn relaxed and enjoyed conversation with adults again; her week had been tense with baby duties, household tasks, and the silent truce with Ward. She looked at him at the other end of the table; he was talking with Eileen Chandler, or rather listening to her.

He looked at Evelyn, and she saw his forehead pucker. He quickly looked away.

She felt tense again. She tried to pick up on what Kip was saying, but she couldn't concentrate. She just hoped the meal would end soon.

Finally everyone was ready for dessert. She cleared the dirty dishes onto the tea cart, took it into the kitchen, and unloaded the first stack onto the countertop next to the empty cocktail glasses. But as she turned back, her elbow hit the stemware, and it crashed down like bowling pins, glass after glass.

Anna came into the kitchen with Ward right behind her. Evelyn was just staring at the wreckage, helpless.

Ward said, "What have you done now, Evelyn? Those things cost fifteen dollars apiece."

She felt like a child caught guilty in a world of adults. She shook her head, wordless.

He got the broom and began sweeping up the glass that littered the floor. "Anna, I'll manage. You don't need to stay here."

But Anna was already holding Evelyn, trying to comfort her. "It's all right, dear. It's just glass. They're just things. Nothing's lost that can't be replaced."

The kindness loosed Evelyn's tears, and she cried all over Anna's slight shoulder. Ward continued to clean up the mess she had made.

As soon as she could stop crying, she thanked Anna and began putting the dessert and coffee on the tea cart. Ward went back into the dining room, telling the guests that everything was all right. She started to follow with the dessert, but Anna stopped her. "Let me clean your face a little, Evelyn." She washed her with one of the baby washcloths Evelyn used for the children.

The next morning Anna called her. "I hope I'm not too early, Evelyn, but I thought the children would probably have you up."

"Yes. Elaine begins our days at six-thirty."

"I wondered if you would bring the children over for coffee and rolls so we could talk, just the two of us."

"Why, yes, that would be lovely. Ward spends the weekends working on his dissertation."

"And Judd is making rounds at the hospital. Come over whenever you're ready, dear. The coffee is made."

They sat in the Adivinos' well-stocked library, on the other side of the house from Judd's office and the Knights' house. Ted lay sleeping on the couch, and Elaine prattled to a cloth book Anna had given her.

Anna stirred her coffee. "Evelyn, I asked you here because I'm a nosy neighbor. I wonder if you're well, dear."

Evelyn looked away from her kind face. "I—think so. It's not time for my six-week checkup yet, but my obstetrician said everything was all right when I left the hospital."

"Let me bore you with some things about myself to explain my nosiness. I have multiple sclerosis."

Evelyn interrupted with a quick "Oh!" and indrawn breath. She reached across the table to squeeze Anna's hand. She didn't know much about the disease, but she knew that it was serious.

Anna went on, her voice careful, hesitating, but warm. "I'm in remission, so it doesn't bother me right now. But when I have symptoms—and they come without pattern or warning—I feel the way you seemed to feel last night, that the world is crashing down around me. There are other things that make us feel that way too, especially women; you know how blue just the monthly cycle can make us.

78

You've just had a baby; sometimes women have postpartum depression from all the hormone changes, and it can be worse if—other things can make it worse."

Evelyn looked at her own hands lying on the table. She didn't know what to say. She was embarrassed that this woman no more than five or six years older than she, a total stranger until she and Ward had moved next door, should see so well how weak she was. She said, "I'm all right—most of the time." But the tears started down her cheeks as she spoke, and by the time she finished, she was sobbing. Then she didn't care. She tried to tell Anna how she felt, how she and Ward argued, even about her irrational jealousy. Anna moved her chair to sit beside her and rubbed her hands and didn't interrupt except to say "Poor girl!" a couple of times.

When Evelyn had had her cry out, Anna said, "Things can be done about it, you know. You can have your obstetrician prescribe drugs to balance your hormone level."

"You talked with your husband about me!"

"Yes," Anna admitted. "He says he's going to take me to court for practicing without a license. But being sick is nothing to be ashamed of and hide, Evelyn; we don't have control over everything that happens to us."

Evelyn thought that she should at least be able to control her own body, emotions, and mind. When she went home, she looked in her medical encyclopedia for postpartum depression. It wasn't there, although of course she had heard the term before. That this wasn't even a recognized illness somehow seemed to belittle her still more.

Nevertheless, she did see her obstetrician and get a prescription and begin to recognize herself again. She didn't tell Ward any of it, but one day when they were planning an evening out, he said, "Since you dislike Diane so much, do you want to get another baby-sitter?"

"No; Diane's fine, and the children are used to her."

"I guess you're all right now then?"

"I guess."

"Thank goodness. I thought for a while you were going crazy."

She didn't answer.

Ward had worked hard those first years to finish his dissertation while teaching. He had resented the demands of maintaining *her* house and *her* yard because they delayed his work on the dissertation, and he was impatient at the revisions his first reader required. But he was happy when he passed his oral defense and was assured the degree. Harper was old enough but not large enough to disregard distinctions between *Mr.* and *Dr.* in addressing professors, and she saw his pleasure in being addressed as "Dr. Knight."

He was disappointed in another expectation; he had thought he would be made chairman of the Biology Department when he received the degree, but he wasn't. He explained to her that this was only because Dr. Weiss, the current chairman, whom Ward referred to among friends as "Dodderer Weiss," was the dean's golfing buddy. Ward, who abhorred golf as a waste of time, kept saying that at Harper who you knew was obviously more important than what you knew.

Evelyn was glad that finishing the degree would give him more free time for the family. Elaine was four and Ted was two, and Ward had missed much of the joy of their development. Her semester's leave of absence after Ted's birth had stretched into a year and a half, and she had prized that opportunity to watch their early achievements.

Ward began joining various campus and village organizations, the Rotary Club and Kiwanis; he said that he needed contact with the people who had power in the community. He persuaded her to join the Meadorsville Garden Club with him: most of the members except a stalwart corps of widows and old maids were couples, the husbands emphasizing horticulture, the wives flower arranging.

She went to the meetings until after the first workshop on flower arranging, when she learned that the club members followed an endless list of rules. Some made sense, like relating the greatest dimension of the arrangement to that of the container. But many didn't. The members even insisted on hiding the graceful, natural stems of flowers when using a clear vase; they wrapped the stems in iris blades as they would hide legs in a petticoat. Ward remained a member and entered competitions; he began regularly to win prizes for his vegetables and flowers in the county fair.

When Elaine was old enough to be a Brownie, Evelyn became a troop leader despite her experience with the garden club. But Elaine decided rapidly that she would rather spend her time free, wandering in the ravine and woods, then meeting with the troop to stitch yarn onto Styrofoam trays. The two struck a bargain that if Elaine finished out the year, she would never have to join anything again. Ted, on the other hand, joined Cub Scouts as soon as he could and enjoyed every minute with his friends. Evelyn was a den mother from the time he first joined through his Webelos year.

Ward became an assistant scoutmaster the next year. He had been passed over when Dr. Weiss retired and a younger faculty member had been named chair of Biology; he was soured on work and spent extra time with Ted. The two practiced knots and Morse code and studied first aid and citizenship. Evelyn was pleased that they were together so much, although nothing short of perfection satisfied Ward and he gave the boy more criticism than praise.

Before Roundup time for Ted's second year as a Scout, Ward reminded him at dinner that they had to register that Saturday.

Ted said, "I don't want to be a Scout this year."

Ward put down his fork. "Why not?"

"It's just no fun anymore."

"Don't you like playing with the other Scouts and going camping?"

"Yeah."

"Say *yes,* not *yeah.* What's the matter then?"

"I just don't want to spend all my time trying to get some stupid badge. I don't care if I'm ever an Eagle Scout or not."

"One of the advantages of Scouting is that it disciplines boys in setting goals and working to achieve them. You need that kind of discipline. Don't you think you ought to give it another try?"

Ted sat looking at his plate. Finally, with all the enthusiasm with which he ate braised liver, he said, "I guess so."

Ward pushed back his chair and flung his napkin down. "Nobody's going to force you to help yourself. If you don't want to do it, you'll just have to do without it." He stormed upstairs to the library.

On Saturday morning, Evelyn asked Ward if he was going to Roundup to register as a scoutmaster.

He gave her an indignant look. "Why would I do that when my own son won't participate?"

For the most part, Evelyn's extracurricular interest at school centered on Community Council, the body for student-faculty-administrative debate. Harper students were far from radical, but the liberalism of the sixties raised issue after issue: long hair on male students working for the food service, censorship of student publications, elimination of chaperons for campus parties (a liberalization the faculty, their ears assailed by electronic amplifiers, wanted as much as students). Evelyn thought that effective action by Community Council encouraged students to work for reform through legal channels.

During the mid-sixties, Harper had made a real effort to recruit black students. It was not easy, for they mostly went to nearby Fisk or Tennessee State University, virtually all-black schools. But by 1968, about 5 percent of the students at Harper were black and there were four black faculty members out of almost a hundred. The assassination of Martin Luther King, Jr., shocked the whole campus, but it hit the black students particularly hard; their generation had looked to him, Evelyn realized, the way she had looked to John Kennedy to cure the ills of a sick nation.

Kennedy's assassination had struck Evelyn like a personal tragedy. She had admired his seemingly genuine concern for civil rights and his perception of the importance of the arts. Most of all, she had admired the intelligence of his words and actions. After his death, she had watched the endless television reports and read the countless articles and cried over all of them.

So she was eager to help when Willard Percy, a black professor of psychology, called and asked her to solicit donations: some faculty were trying to organize a trip to Birmingham for Dr. King's funeral for those black students who wanted to go. It turned out they all wanted to go, and some white students did too, and the group needed to charter a bus.

She began calling the faculty and administrators assigned to her at once.

When Ward came home from class, she was still calling. He listened to her conversation until she hung up, then said, "I don't think you ought to be doing this."

"Why in the name of heaven not? I can't think of anything better to do."

"There's no practical result from attendance at a funeral; it's just a social gesture." He waved his hand in contempt.

"It means something to the students; expression of feelings is important."

"I don't think it's good for Harper's image. A college is supposed to search after truth, not advocate some political position."

"They said that in the German universities before World War II."

"Well, they were right, then."

"Ward, I can't believe you really said that. What good does it do to find truth if we don't act on it? And if that means political action, I intend to go ahead."

He shrugged and left the room.

She thought of the differences between their fields: the scientists looking for facts in the material universe and rational explanations for them, the humanists looking for psychological and philosophical truths about people's relations to themselves, each other, and that elusive ground of being. Every day her classwork made her think of feelings; Ward's emphasized mechanical and chemical processes. Their very disciplines made their views split apart. Or had they chosen divergent areas because of their different natures? She dialed the next number.

One night when Ted and a friend were supposedly sleeping in the yard in a tent, he knocked on their bedroom door until he woke her and Ward. When she opened it, she found him crying. With ten-year-old daring, he and his friend had been sliding down the roof of the outside garage into the spruce trees next to it, and he had run his eye into a spruce twig. The white of his eye was all red, and there was blood.

Evelyn said, "Ward, call Judd." She led Ted into the bathroom and started splashing the eye with water to remove the surface grime and see the extent of the damage.

Ward followed her to the bathroom door. He said, "Leave him alone. I'll take care of him."

"But he needs a doctor."

"How do I know that? You won't even let me see him. You're always hovering over him. You always keep him away from me."

She stood up and turned the boy toward his father and went back into the bedroom. She listened as Ward determined that they did indeed need to call Judd, and she listened to what Judd said when he came. But she stood in the doorway and said nothing.

Ward's words and his bitter tone had revealed a distance between them that she had not known, and ironically the words created a distance between her and Ted. After that, she held herself back to let Ward direct him alone. It didn't make much difference; both children still came to her with their problems and told her things they never would have told Ward.

That was when she first began to think about divorcing him. But then she really would be keeping Ted from him. And Elaine. She certainly wouldn't give up the children herself. And she remembered the time when her own mother and father were separated and the pain that had caused her. She didn't want to hurt Elaine and Ted that way.

Also, in a sense, she felt that she was being unfair to Ward. He was, after all, the same as he had always been. She really shouldn't penalize him for not changing after their marriage just because she had expected him to become more tender. If anything, he had become more critical. She knew that she too had changed; she no longer tried to warm him with her own affection. Perhaps if she had tried harder . . .

But her hope that he would respond had died, and she couldn't. Whenever they had sex, she found herself involved physically, not emotionally; she was guarding against hurt. She felt remiss about not giving herself fully to him. But she never felt that he gave anything but his body to her; she told herself he didn't know the difference. Maybe there wasn't any; maybe the feeling that she had given him all of herself at the beginning of their love was just a self-aggrandizing illusion. Maybe there was nothing to give, nothing worth giving, except flesh.

She went to a noon recital of Mozart piano music and found it an irritation rather than the peaceful oasis in the day that she had sought: the pianist played with virtuosity, but without feeling. Even the melody was suppressed. She felt cheated.

After the second movement of the first selection, Nina Wilton got up from her central seat and walked out. Evelyn looked after her enviously; she didn't follow, although she left at the end of the selection.

She stopped at Nina's office to express her admiration.

Nina smiled. "One of the rewards of growing older is caring less what others think of one. Besides, I was making a statement for Mozart."

"Thanks; you spoke for me too." She started out again.

"Evelyn—wait a minute. Wasn't Greg Beall here when you were a student? It seems I remember he dated Jessica."

Evelyn's heart lurched. "Yes. What about him?"

"I just read in the alumni news that he was killed in Vietnam."

"Oh!" She put her hands over her mouth. *It can't be. Not Greg.*

But Nina handed her the magazine with the news item. "I'm sorry. I didn't mean to shock you so."

"That's all right. He was . . . a good friend." Evelyn read the words without knowing them and walked out. She felt numb. Only when she reached her own office did she realize that she still had Nina's alumni magazine.

No one was at home. She went upstairs to the library and pushed behind the off-season clothes in the library closet to the door at the back leading into another closet under the eaves; she left both closet doors open but didn't turn on the lights.

She put her head down on a suitcase in the eaves closet and cried, cried for him and herself too. She could see his young body, his dear body, blasted and torn, with blood on his open, loving face. Gregory Douglass Beall, with two *s*'s. She had lost him before, thrown him away. But he had still been alive. Somehow, she had still had him. Now he was truly lost to her. She wished that everything had been different.

Then she heard the children coming in from the school bus. *No, I wouldn't want not to have them. I wouldn't have had them. They're worth it.*

She got up and dried her eyes and went downstairs and hugged them.

Elaine said, "Mommy, what do you have on your face? There's funny letters, all backwards."

Evelyn felt her cheeks; the left one certainly had strange indentations. She looked in the mirror and saw the letters in their proper order: EAK. She had been branded by the monogram on one of the leather suitcases Ward had bought for their trip to Europe on his first sabbatical. She felt that Greg had branded her heart.

Ted was not particularly tall until his ninth-grade year, when he shot up like a beanpole. His growth shifted the balance of power with Elaine somewhat: she had been able and inclined to bully him before, but his new height gave him the psychological boost to resist her.

It also attracted the attention of the high-school basketball coach, who asked him to go out for the team. To Evelyn's surprise and Ward's pleasure, he made it. He began running in the afternoons, and Ward insisted on putting up a hoop in the driveway and buying weights so he could work out.

They went to all the games, at home and away. Elaine had been dating one of the starters, so she had been a loyal fan before. When Ted didn't ride on the team bus, Ward used the ride home to critique Ted's performance.

One night when Elaine had begun college and Ted was a junior, he made a last-second goal that won the game. Evelyn shouted till she was hoarse and clapped till her hands hurt. When he came out of the locker room, she hugged him and said, "That was a wonderful shot."

"Thanks," he said. His teammates were slapping him on the back as they left, and he was beaming.

Ward said, "Well, let's go home."

The traffic on the way out was heavy, as always, and Evelyn closed her eyes as usual to avoid seeing the near misses as Ward bluffed other drivers and nosed into moving lanes.

Once on the highway, Ward said, "About that last shot, Ted."

"Yes, Dad?"

"I know you made it, but you shouldn't have. You were too far out to risk it, and there was no one to stop you in front. You should have moved in closer before you tried; you could have lost the game right there with an attempt that would make you look foolish when you could have waited for a sure thing."

"I knew I could make it. And I did."

"But that was sheer luck."

"Even if I hadn't been sure, I'd have tried. Didn't you ever do anything foolish?"

Ward didn't answer, and they all sat silent for the rest of the ride.

That night Evelyn lay awake next to Ward long after he slept; she felt cold and hard. When she finally slept, she dreamed that she was peeling something tough off his heart. It was like the hull of a chestnut, only thicker; it would tear but wouldn't break loose. It had to be pulled and tugged. She had no knife, so she had to use her teeth to pull it off like the rind of an orange.

She awoke with her teeth clenched and her jaws aching.

In the late summer, Evelyn's gynecologist warned her that some abnormalities had appeared in her tests and recommended an exploratory operation.

"Do you think there may be serious trouble, Dr. Wang?"

"What is your family history?"

"My mother had a complete hysterectomy because of . . ." She tried to remember the phrase Mother had used. ". . . cellular abnormalities not long after my brother was born."

"How old was she then?"

"About forty. And my great-grandmother on my grandfather's side—Mother's grandmother—died of uterine cancer."

"Do you want more children?"

Evelyn remembered Ward's vasectomy and smiled. "No."

"Then if the exploratory operation indicates it, you would have no objection to a hysterectomy?"

"No. Do you mean the ovaries too?"

"That depends on the findings. But that's safest; then there's no worry about ovarian cancer either. Hormone replacement therapy can help you through the chemical changes and give some general benefits too, like preventing osteoporosis and even heart attacks, we think."

When Evelyn told Ward, he shrugged. "It doesn't make any practical difference, does it?"

"I don't think so; the doctor says that after complete physical recovery, it doesn't affect libido, if that's what you mean."

"Then why not?"

During Christmas break, Evelyn had the exploratory operation. She had many fibrous tumors, prolapse, extensive endometriosis, and ovarian cysts, so Dr. Wang removed the ovaries and the uterus. The hospital papers called it "surgical castration." Evelyn took a month's sick leave and stayed at Cedar Springs, where Granny could take care of her. She had scarcely ever taken a sick day and had an incredible accumulation. Her mother helped too, of course, and she felt like a child again. A prepubescent child, genderless.

In the fall of 1978, she and Ward worked on the same ad hoc committee to revise the core requirements for general education for all students. Some obvious changes were needed, for instance, the requirement of an introductory computer course. The usual friction between advocates of the students' liberal-arts education and those promoting specialization for careers ignited the meetings, and there were additional turfmanship battles.

Ward led one of these. The natural sciences were pushing for more credit hours, five instead of four, for introductory courses meeting the core science requirement. The scientists' argument was that the explosion of information over the past two decades made it impossible to cover the fields adequately in four-hour courses, even with the extra contact hours allotted for labs. The humanists and social scientists argued that the reason all students needed science courses was to learn the scientific method, not to acquire all the information available, and they could learn the scientific method in four-hour courses; science majors would take additional courses to learn the information they needed. The career-education committee members always opposed core requirements because to them a degree represented only a union card.

Ward saw that the natural scientists were outnumbered and never moved the adoption of his plan.

A month later the minutes of the curriculum committee showed the revision of every single science course in the core curriculum: the credit had been raised to five hours.

Evelyn went to Wyatt Troutt, the English representative on the curriculum committee, at once. Pointing to the offending paragraph, she demanded, "Why did you all approve this?"

He was obviously astonished. "You of all people ought to know; Ward was the one who made the presentation. And aren't you on the General Education Revision Committee?"

"Yes, I am! But we never voted on it, much less approved it. Ward launched his proposal there and pulled it back when he saw it wouldn't float."

"But he said . . ." Wyatt looked puzzled. "Let me get my copy of the proposal."

After outlining the same arguments that Ward had raised in her committee, the proposal read, "Having previously discussed and obtained approval of this proposal within the departments and division involved and brought it before the General Education Revision Committee, the natural science departments recommend the following changes."

Wyatt and Evelyn looked at each other, and Wyatt raised his hands. "Okay, okay, so it just *seems* to say your committee approved it. He's your husband."

She started to expostulate, closed her mouth, shook her head, and left. Ridiculous as it was, she imagined strangling Ward with her bare hands.

She had afternoon conferences about research papers, and Ted had left on the team bus for an away game, so she and Ward had agreed that morning to meet for dinner at the local motel restaurant before driving to the game. Granny was living with them then, but Lucy Taylor, who looked after her all day while Evelyn was at school, would feed her and put her to bed.

Evelyn arrived early; the dining room was almost empty. It was set up for dinner with burgundy tablecloths and white napkins. The napkins were folded in triangles and stuffed into water goblets so that one point angled up and the other two arched out on each side. Birds trying to fly away. The idea of their imprisonment hurt her. When she sat down, she took hers out at once and laid it flat on the table, a piece of white cloth again.

When Ward came, she said, challenging him with her look, "I saw the curriculum committee minutes."

He grinned. "I won that one."

"Winning! Is that all you care about?"

"It matters. Or don't you mind losing?"

"Yes, I mind. I mind because of the consequences to the students. But most of all, I mind because of the dirty, low-down, under-handed, sneaking, manipulative, lying way you did it."

He turned red and looked around. "Not so loud. People will hear you."

She thought of Archie Bunker telling Edith to stifle. "I couldn't care less."

"Here comes the waitress."

Evelyn ordered only a cup of coffee. Ward chose his usual special. They sat in silence until the waitress brought the coffee and left.

"What are you going to do about it?" Ward asked.

"I'll talk with the dean tomorrow; I've already made an appointment."

"He'll approve it anyhow. Chandler and Phillips have him in their pockets."

"Yes, he probably will. But I'll make the effort regardless."

The waitress brought his food.

He considered his fingernails. "I'd rather you didn't see Hasrow."

"Why not?"

"Well, of course then he'd know you don't agree with me."

"Ward, I don't care who knows we don't agree. We haven't

agreed about most things in the last twenty years. Twenty-four. I don't know how we've stayed together this long. And I don't intend to stay with you any longer." She hadn't thought it out before she said it. But she knew it was what she wanted.

"You can't mean it. You can't leave me just because of a fight over credit hours." His neck was red, the way it always turned when he was angry.

"No. It's because of lots of things, most of which you never even noticed."

"I suppose I'm too crude and common to notice what exalted, sensitive types like you would. Well, just let me tell you, it's been no picnic all these years to put up with you and your eternal rightness."

She disregarded his sarcasm. "Granny may call for me during the night; it would be better if you moved to a room upstairs. The beds are all clean. I'll gather your clothes together when I get home."

"I'll get them myself. And I'll find some other place to sleep. No place could be worse than your bed."

She disregarded that too as she laid down the money for her coffee and a tip. Then she left the dining room to drive to the basketball game.

At first she felt free, released. "And I am glad, yea, glad with all my heart/ That thus so cleanly I myself can free." Then she remembered the rest of Drayton's sonnet, which showed the narrator's willingness to resurrect love if the lover was willing. She felt confused and alone. Their angry words seemed part of a dream to her, something that couldn't really have happened. After all those silent days, how could she have spoken? Yet she knew that the words had been real, an explosion that had blasted away a facade like stones sealing a cave; they had released the fetid odor of death, the death of their marriage. She did not believe there would be a resurrection.

She realized too that she had not even now addressed the real issues of the marriage, the feeling that she was not loved, that she was even more alone in this coupling than if she had no one. She wondered, *Are we, each of us, ultimately utterly alone?* That seemed true in some respects. Then she thought of her own parents and of Judd and Anna Adivino; those couples seemed truly to have become one. But she and Ward had failed to touch each other except with their flesh.

When she sat down on the bleachers, she started shaking and couldn't stop; she hoped that people thought it was from the cold.

Ward was still packing when she heard Ted's car pull in the drive. She went to the bedroom and said, "Do you want to tell Ted, or should I?"

"This is your decision. Do your own dirty work."

She couldn't stop staring at the small raised mole under his left ear. When they were first married, that had always been the last place she kissed after they had made love. She had to restrain herself from reaching out and touching it.

He stopped packing and glared at her, and she left.

She met Ted at the top of the basement steps. "Nice game. You did an especially good job in the third quarter."

"Yeah. Thanks. Where was Dad?"

"He was there. We just didn't sit together."

He looked at her. "Something wrong?"

"Yes. I've asked your father for a divorce."

He set down his sports bag. "Well . . ." His long fingers interlaced, bent backward, separated, and fell at his sides.

Her chest felt tight, and her throat swelled. "I don't want to hurt you and Elaine."

He shook his head. "You aren't, Mom. I just . . . don't know what to think yet."

She nodded. "Talk to me whenever you're ready."

He nodded.

"Your father's in the bedroom."

"I saw his car in the drive."

"Talk with him about it," she suggested.

He shook his head, picked up his bag, and headed for the stairs to his room.

When Ward left, he didn't say anything. She said, "Good-bye."

She took his towels down in the bathroom. Then she stripped and changed their bed. She took the dirty linens downstairs to the utility room instead of putting them in the hamper. She would have washed them, but she was afraid of waking Granny. She took a bath, washed her hair, and put on a clean gown.

As she lay down in the clean bed, she remembered the last time they had made love there. They had been to a party at the Chandlers' and giggled about Kip's drunkenness, which always made him sage. They were still a little high themselves and joked about not scandalizing Ted with their undignified fun.

She realized that she was crying. She had loved Ward. But the love had died. Could it have died if she had really loved him? She would never be able to trust her love for anyone else. Her chest felt heavy. *The heart really does ache.*

ॐ

They didn't have to tell many people; word traveled fast in the tight world of the college and the town. People spoke as if Ward were dead if they spoke of him to her at all. She tried to avoid seeing him and was sure he avoided her.

She started sorting out their books and records, making stacks of those they had bought together and would have to divide. And she kept finding other things of his that he had left, his camera, a poster he had bought in Italy. She put whatever she found together in an upstairs bedroom, out of sight. But even after he had gotten settled and come for them and they had gone through their common chattels together, talking like two strangers at an estate auction—even after that, everything about the house reminded her of him, the very paint on the walls and landscaping in the yard. How could she put their world together out of sight? Or out of her mind and heart?

There were no acrimonious disagreements. Evelyn's and Ward's lawyers met and worked through the drafts of their settlement. Ward had never been rapacious, and they were both civilized, she thought. That was the word. Like *natural* for a corpse.

Two months after their separation, Ward had brought Mary Will

Benson to an Artist Series presentation. After that they appeared together regularly, and that summer they told friends that they planned to marry as soon as the divorce was final. Many people thought that Ward had left Evelyn for Mary Will. That was fine with Evelyn.

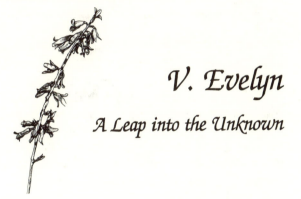

V. Evelyn

A Leap into the Unknown

$\mathcal{A}$s Evelyn gave instructions and the students began writing, pressure spread through her eye and into her brain like a fog. She kept telling herself that she could make it through this last class; she would have the rest of the afternoon, Thanksgiving, Friday, and the weekend off. She could live through one more hour. All she had to do now was sit and answer any questions the students had about the test. She could bear that.

She had planned to read the first assignment in *King Lear* for the Monday morning class while the students were writing so that she wouldn't have to do it over the break. But the headache prevented her even trying. She just sat and looked at the students: Tim Haynes in his leather jacket and motorcycle boots, modern armor against the world; Teresa Graham with her moussed green-dyed flattop and five-hued eye shadow; the universal tight jeans worn with T-shirts advertising their wearers' sexiness. How different from her own restrained college persona—hers and Ward's. But then they had been part of the Silent Generation.

Tammy Smith came in five minutes after everyone else had been writing. As usual. Instead of taking an empty seat near the door, she wound through the rows to her accustomed spot, knocking Harris Creasy's papers off his desk. He glared at her as he picked them up, but she was oblivious. She dropped her books on her desk with a thump. When she realized that she needed the test questions, she retraced her steps to Evelyn, who was holding out a copy. Harris held his papers down with both palms each time Tammy passed his desk again.

Tammy looked up after the questions and asked at normal volume, "Are we supposed to do two under *A* and one under *B?*"

Faces all over the room frowned at her. Grateful that at least she had read the instructions right, Evelyn nodded. *I wonder how many credit hours we should give for a remedial course in manners,* she thought.

The Silent Generation had been trained in that: white gloves, hats for afternoon teas, formal receptions, which flatware for what, all the no-white-shoes rules, speaking when spoken to (which accounted for their silence). Of course, there had been special rules for girls: no slacks worn to class unless the temperature fell below forty degrees, no panty lines or (heaven forfend!) nipples showing through clothes, no crossed knees. Rules had governed color combinations: no green with blue, no red with pink. Her mother was horrified with the printed fabrics used for Jams now.

Her generation had always taken the rules so seriously, just like the earnest songs of the era: "Love Is a Many-Splendored Thing," "All the Way," "Young and Foolish," which they had never dared to be. Earnestness seemed to produce melodrama too.

Ward had always been the perfect gentleman, even after they had married, holding doors and offering his arm. She was sure he still did for what's-her-name.

You know perfectly well what her name is. Mary Will Benson. You've known her fifteen or twenty years. Know as much about her as about your own younger sisters. After all, Meadorsville, Tennessee, isn't New York City. And you ought not blame her for marrying the man you're divorcing. Have divorced. As of nine forty-five this morning, you have divorced Ward.

And he's free to marry Mary Will Benson tomorrow. Could have today, but wanted the children to be there. My children.

And you ought to be giving thanks now. You wanted this divorce. Asked for it. Still want it. Now just pity poor Mary Will Benson.

So why do you have this headache if you're so happy about getting what you want?

She heard the echo of Ward's voice whispering in her ear. "Is this what you wanted?"

The smell of pine needles beneath them and dry maple leaves. The night black, no stars, no moon, just the solid earth underneath and the night sounds around and the feel of each other.

"Nothing else worth wanting. Not that I know."

So what do I want now?

Evelyn trudged with the blue books back to her office through the cold rain. Rob McFergus and Sue Hart, Evelyn's office neighbors to each side, were chatting in the hall. Sue, not a reticent soul, said, "Well! I was about to congratulate you on your independence, but you look as if commiserations are more in order."

"For this headache, yes. For my freedom, well, it's limited: I'm taking thirty-five sophomore exams on *Brave New World* home to entertain myself over the holidays."

The others groaned and shared their paper count and holiday plans. Sue, who was twenty-eight, single, and dating a penniless Vanderbilt graduate student four years her junior, was spending the vacation with him in Nashville. Rob, Marcia Lee, and their four-year-old son, Trey, were traveling to Memphis to visit her parents. Marcia Lee always arranged for them to go to her home for holidays.

"What are you doing, Evie?" Sue asked.

Sue was the only person besides Jessie who called her Evie. She had asked if it was all right soon after they had met, and Evelyn had said yes at once; it sounded friendly, and Sue was such a warm, vivacious girl that it fit the speaker.

Evelyn answered, "I'm cooking the traditional for Granny and Judd Adivino and myself at noon and warming up leftovers for the kids after they see their father properly married again."

"At least Mrs. Arnold will have everything cooked when we get there," Rob said.

Sue sighed. "That's the price I must pay for my passion; not only do I have to cook for Jeff, but I'll have to buy the food and take it with me. And Thanksgiving *would* come at the end of the month just before payday."

Evelyn thought of the hoary-bearded carrots and rotten celery that doubtless lurked in her refrigerator. Unless she wanted to cook a meal for necrophiliacs, she'd have to go to the grocery store too. At least she had bought a pair of frozen roasting hens already; Granny didn't like turkey much, and it was hard enough to get her to eat what she did like. "Maybe I'll see you at the cranberries, Sue. If there are any left."

"You'll have to hurry if you do. I haven't seen Jeff since the middle of October, and I'm going to write Kroger my bad check and leave this town as fast as a sex-starved female can." Realizing what she had said, she shook her head. "I'm sorry, Evie; I do have some human feelings when I don't let my rattletrap mouth run them down."

Evelyn smiled. "That's all right, Sue. Enjoy life. I intend to."

Sue hugged her, said good-bye to them both, and left.

Rob said, "I have no doubt that *she* will."

"And I?" She immediately wished that she hadn't asked. Rob seemed so much like her younger twin sometimes that she was afraid he knew how hollow she felt.

He smiled but raised his eyebrows. "I'm sure you *intend* to. Do you know how?"

She smiled back and shook her head. "I don't have even a clue. I wasn't brought up to enjoy myself."

"High time you learned." He looked at her, then away. "Well, I'd best be off. Marcia Lee will have the suitcases ready for me to load into the car."

Lucy Taylor, Granny's companion, left without their usual chitchat as soon as Evelyn got home. Lucy was eager to see her son and his family, who were coming from Huntsville for the holiday, and the rain was threatening to turn into ice.

Granny was in bed. As Evelyn put up the groceries, except for the stack she would use that night, she wondered if Lucy had let her stay in bed all day. At nearly eighty-three, Granny suffered from congestive heart disease, and she preferred to lie in her warm bed and do nothing, the worst treatment for her condition possible, according to Judd. But Evelyn was tired of fighting the battle to get her to exercise. She understood why Lucy gave up. Sometimes she thought it would be better for Granny if she did die; her life seemed painful and pleasureless. Sometimes Evelyn even became impatient with the cajoling and cleaning up and wished for her own freedom. But then she felt guilty, as if she had wished for Granny's death.

Granny was still sleeping, so Evelyn tried to call Elaine to see if she had left Danville yet. The phone rang without an answer. Evelyn wondered if she had dialed the wrong numbers. Or maybe, as many times as she had called it, she had misremembered this time. Was that really the right number? Or some other number that used to be important to her that wasn't anymore? She dialed again, and the rings began again.

Then there's the sly way numbers have of slipping around on you. Just when you think you've caught them, they've changed to something else: you think it's the 1812 Overture *plus one, and when you look, it's 1318.*

Not like words—they carry their own odor and can't be mixed up. You can't confuse cloister *with* cabaña. *Words mean something even when they're misspelled, like* recieve *or* veiw.

Oh, yeah, babe? What about united *and* untied? *Or* sacred *and* scared?

There was no answer, on the phone or in her mind.

When she checked again, Granny was awake. Evelyn lifted the bed-clothes and looked at her ankles despite complaints about exposure to the cold. Their swelling told her that Granny had not exercised lately, if at all that day. She didn't ask Granny; her truthfulness could be trusted, but her memory couldn't.

"Granny, you need to walk around awhile. I'll get your housecoat and slippers and walk with you."

"Oh, child, I don't want to get up. Can't you just leave me here where it's warm and let me rest?"

"Now, Granny, you know if I do that, your ankles and legs will swell more, and the skin may break again. We don't want that to happen." She remembered the last angry red lesions on Granny's thin, taut, blue-white skin. They were slow to heal, even with vita-min E oil. She got Granny's walker and cajoled her out of her nest.

Whether it reduced the swelling or not, the walking made Granny think more clearly. After a few rounds, she asked, "When will the children be here? Didn't you tell me they'd be home today?"

"Yes, they're coming, but neither will get here until late tonight. And tomorrow they have to go to a wedding." She had quit trying to explain to Granny about divorcing Ward; Granny forgot the fastest the happenings she liked the least.

"Well, call me when they get in. I've not seen them either one in a long time."

"Yes, that's because they're away at college. But you'll see them in the morning, and they'll be back by suppertime. And Judd Adivino will be here for Thanksgiving dinner as usual. The Wiltons would have come again too, but they were invited to the wedding, and I urged them to go."

"Well, I like Nina and Andy and Judd, and he's a good doctor, though I reckon he's a Jew."

Evelyn reminded herself that Granny called all the news except state and local "the foreign news." "Yes, and he's been a lifesaver to me all year." She had depended on Judd for all the problems about maintaining the house and yard since Ward had left. She had hired the Stamps boy to do the yard work since Ted had left for college, but Judd had had to teach them both how to start the lawn mower and the leaf blower and to answer all her questions about furnace filters and car care.

Granny said, "Is Anna coming with Judd, Evelyn?"

Evelyn was startled: Anna Adivino had died more than five years before, and Granny had known all about it, known all through the long illness that Anna had borne so patiently.

"No, Granny, she's dead. Remember?"

Granny ignored the question and asked another: "Is Elaine or Ted either one ever going to have any children? I was a grandmother a long time before I got to be as old as you are now."

"Yes, I know, Granny. You were only thirty-eight, and I'm nearly forty-four already. But people don't marry now so young as they used to."

"I reckon the whole world's not the same as it used to be."

"No, I guess not."

They had walked quite a bit when Granny asked, "Evelyn, where's Gavin? Is he hiding from me? I can't think when I seen him last."

"Granny, he's gone." *Dead two years, after a year of fading to nothing, a dwindling that she watched over every minute like watching her own life's blood seep out.*

"Well, poor old thing. He couldn't get better nohow."

"No. He's better off." She mouthed the piety for Granny's sake, not because she felt its truth, just as she had used the euphemism for dying to spare her feelings.

After they had walked awhile more, Evelyn let Granny sit down in the living room and propped up her feet. As soon as she was settled, Granny's face showed that she had left Evelyn and was somewhere a long way away. Her wrinkled profile was as still as a marble statue. *Realistic Roman, not idealized Greek,* Evelyn thought as she went to the kitchen to finish their supper and begin preparations for the holiday feast. She wondered with a tightness in the ribs if it would be Granny's last.

Evelyn was sleepily waiting for the Thanksgiving pies to come out of the oven when Elaine drove into the basement garage. It would take Ted longer to get home from Durham. But as if she could hasten their coming, Evelyn had turned the lights on in both their bedrooms and the floodlights on the drive at dusk despite the energy conservation program.

Elaine looked tired but healthy. She had let her blond hair grow out again. They hugged and unloaded the car and hugged again and sat at the kitchen table to talk. A junior psychology major, Elaine complained, "This wedding's going to interfere with my plans for academic excellence. I have a paper to finish by Monday."

Evelyn felt good about Elaine's dedication. She knew that she had given the children more freedom than she had had growing up, but the price of their freedom, especially for Elaine, had been discipline. She had done well without it in high school, then had had two hard years learning it in college.

But Evelyn had more pressing concerns. "How do you feel about the wedding, hon?"

"It's fine. If that's what Dad wants to do, it's fine with me. How do *you* feel about the wedding, Mom?"

Evelyn considered. "That's a good question. I certainly don't have any right to complain. But part of me is jealous still, I guess. Funny how I don't want him, but I don't want anybody else to have him."

"That sounds like an honest answer."

"I think it is. And while we're being honest, how do you feel about the divorce? I was terribly upset and torn between them when I thought your grandparents were going to be divorced when I was about fourteen." She tried to keep her voice steady.

"But I'm not fourteen. I guess part of me is angry. You're breaking up my family, my security. But I've known for years that you and Dad weren't happy with each other, and I can see that you're free of that now, and he's probably freer too. So I can be glad for the both of you, and I don't have to be careful with the two of you because you aren't together."

Elaine was twisting her hair as she talked, and Evelyn wondered if her words conveyed her full feelings.

Elaine went on, "I guess I do have one question: Are you going to marry somebody else too?"

"No. That's the last thing I want at this point."

"Then—that wasn't why you broke up with Dad?"

Evelyn was a little shocked that Elaine could have suspected her of that. "No. I didn't leave your father because I was . . . There's no other man."

Elaine didn't say anything, and after a bit, Evelyn continued, "What about you? Have you fallen in love with anybody yet? You've talked a lot about that fellow Bill."

Elaine laughed. "No, I'm not in love with Bill Jackson. I'm afraid I'm nothing but an egoist, Mom; I'd love it if he'd throw himself at my feet, but I'd just walk away and leave him there on the floor. Or walk over him."

"Well! I hope for his sake he has better sense than to lie down, then. Not having met him, I won't make any comments about pearls and swine."

"That's the best thing about him. He's so stuck on himself there's no danger of his falling in love with anyone else, especially me. It's a perfectly safe relationship."

"Is that what you want, a safe relationship?"

"Right now, yes. I don't want to get tied to anyone, and I don't want anyone tied to me emotionally."

Evelyn hesitated but then voiced her worry. "I guess one of my fears about divorcing your father is that it'll make you and Ted afraid of marriage."

"Well, I don't know whether or not I want to get married. But I don't think it has much to do with your divorce. If anything, that frees me from the feeling that if I marry and it's a mistake, I can't get out of it."

"That's certainly a new slant on the matter. But you always do see things differently. Remember your argument for not learning to cook? 'If I don't know how, no one can expect me to.' "

They both laughed, knowing how Elaine had picked up early on Evelyn's thinly disguised dislike of having to cook all the time. *Though it can be a gift I enjoy giving—like cooking for Granny and the children and Judd tomorrow.*

She went on, "But you like to cook now. And I guess I worry that you'll put off marrying until it's too late and then wish you had."

"What's too late? Granny married Grandad Gavin after she was fifty."

"That was too late to have children at least. You realize that your grandmother and great-grandmother had children long before they reached your advanced age."

"But you didn't. You finished college before you married and had me. And I intend to finish grad school first. And postdoctoral work. And win the Pulitzer Prize. And the Nobel."

"All right, all right. That's fine with me. I don't really want to push you into motherhood."

"That's good. Because I'm not ready to start chasing rug rats yet. And if and when I am, they'll be mine, not yours, you know."

"That sounds like a warning to keep my hands off."

"You got that right, lady."

"Fair enough. I wouldn't let your grandmother or grandfather tell me how to bring you up. As you know from the sass I take from you. Grandma would certainly never have put up with that."

"Then it's a done deal. If I ever marry at all, that is. Or if I have kids at least."

"In my day, the two went together."

"And how many miles did you walk to school every day?"

"Oh, go to bed and pray for some filial piety."

"Well, bed sounds good anyhow. Sleep well, Mother."

"Sleep well, baby girl."

Evelyn knew three worlds: the everyday world of routine, where she worked and talked and planned and did whatever had to be done; the world of light, that touched her like sunshine through the leaves in a woods; and the underworld of spiderwebs, catching her, tangling her, binding her. It smelled of death, and she knew that bones lay there in the darkness. Most of the time she moved in the everyday world, but sometimes she had glimpsed the sunlit world, usually when she was in love or her children touched her. And she had felt and feared the underworld, Dostoyevsky's *podpolya*, the crawl space under the house. She knew that she had stayed up so late partly to tire herself because she was afraid that otherwise she would lie awake thinking of the divorce and staring into the dark where the spiders and vermin lurked and the bones rotted. She didn't want to think about the effects of the divorce on the children. Or about what she would do with the rest of her life. Or about Granny's illness.

When she finally went to bed, she did fall asleep right away. But she was trapped in another landscape, sterile and hard, as alien as the spiders' world. Atop a high brick wall, she couldn't get down. Then she was in the darkness outside a house with no doors, looking through its closed windows at a party going on inside brightly lit rooms. Rob McFergus and Sue Hart with her Jeff were there. But no one helped her in.

Evelyn awoke to the sound of Ted's car pulling into the drive about three in the morning. When it stopped, she heard the steady pounding of rain. As she opened the side door to greet him, she was glad that at least the roads were not icy. The rain was misting into clouds of fog; a warm front must have moved in. She and Ted hugged and exchanged brief accounts of the previous day, but they had no long talk before retiring.

About ten that morning, as she was mixing the cornbread dressing, he came into the kitchen, dropped his bag of dirty laundry by the basement steps, kissed her again, then stretched his long frame lazily and yawned. "What's for breakfast, Mom?"

"There's a package of bought rolls in the bread box, or there are eggs and bacon in the refrigerator."

"Fine welcome a guy gets after driving half the night to see his mummy." He patted her head hard with his big palm in mock affection.

"Well, his mummy would be dead sure enough if she fixed a big breakfast *and* dinner *and* supper."

"Smells good in here. Wish I could stay and eat whatever you're fixing. But I guess that's all for old Dr. Adivino next door."

She felt guilty again. "Are you jealous, Ted? I didn't divorce you, you know, when I divorced your father. And you know Judd's just a good friend."

"Yeah, yeah, that's what they all say."

"It's certainly what you've always said about your harem." Since he had learned to talk, Ted had struck up conversations with total strangers wherever she had taken him. He reminded her of her own charming father, although his handsomeness was more like Ward's; he and Elaine both had Ward's blond coloring. She had given him her own views on getting along with the opposite sex: "Pay attention to a girl, and she won't be able to resist you." Whether because of her sage advice or his own attractions, Ted always had at least one girlfriend since nursery school. Throughout high school, he had traveled with a swarm of girls; he had taken two to his senior prom. But he had never gotten serious about any. Now that he was in college, he still played the field.

"You know I have to share the wealth, Mom; it wouldn't be fair to all the other girls if I tied myself down to just one."

"Yeah, yeah, that's what they all say. But what time do you have to leave to go watch your father tie himself down again?"

"The wedding's at twelve-thirty, and the dinner's not till after that. Weddings don't take long, do they? 'Cause I'll probably expire of starvation right there in the middle of the ceremony if I have to wait too long, going without breakfast and all."

"If you go without breakfast, it'll be your own fault: there's food here."

"Yeah! There's two perfectly good pecan pies sitting neglected on the counter over there. A piece of one of them would be better than any old boughten rolls."

And more nutritious, Evelyn thought. "All right. Help yourself."

"Thanks. You're a good mummy after all."

"I know it." *At least I try to be.*

Elaine had volunteered to care for Granny's morning needs. Evelyn was glad; she had a hard time dealing with the role reversals as well as with the tedium and dirtiness of the tasks. When Granny was aware of her dependence, Evelyn hurt for her pride. When she was not, Evelyn grieved over her slipping mind. Whatever happened, Evelyn felt helpless, watching the woman she had depended on all her life, her second mother, reduced to dependency herself. She couldn't imagine life without Granny.

When Elaine finished, she came into the kitchen with her dirty laundry and offered to help cook.

Evelyn said, "Thanks, but it's eleven-fifteen already. Ted said the wedding's at twelve-thirty; you'd better get dressed."

"Shall I wear all black?"

Evelyn wondered if this was a playful expression of sympathy or a test. "Of course not! Wear your light blue taffeta and let everybody tell you how much your eyes look like your father's. It's his day."

She sent a gift by Elaine, Nana's silver ice bucket that Father had given her when she and Ward had moved to Meadorsville. Ward had always prized it, and it would fit right in with Mary Will's antiques.

The dining table seemed pitifully empty with just the three of them there for the feast. Evelyn thought of the many Thanksgivings she and Ward and the children had shared there with Nina and Andy Wilton and Judd. And Anna. She did miss Anna. Judd must too.

Then she thought of Sue Hart and her celebration. The food probably wasn't the *pièce de résistance* of the day there!

Granny was more like her old self. After Evelyn remarked that it was the sixteenth anniversary of the assassination of John Kennedy, Granny remembered that Evelyn's other grandmother, Evelina Lanier, had been born near Thanksgiving and had usually celebrated her birthday then.

Evelyn thought of Nana's customary reserve and her sudden smile, like Father's, when happiness surprised her. "Yes, and Jessica's birthday was last week."

"My birthday's the twelfth of November," Judd said.

"Oh! I forgot it this year," Evelyn said. "I'm sorry, Judd; you're a dear friend, and I don't forget *you*. Funny how birthdays cluster like that. The other busy month for us is January: Father and Jonathan and I were all born in January."

Granny said, "Where are Clara and Jourden, Evelyn? Why aren't they here?"

"Now, Granny, they've been in Europe practically all year. Remember? They're traveling all over, wherever they take a notion to go."

"Well, I don't know why they had to go clear across the waters. Reckon we've got a good enough meal here for anybody."

Judd said, "That you have. I give thanks every year for neighbors kind enough to ask me over, especially while Anna was sick and since she died."

Evelyn said, "It wouldn't seem like Thanksgiving without you, Judd. But you may have to do something else next year. I'll be on sabbatical, and I don't know whether I'll be in Meadorsville for Thanksgiving or not."

"I've never really understood this sabbatical thing at the college, Eva. Now I have reason to dislike it too. How does it work? Every seventh year you get off?"

"No, that's the way it works in the Old Testament. But you know that. The Presbyterians who founded Harper let faculty have a year off for study or research every *eighth* year."

He grinned. "I guess that settles the debate about whether Scots or Jews are stingier."

Granny got the joke too and laughed despite her Scottish blood. But then she began asking for Gavin again, and Evelyn had to tell her again that he was dead.

Elaine and Ted came home about four, after Judd had left and Evelyn had gotten the last load of dishes in the dishwasher. They described the wedding and the guests; many of the college people were out of town for the holiday, and others had told Evelyn they didn't intend to go, although she had tried to free them from feeling that their attendance would betray her. But there had still been a houseful of guests. Both the Wills and the Bensons had had buildings named for them at the college, and the old townsfolk had come for Mary Will and the newer for Ward, who had been active in town politics and civic clubs.

Elaine commented that Mary Will looked older than Evelyn.

"I can't say that makes me unhappy, hon, but I certainly don't wish her any ill. She's been a model member of the community, volunteering for everything she should have and writing all the right notes and doing all the things expected of her. And I think getting married is probably important to her; it is to most women of my generation." *Certainly was to me.*

"Why didn't she ever get married before? She's not really bad-looking, and she's got money—old money."

"I think there probably wasn't anybody around good enough for her when she was young, and then there probably just wasn't anybody around." She didn't tell them the gossip about Mary Will and Jack Meador, who had gambled away his father's money and reportedly part of hers before he disappeared. Or about Mary Will's long courtship with one of Ward's colleagues, who was rumored to prefer men. "I hope she and your father make each other happy."

As usual, Ted had left the talking to his older sister. But he said, "Well, I just hope they don't expect me to call her Mother."

Evelyn gave him a one-armed hug around the back. "I doubt if Mary Will wants the title from a big, grown-up hooligan like you."

"That'll be fine with me." He returned the squeeze. "Got any more of that pecan pie, Mummy? Or did old Dr. Adivino gobble it all?"

"I think you'll find plenty. Help yourself. But don't spoil your supper."

108

The newlyweds had flown to Jamaica for a brief honeymoon before returning to Twin Elms, the Bensons' family house, where Mary Will had lived alone during the fifteen or so years since her elderly mother had died. So Evelyn would not have to share Ted and Elaine with Ward this holiday. The kids were still sleeping after getting in late the night before, and she had already cared for Granny. So she could start grading her sophomore papers.

The main question on the test was a comparison of *Brave New World* with *1984*. Despite all the class discussion, many of the students thought Orwell's dystopia was worse than Huxley's; they didn't see that the worst in Orwell, loving Big Brother, was the norm in Huxley. Maybe they were right. Maybe being comfortable is worth more than being free. She'd find out.

She awoke from a particularly boring answer to find herself staring at the closet door in the library. Just after she and the family had moved into the house, she had discovered the medieval woman trapped in the wood grain of the long central panel there. She had never shown Ward; he would have said she was crazy. But she had even named the phantasm—Cressida, after Chaucer's sweet, pliant, fearful lady whose name had become synonymous with perfidy. She also thought of the mirage as Viviane, the witch whom Merlin had made so skilled in his art that she bound him in wood. Viviane or Nimue or the Lady of the Lake—whatever she was called, Evelyn thought of the door as Merlin's revenge: the enchantress entrapped. For surely she could not have bound Merlin without binding herself. The figure had no feet with which to get out of the door.

The grain lines where Evelyn saw the lady most clearly outlined her face, her long neck and gracefully sloping shoulders, and her delicate left arm and hand, which bore a large dark whorl like a ring. Another whorl, crowning her Nefertiti-like headdress, was clearly her misplaced left eye. Her right eye, in its expected place, and her eyebrow and nose formed another graceful line. Her lips, like those of Hendrickje Stoffels in some of Rembrandt's paintings, were fuller, more vulnerable, than medieval fashion dictated; they were closed. Her flowing, fitted robe and sleeve showed her era. She was pregnant, as Evelyn, carrying Ted, had been when they moved into the house.

Evelyn remembered the sharp turning in her own abdomen after her hysterectomy. There would be no child out of her body again. And she was not likely to see what Cressida would bear in her bondage.

Ted's friend Kevin Beaty came over after lunch to work in the basement with Ted on the model airplanes they crashed at the football field or some park. When Evelyn had finished putting the food away and started the dishwasher, she found Granny lying with her arms out from under the covers spread wide on each side, breathing rapidly, her eyes fixed on the ceiling.

"What's wrong, Granny?"

She gasped her words. "I don't know, child. Seems like I can't get my breath."

"I'll get the doctor." Evelyn ran up the stairs and called Elaine to get Judd, then went back to Granny, who was still panting. She knew nothing to do but prop Granny up on her pillows and hold her hand. She felt panicky. *Granny's all I have now.*

By the time Judd arrived, Granny's breathing was slower than normal but still labored. He listened to her chest carefully and told them that there was nothing to worry about; it was called Cheyne-Stokes breathing and was a common symptom of her condition. "But just to make sure nothing else develops, maybe we ought to put you into the hospital, Mrs. O'Neill."

"Oh, no, I don't want to go. Don't take me away from my own bed. If I'm going to die, I'd rather it was here."

"Now I don't want to hear any more talk about dying. You're not that bad off. But I don't want Eva to be up all night worrying about you, either. You can go where somebody'll be paid to take care of you and she can get some rest."

Granny said nothing to that and submitted to their bundling her up for the trip.

Evelyn said, "Should we call an ambulance?"

"No; close as the hospital is, there's no danger in driving her. I'll go with you. Come help me get the car ready. Get some pillows and blankets.''

He closed Granny's door and took Evelyn's hand. "I don't want to alarm her any more than she is already by calling an ambulance. And I really don't think there's any immediate danger. But at her age, Eva, and with her condition, nobody can be sure. She may last another year, or she may go tonight. I want you to know that; you need to get used to the idea." His brown eyes looked at her intently, and he squeezed her hand.

She nodded. "I'll get the pillows." The words came out thickly.

"Get your keys, and I'll warm up your car. I'd use mine, but yours is bigger."

She nodded and brought the keys. She didn't try to talk again.

Evelyn rode with Judd and Granny, leaving Elaine to follow with the boys folded into her little car. At the hospital Elaine worked out a schedule for all of them to sit with Granny in shifts, and she insisted that Evelyn stay first. "Otherwise, you'd be pacing the floor at home wondering how she is. This way you can be with her long enough to see that she's all right and settle down. Ted and Kevin can stay during dinnertime; they've been nibbling all afternoon and won't be hungry anyhow."

The boys denied foraging but agreed to stay. "We can always send out for pizza," Ted said. That was the mainstay of his diet. "When are you going to take your turn?"

Elaine said, "I'll stay after you till they chase me out. Granny'll be asleep by then, and I can do some work on my paper. *Some* of us are serious students, you know."

Amid rebuttals and recriminations, the crew left. Judd had left earlier, saying the air was not too brisk for a walk home.

Her breathing eased, Granny slept. Except for the time she broke her hip, she had not been in a hospital before. The room was cold, and Evelyn retrieved the extra blanket from the closet, then went to the nurse's station to request another; the cotton thermal weave seemed scarcely thicker than a sheet. She spread Granny's robe over the blankets.

Then there was nothing to do. She had not brought her ungraded exams and could not have read them fairly in her upset condition if she had. Nor had she brought *King Lear* to read; the decline of the aged king was scarcely a subject she wanted to think about. She tried to compose a poem about cold hospitals, but nothing came. *I have had no tranquillity in which to recollect this emotion,* she thought. And the only poems that she could remember were like Dylan Thomas's "Do Not Go Gentle into That Good Night." She didn't want to think of those.

Finally she thought of a song her mother often sang, and then she tried to remember as many songs as she could. She sang them softly like lullabies as she sat watching the still face under the oxygen mask.

When she got home from the hospital, she called her brother Jonathan and her sister Jourden Marie, both still in Cedar Springs with their families, and told them about Granny. She decided not to call Jessie and Annette, both too far away to do anything but worry. She wondered if she should call her parents. But she didn't know what to tell them: according to Judd, there was no way to know whether or not they should come home from Florence. So after supper, she wrote them a letter instead and drove it to the post office, knowing that it would not go out until the noon mail truck the next day anyhow.

Then she drove across town to the hospital to check on Granny, who was awake and talking to the boys as they finished their pizza. They shooed Evelyn home, saying she didn't trust them. She would rather have stayed, but went home.

The boys reported that Granny was sleeping when they left at seven-thirty, and Elaine reported at ten-thirty that she had slept the whole time she was there, and all the monitors had shown normal vital signs. Evelyn went to sleep about midnight.

She called the hospital as soon as she got up, and learned that Mrs. O'Neill had rested well. Judd knocked on her door while she was cooking breakfast and told her the same; he had already been to the hospital. He accepted her invitation to breakfast, and over coffee he promised to release Granny if there was no contraindication by ten.

The smells of coffee and warm maple syrup brought her children and Kevin to the table. Discussing the JFK assassination, she and Judd told about the shock and grief, and Evelyn actually forgot about Granny until Judd got up and said, "I'd better leave to check your grandmother out before they charge you for another day and send all you Scots into shock so I have to treat the lot of you."

Elaine volunteered to go with him.

When Evelyn said that she would, Elaine said, "You stay right here, or I'll thump you upside the head with a puddle. You'd just work yourself up over nothing. We'll be right back."

Evelyn said, "What a way to talk to your mother."

Ted said, "That's how she's bossed me around all these years. It's high time somebody else had to put up with it."

Evelyn said, "Well, I guess if I boss my grandmother around, I'll have to get used to being bossed by my daughter."

Elaine said, "Glad you're shaping up, Mom. I'll get my coat, Dr. Adivino."

Evelyn's heart felt lighter. Surely everything was going to be all right.

Granny seemed as healthy as she had for months, so with Judd's approval, Evelyn walked with her that afternoon and treated her normally. They sat in the sunroom and watched the birds at the feeder. Evelyn enjoyed the drama of their competition, but Granny just sat. Evelyn fed her and put her to bed early because she was tired.

Elaine was with Amy Lund, a friend from high school. Evelyn had always felt sorry for Amy because of her drunken father and promiscuous mother. When Amy was thirteen, her mother had run off with a married man, leaving two younger daughters as well as Amy and her father. She had come back after three weeks but left for good with another man a year later. After high school Amy had gotten a job, but she still lived at home and did what she could for her sisters and father.

Granny's absence made it an ideal time for Evelyn to prepare cheese fondue for all of them, including Kevin and Judd; Granny didn't consider fondue real food anyhow and didn't approve of the wine in it or with it. They had fun; it seemed like a real party.

Sunday morning both children had to leave early for their schools, Ted with his long drive and Elaine with the necessity of typing her paper before Monday. After they were gone, Evelyn graded her sophomore tests until Granny woke up, then fed and bathed her, changed her bed, and walked with her awhile. Granny asked for the children and fretted about not seeing them before they left, but both women knew that the eldest, who always had gotten up with the sun, now preferred to sleep her life away.

Evelyn finished grading while Granny took her afternoon nap. The day was bright, and when Granny awoke, they sat in the sunroom and talked sporadically until suppertime while Evelyn knitted on a sweater for Ted. The colors and textures and growing design of the yarn comforted her with their order.

After dishes and Granny's bedtime, Evelyn realized that she had free time, and she knew what she wanted to do with it, had wanted since Wednesday. She went upstairs to the library and took down Keats. She intended to o.d. on poetry.

And she did. She started reading the odes and planned to read them all, but the "Ode to a Nightingale" sent her to Whitman's "Out of the Cradle Endlessly Rocking," where the more familiar mockingbird sang rather than the nightingale. It was not the bird but the sea, the endlessly rocking cradle, that answered the questioner, and the tolling word was not *forlorn* but *death*, "the word of the sweetest song and all songs." She quit when she had finished reading that and went to check on Granny. She lay breathing quietly, so quietly that Evelyn bent over her in the dim glow of the night light to be sure that she was still breathing.

The two weeks between Thanksgiving and Christmas vacation were always difficult. Students didn't have their minds on classes, and Evelyn was already feeling the pressure to finish the semester's work by exam time in January. This was particularly true in her freshman composition section. She had gotten used to students coming to college with no sense of what a composition was, no idea of focus or organization or development. But this freshman section had been especially slow. They were one whole paper behind and would have to work extra hard to make up the time they had lost.

On Monday after Thanksgiving, they had discussed the reading for the day, an essay on different types of families in modern American society, when Evelyn gave the assignment for the next paper: They were to define *family*, using examples they had observed or read about. "Your first draft is due Wednesday," she said.

A groan went through the class, and Michelle Quinn said, "You never give us enough time for papers."

At another moment, Evelyn might have been able to control herself. But just then, Michelle's words ignited her, and irritation raised her voice. "You are already one whole paper behind schedule."

Michelle flashed back, "Well, you shouldn't have spent so much time at the beginning on all that boring stuff about thesis statements and topic sentences."

"It is precisely that boring stuff that you have never mastered that has meant most of you have had to rewrite your papers far more than the average class." She didn't stop. She went on about how students were less well prepared and less well disciplined every year, even about how they seemed to expect the teacher to give them good grades whether they worked for them or not—"without expending any energy," she heard herself say, knowing that falling into Latinate diction was a sure sign of the inflation of her emotions for dramatic effect.

The class sat silent, eyes down. Only Michelle still looked at her, totally hostile.

Evelyn apologized. She said that she was sorry for losing her temper, for addressing them all when her dispute was with one student, and for wasting class time.

They sat looking at their desks. When she began talking about the form of a definition, they diligently wrote without stopping everything she said. *Probably they're writing without thinking too,* she thought. When the period ended, she announced, "That's all for today. See me in my office if you have questions before Wednesday. I'll be happy to check any outlines you want to show me." They all gathered their books immediately and left without the usual talk. She was glad to leave too, even to go outside into the winter drizzle that seemed to have set in permanently.

The next day, Lucy called Evelyn at work; Granny was having another episode of labored breathing. Evelyn instructed her to call Judd and arranged to go home as soon as she could. But before she left the college, Judd called her.

"It's the same as last week, Eva. This isn't in itself fatal but is another serious symptom of her condition. I suggest that you put her in the hospital again and leave her there a few days—till Saturday, when you'll be home again, at least. It can't do any harm and may be helpful."

"You mean for me."

He laughed. "Partly. But for her too. Even you can't monitor her all the time. The machines can."

"Machines aren't people." She paused. He started talking at the same time she did again, but she went ahead; she had to say it now that she had started. "Judd, I don't want her to be alone when she dies. I want to be with her."

"Eva, that's not rational. You can't stay awake all the time for an indefinite period. And she doesn't know whether you're there or not most of the time; she probably will go in her sleep. And you have responsibilities to others in your family."

"She's all the family I have at home now."

"To your students, then."

She had no answer for that. She obviously couldn't leave her classes and spend all her time with Granny; there were no substitute teachers in college, and no one else knew exactly what she had been doing anyhow. "All right."

"Good. Now you can begin letting go by letting Lucy and me take her to the hospital. There's not a reason in the world that you should come home before your duties at the college are over."

"All right." As she hung up the phone, she closed her eyes. *Ostrich!* she accused, and opened them. She walked to the window and looked out into the dreary rain. It was a moment before she realized that she was looking toward the unseen hospital.

The next day, Michelle Quinn was not in the comp class. At first Evelyn was relieved, but then she reflected that she would have to contact Michelle if she didn't come Friday.

Michelle did. Without saying anything, she handed Evelyn her first draft as she came in. It was late, of course, but Evelyn also said nothing. She read it rapidly, making brief notes to herself, then took it back to Michelle's desk and gave her an oral critique so that she could revise with the rest of the class that day. Michelle made a few responses and asked a couple of questions. Student and teacher were both businesslike.

That weekend, when Evelyn was going through the revisions, she absorbed the contents of Michelle's paper. The girl had used the broadest definition of family, a group of persons associated by ties of blood, marriage, or adoption. She defined by contrast with ties of common habitation and of love; using her own family as an example, she asserted that they were still a family, although her parents were divorced, her demanding father had remarried and was not interested in her, and she had no real home but stayed with some friend during college vacations since her mother had driven her out of the house after a quarrel about the mother's boyfriend. She gave detailed evidence of the family's mutual alienation.

I guess I'm not her only problem. I'm not even very high on her list. Then she thought, *What if this were Ted or Elaine?*

Her endnote praised the clear focus on the assignment and the convincing anecdotal evidence. She added, "Talk with me about your situation if I can help."

Rob stopped by her office to ask about a problem with Trey: he was eating practically nothing. Remembering what she could from Elaine's and Ted's toddler years, she reassured him. "All the experts say children won't starve themselves. Just don't let Trey think he can use hunger to get attention or junk food instead of what he rejects."

"He already gets attention; Marcia Lee spends every meal coaxing him or threatening him about his food."

"That'll just make it worse. I'll look at home for some books on the subject."

"I'll be grateful. I've lost my own appetite just watching them square off against each other every meal."

Each day after classes Evelyn went to the hospital. Although she still felt trapped by Granny's illness, it was in a different way, confined in her schedule by the college and the hospital. And through necessity she learned to use her time there. She brought a lapboard to make a desk out of the visitor's chair. Granny often dozed, and Evelyn graded papers or prepared for classes then as she had during the children's naps when they were small. She knitted when Granny was lucid, and they talked. Sometimes Evelyn scarcely knew whether Granny was awake or not: her eyes could be open without her responding, or she would close her eyes but still talk.

Sitting with her, Evelyn often fell into reveries herself, mostly memories of childhood when she was visiting Granny or living with her. Jessie had been Nana's favorite grandchild, and Annette had been Grandad's shadow, playing in the fencerows while he plowed a field or riding on his horse sledge to take the milk cans to the road for the milk truck. But Granny had belonged to Evelyn. Granny's bed had even been where she slept when Father was gone to the war and she and Mother and Jessie were living with Granny and Grandad before Annette was even born. Jessie slept with Mother, and Grandad slept by himself in the little bedroom next to Granny's. Uncle

Nathan was gone like Father, but he wasn't in Europe too. He was on a big boat, Granny said. Every night Granny would listen to her say her prayers, and then Evelyn would ask Granny to say her own prayers. And every night, when Granny got to "God bless," the first one would always be "God bless Nathan and his ship. Keep them safe."

After "Amen," Evelyn liked to have Granny talk with her. She would tell Granny everything that she had done when Granny wasn't around. That wasn't very much sometimes because she stayed with Granny as much as she could. She handed her the clothespins when she hung out clothes; Granny always saw four-leaf clovers in the grass then, and she would point them out for Evelyn. Or Evelyn hoed and pulled weeds beside her in the garden. Sometimes by mistake Evelyn would pull a flower or vegetable, and Granny would show her so she'd know it next time, but she wouldn't fuss the way Mother would. Granny let her cut the gladioli and dahlias and sometimes even the roses for bouquets, though Granny never cut any herself; she said she liked them better outside. And she showed Evelyn how to break asparagus and pick tomatoes.

But sometimes Granny had to go tend somebody sick and she couldn't go along, or sometimes Mother took her and Jessie to visit Nana or shop in town. Sometimes Mother would buy them a new coloring book or a paper-doll book and help them choose the right colors or cut out the pretty dresses. Once Evelyn got a paper-doll book with seven dolls that were supposed to be the same little girl from a baby to a seven-year-old. Evelyn named her Shirley. Each doll looked different and had different clothes. When she was seven, she was almost grown-up. Evelyn would be six her next birthday. Shirley was her favorite paper doll. Granny liked to hear about what Shirley had done. Evelyn could make her do whatever she wanted her to; Shirley wasn't like Jessie, who had a mind of her own.

When they lay in bed, Evelyn asked Granny about the news too. They always listened to the ten-o'clock news right before they went to bed, and Evelyn knew it was about the war that took Father and Uncle Nathan away. Sometimes there would be parts that were hard to hear called "News from the Front," and Granny and Mother and Grandad always listened hardest to that. If Evelyn or Jessie tried to say anything then, one of the grown-ups would say, "Shh!" and not even look at them. They would hear loud noises in the background like firecrackers and a lot of high whining that the grown-ups called airplanes. Father flew a plane; Evelyn remembered seeing him climb into a plane and go up into the air when they lived somewhere else before Father left for the war and they came back to stay with Granny and Grandad.

One night in August, it was too hot for Evelyn to go to sleep. They had all the windows open, but there was no air stirring. Granny couldn't sleep either. At least, she didn't hush Evelyn the way she usually did. There had been a lot of "News from the Front" that night. Granny sang to her, "Go tell Aunt Rhoda that the old gray goose is dead" and "Oh, where have you been, Billy Boy, Billy Boy?" and all the other songs she liked best. But she still couldn't sleep.

Then they heard the first mosquito. It whined a high, sharp sound that went through Evelyn's head the way a mosquito bite goes through the skin. Like a needle. Granny got up and got the flyswatter out of the kitchen without turning on the bedroom light. But when she turned it on, she chased the mosquito around, climbing on the bed to try to reach it. She didn't swat at it until it lit. Then she hit it hard and killed it and turned out the light and came back to bed. But not long afterward they heard another mosquito, and she turned on the light and killed it too. And all night long there were mosquitoes, and Granny got up and killed them. She killed every one.

The next day they learned that Uncle Nathan's ship had been bombed and had sunk. His body wasn't even found. Before he went off to the navy, he used to play his guitar for Evelyn and Jessica. Evelyn tried to keep remembering what he looked like.

Michelle Quinn had finished the definition paper with a good grade, but she had missed the next couple of classes. Evelyn meant to call her but kept putting it off. Then she saw Michelle in the Center, watching a group of cardplayers.

Invading the students' territory, Evelyn threaded her way to the card table and touched Michelle's shoulder. "Michelle, would you see me for a moment."

The girl jumped, but moved to the periphery of the room. She looked guardedly at Evelyn.

As quietly as she could, Evelyn said, "I'm sorry for the quarrel we had in class. I don't like to lose my temper, and I shouldn't have. But certainly you shouldn't let that influence your work. You're bright enough to finish this course, and you'll be doing yourself a disservice to fail it if you don't come to class."

The girl still didn't look at Evelyn, but nodded and said, "All right. I'll come."

Evelyn felt better as she resumed her route to her office.

Later that day, she stopped in on a reception for the retiring public relations officer for the college and saw Ward ahead in her path. They had seen each other across the room in meetings and at public programs since the divorce decree, and they had talked on the phone about arrangements for the children, of course. But they had not met face-to-face. She looked at him as she might have assessed a stranger. He was still handsome. *Distinguished* was perhaps the right word now; the ash-blond hair at his temples was silvered, and his expression was solemn, as it always had been.

He stepped aside, but she walked straight toward him.

"Hello, Ward. How are you?"

"All right."

"Did you enjoy your trip to Jamaica?" *Now there's a faux pas for you—"Did you have fun on your honeymoon with Wife Number Two?" asks Wife Number One. But I don't even have the grace to blush. Or the courage to smirk.*

He didn't seem to notice the gaffe. "Yes, though of course we weren't there long. The scenery's beautiful, and the weather was perfect—not like this rain we've been having."

No, I won't degenerate into talking about the weather. "I haven't seen you to congratulate you since the wedding. Do give my regards to Mary Will; I hope you're both very happy." She meant it.

He seemed to see that. "Thank you. And thank you for the ice bucket; you know I've always admired it."

Of course Mary Will had already sent her thank-you note.

121

"May you have many reasons to chill champagne in it." She held out her hand, and he took it, and they let go as easily as fish slipping through water.

The measure of our distance is the ease.

Evelyn tried to work herself up to getting out the Christmas decorations and putting them up. At least the house would not be so empty then. But she still delayed until the recess began. She knew why. She could not face the memories, not all of them unhappy, of the Christmases spent there with Ward and with Granny. At Christmas the house did not seem dowdy. They had always strung lights on one of the forty-foot spruces at the front until the energy conservation ban on outdoor lighting. Even the living room took well to Christmas decorations. The fireplace on one side and the balustrade on the other offered backdrops for candles and garlands. And the nine-foot ceiling accommodated a tree large enough to maintain a presence in the long room. Her children remembered Christmas in no other place: Elaine had been two when they had moved in, and Ted had been born there.

Granny was still in the convalescent wing of the hospital. The year before had been Evelyn's first Christmas without Granny herself making fried dried apple pies, the clove-scented turnovers that were more a part of Christmas than jam cake or boiled custard or country ham to Evelyn. Last year she had made them under Granny's watchful eyes. She would make a few this year and take some to Granny, but with only herself and the children at home, they wouldn't be the same. And the children would be with her only half the time; she had to share them with Ward and Mary Will now.

The house came alive when the children got home. Ted was out first this vacation. But he wasn't home much. He was with his friends from high school most of the time. Evelyn didn't mind; it was good to see him happy, doing all right in school, talking about new friends

122

and keeping the old, with his own car and bank account and part-time job. He had all the freedom of an adult without all the responsibilities.

Elaine too showed more youthfulness than at the busy Thanksgiving holiday. Always a trickster, her favorite game even as a toddler had been to pop her head between her father and his book. Evelyn's credulity had been her frequent target, and even her college professors were hoaxed with crashed computers and vanished lab setups. Few things lit Elaine's face so much as the success of some prank.

The second day she was home, she spent a lot of time with Judd's housekeeper, Earline Wilks, and wouldn't tell why, but Evelyn knew it had something to do with party decorations. Evelyn had asked the Wiltons, Sue Hart, Rob and Marcia Lee McFergus, and Judd for a holiday dinner. Elaine complained that there would be an uneven number at the table, and Evelyn asked her if she wanted to invite someone. She said she would but wouldn't say who. And on the day of the party, she closed the doors to the dining room and kept her mother out; she insisted that she would do all the table setting and decorating. She also made the dessert, a chocolate almond pâté. Since Lucy Taylor, Granny's companion, still came once a week to clean the house, all Evelyn had to do was prepare the soup and main course.

When all the guests except Elaine's had arrived and the dinner was ready, Elaine revealed her arrangements: Judd's medical-school skeleton, Mr. Bones, occupied the foot of the table, elbows inelegantly propped on each side, but tie and coat (no shirt) suiting him to the occasion. Blue Christmas lights shone from his eye sockets.

Evelyn blushed. Her knees felt so weak that she sat down, hoping that in the surprised shrieks and laughter no one would notice. Her immediate assumption was that Elaine was accusing her of somehow killing Ward, replacing him with a dead man.

But her daughter's face was mischievous, not angry. And the place cards revealed that Elaine was claiming this old friend as her own escort for the evening, "the only man who can't get away from me," her false modesty eliciting the expected protests from her mother's friends. She explained how she and Earline had accomplished their "skulduggery." Judd's predecessor, Dr. Martin, had built his office onto the side of his house, so she had limited time to act. But she and Earline had robbed the crypt while Judd was making hospital rounds; they had smuggled Mr. Bones into Elaine's closet and kept him there until the previous night, when she had dressed and seated him.

While Elaine burbled to the guests, Evelyn reflected that Elaine's interests were perfectly consistent. As a child, she had been fascinated with the skeleton whenever she was in Judd's office. She had collected her own skeletons wherever she could. Throughout her childhood there were new diggings in a plot of lawn appropriately close to what she called the people cemetery next door where she often (cajoling Ted into helping) buried roadkill or dead pets to be transformed into skeletons. Occasionally there were lucky finds like the squirrel bones from Granny's woods. Ward, of course, encouraged her and was sure she would become a zoologist. Her closets still contained shoe boxes labeled RACCOON, POSSUM, or for more familiar denizens, FLUFFY. But she always preferred Mr. Bones, and Evelyn never urged her to read *A Tale of Two Cities* lest she imitate Jerry Cruncher and resurrect some of their people-cemetery neighbors.

Despite the plausible explanations for Elaine's prank, Evelyn couldn't avoid thinking that she might subconsciously be reminding her mother of the blue-eyed Ghost of Christmas Past, who would never occupy the foot of her rosewood table again.

Elaine and Ted had both baby-sat for the McFerguses' son, Trey, so they asked about him. Rob said the boy's newest interest was origami, producing mostly paper hats, cups, and especially airplanes, for which he had a passion. Ted offered to visit while he was home and show Trey some of the model planes he had built. He and Rob tried to set up a time, but Marcia Lee had already planned every minute of the vacation.

She was a wan blonde who wore uncertain colors, grays that could be blue or orchid. But there was nothing uncertain about her opinions. All the faculty wives had heard her housekeeping dicta, including instructions on cleaning out a refrigerator: one must end with a rinse of vanilla water to make it smell good. She had once taken Trey home early from a children's birthday party because another mother had dared dispute Trey's right to take away her daughter's toy.

Sue asked how Granny was.

Evelyn said, "Oh, about the same." She noticed Ted and Elaine exchanging looks; they had both gone to the hospital several times since they had been home. She asked them, "Don't you agree?"

Ted said, "Mom, you see her every day, and she doesn't seem much different. But we both thought she'd . . . broken a lot since Thanksgiving."

Evelyn didn't know what to say.

Talk turned to the new college president, Dr. Swanson. He had come at a busy time, two years before the college calendar was to change to early semesters and the year before the accreditation visit from the Southern Association. And he had brought a sheaf of proposals for his own changes—revision of the organizational structure of the divisions, granting of credit for work experiences by portfolio evaluation, revision of placement testing, the development of a satellite campus.

Judd said, "Is he advocating change for its intrinsic merit or for cosmetic effect?"

Andy Wilton, who taught political science, said, "Some of each, I'm afraid."

His wife, Nina, an artist and art professor, said, "When I've been in meetings with him, he seems to pick up ideas like lint on black wool, and they stick or fall off purely by chance." Her long earrings bobbled with the toss of her head.

The guests laughed. Nine was one of the few faculty members outside the English Department who met weekly to discuss their creative writings. Her specialty was acerbic little epigrams which had no general market at all but were prized by the members of the group, who knew her victims. Despite her acid tongue, she had a kind heart and would help anyone who needed it.

Sue said, "That sounds a lot like my students, except I'm not sure any ideas ever stick to them."

Rob said, "I have a new candidate for the most unrealistic student of the year. One of my freshmen has turned in every paper late, can't remember to turn in her record sheet with each paper, and staples the pages not only in the wrong order but upside down. Guess what her career goal is."

"Copyediting?" Sue ventured.

"No, but you're close: accounting."

Before the laughter ended, Marcia Lee complained of the general lack of carefulness. "I can't get anyone to clean decently for me."

Nina suggested someone, but Marcia Lee had already tried her and found her wanting. Evelyn didn't want to subject Lucy to Marcia Lee, so she said nothing, though it would be a picky housewife indeed who could fault Lucy.

Elaine asked Evelyn in an aside if it was time for dessert, and Evelyn agreed. They cleared the table together, and in the kitchen Elaine began slicing the pâté into curled diamonds.

Evelyn asked if she could help, but she knew Elaine was very much into presentation these days and would probably want to do it herself.

"No. If you have to do something, whip the cream."

"What goes into it?"

"Nothing. Just cream."

Without saying anything, Evelyn put in a couple of tablespoonfuls of sugar; it needed that at least, she thought.

Everyone admired the flowerlike arrangement and praised the rich confection.

"My arteries will suffer, but my palate is rejoicing," Judd said.

Elaine glared at her mother. "You put sugar in the cream."

"Just a little—I thought it needed some."

"The pâté has enough sugar, and the cream shouldn't have any. I told you not to put any in. You just think nobody else can do anything as well as you can."

"I'm sorry." Evelyn thought that Elaine really should have said *"so* well as you can" after the negative, but that was scarcely the time to bring it up. It was an old, formal rule, one Nana had taught her, and trotting it out now would just prove Elaine's assertion. And she *shouldn't* have added the sugar; it was Elaine's recipe.

After Christmas dinner the children moved themselves and their suitcases to Ward and Mary Will's to spend the rest of the vacation. Both assured Evelyn that they would be in and out to see her at home and at the hospital until they left for school again.

But she still needed to get out of the empty house, emptier now than it had been before the children came home, she thought. She spent the rest of Christmas Day and the next morning at the hospital, and that afternoon she began raking leaves in the yard. Along the fence, they had accumulated and were smothering the periwinkle.

The periwinkle leaves—*Vinca minor,* Ward called it—were still green under the dry leaves. She looked around for other winter leaves, magnolia, rhododendron, holly, and azalea, glossy like the periwinkle. Leathery. The surviving blackberry leaves in the ravine were thinner, red as if stained with the juice of their own berries. Winter leaves. Leather leaves. She played with the phrases.

About four o'clock, Judd came out his back door and walked over. "Hello, Eva. I thought Mark Stamps did this kind of thing for you."

"Hi, Judd. He did, and he did all right till football season began, but then I had to call to remind him about every little thing to be done, and sometimes he did it, and sometimes he didn't."

"Does he play on the team?"

"Oh, yes. Betsy showed me his picture every time it came out in the paper; she and Gordon hope he'll get a football scholarship to UT or 'Bama."

"Well, you'll have to find a new yardman then."

"Or do it myself. That's what I've been doing lately."

"Well, you probably need the exercise."

"Yes. I always intend to start an exercise program but never do."

"I go walking every day. Maybe you could join me."

"If I ever found the time."

"Look—a deer!" He caught her arm and pointed.

The doe was running through the woods at the back of Evelyn's property. She leaped over the ravine and branch and ran across the lawn toward the driveway, hesitated a moment at the road, then ran across in two leaps to the yards on the other side that abutted on the college golf course and the dormitory area. She disappeared behind Mrs. Tibbets's garage.

"She's lucky there were no cars coming," Evelyn said.

"She's running dangerous paths, all right."

"I wonder what's worth the risk. There's more open land on this side of the road."

"She may not know that. Or maybe she just wants to find out." The shadows from the late-day winter sun emphasized the quizzical curve of his mouth.

Ted and Elaine were coming out of Granny's room at the hospital when she arrived the next day. After greeting them, she asked, "How long have you been here?"

"About five minutes," Elaine said.

"Don't you think you ought to stay a little longer?"

Ted shrugged, went back in, and sat down.

Elaine said, "She really doesn't want us here, Mom."

"Not want you? You know how much she thinks of both of you."

"Not now. I don't think she cares anymore."

The words twisted Evelyn's heart. They couldn't be true. She approached the bed; Granny's eyes were closed. "Hello, Granny. How are you today?"

"All right."

"Ted and Elaine are here."

"Yes."

"Don't you want to sit up and see them? They'll be going back to school soon."

"No. I just want to sleep."

"But you can't sleep all the time. Why don't you sit up and talk a little with us?"

She opened her eyes then and looked bullets. "Leave me alone. Go away. Don't aggravate me."

Elaine put her arm around Evelyn and led her out. Ted followed.

VI. Annie Bee

The Stairway to Heaven

*T*hey've all come, and the room is so crowded it's hard to breathe. There's something over my face too. If I could just get this thing off my face and get back home in my own bed and rest without somebody bothering me every five minutes, I'd be all right. I just need to sleep a little.

There's a bird flying around in the room too. They ought to know better than to let a bird in here. Why don't they shoo it out?

Open the window and let it out, you all.

Can't they hear me?

I don't think I heard myself. Maybe I didn't say anything.

Gavin'll let it out. Gavin? Why don't you let it out?

Remember the chimney sweeps that got in the chimney at home while we was living in Old Hickory when we first got married? We'd decided before we ever got married to move to your house and sell mine, and so we put the farm up for sale, and I packed up and moved in with you, into the house you and Mary had bought when you first moved down there.

And I tried to like it, partly because I still felt funny about living with you in Cedar Springs and sleeping with you in Ral's bed. But in

129

Old Hickory I just couldn't get used to the noise and the streetlights shining outside so it was never dark like real night so a body could rest. And I missed having big trees. We didn't even have any yard to speak of, just a little postage stamp with cement all around it and people cutting across all the time, trampling what little green grass and flowers a body could grow. And I nearly never got to see Clara and the babies 'cause they all were so far away.

So you come in one day and said—I can hear you now—"Annie, ain't you tired yet of fooling yourself and trying to fool me making out like you like it down here? Why don't you just give in and say you're homesick, and we'll sell this place and move up where you can see Clara and the grandbabies." And I just hugged you and started packing.

But when we got home, we found things was in a mess sure enough. Moles had burrowed up the yard, and creeping jenny and darter was taking the place, and spiders had filled all the corners of the house with cobwebs, and it took a week just to get the house scrubbed and swept out. I don't blame Clara; she'd just had Jonathan then and had enough to do with the four she had before and couldn't see to my place too. We stayed at Clara's till we got the house cleaned up enough to move in at least, and she and the big girls helped us, though she was still nursing the boy.

But the first night we tried to sleep at home, we warn't no sooner in bed—and you'd made me change my rooms all around and brought your bed from Old Hickory to pamper my silly notions, and it was a fine maple bed you'd made yourself that I was glad to bring, aside from my notion about sleeping in Ral's bed—anyhow, we'd no sooner gone to bed than there was a racket in the living room, and we found those dratted chimney sweeps had built in the chimney. And they wouldn't be quiet, but kept on setting up such a racket we couldn't sleep.

And the next day you wanted to light a fire in the fireplace to smoke them out, but I wouldn't let you till after you'd tried to poke them out from below with a beanpole, and that didn't do a thing but send down a lot of soot and mess, and then you thought maybe you could hook their nest out with a bent clothes hanger on a long line, and you rigged it up and weighted it, and you didn't get anything for that but a lot of squawking and a faceful of wings when the mammy and pappy birds flew up and tried to flog you. So finally I let you light a fire in the fireplace, and those birds set up a racket that was ten times worse than anything before, but they didn't leave, and the nest was blocking the flue so all the smoke just backed out and filled the living room, and we had to close it off and open all the doors and windows, coughing and choking ourselves to death the whole time.

And you sat down in the swing and began laughing, and I caught it and couldn't do nothing but laugh either, and Clara came over and found us there, and ever' time we'd try to explain, we'd start laughing all over again. And she called Jourden, and he called an exterminator out of Nashville to come out and get rid of those pesky birds.

But it's Evelyn here instead of Gavin. She's gotten awfully bossy. She won't leave me in peace five minutes but has to be making me walk all the time, taking the covers off when it's cold and making me eat when I don't feel like it. But she's not going to make me walk to Old Hickory. Gavin's here, and there's no need to walk back to Old Hickory, 'specially in my bare feet. Ral might not like it, but I've took him the way he is, and he'll have to do the same for me. And I won't give up Gavin again.

That bird is still circling around and around the room. I don't know how it can fly; it don't have feathers. It's nothing but bones, just dry, hard birdbones, circling around and around, its wings sticking out sharp as its beak. It's a blackbird, but it's lost all its feathers.

There was a mockingbird flitting around Evelyn's house last year after Christmas, when the birds start getting mean to each other ever' year. It had feathers; the white stripes on its wings went up and down, around and around, in white circles like pleated ruffles. Like a girl's fan flirting upside down. And it drove the other mockingbirds away. It built in that big cedar by the outside garage. It's going to again this year, I imagine.

It's so cold. Why can't I get warm anymore? Not since Gavin died. The river was frozen over, and I couldn't get home to Mammy. Mammy was dead, and Callie Jane was dead, died having a baby, the baby dead too, me or Mammy not there to help her, her four others not grown yet and the least one of them barely three years old for Warren to raise by himself. And that baby's grown now and Warren's gone too. Callie Jane's hair never bore a touch of white.

Nate's dead too. Or was that Nathan? I never even got a body for Nathan. His bones'll never be dry, lying there at the bottom of the sea. Do bones rot, or will they turn hard like shells? Or maybe they'll be ground up into sand by the waves. Maybe his bones are all sand by now.

I never saw the sea.

I think Nate's dead now too. I think they're all dead—all my brothers and sisters, all Ral's too. Leathie gone these many years, buried with Ral and Mary and all up in the Hendersons' cemetery. And Gavin.

All Gavin's brothers and sisters were dead by the time I married him; he was the baby of the family.

I never could give Gavin a baby. That's one of the things we gave up. But I had more than I ever thought I'd have. I had enough. We had enough. I was glad he loved Clara's babies so. I gave him grandchildren at least.

Before he died, he was a fox. He lay there on the pillow with his flesh all wasted away and his bones sharp up to his nose. Funny how we change so. Old Mr. Henderson was a weasel before he died, crawling back into his hole, just his eyes shining out of the dark. He didn't know nobody—not his own children. And I couldn't tell if there was something looking at us from behind his eyes, or if there was nothing. And I didn't know which was scarier.

But Gavin knew me. He'd try to grin at me, try to say something. And then all at once he said, "Annie, help," and I tried to raise him up so he could breathe better, and I called, "Clara, come help me; Gavin's took bad," and she come in the room and said, "Momma, he's gone," and I said, "Oh, no, don't tell me that." Oh, no, don't tell me that.

There's still Clara. And her children. But she don't need me; she's got Jourden. And they don't either. Evelyn'll miss me the most. But she'll forget too.

That bird's coming back around again. I wonder why it's come and why they don't shoo it out of here. It wants out. I know it wants out. I can feel it circling, circling, looking for a way out, like me. That's what I want too. I'm circling around and around, trying to get out.

And I will. I'll go out the window with the bird, into the light, and we'll fly out of here and go find Gavin. He'll make me warm again.

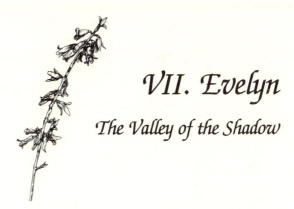

VII. Evelyn

The Valley of the Shadow

*A*s soon as the phone awoke her, Evelyn knew that Granny had died. *Alone. She was alone. And I could have stayed with her,* she thought as the nurse's voice confirmed her supposition.

"What time?"

"The monitors rang the alert at four minutes after four. She didn't suffer; she had been asleep. The night nurse went in at once, but there was nothing that could be done."

Yes. Sure. So much for the advantage of her being in the hospital.

But you didn't stay with her, did you, Evelyn?

"Thank you for calling. Is she still there? Can I see her?"

"She's been taken downstairs, Mrs. Knight. I don't advise you to go there."

She means she's in the morgue already, kept cold, with no one she knows to touch her, dress her, lay her out. "What will they do with her?"

"They'll keep her there till the men from the funeral home come. But we need to know what funeral home to call."

"Loveless at Cedar Springs." Granny had given Evelyn and Mother and Jessica all full instructions fifteen or twenty years before—the funeral home, the burial clothes folded in tissue paper in the cedar chest, the preacher (who had up and died before her despite her wishes), the hymns, the resting place beside Gavin.

That was determined before Gavin took sick and died, regardless of where he was to be buried, regardless of where Grandad was buried.

As it turned out, when Grandad had been killed by the horse, his older sister Molly Lou had said she'd be buried with her husband, Haskell Gwaltney, in his folks' cemetery and Grandad should be buried in her place in the Henderson cemetery in Stone's Creek. So they had put Grandad in the place for Haskell, and there had been two spaces between him and his oldest sister, Mary, Gavin's first wife, and Granny had buried Gavin next to Mary. That left Molly Lou's space for Granny herself to fill out the row, her between her two husbands and Gavin between his two wives, sisters-in-law and brothers-in-law, brother and sister all together. *Tidy*, Evelyn had thought. *And not quite incest, but certainly a kind of ingrownness.*

The nurse was giving other instructions, but Evelyn realized she was not capable of understanding them at the moment. "May I call you back?" she asked. She scarcely waited for the response before thanking the woman and saying good-bye.

She sat by the telephone, the house quiet around her. Empty.

She had not gone to the hospital the day before because she had been afraid she was coming down with a cold, and the visit before that, Granny had been somewhere far away, as she so often had been lately. But the day before that, they had talked a little more. Evelyn had told her what the children were doing, and Granny had asked if she had heard from Mother and Father. When Evelyn was bundling up, she said, "I have to go now, Granny. I love you."

Granny said, "You know, don't you, child, that I've always loved you?"

"Yes, Granny, I know." She had hugged Granny, and they had kissed each other good-bye.

It was such a little thing to have to hang on to.

She imagined Granny lying dead on her bed, growing younger, her hair darkening again, her skin smoothing, looking as she had when Evelyn was a child. Evelyn felt a band around her ribs, so tight that it hurt her to breathe. She remembered when Granny had had pneumonia and had trouble breathing. They had all been afraid she would die then.

She dressed, made the bed, and opened the draperies. It was getting light, for it was after six o'clock. The frost looked like dead snow.

She called the hospital and made arrangements to get Granny's things; the hospital had already called the funeral home, and the hearse was coming from Cedar Springs. She said that she'd bring a picture for the mortician. She wanted Granny's hair in its usual braided coronet, not the bun on top that the nurses had found easier.

She telephoned her parents. She didn't know what time it was in Rome, but she thought it was evening. She hoped that Father would answer, and he did.

"Father, it's Evelyn."

"Hello, Li'lun! We were just talking about you, planning ourselves to call. Happy birthday!"

"Oh!" She hadn't thought about that.

"Why, isn't that why you called? Is there something else?"

"Father, Granny died this morning."

His voice was carefully neutral. "Do you want to speak to your mother?"

"No; you tell her. I'll hold the phone and talk to her afterward, or to you if . . ."

"We'll be back with you in a moment."

Evelyn heard the click of the receiver on the table, then her father's voice, then her mother's outcry. It was not long before Mother said, "Evelyn?"

"Yes, Mother." Both were crying.

"Did she suffer?"

"No, she went in her sleep."

"Well, thank God for that. Your father says we'll come home. We'll make arrangements right away and let you know as soon as we can. Can we do anything else? I feel so guilty, not having even seen her."

"No, and don't blame yourselves for not having come. There was no way of knowing when it would happen, and she hasn't . . . known whether we've been with her or not most of the time."

"I still wish I'd seen her."

"I know. I wish I'd been with her."

They both tried to compose themselves. Her mother recovered first. "Thank you for calling, dear. We love you."

"You're welcome. I love you and Father. Good-bye."

She called Jonathan and Jourden Marie in Cedar Springs, Jessie in Houston, and Annette in Memphis. Jessie remembered that it was her birthday.

She called Wyatt Troutt, the chair of the English Department, and told him. He offered to cancel her classes, but it was the last day before exams, and she refused. "I'll get someone to cover anything I can't. There's nothing I can do for her now anyhow." She knew as she spoke that she was protecting herself—forcing herself to fill her time so that she had none to think about Granny.

She still needed to call the relatives in Stone's Creek. She couldn't even remember her cousins' names. She began rummaging for her address book. But she was interrupted by a light knock at the door.

It was Judd. When she opened the door, he looked at her, then hugged her, saying, "I'm sorry, Eva."

"How did you know?"

"The hospital called me. I thought you'd be up, but I didn't want to wake you if you weren't, so I didn't call."

"I've been on the telephone anyhow."

He had taken her hand, and she led him into the living room, where they sat on the couch. He took the other hand and held both. She knew they were icy cold.

He said, "How are you, dear?"

She started to say, "All right," but she broke down in the middle, and he held her until she stopped crying and blew her nose.

Then he took her cold hands again. "You did everything you could, you know."

She shook her head; she didn't trust her voice.

"Yes, you did. She was only half alive for the last month. But I know from Anna that we always think of the things we might have done or said that we didn't."

She nodded.

He said nothing awhile, but put her two hands together inside his and stroked the top one. It was a comfort, a bond to another human, and she closed her eyes and leaned her head against his shoulder. He released her hands, and she realized they were warm.

He said, "I was going to wish you a happy birthday today, but now I won't. I will remind you that the pain you have now is because of the happiness she's given you all these years, and when the shock is gone, you'll remember those things more than this. That's how it's been about Anna, anyway."

"Thank you, Judd. I'm glad you're here; you help."

"What can I do now? Do you want me to bring her things from the hospital?"

"I'd like to go myself. If I can, I'd like to see her before they take her away. But I'd be grateful to have you with me."

"Fine. I'll get my car and meet you in your drive."

There weren't many of Granny's things at the hospital, and the staff had already put them in a plastic bag and put her personal hospital equipment, her thermometer and so forth, into the plastic basin they had used for washing her. Evelyn looked through the bag while Judd was checking to see whether the hearse had gone; Granny's Bible was on top, and Evelyn opened it to Isaiah 40:

> The voice said, Cry.
> And he said, What shall I cry? All flesh is grass, and all the goodliness thereof is as the flower of the field: the grass withereth, the flower fadeth: because the spirit of the Lord bloweth upon it: surely the people is grass.

She closed the book. All the gold on the edges of the leaves had disappeared, and they bore only thin red lines like paper cuts.

Judd came back and shook his head; the hearse had already left. She couldn't even send the picture.

He drove her to Harper and arranged to drive her home after her classes. She called Jourden Marie and asked her to take a picture of Granny to the funeral home.

She had two classes, sophomore literature and freshman composition sections, with no break between. She thought about asking Sue or Rob to cover them. But what would she do—sit in the office and cry? Besides, in literature, she was pulling together all the previous discussions of *King Lear*, and in composition, a few students were having trouble with the final revision of their last papers. It would be hard for anyone else to pick up, and she really needed to do it herself.

In the literature class, she asked the students to compare the imagery and themes of *King Lear* with those of *Oedipus Rex*, which they had studied earlier. First someone worked out that in both plays sight equaled understanding, and out of this imagery someone else realized the theme of self-knowledge in this play as in the earlier. She told them one of her favorite quotations, from Robert B. Heilman's criticism of the two plays: "The joy of knowing is a sad joy, but those who have tasted it would not exchange it for the bliss of ignorance." That led into the discussion of the nature of tragedy that she wanted and to the consideration of Edgar's speech to his father when Gloucester wanted to kill himself:

> Men must endure
> Their going hence even as their coming hither.
> Ripeness is all.

Some of them saw that ripeness summarized Lear's and Gloucester's psychological development and redeemed the darkness of their tragedy. She did not have time to pull together everything they had discussed; there was always too much to get in. She allowed time for them to ask last-minute questions about the final examination and told them that someone else would administer it.

She had gotten through. She had thought of Granny with every reference to death or aging or loss and had had to control her voice. But the play had helped her put into perspective again the realities of living. Granny's life had been full, and she had known ripeness. Evelyn couldn't call her own knowledge joy, but it was a sort of peace.

On her way back from class, everyone she met in Will Hall seemed to have heard. They offered condolences, hugs, and kisses. She finally got to her office and had closed the door when Rob knocked and came in at her response.

He didn't say anything. He just offered his arms until she stood up, then held her. When he did let her go, he said, "Evelyn, Evelyn, why didn't you ask me to take your classes this morning? I didn't know anything about it till Wyatt told me."

She explained and added, "Talking about Lear probably helped me deal with it."

He nodded. "I can understand that. But I did want to tell you how sorry I am. I know you were as close to your grandmother as most people are to their mothers."

"Yes. I should be grateful that I had her as well as Mother. And that I had her so long."

"Did you know that I lost my own mother when I was nine?"

"No. I'm sorry, Rob."

He shrugged. "It was a long time ago. Things might have been different if she had lived. If she hadn't been sick so long."

You probably wouldn't have had to marry such a managing woman at least, she thought. But she said, "I've been really lucky to keep my parents and her so long. I'm older than you."

"Nine years," he said.

She was surprised that he knew and a little insulted that he said it. She had enjoyed being a young faculty member, close to the students' ages, when she had begun teaching. Now at forty-four she was conscious of how many colleagues were younger than she. But all she did was thank him again and accept his offer to proctor her finals.

Ward telephoned his condolences and offers of help. *Yes, the word is still civilized,* she thought. She wondered as she hung up how he had heard, but of course on a small campus, word spread fast; probably everyone knew by then.

❦

Judd drove Evelyn home after classes, and they set a time to go out to dinner. She heard the telephone ringing as she unlocked the door. It was her parents saying that they were leaving Italy the next day— early morning Tennessee time—and should arrive about ten at night in Nashville. They discussed funeral arrangements, and Evelyn promised to contact all the stateside relatives. Her mother even remembered the names of the cousins in Stone's Creek.

After dinner Evelyn spent most of the evening on the telephone, calling relatives or arranging for the church, music, minister, flowers—all the ceremonial parts of the rites. When she had called all she could think of, she went into Granny's room for any possessions to take with her to Cedar Springs. There were a few clothes that could be given to Goodwill, others that should just be discarded, nothing of any importance.

It was as if Granny had been sucked up by a tornado and all the pieces making up her life—the letters, the plants and rings and diapers and ribbons—had been scattered over the countryside, unrecognizable bits sown like seed with no germ to bring forth life.

❦

Sometime in the night she awoke to hear the Canada geese flying overhead honking, lost in the clouds. She went back to sleep but remembered them when she awoke and started a poem. She tampered with it until she had a complete draft at least, altering the time to dawn, expressing her feeling of loss and isolation through the lost geese. She wasn't happy when she reread it. *Poor. But I need it. I'll work on it later.*

What shall I call it? "A New Day," with irony? No—"Daybreak." Break, break, break.

But I don't intend to break. I have to live while I can. Somehow, I have to live.

Book Two

Spring

For ever wilt thou love, and she be fair!

—John Keats, *"Ode on a Grecian Urn"*

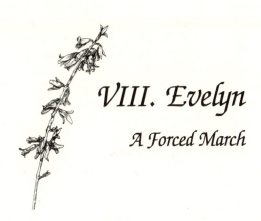

VIII. Evelyn

A Forced March

*T*he beginning of February, when the crocuses were already up and budded, brought the rare snow that December and January had not. On the first day of classes for the second semester, Evelyn opened her bedroom curtains to see the apple trees outside bowed with heavy loads, and huge, feathery flakes were still coming down. Wet snow like that packed into slickness and iced over; she decided to walk the few blocks to Will Hall rather than drive and park on the hilly lot.

The streets had not been cleared, much less the sidewalks. She was grateful for the verticals along her route, the trees, fences, and street signs; without them, she could imagine wandering off into a fog of white. As it was, sometimes the familiar trees didn't appear until she reached their leeward side and saw the dark trunks, or she couldn't be sure whether what she thought she saw a little distance away was a tree or just a mirage of snow and wind.

She was trudging through the snow to begin another term, to start all over with a new group of students, to do the same things again. She wondered whether she was really getting anywhere through the blinding snow or just moving, treading a wheel.

Her upper-division class for the semester was Nineteenth-Century Poetry, and she had one section of Freshman Composition II, which she loathed because of the research paper, and one sophomore literature section.

Michelle Quinn, who had passed Comp I, came by Evelyn's office to express sympathy for her grandmother's death; Rob had told Michelle's class about it when he had proctored the final exam for Evelyn, who had not seen Michelle since the last class meeting. Michelle explained that she was taking Comp II under another teacher because of a lab she had to have. She made it sound like an apology, and Evelyn wondered why; at the same time, she was relieved that the girl had no hard feelings about her outburst.

She was also pleased that Katy Cohen was on her roll for the poetry class; Katy had brightened Evelyn's composition class a few semesters before. She looked forward to seeing her on Tuesday.

By the time she had met her two Monday-Wednesday-Friday classes and finished all the minutiae of a first day, it was well past the end of her office hours. She felt exhausted. She bundled up for the trek home. At least it had quit snowing, and the clouds were gone. But the wind that had blown away the clouds was cold. Still, it was a spring wind; it chilled her skin, not her bones.

She was glad that she hadn't driven. Cars had been left in the parking lots and abandoned along the streets. Two inches of snow in Meadorsville were as treacherous as a foot farther north because the town and college lacked equipment for clearing away snow and because local drivers were unused to the hazard. And the town had gotten over four inches, she guessed, of this late heavy snow.

A car sat in the ditch in front of her house. It had evidently been kept in a garage the night before, for it bore little snow itself. As she plodded toward it, she read and reread the license number: URL 226. It transformed itself in her mind into a chant: You are ill—too too sick. You are ill—too too sick.

She bumbled into the house, took off her wet outerwear, and collapsed onto the living-room couch. She wrapped one of Granny's afghans around herself, insulating against the world, and wished she had the energy to get up again and close all the sheers, all the drap-eries in the house, so that she could lie inside layer within layer. A mummy, not a chrysalis. She didn't want any new beginnings—not of the term or the spring or herself. She just wanted to sink into some soft nothingness, a snowdrift or woolly fog. She saw herself melting like a Dalí watch and draining down into an icy puddle on the floor.

The phone awoke her. Ted told her he had arrived back at Duke safely and was able to change a class that they had talked about. She was scarcely able to concentrate; naps always made her feel as if she had been clubbed.

Ted said, "Are you all right?"

"Yes—just old and tired."

"Maybe you should see a doctor."

"Oh, there's nothing really wrong."

"Would you send us to the doctor for the way you feel?"

"Probably—to see if you had mono."

"Do you?"

"If I do, I didn't have any fun getting it."

"Well, if you don't feel better soon, do something about it, Mom."

"Yes, son."

The next day's sun melted all the snow except that in shadows, which still bore remnants of beauty. By the day after, there were only dirty patches. Evelyn felt like that, sodden and grimy. Each morning her mind would awaken first, and then she felt as she had every morning just after her hysterectomy when her flesh would shudder awake. After a few days, expectation of the shudder had been the first thing her mind knew. But now what she expected each morning was not pain in the flesh. It was the awareness of an ab-sence, a loss. And then she would remember Granny's death and be fully awake in the quiet house.

After a week of classes, life settled into a comfortable routine, although she still felt tired all the time. Her course schedule, meetings, and conference appointments regulated her days, and grading and class preps filled her evenings.

The weather warmed but turned drizzly. She noticed that her skin felt like spring again, moist and soft, and she quit using moisturizer after washing her face. The air was like dew. Her skin was still pale, of course, but it had more color, as if she were a tree and her blood flushed it like spring sap rising. The finches at the feeder were growing more colorful; the male purple finches were deep rose and the male goldfinches lemon, and even the female goldfinches had changed their drabness for a rich olive. Evelyn remembered Chaucer's writing that the birds dressed their brightest for St. Valentine's Day, when they chose their mates.

Occasionally, she had time to go to or give one of the small dinner parties that constituted the social life of most faculty members. And, of course, there were the perpetual series: the Film Series, the Lecture Series, and the Artist Series. These were better attended on a percentage basis at Meadorsville than the many cultural events in New Orleans when Ward and she had been in graduate school. She had decided long ago that this was because people prize food more when faced with a famine than when confronting plenty.

She was invited to Rayna Hull's house following a Thursday-night Artist Series concert for two classical guitars. Most of the speech, music, and English faculty were there and all of the eligible men on campus near Rayna's age.

Evelyn arrived a little earlier than the other guests and offered to help in the kitchen. Rayna, a speech and drama teacher, prided herself on theme parties, and she had dressed as a Spanish *doña* and hired a music major to play Segovia arrangements; she served fruit, cheese, and Mateus.

Evelyn asked if Ward and Mary Will would be coming. She had seen Ward routinely, but not with his bride.

"Yes. I hope you don't mind."

"Oh, no." It might be uncomfortable, but it would have to happen sometime.

146

"I'll be glad to listen anytime you want to talk about . . . anything." Rayna was the campus expert on marriage and divorce, having had four of each.

"No, I have no deep unresolved feelings, I think," Evelyn said.

"Then you weren't—that is, Ward wasn't seeing Mary Will before you decided to divorce?"

Evelyn smiled. "No, I don't think Ward would have thought of doing that. And I'm not jealous about his marrying so soon, I think. If anything, I feel guilty."

"Now, don't tell me: Did you match them to get rid of Ward?"

Evelyn laughed outright at that. "No, I never thought of anything so clever."

"I did, you know, with Fred; he and Winnie were much better suited than we were, and I figured it would be doing us all a favor."

"Well, congratulations; they seem to be a very happy couple."

"Thank you."

Rayna's self-satisfaction showed that she wasn't thinking of her own abortive fourth marriage after Fred to Leon, who had evidently chosen her successor himself.

Still, the idea of freeing oneself of a husband by interesting him in someone else amused Evelyn. She could have done something like that! If she had been manipulative.

But saying she felt guilty must have misled Rayna; maybe she thought now that Evelyn had broken with Ward because of an adulterous affair she had been having herself. She tried to explain. "No, when I said I felt guilty, I meant for failing to keep the marriage alive."

Rayna didn't reply, and Evelyn reflected that it hadn't been very tactful saying that to a woman who had let four marriages die. She took a tray of food out of the kitchen and resolved to try to think more before she said anything.

Sue Hart, who had just recovered from flu and still looked unwell, sought Evelyn out. "Evie, would you have some time tomorrow when we could talk?"

"Sure, Sue—anytime after ten."

"I'll be in around eleven, then; I have a ten-o'clock comp class."

Evelyn wondered, but she obviously would have to wait to see what Sue wanted.

Joe Jamison, a music professor with some background in guitar, was talking with Rob and Marcia Lee McFergus about the concert. The older guitarist, Lesley Parman, had been the more skilled, he said, and elaborated on his technical strengths.

"He really wasn't very well dressed," Marcia Lee said. "His shirt looked yellow, and the tails on his coat needed pressing." Marcia Lee judged people by laundry and houses by window glass.

Evelyn said, "I couldn't help watching him all the time. It was strange; Braswell moved much more. He contorted his face, and his fingers moved frantically. But Parman's quietness riveted me."

"I felt that too," Rob said.

Marcia Lee gave him an annoyed look. "Rob, I need some more wine."

"Do you want anything else?"

"No, dear."

Rob offered, "Evelyn? Joe?" At their refusals, he left with Marcia Lee's glass.

Marcia Lee turned toward Joe and asked when the next student recital was scheduled. After his answer, she began a long, rapid, unpunctuated list of the recitals she had attended in the last two years.

Evelyn, in effect cut out of the conversation, moved toward a gesturing colloquium of speech teachers, then veered toward a solitary piano teacher, Willabeth Waring, who knew every city east of the Mississippi by its major department store. Until Evelyn saw someone else leave and could decently depart herself, she could seem to listen to Willabeth with little effort and less strain to the eardrums than with the speech teachers.

Then we'll all leave like lemmings, she thought, *plunging back into our solitary worlds of vicarious knowledge.*

She could still hear Marcia Lee's voice in the background, and her tabulation of concerts provoked description. *Her words are lemmings, uniformly round, brown, and huddled, bunched like cobblestones, rushing toward destruction. I'd rather sound like a boa constrictor, my sentences winding, sinuous, svelte, punctuated by bulges that, we can hope, are lemmings.* She worked on the phrasing, seeking a rhythm, while Willabeth complained about the pay given rock and country stars compared with the income of serious musicians.

Evelyn's glance lit on Ward across the room, Mary Will on his arm. She was looking up at him, and Evelyn thought, *That's what Ward has always needed. Not competition at home.*

Then she reflected, *Ward would say that lemmings and boas live in different habitats.*

The next morning, Sue appeared in Evelyn's office promptly at eleven carrying *Women in Love.* "Have you ever taught this, Evie?" she asked.

"No. I've taught *Sons and Lovers* with some success; our students relate to the parental conflict. But I'd think this would be harder to teach. Are you teaching it this term?"

"No; I'm considering it for fall if I do Modern Fiction. What do you think about using it?"

"Well, I have a harder time with it myself than with *Sons and Lovers;* Lawrence's attitude in it doesn't seem consistent."

Sue dumped the book onto the floor by her chair. "You know, I keep looking for the book Lawrence didn't write—one about a woman who was equal to a man, or at least important to him, outside of bed."

"Then *Women in Love* certainly isn't your book. I mean, Birkin even pants after Gerald. And Lawrence probably isn't your man. He says in nonfiction somewhere that man must lead and woman follow, which means, of course, that he's free to direct himself, but she isn't."

"Maybe the real reason I want to teach the book is that very first conversation between Ursula and Gudrun, the one where Gudrun says that marriage is impossible, that the man makes it impossible."

Evelyn waited a moment, but Sue didn't go on, so she said, "Is that what you really want to talk about?"

Sue took a deep breath and huffed it out, then said, "I'm pregnant."

"Well, I don't know whether to congratulate or commiserate."

"I don't know, either."

"How does Jeff feel about it?"

"I haven't told him. You're the first person I've told."

"Really! I'm honored."

"You've had children, but you have a life too. I guess I want to know if I could."

149

"But I don't have a husband anymore."

"Yes, that's part of it too. I've had a lot of fun with Jeff, but I somehow can't see him as the devoted father. Cripes, he's just a big kid himself."

Evelyn bit the earpiece of her reading glasses. "It would have been a lot harder to bring up Elaine and Ted without Ward. It was hard to do it *with* him sometimes; we didn't agree on how to treat the children. But it would probably have been harder without."

Sue shook her head. "I can't imagine marriage." She grinned wryly. " 'The man makes it impossible.' But I can't imagine having an abortion or giving a child up for adoption or having a real life while teaching with a baby. I probably wouldn't even get tenure if I had a baby 'out of wedlock.' Maybe not even a contract for next year."

"When is the baby due?"

"The end of September or the first of October. I can't take the pill, and we got careless a couple of times around Christmas."

"So you'll need to ask for maternity leave from classes in the fall. Too bad you couldn't deliver a month early or so."

Sue laughed hollowly. "I know a woman who had a C-section just before the end of the year so she and her husband could claim the child as a tax deduction. Never thought I'd be tempted to imitate her." She got up. "Well, I'd better leave you to your lunch and take my problems with me. Thanks for listening, Evie."

Evelyn stood up and hugged her. "I'll do anything I can to help you. I mean that; let me know if I can."

Sue nodded and left.

Evelyn had tended Granny's houseplants since she had first moved in with Evelyn and Ward a year and a half before she died. Several of the plants had died too, but Evelyn felt bound to care for the survivors as long as they would live. After the winter, several were in bad shape. The African violets were not blooming, so she bought fertilizer, choosing one with a high middle number on the label to produce blooms as Ward had advised her years before. She repotted those violets that were obviously crowded, cut off the many small plants that were trying to grow on the sides, and even stuck the larger of those in moist sand to see if they would root. She wasn't sure why. But there was guilt in letting flowers die.

Most of the leaves on a big tropical thing that someone had sent when Gavin died had fallen and turned brown. She had left it on the screened-in front porch, and it probably had gotten too cold in the winter. She decided on radical surgery: she cut off all the brown and bent-stemmed leaves, leaving only three obviously new, green leaves furled and upright. Under the old leaves she found a tag calling the plant a spathiphyllum. She watered it. It would live or die; that was all she could do.

She remembered Granny's old policy that she and Ward had always laughed at: Granny "gave a chance" to an ailing plant. She would set it outside and leave it alone in the sun and the rain. If it lived, she reinstated it in the house. If it died, she dumped it out and stacked the pot for reuse. Ward said the chance she gave it was the chance to overcome the natural laws of the universe.

The crocuses finally opened the last week in February, first the chrome yellow, glaring in the spring light, then the cream and white and purple. Evelyn stood at the sunroom window and looked across the lawn into the woods bordering the ravine. Sunlight cast shadows of the tree trunks across the ground, over the old year's leaves, through which no green shone yet. The sun shone on the ghosts of beech leaves, the brown oak leaves, and the dead dark seedpods on the lilac bushes. The tips of the boughs were yellow and red with sap; the buds were swelling. Birds clamored. Dull roots stir before April in Tennessee.

The first weekend she could get away, Evelyn went to Cedar Springs. Mother and Father were in Memphis visiting Annette, but Evelyn was supposed to go through Granny's things at her farm to see if there were any mementos she wanted. She stayed with Jourden Marie and Clark.

Friday night, she and Jourden Marie stayed up late talking; she told about her divorce, and Jourden Marie told about her and Clark's efforts to have children. They had gone through all the testing Clark and his doctor friends had heard of and had found no cause for infertility, but after seven years of trying, they still had no child. Evelyn ruefully wished that Sue and Jourden Marie could change conditions.

Ten years older than Jourden Marie, Evelyn knew less about her youngest sister than about either of the others. She went to bed feeling a little closer.

The next morning, they both went to Granny's, unoccupied since Granny had gone to stay with Evelyn "for a little while." Jonathan's farm workers had kept the grass cut, but the place still looked abandoned. Its bare-limbed trees rose above the house like skeletons. Evelyn remembered the big trees in summer, the maples and box elder and hackberry, the elm, not hit by the Dutch elm disease, not yet, anyhow, rising over the house, shading it from the merciless sun. Granny had told her about planting the trees with Grandad when they had first built the house.

Winter storms had blown down limbs, which Evelyn started picking up till Jourden Marie said, "Why bother with those? Jonathan's men will get them before they mow. If it's not sold by then. He thinks we should put it on the market right away."

Evelyn nodded. "I know. But I can't leave all these limbs lying around. She did hate so for the yard to be untidy." She bent for another.

Jourden Marie nodded and helped Evelyn carry the heavier limbs back to the burn pile in the garden.

Evelyn was dragging a large limb when it broke; it was rotten through. She burst into tears, and Jourden Marie looked at her, wondering.

Evelyn shook her head and tried to smile. "It's a hopeless job, tending old trees." She had to catch her lower lip in her teeth to keep it from trembling.

They went through the house, Evelyn picking up a few things she remembered Granny using, requesting a few pieces of furniture if no one else wanted them, thinking that they would be good for Elaine or Ted in a few years when they set up housekeeping. She certainly had room to store them.

"Do you want to go through the outbuildings?" Jourden Marie asked.

"Yes, just to remember them; I don't imagine there's anything I'd want there."

Both were surprised to find full fruit jars in the cellar. Granny had frozen her produce for several years before she left the farm, and they wondered how old the canned food was. Jourden Marie asked if it would be edible and decided to take some, so they found boxes and packed them. When she had selected all the cans that she wanted and they had loaded them into Evelyn's car, Evelyn went back to the cellar; she was trying to remember something there.

The memory came when she closed her eyes and smelled. Granny had led her and Jessica down the stone steps in the dark, although she had carried a flashlight. It was cold, and Granny said they were going to see a flower, a night-blooming cereus; it would close up if there was too much light. She even shut the door after they were inside to keep out the faint starlight. Evelyn wasn't scared, but she didn't like being in the dark cellar. She noticed the musty, earthy smells more than she had before.

Then Granny shone the flashlight on a dark green plant with flat leaves. It had a white bloom about five inches across that was like a lily or a star with a whole row of white stamens pulling her sight in toward the center, as if a secret lay there. It was so white that it seemed to shine in the darkness. They had looked at the white flower until Granny turned off the light. Then they had gone back to the house without talking.

One night when they were talking on the phone, Evelyn told Elaine about her aunt's trouble conceiving.

Elaine said she couldn't imagine going through all the tests and tedium of basal-temperature thermometers and such that people put up with just to have children.

"I'd have done it to have you," Evelyn said.

"Well, of course, but I'm special."

"And you don't think your children would be."

"Here we go again on the grandmother kick. All right, I'll have children, but I don't want my genes diluted with anybody else's; I'll have to have my kids by cloning."

"Your father can clone his orchids. Are you that rare a plant?"

"But of course. Either that, or I'll just have to be reincarnated like a phoenix: the world can't do without me."

"I see your self-esteem is healthy. Or does the lady protest too much?"

There was a heartbeat's too much silence on the phone. Then Elaine said, "You know me too well. Actually, I'm feeling pretty down."

"What's the matter?"

"Oh, Mom, I've gone and let myself get too attached to Bill, I'm afraid. I don't want that now."

"And how does he feel?"

"I don't know. I've broken up with him; he's just not the right one for me. It's not smart for me to like him."

"Why do you say that?"

"Well, he's really just not interested in the sort of life I want. He doesn't plan to go to grad school—just wants to work for his father and take over his business and get married and have kids."

"Does he want to keep you from doing what you want?"

"He just better never try!"

"Would he if he could?"

"No-o-o-o, I don't think so."

"Then basically, you're objecting that you can't make him do what you want him to do."

"Mother, you're mean."

"I hope not. But Nana always said a person had a right to do with his or her own life whatever he or she could, so long as it didn't infringe on someone else's rights."

"That's another of your rules."

"Yes, I know; I have hundreds. Maybe some of them are worth something."

"Maybe."

That week at the writers' meeting, Rob read a difficult episode from his novel. The protagonist, Keith, a twenty-five-year-old man supporting his manipulative mother and alcoholic father, had met Valerie, whom he was attracted to. Returning home after that encounter, he confronted his mother about his desire for independence. Rob's problem was to show the mother's hold over Keith, to account for his not simply leaving. Rob had used the parents' financial needs, but the group didn't find that sufficient motivation.

Brandon Martin, a young English instructor and Rob's tennis friend, suggested Oedipal conflicts, but Rob thought that that ground had been turned too often. Nina Wilton said that Keith could be latently homosexual and use his mother as an excuse for avoiding the heterosexual attachment, but Rob didn't want to take the novel in that direction. Thinking to find a path, Evelyn asked if he knew how the novel would end, and he said no. She knew that novelists and even poets wrote that way sometimes; she couldn't imagine herself writing without knowing where the work was going. The discussion trailed off without finding a solution.

Brandon read the latest chapter of his own work, a satire, and they discussed it. Evelyn was next. She read the draft of her poem written after Granny's death:

Daybreak

After light I heard the geese's calls.

> They settle here for winter,
> Glean the corn too scant for harvest,
> Swim the uniced pond
> In flocks.

But these were two
Parted by the fog.
They cried to each other,
Tried to meet again,
Their voices smothered, lost.

> And I am tied below the fog
> In blankness.

Rob said, "The poem conveys emotion, but it's less polished than what you usually write, Evelyn. The diction seems a little off. For instance, *uniced pond* calls too much attention to something accidental to the poem."

Nina said, "Makes me think of a naked cake."

While they laughed, Evelyn looked at the line. "Would *iceless* be better?"

Rob said, "Certainly the sound is—the soft *s* instead of the intrusive *t*. There's less consonance with *pond*, too."

The others agreed.

Wyatt Troutt said he didn't like the first line somehow. "I think it's the diction again. *Heard* is too passive."

Rob said, "What about *woke*? That picks up on *Daybreak* and suggests psychological as well as physiological action."

Evelyn considered. "Yes, that'd help. Maybe you should be a poet, Rob!"

"Maybe so. I don't seem to be having much success with my novel."

That evening, Evelyn was struck with the possibility of introducing another angle into Rob's plot. What if the son were tied to the mother by the need for emotional security and feared risking that for the young woman? She thought of T. S. Eliot's poem "Animula," which always seemed to her an abstract of "The Love Song of J. Alfred Prufrock": the small soul, warped by the hand of time, "Fearing the warm reality, the offered good." It was a more nearly universal modern problem than financial need or homosexuality or even perhaps the Oedipal conflict. It would change the focus of the scene; it might change the novel. But that would be Rob's choice.

She called his number.

Marcia Lee answered, and Evelyn announced her name and asked for Rob. "I wanted to talk with him about some writing we were discussing today."

"He's busy right now. I'll tell him."

"It's rather complicated. Please have him call me back when he's free."

"He's going to be tied up all evening. You can tell me whatever you want, and I'll tell him."

Evelyn explained the best she could, then said, "Good-bye; thank you for your help." She heard the click of Marcia Lee's phone before her sentence was done.

Evelyn continued to feel dragged out. Just getting up in the morning was a struggle. She went to bed early, but she lay tossing and turning for hours, too stupefied to read but too upset to sleep. Or she dozed and woke, dozed and woke. But she had nothing to be upset about; all her long-standing problems had come to an end. She couldn't understand it.

Finally, she acted on Ted's suggestion to see a doctor; she made an appointment with Judd. She had had her routine mammogram and gynecological exam from Dr. Wang in October, but she had not seen Judd professionally in ages. She felt a little awkward. It had been years, she realized.

He noted the fact. "Well! My neighbor remembers to check on her health! You know, if all my patients saw me no more than you, I'd starve to death."

"I eat my apple a day religiously; that means I'm not supposed to have to see you." Her light words hid tension between their friendship and this professional relationship. She felt even physically awkward, exposed, in her skimpy examination gown.

He sighed. "The bogeyman and me—no one wants to see either one of us. But since you're here, you must have been driven by something still more frightful."

"I don't know, Judd; I don't really feel sick, but I don't feel well, either."

"Well, we'll see if we can find out what's bothering you."

He asked then about virtually all her systems, listened to her heart and lungs, shone lights in her eyes, ears, nose, and mouth, and instructed his nurse about other tests. Then he told her the office would call when they got her lab reports.

She revised "Daybreak" that night:

> After light I woke to calls of geese.
>
>> They settle here for winter,
>> Glean the corn too scant for harvest,
>> Swim the iceless pond in flocks.
>
> The two that woke me flew alone.
> Parted by the fog,
> They hailed each other,
> Tried to meet again,
> Their voices smothered, lost.
>
>> And I am bound below the fog.

It still wasn't right, but it was a little better.

At her follow-up appointment, Judd told her the reports gave no indication of anything abnormal. "That doesn't mean you aren't sick. It can mean some problem isn't revealed yet, and we could put you in the hospital and give you more tests. But I'm not really sure your symptoms warrant that. Your body may just be reminding you that you need to take care of yourself and haven't been."

"You mean a psychosomatic problem."

"You say that as if it were a weakness of character."

She didn't answer at first. "I guess that's how I think of it."

"Then try to think of it this way: Sickness can be a natural reaction to hurt or grief, particularly in people who won't give in to it in other ways."

"So if I grieve properly, I'll cure myself."

"I'm sure you've already grieved properly. I'm telling you that you may have to grieve improperly—let your feelings of pain and loss for the last two years out in some outrageous, totally unacceptable, appallingly human way."

"You think I'm—repressed, inhibited—"

"I think you're a strong-minded, strong-willed, strong-conscienced woman who does what she has to—or thinks she has to—so much that she never asks what she wants."

"All those *strongs* seem to add up to something sort of stubborn."

"They add up to *strong*. But even strong people need advice sometimes. So I'm telling you what you have to do for a while. If you don't do it, you're disobeying explicit doctor's orders."

"And what are your explicit orders, doctor?"

"You're asking so you can reject them."

She had to smile. "Maybe not. I have to hear them first."

"Well, thank goodness that your liberal education makes you at least listen before you refute what I say. The first thing I want you to do is promise to walk every day. Your lifestyle is altogether too sedentary. That should help your weight, which I shouldn't mention if I were merely a gentleman but am obligated to as a doctor; you've gained about twenty pounds since you first started teaching at Harper, almost all in the last five years. More important, walking will help you avoid osteoporosis, toward which you may have inherited a tendency from your grandmother; you're a good bit taller than she, but you're small-boned and fair-skinned like her, both predispositions to osteoporosis. And walking will get you out of the house some. I see you fill your bird feeders every morning; it's time you touched nature, saw it without a plate-glass window in between."

"How far must I walk to satisfy your commands, sire?"

"Well, as with all exercise, you shouldn't overtax yourself at first. For a week, try just walking to school and back every day. You ought to work up to about forty-five minutes a day, all at one time. That's what I try to do to keep from falling into a more advanced state of decrepitude."

"You aren't all that old."

"My last birthday was the half-century one."

"And I forgot it."

"Proper treatment entirely for that particular age. Now, the walking is only the beginning of my prescription. The rest is to take a real vacation just as soon as you can: get away from Harper and Cedar

Springs and all your relatives and go somewhere you've never been before. And I don't mean to do research on some poet you teach."

"You mean you won't let me go to California to see the places Robinson Jeffers wrote about."

"Is that what you want to do?"

"I thought of it when you said I should go somewhere I've never been before."

"Then do it. As soon as you can."

"That may not be such a bitter pill after all, Dr. Adivino."

"I aim to please, Mrs. Knight . . . Ms. . . . ."

"Eva. What you've always called me. But 'Mrs. Knight' is still on my syllabi."

That evening in the library, she looked up from her grading to see Cressida-Viviane trapped in the door. In grain lines beyond the figure itself, lines that she hadn't noticed before, she saw the wavering movement of flames around the prisoner, as if she were a witch being burned at the stake. Or Jeanne d'Arc.

All at once the imprisonment seemed unbearable; better to take down the door and literally burn it, free the captive spirit in real, cleansing flames.

You're crazy, lady.

She picked up her papers and turned out the lights and took her work through the dark, empty house to her bed to finish.

She dreamed that Greg Beall came back to her from the dead, but he was on the other side of a wall. His eyes were darker blue than she remembered. He smiled his beautiful smile and beckoned for her to join him, and she crossed through the wall between them. She was surprised at how easy it was to pass through the wall and how willing she was to go. He held her, and everything else faded away.

She awoke to see the wide, white louvered closet door on the wall opposite her bed. The room seemed gray and dull in the dawn, but she knew there were green trees outside it. And she envisioned the louvered doors folding back, releasing a smooth, flowing whiteness that she could pull up from the floor like a Roman shade. She knew that her will pulled the shade. She could lie there on the bed and without moving a finger pull up that white nothingness to engulf herself and extend outward infinitely.

And then she was really awake. She wished for sleep again, wished for the unimaginable, imageless verge of never having been.

IX. Evelyn

The Primrose Path

*B*etsy Stamps continued to make excuses for Mark's not getting Evelyn's yard work done; she seemed more interested in her son's keeping his job than he was. Evelyn remembered the rush Ted had been in the year before, choosing a college, getting ready for prom and graduation, and finding a full-time summer job, so she didn't blame Mark. But she didn't know anyone else to do her yard work. Mowing wasn't a necessity yet, but there was perpetual debris to clear away, and the shrubs should be pruned of their budless limbs.

So she attacked the job one Saturday morning. The calycanthus especially seemed to have lost several main shoots. Probably the series of drought years were taking their toll. At any rate, the scissors pruner couldn't cut the larger dead limbs; she had to get the tree loppers. The wood assailed her nose; the sappy parts smelled like sassafras and the woody like rosin, and their scents were potent, like the strong, spicy odor of the shrub's blossoms.

"I see you're taking my advice to get outside," Judd said.

She jumped; she hadn't heard his approach.

"Yes. I was just thinking that my exercise would please you," she said.

The morning sun shone out of the June-blue sky onto his smooth face, which had a kind of planed squareness—rectangularity, actually—about the jaws, the eyebrows, and the high forehead. But he smiled. "How is the walking?" he said.

"I've been doing my stint to and from classes, rain or shine. But that takes less than ten minutes. I know you said I need to add a longer walk each day, but I haven't found the time."

"Made the time?" He raised his eyebrows.

"You're ruthless."

He grinned. "It's my job. But I do know how hard it is to schedule an exercise program. I'm willing to help. I walk every evening after dinner. The old British constitutional. Would you join me?"

"That's certainly more attractive than walking alone. But I'm probably not up to your level yet."

"Then you may walk as far as you are up to and then desert me. I'll be grateful for your company as long as I have it."

"As Elaine would say, it's a done deal." She took her hand out of her dirty glove, and they shook on it.

They talked about Elaine and Ted and Judd's sister Rachel in Baltimore, who had recently broken her wrist in a fall. Just as he was leaving, Evelyn called him back. "Earline doesn't come on weekends, does she?"

"No."

"Then why don't you come over for dinner before our constitutional tonight? Without anyone to cook for, I probably don't eat well enough to suit my doctor either."

"Contrary to popular opinion, I'm not a helpless male who can't stir-fry some chicken and veggies, but I'm delighted to accept your invitation."

They set up a time, and Evelyn began planning a menu and schedule as she carried the dead limbs off. She started singing to herself; her day now had a destination. And she realized that her life was her own, that she could decide to do things with it.

The fine weather continued through the day, although it was windy. Rays of light shone through cracks in the cumulonimbus clouds.

Judd brought an armful of forsythia blooms, golden boughs that Evelyn put in the crystal vase that had been Nana's. The petals seemed stiff, frozen. But their gold lit the sunroom table next to the shadowy living room. She and Judd enjoyed the advancing spring through the sunroom windows. The small leaves on the tree outside were quite distinct, and new green growth veiled the bare limbs of the trees along the ravine.

After dinner, they walked past Judd's house, the last in town on Franklin Pike. Collins Lane, blacktopped only a couple of years before, turned off the pike beside his property and meandered toward outlying farms. Judd directed Evelyn down it. "This is the way I usually take. There's less traffic and more to see."

The fields on their right rose into hills, the first mostly in pasture, the farther ones wooded. It took a while for them to adjust their paces to each other, but as soon as they did, she forgot the walking and focused on the scenery. The late sun shone on the soft tan carpet of the old year's leaves scored with dark trunks of fallen trees.

She said, "I know the leaves are already budding out, but it seems as though everything is still waiting for the year to start."

"Maybe that's because the time of day doesn't accord with the season; sunset and spring don't go together. And the sun's not setting yet, but it soon will."

"You're right. But I like this sort of wavering spring light, not quite certain yet. It keeps the scenery from looking hard like picture postcards, all seen in bright sun with no shade, no shadows—no variations, just a flat, sharply outlined world." Her speech had streamed out like a waterfall, unexpected and unplanned, unthought till she said it. Maybe that came from her being alone so much. She realized that she wasn't used to sharing her thoughts like that. It made her feel suddenly shy.

He said, "You write poetry, don't you?"

"Yes, but I've not written much for a while now. Too long. And not much that's any good." The admission was more to herself than to him.

"Maybe you'll want to keep a walking journal."

"That sounds like a good idea. You should be a writing teacher!"

"Just trying to interest you enough to keep my walking partner."

That night she wrote a few notes about the walk and played with images of the sunlight in the woods. Expectancy emerged as the dominant emotion. But then she remembered the sunset, glowing pink with silhouettes of the nearly bare limbs; although the light had lain on the distant hills, they had walked down the road in shadow.

The next evening before their walk, Judd came by, bringing her a blank octavo book for a journal. It was bound in flame-stitch print in reds and blues and had unlined, heavy linen-weave paper with gilt edges. The heft of it in her hands pleased her.

The sophomore literature class progressed smoothly. The Comp II plodded through exercises on quoting, paraphrasing, and summarizing, difficult tasks for imprecise students and maddeningly boring for Evelyn to check. And the current-affairs subjects themselves held little interest for her; subjects didn't vary much from year to year. She realized one day that all the time she had been conferencing—relevantly, she believed—with a student about his use of sources on Islamic fundamentalism, she had been woolgathering about Wallace Stevens's peignoired woman incongruously escaped with her cockatoo to a weathered farmhouse Judd and she walked past, the porch of which was bordered with lard cans filled with sultanas, coleus plants, and Joseph's coats—nothing at all to do with Shiite Iran. She forced herself to focus again on the student's research.

The Nineteenth-Century Poetry class began Keats. Evelyn always feared and delighted in the encounter. Her students either loved or hated his poetry, and she responded so deeply to it herself that their responses mattered more than for most works. She began with the medieval narratives "The Eve of Saint Agnes" and "La Belle Dame Sans Merci," luring the students with story and emotion. She spent most of the class time eliciting the way Keats used contrasts: cold and warmth, food and starvation, color and darkness, sex and death, love and cruelty.

Michelle Quinn came by the office to complain about her new teacher, Wyatt Troutt. She said that he was cold and didn't care about the students, and Evelyn realized why she had become Michelle's confidante: no one else, parent or teacher, had cared about her enough even to be angry with her. Seeing her as a child, Evelyn wished that she had a real mother. She listened and tried to guide Michelle toward better communication with Wyatt and hugged Michelle as she left.

Rob poked his head into the office and said that he wouldn't be able to make the writers' group. "As a matter of fact, I probably won't be able to come anymore. Marcia Lee has enrolled Trey in a swimming class in Franklin every week, and she always has her hair appointment the same afternoon, so I'll need to take him."

Evelyn thought, *And far be it from Marcia Lee to change her hair appointment so Rob could do something he wanted.* But she only said, "I'm sorry. We'll miss you."

"I'll miss the group's help too."

"What did you think about the suggestion I phoned you about?"

He leaned against the doorframe and puckered his brow. "I'm sorry. I don't remember. I must be losing my mind."

"You know—you couldn't come to the phone, so I told Marcia Lee about it." He still looked blank, so she went on. "The possibility of having Keith's conflict be his *emotional* dependence on the mother."

He came all the way into the office and sat down. "She didn't tell me. You mean just his fear of being on his own."

"Yes—the old bit about not wanting freedom but merely a kind master."

"Well, that certainly has possibilities. It also links to his fear of forming a relationship with Valerie."

"Yes. More Prufrock than Oedipus. With maybe some manipulation from the mother."

"I like that. It seems like something I've meant without knowing it."

"It certainly fits with the earlier scene at the picnic with the father."

"Yes—and with Keith and his mother on the visit to the aunt."

They talked about the relations already established in the novel to see if any would need alteration. When that subject trailed off, Evelyn sensed that he was about to leave. But she knew that she could hold him there in the chair. She said, "What about the situation of Prufrock for the travel episode? The poem is a journey with self as the companion; the mother is the companion in your version."

He settled in again, and like a couple of hounds after a fox, they chased the possibilities smelled out until each was caught or run to earth. This time she released him. *No wonder Marcia Lee controls him; it's so easy to do. Or has she just trained him that well?* She felt devious as he left.

And why didn't Marcia Lee give him my message?

"Where did you get a name like Adivino?" Evelyn asked Judd as they walked. "I thought for ages that you were Italian."

"Actually, I got it—or my ancestors did—in Spain. It was common for the Sephardic Jews—those in Spain and Portugal during the Middle Ages—to translate their Hebrew names into the local language."

"What does *Adivino* mean?"

"*Prophet,* I think. One who divines."

"Well! I'll have to watch what I think around you."

"You think I have ESP?" He grinned. "The name probably just means I had some ancestor who forecast a drought or something."

"Like the woman that the weather forecasters consult every year to find out how many big snows we'll have."

"Yes, someone like your grandmother, who used to count the fogs in August or the hairs on caterpillars."

"Maybe so. But I still think you must have had a wizard in your family tree to get a name like that. I've no such glamorous ancestry; *lanier* just means a fastening, like *lanyard*." She thought of her old pseudonym, Vivian Bond.

"Ah, but you don't need a name to announce your powers. Better to hide them; in the Middle Ages you'd have been burned at the stake anyhow."

"Whyever do you say a thing like that?"

"Eva, dear, you couldn't have stayed orthodox, and you couldn't have stayed quiet."

"You think I'm not orthodox?"

"I think beneath all those social wrappings around you, something flows—water, the sap of a tree, or the lava of a volcano."

"And that's what you divine."

"Yes, like a water dowser. Or a seismologist." He raised his hand and pointed. "But look—there's a bluebird. The first I've seen on this farm."

They talked of the bird then, its vivid color in the sun and its quick flight. But she thought about his assessment. It was bold of him to make such personal judgments about her. And exaggerated. Volcanoes!

As if aware of her resistance, he kept the conversation on their outer world for the rest of the walk.

When they were returning, she saw atop the first hill the single row of newly leafed-out trees blowing against the sky. Their trunks were like long legs, and they reminded her of horses running. She wondered where the herd was going. She didn't ask Judd; she was half afraid he might know.

The academic calendars for the three schools affecting Evelyn never synchronized. She and Ted shared a week for spring break, but Elaine would not be off until the next week. Ted had asked Evelyn to go with him to Cedar Springs to see Granny's house. He and Elaine had both spent happy times there before Granny had needed care and come to live with them in Meadorsville. And Ted had been Granny's favorite great-grandchild, probably because of the son she had lost; he was the oldest boy in his generation. Ted and Evelyn planned to visit Jonathan and Carolyn and their brood that night; Jonathan, fifteen years closer than Evelyn to Ted's age, had assumed an older-brother role toward his nephew.

So Ted and Evelyn drove north to Cedar Springs Tuesday. The spasmodic showers didn't mar the pretty drive. Grass and trees flaunted fresh green, and daffodils blew in the March wind.

The daffodils—buttercups, Granny would have called them—around her house were in full display. They were not the large, named varieties that Ward had planted in Meadorsville, King Alfred and Mount Hood and the others ordered from Wayside Gardens and White Flower Farm, but the early, common small yellow buttercups that every farmyard in Tennessee paraded in March. They had multiplied through the years into a thick, irregular row inside the rock fence on all sides except the garden, where Granny had planted monthly roses inside the fence and floribundas on it. The lines of rock and flowers had protected the house like a fortification. Granny always said only trash gave their chickens the run of the yard.

But the fluttering daffodils were the only visible life at the house. Evelyn and Ted talked about the lack of chickens and barn cats and cattle in the fields; the empty windows were in her mind and, she was sure, his, but neither mentioned them. The daffodils and fence had not fortified the yard enough to keep out something that had gotten in and stolen everything dear to her out of the house, leaving the trees to shade nothing. She silently resolved that unless she had to, she would never come there again.

Wanting to cut flowers to take to Lanier Bluffs, Evelyn found an empty fruit jar and tried to fill it, but the backyard pump was evidently broken; its handle seemed attached to nothing. She looked in the old hiding place inside the bird feeder and found a house key, so she tried to fill the jar in the kitchen. But of course the water had been cut off. Ted offered to go to the creek and get water.

He had just gotten back and they had begun cutting daffodils and flowering quince when they heard thunder. Snatching a few more blooms, they listened for the first big drops that would come after the thunder. The rain came as they raced to the porch, the big drops and then the torrential sheets. They sat in the old swing awhile, listening to the pelting on the tin roof.

He said, "Everything's dancing, the rain, the buttercups, the trees whipping in the wind."

"Yes."

"You say that, but you don't mean it."

She evaded him. "You're dancing. I can see it in your eyes. Is there someone special you're thinking about?"

He laughed. "I think I've come down with a case of undying love, Mom."

"Well, undying love's easy to dismiss for somebody who doesn't have it. Otherwise, it can be a near-fatal disease."

"That's cynical."

"Yes, but maybe I'm just envious of you, son. The truth of the matter is that most people would rather be sick with that disease than well. What's she like?"

He got out a picture showing him too, evidently one made at a dance, and told Evelyn about her. Melissa Chang, delicate-featured and lovely, had been born in California of parents who had come from Korea.

He said, "Does it make a difference that she's Korean?"

She could see that he had worried about this, so she gave the question full attention to be sure herself and convince him. "No. Neither intellectually nor emotionally. You know the only thing I ever asked you about your girls."

" 'Don't choose an airhead.' Yes, I know. I've wondered: Did you ever tell Elaine the same thing?"

She laughed. "No. You've caught me in a double standard. But women are expected to choose a man of superior intelligence."

"Is that just because you tend to think of men as superior in intelligence to women?"

She stared at him a moment. "I don't know. I don't think so."

"Melissa's two years older than I am. Does that make a difference?"

"More now than later." She realized that he was testing her and that she had some prejudices to investigate.

She also realized that his views were different from Elaine's. Maybe he would marry before she did. Evelyn wasn't sure why, but Elaine had erected more defenses against becoming close to people.

The second child is easier than the first in most ways. I never worried about Ted the way I did Elaine; I never tiptoed in and woke him from his nap because I wasn't sure he hadn't somehow died in his sleep, and when he caught the childhood diseases, I knew what to do, and when he left home for college, I was prepared for it because I had begun imagining it two years before when Elaine left. Now when he registered for the draft, that was a shock; she never had to do that. I thought, What will I do if I lose my beautiful boy? And now when I think about his marrying some girl I don't know and moving off to California—

She said, "California may be the biggest hurdle. Is she infected with the state madness?"

He laughed. "She's been brought up more conservatively than we were, Mom. Or you even."

"Heaven protect the poor child."

A pair of L. L. Bean gum shoes—ducks—arrived for Elaine before she reached home on break herself. Ducks were the preferred footwear at Centre, Elaine's college; she had already worn out one pair there. Shopping was the first thing she wanted to do when she had caught up on sleep missed during the last few weeks. Bound by classes, Evelyn couldn't go with her, but Monday night, she enjoyed sitting in Elaine's room seeing the purchases spread out on her bed. The first acquisition was a pair of bathtub rubber ducks, bright yellow, of course.

"Whatever are those for?" Evelyn asked.

"They'll make my fashion statement for the spring. I'll make a slit in the bottoms right here and slip them over my Bean ducks. See? Ducks on ducks."

Evelyn shook her head. "What else did you get?"

Elaine was planning to be a teaching assistant in graduate school after her senior year, so she had gotten a blazer and a couple of skirts and blouses to add to her professional wardrobe. At Centre, dress ran to jeans or shorts, depending on the weather, and vastly oversized T-shirts or sweatshirts. Evelyn had complained about the ugliness of such clothes, but Elaine had told her that coed dorms had destroyed glamour; there was no point looking fabulous for class when the guys had seen the women in curlers and grubbies the night before. All in all, it seemed a more realistic way for fellows and girls to get to know each other, but Evelyn was still glad that Harper, more conservative, kept separate dorms for different genders.

The girls at Centre compensated for the lack of glamour on the outside with frilly undies, and these constituted the remainder of Elaine's purchases. Evelyn asked if she had bought them at Frederick's of Hollywood.

"Mother! That's *déclassé*. They're from Victoria's Secret. Nobody would wear anything that wasn't from Vickie's."

"Oh. Pardon me."

Evelyn called one garment a teddy, and Elaine corrected her on that too. "These loose ones are teddies; they're to wear at night. And the fitted ones are bodysuits. I'm not sure what this one is." She held up a black lace nothing with red hearts strategically placed, but small.

"Fantasy," Evelyn ruled.

Elaine laughed. "You may borrow it anytime you want, Mother."

"Gee, thanks."

"You ought to be grateful that I'm maintaining my femininity; I do it partly for you."

"I know I have some hang-ups about traditional roles; your brother and I touched on that when he was here." She told Elaine about her conversation with Ted.

Elaine said, "You know, I think the hardest thing for me to understand about your attitudes is simply the importance you put on marriage. Sex, yes, but why marriage?"

Evelyn thought. She wanted her children free to establish their own values, but balancing that freedom with her own views was not easy. So far, she had been lucky. They had given her and Ward no real anxiety and were independent, responsible young adults. She knew that Elaine was not advocating a life of senseless promiscuity, and she didn't fear her daughter's getting pregnant and bringing home a fatherless child. But she wasn't sure how to answer the question.

"Maybe it's mostly the way I was brought up. But children do need to have two parents. Also, each person needs to relate to someone else in a basic way. Marriage is the only social arrangement which brings two people together so they have to deal with their basic differences permanently and almost constantly and certainly intimately. In writing about Poe, D. H. Lawrence said that that is what is wrong about incest, that the two involved intimately with each other are so like each other that they have little adjustment, little growth, and really they are each involved in self-love."

"Sex gives intimacy."

Evelyn thought about saying, "How do you know?" But she didn't. "Superficially, yes. But sexual partners sometimes have almost no intimacy at all emotionally. Real intimacy means feeling safe enough in the relationship to be honest with each other, to show even the fears and anger about the other. It means being sensitive to the things a partner doesn't say. Then the two have to love each other enough to accept one another for what they really are."

"Did you and Dad love each other that way?"

172

"No." Facing it before didn't make it easy to say, especially to her daughter. She couldn't look at Elaine.

But Elaine let her off the hook. "How can people tell before they marry whether that kind of intimacy will develop?"

"If I knew that, dear, I wouldn't be divorced. I think sometimes—maybe all the time—we just have to risk it. And if we fail, we have to decide if we can risk it again. Few things in life are really irrevocable, I believe; most of the time we can undo and try again."

"What things are irrevocable, Mother?"

"Murder, suicide, and having children. I've committed one twice. And have no regrets."

"But someone else might say that every act of our life is irrevocable. I can't turn a corner on a street without changing something about me and maybe something about someone else."

Evelyn nodded. "Of course, that's true too. Living with those contradictory truths, plus everything that happens that we have no choice about, makes the human condition. I certainly can't give you the answer for that; I just try to take whatever happens to me, choose the best I can when I can, and live with the consequences or try to change them."

"Well! Evelyn Lanier Knight's guide to life!"

"Yes. Work out your own." *With fear and trembling.* Evelyn looked down from Elaine's window into the top of one of the apple trees; the spring wind was ripping the petals off. They flew down like snowflakes and heaped up in the shining grass. *Petaldrift. Or are they whitecaps? Petalfoam. To drown in apple blossoms. Or orange blossoms?*

Tuesday, Amy Lund came over to eat dinner and spend the night with Elaine after Amy finished her shift at a local restaurant. She looked like her errant mother: their classic features and long, straight hair gave them an innocent look. Ironically, Mrs. Lund had somehow been innocent, despite her affairs. Or perhaps naive or even lost was more accurate. Evelyn knew that Amy was not innocent either; she had slept with many boys her age, as Elaine had told Evelyn. But Mrs. Lund had not known; she had offered to help Amy get birth-control pills as soon as she turned eighteen, long after Elaine and even Evelyn knew Amy was sexually active. Fortunately, Amy had been less naive than her mother—savvy enough at least to insist on birth control. Evelyn hoped the girl would grow to be more mature and responsible than her mother as well. She had warned Amy herself about the care necessary in choosing a husband. *As if I were such a great expert!*

Before Elaine left to spend the last half of her vacation with Ward, she took a stuffed dinosaur to Trey McFergus, her former baby-sitting charge, for his birthday. She complained that Mrs. McFergus had rushed her visit, not seeming to want her to play with the child.

Evelyn told her about Marcia Lee's keeping Rob from attending the writers' meetings and not relaying her telephone message. "It's almost as if the woman is jealous of me, Elaine."

Elaine giggled. "You can put an end to that."

"How?"

"Next time you see her, just make a pass at her."

"Oh, you're impossible, child!"

"What's wrong? It'd give her all sorts of new things to think about."

Mother and Father called from Houston, where they had been visiting Jessica. They planned to come to Evelyn's next; they were visiting all their children before returning to Europe for their interrupted tour.

Evelyn looked forward to the visit. Losing Granny and Ward had increased her need for other ties. Also, she asked Mother to redecorate Granny's room while she was there; the colors reminded Evelyn of the depression of Granny's illness and death now every time she went into the room. Mother sounded glad to help.

After she hung up the phone, Evelyn wondered if she should redo the whole house, make it her own, make it fit her new life. But how could she do that when she didn't know herself what her new life was like?

174

Sue Hart came into Evelyn's office the next day and closed the door. "I may want to join your writers' group, Evie."

"Well, great! Rob's just dropped out. But I didn't know you wrote."

"I don't. But I'm going to start a project: rewriting *Pygmalion* for the eighties."

"And what's your angle?"

"I'm doing role reversal: the woman is going to be the shaping influence."

"Sounds like a lot of John Fowles. But is this another kind of indirect announcement?"

"You know me too well."

"Let's say that I'm coming to understand your style: you approach sensitive subjects through literary allusions. Now quit beating around the bush and tell me. From the way you look, the news must be good."

"It is, I think, Evie. I told Jeff about the baby, and he said we should get married right away, and he's been badgering me so I think he really wants it. And I guess I do too. So we'll do the old-fashioned thing: marry privately and announce that we've been secretly married for ages. Isn't that positively Victorian?"

"Quite. But it sounds like a happy ending—or beginning. I always confuse the two."

"I think it can be. That's where *Pygmalion* comes in. I think Jeff can really change. Do you think people change?"

"Well, I couldn't teach if I didn't. Just remember that students change us too."

"I could probably do with a little. And the baby will change us both."

"That's for sure."

Right after Sue left, Rebecca Cane, an art student, stopped to talk about Frost's "Fire and Ice," the subject of the sophomore literature class the day before. She had brought a tape of Leon Russell's song, which Evelyn hadn't known, and they listened to it and discussed how the music used and enhanced the poem. Rebecca wanted to paint the poem, not, she explained, as an abstraction or a representation, but as an allegory, two figures in opposition like yin and yang, a male in icy green and a female in complementary red, maybe both in carnival costumes.

Evelyn gratefully added Rebecca's name to her short list of students with synthesizing, creative minds; her greatest reward in teaching was knowing those. She celebrated them.

So far, it had been a terrific day.

The discussion made Evelyn arrive late at a meeting of the committee selecting the sophomore literature texts. She took a chair between two places already claimed by books and papers on the table; their owners were evidently getting coffee and some sweet rolls that someone had brought.

Rob took the chair at her right. They greeted each other, and he smiled. She looked away. But she still felt his presence beside her.

He leaned toward her. "Would you like me to get you some coffee?" He put his hand on the back of her chair.

Although his hand wasn't touching her, she felt it like a weight against her, stopping her breath. She couldn't bear it but stood up. "I'll get some myself," she said, smiling apologetically. "Thank you anyhow." Then she just stood.

He looked at her, his eyebrows raised, leaving his hand on her chair. When he took it off, she could move away toward the coffee.

When she returned, she felt that she could control herself, but all her senses were alive to everything around her. The colors in the covers of the texts that people had brought to talk about glowed as if they were fluorescent. She was acutely aware of the noise of the air-conditioning, the smell of cinnamon and coffee and chalk dust. The spring sunlight pouring through the windows seemed the brightest she had ever seen. Most of all, she felt the substantiality of her own flesh: the angle of her waist and shoulders, the extension of her legs and feet, the touch of her fingers against each other.

Irrelevant and sometimes irreverent ideas about what her colleagues were saying flew into her mind, and she shared the better ones with Rob. He responded, so they kept a private conversation going at the same time that they followed and participated in the general discussion. When the coffee urn was passed, he refilled her cup without asking, his left arm again across her chair. She thanked him, but when she tried to drink, she couldn't swallow. His long fingers moved restlessly; she wondered if he had long toes. Seeming to look at someone past him, she covertly studied his face. His expressions shifted restlessly too; something about him seemed hungry. Someone mentioned Sappho, and she thought of a line: "A thin fire races under my skin."

She lowered her eyes. *This is ridiculous. And wrong. He's married with a young child. He's nine years younger than I am. Nine years.*

Then she looked at him, the dark hair, the neat profile, the dark blue eyes. He was listening to something Wyatt was saying, and when Wyatt finished, he turned and whispered to her, "Wouldn't it just!" His smile was boyish.

She didn't have the slightest idea what he was talking about, but she smiled back and nodded. She couldn't think; she just wanted the meeting to stretch on forever, the way meetings seem to when they are dull, keeping her and him together, insulated from the rest of the world by the invisible fog she felt screening them.

Finally, the group chose some texts, named others for consideration at the next meeting, and adjourned.

Rob stood up, saying, "I have to pick Trey up at the nursery school. I'll see you tomorrow."

"Good-bye." She didn't look at him. She wondered if he had known her agitation. Had he felt anything himself?

She didn't remember the walk home. She called Judd and begged off their constitutional; she said it was too late because of her meeting, although the evenings were getting longer and they had walked through the dusk several times. Judd didn't urge her. She ate a tuna-fish sandwich and settled down in the library to look over the texts being considered.

Then she remembered something she had seen when walking home. Two children had been playing in a yard. Just as she went by, they ran out of the spring sunshine into the shade of a lilac bush, and the yard had gaped empty.

She reached for the journal Judd had given her. But instead of writing prose, she set up her words as poetry. Then she rewrote the whole poem on a loose sheet of paper, taking out all the punctuation and capitalization:

> in this may-world
> sun-children careen through grain
> trampling shouting
> picking daisies
> flinging
> petals to the sky
>
> hush
>
> see the smiling
> private
> shadows

She walked to the bathroom mirror and looked at her face. It glowed as though lit like a jack-o'-lantern. *This is the face of a woman who wants another woman's husband.*

X. Clara

The Even Tenor of Her Ways

*C*lara rinsed each dish before she put it in the dishwasher. She knew that Evelyn put them in dirty, but they ought to be at least rinsed first. Evelyn might be bright and have degrees and teach college, but she hadn't ever paid the attention Clara had to housekeeping. "So what do you think about your father's health?"

"The tan he got in Houston certainly looks good, and I don't think he's fair enough that it'll hurt his skin. Why do you ask? Has he been sick?"

"No, but he's not as young as he used to be. And both his parents died young." *And with Momma gone, he's all I really have now.*

"Now, Mother, you certainly can't think he's doomed to an early death because his mother drowned at sixty-two. I don't know about Grandfather Lanier; he died of a stroke, didn't he?"

"He was sixty-eight when he died, but he was nothing but a burden for your poor grandmother for six years before that. And your father's sixty-seven now."

"But his father was a different kind of person, a Type A personality if ever there was one, from what you've said."

"The other night, I dreamed that your father had died. And

someone strapped me down on my stomach and poured hot wax on my back, and when they peeled it off, my skin came off with it." She hadn't told anyone else about the dream. It made her feel practically ill to think about it, but she hadn't been able to get it out of her mind.

"Oh, Mother." Evelyn put down the platter in her hand and hugged her. "But it was just a dream."

"I don't know what I'd do if I lost him." *Let me go first. Please, let me go before him.*

Evelyn didn't answer her for a minute. "No, I don't know either, Mother. You don't have many interests apart from him."

"I never had time; I've always been too busy seeing to everyone else's needs."

"I know that, Mother. You've brought up the five of us and helped with Granny and the grandchildren. But now you could certainly have some time for yourself. Maybe you should build some interests of your own."

"What? The only thing I've ever done was the interior decorating, and I really don't want to get into that again. Except for projects like yours, I mean," she added. "Of course I enjoy doing it for family. But I don't want to have a shop again or anything like that."

"I'm really grateful for your help in redoing that bedroom. I couldn't face it the way it was, reminding me of Granny all the time. Thank you again."

"You're welcome, dear."

Evelyn was just standing without raking the leftovers into the plastic containers she had gotten out to put them in; she was always easily distracted. She said, "Maybe you could continue to travel."

"I wouldn't enjoy it except for your father. It just disrupts the order of things—always packing and unpacking in some strange place without enough drawers."

"You've enjoyed reading; maybe you could do that more."

"It's no substitute for living, Evelyn."

"Yes. I know that, whether I practice it or not. What about your music? You've always sung."

"My voice isn't what it used to be. Now I sound like some old woman sometimes, wavery as water. And I don't have the training to play for church or direct the choir."

"What about your own health, Mother?"

"I'll probably live to be eighty like Momma." *What would I do to fill all that time without Jourden?* "The cancer's all that's ever bothered me, and that's not come back anywhere else. I do get checkups."

"That's good."

"What about you, Evelyn?"

"I get my checkups regularly too. I've also been walking lately; Judd Adivino told me I should, and he nags me unmercifully if I lay out a few times."

"Good for him. And it must be good for you; you look much better than you did when we came home for Momma's funeral or even before we left for Europe." *She can be pretty when she takes care of herself; not striking like Jessica, of course, but she has good bones and regular features. All our children look good. And our grandchildren.*

"Thank you."

"You're welcome. And you've started taking care of yourself again. You're wearing makeup and perfume."

"Yes, but I changed scents."

"You don't use Chanel No. 5 anymore?"

"No, nor anything similar. I've tried several scents. This is Charlie. Do you like it?" Evelyn held out her wrist to be sniffed.

"It's all right; it's young. It's a little too musky for me. Your father prefers florals and spices."

"How long have you used Tabu?"

"Since 1935. Your father gave it to me that Christmas." She laughed at herself. "I guess I don't experiment with perfumes much."

"Nor men either."

"Well, of course not!" *I shouldn't be so sharp; she's thinking of Ward. I already said too much about that when she first told me she'd asked for the divorce. But Ward wasn't a bad husband; he was never unfaithful, I'll bet. And he provided well.*

Evelyn said, "Elaine's been going with the same man for over a year now, and Ted seemed to be getting serious about someone when he was home for spring break."

"Well, I know they're growing up. But they seem too young to settle down. And I'm too young to be a great-grandmother!"

"Granny was a lot younger than you."

"Yes, but times were different then. Women didn't have much they could do except get married and raise a family." *Which is why I don't know what I'd do now without Jourden. What I'd be.*

They finished putting away the food, and Evelyn started the dishwasher, so they went into the sunroom, where Jourden had set up his easel and was painting the tree outside the window. It was a nice picture, all full of sun and shadow. After they had all talked about it a few minutes, she could tell from his face that he was still engrossed in the painting, so she suggested to Evelyn that they sit in the living room. She turned on the television set, and Evelyn laid out a hand of solitaire.

There was nothing very interesting on television, so she turned the set off and watched Evelyn's game. After a minute, she said, "That's not right. You're playing with eight stacks instead of seven."

Evelyn said, "I'm not playing Klondike. I got bored with that a long time ago. It doesn't give much room for skill."

"So how do you play?"

"Do you want the whole lecture?" Evelyn gave her Jourden's crooked smile; all the girls had it, but Jonathan didn't.

"You mean you've worked out a rationale for the way you cheat at solitaire."

Evelyn shook her head and wrinkled her nose. "That *is* what you'd call it. Look, Mother, solitaire is always the player against Fate. The only area for variation is how much advantage each has. I give Fate better odds by hiding more cards; there are only sixteen in my hand and eight exposed, seven fewer than in Klondike. But I give myself more scope as player, more free will. I don't have to play a card just because I can. And after I've gone through the deck twice, I hold the cards like a regular hand that I play at will."

"But that's cheating."

"Whom do I cheat, Fate? But you still haven't heard the worst. If I have two cards alike that I could play, I try one and turn the card under it over. But if I can't play with the new card, I replace it and the first one I tried and play the second and turn over whatever was under the second."

"Well, that's just not the right way to play; you ought to play like everyone else."

"That's just exactly what I'd expect you to say." Evelyn smiled again.

She watched Evelyn for a few minutes, then said, "You know, I always have a feeling that the face cards are like people. Isn't that silly?"

"I don't think so, Mother. I suspect a lot of people think that. You know *Alice in Wonderland,* where the cards are characters. And even the nursery rhyme about the queen of hearts. That's a sneaky way of telling some scandal, you know."

"Really?"

"Yes. Didn't I ever tell you about Little Jack Horner?"

"What about him? I don't mean the rhyme; you know I know that."

"Well, he was an official under Henry VIII when Henry left the Catholic Church and robbed the monasteries. And in taking monastic property for the king, Jack Horner dipped in and stole a plum or two for himself."

"Honestly! It's just a child's rhyme, Evelyn." *Nothing's ever simple to her. Why can't she just take it for what it seems?*

"Maybe so. But lots of the old nursery rhymes could mean more than appears. I always thought Peter, Peter, Pumpkin Eater must have been a wife murderer with an unusual hiding place for the body. And the queen of hearts, that we started out with—that fits the whole courtly love tradition."

"What's that?"

"Well, I *won't* give you the whole lecture on that, but in the late Middle Ages, when a knight was gone for a long time on a crusade, his lady was left home alone with young squires. The lady was above the squires in rank, and of course to them she was forbidden fruit because she was married. But the squires grew up, and they were supposed to honor her, and daily contact had its effect, so sometimes a squire became the second man in a triangle—stole a tart. That's the beginning of the romantic ideas of the lady on a pedestal and love too great to resist and the elevation of the lover to a higher spiritual state through his devotion to the lady."

"Well, I never! It's just a way of fancying up adultery."

"Ye-e-e-s. But you know lots of stories about that—Guinevere and Arthur and Lancelot, Tristram and Iseult and King Mark—most of the great love stories, on down to Anna Karenina and her two Alexeys. So each suit of cards—love, death, art, and wealth—has its own king, queen, and squire or jack, who is often called the knave."

"Why does the king of hearts have his sword broken, do you think?"

"Does he? I guess I never noticed."

"Look—see? He holds it up behind his head, but it's either broken off or too short to show on the other side of his head."

Evelyn laughed. "Well! If anyone has a long enough sword, it ought to be the king of hearts!"

"What do you mean?"

"Oh, Mother, you've read enough Freud to be able to figure out what a short sword would mean."

Goodness! I'm glad I never said anything about it at bridge club. "The jack of hearts has a weapon, but it doesn't look like a sword."

"No; I think that's a battleax."

"And whatever it is, he isn't holding it; what he has in his hand is a feather. Is that Freudian?"

Evelyn laughed. "Almost anything can be. Think about it. But I imagine it's supposed to be a quill. And that fits with my interpretation of playing cards as reflecting the courtly love tradition: the squire wooed his lady with his writing, not with force."

"Do you think about stories like that when you play solitaire, based on the way the cards fall?"

Evelyn laughed again. "Not usually. But I do have some other quirks about cards. Even the number cards have sorts of personalities to me."

"Like what?"

"Well, most of them have gender, age, and position. The ace is older, masculine, and powerful. I guess that's Father, the first man in my life. I'm the deuce: feminine, young, and unformed. The deuce means the devil, too; maybe that has something to do with the doctrine of original sin. But I'm also the four as an adult; I suppose it's like the difference in a play between the ingenue and the leading lady."

"Who's the trey?"

"Oh, that's you—feminine, older, and very powerful. Three is a magic number. So is seven, but it's masculine, as are five and six. Those three—five, six, and seven—are the leading men in the cast. Six is nicer than five, but five is strong, half of ten and what we count by, like our fingers. Eight is Granny, and I don't know about nine and ten. I never really worked this out as a complete system, I guess."

"Well, then, there's some hope you're not completely crazy." They both laughed.

184

"Not yet, anyhow."

"I see where Elaine gets some of her odd notions."

"Yes, she's been reading *archy and mehitabel* and started writing verse about being reincarnated as a skunk who pays off debts from her former life."

"Honestly, that child. Will she ever grow up?"

"Not if she can help it. Her current career goal is to be a kept woman."

"Evelyn! Not seriously!"

"No, Mother, not seriously."

"Well, thank goodness for small favors!"

"As a matter of fact, she also says she wants to marry a man named Poole so she can name a son Seth."

"Poor child!" But she laughed.

Jourden came in from the sunroom then. "Well, you all seem to be having a good time." He kissed Evelyn on the forehead, then sat on the couch beside Clara and put his arm around her.

"Yes, we are, dear. Did you finish your painting?"

"I think so. I don't rework them the way I used to."

"They're always fine."

"I know you think so, dearest. I know you think so."

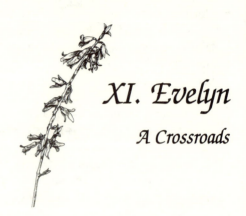

XI. Evelyn

A Crossroads

*E*velyn's journal entry called the day after her parents' visit a day of birds. Walking across campus, she saw a mother killdeer chasing a baby, smaller but marked like the adult and with long scuttling legs like stilts; the fledgling had evidently left the nest before the mother considered that safe, although few nests give less protection than a killdeer's. In a bush outside her office window, two robins pursued the unending task of filling their offspring with insects and worms. As she walked home, she saw a cardinal atop the tallest maple in the neighborhood, catching sunlight on his red feathers. Later, she and Judd paused in their walk to listen to a mockingbird who broadcast all the notes in his repertoire, mocking even himself with his repetitions, until he twirled his wings and flitted his tail across the road and away from them. They also saw red-winged blackbirds, a wren, a kingbird, and, as dusk brought out the night insects, the dipping, swerving swallows. Honeysuckle perfumed the air.

When they reached Judd's property again, he invited her to smell the lilacs in his backyard. She breathed in the odor of the first opening blooms. *Yes. That's what it is—like nothing else. How could I have forgotten?* She inhaled it again.

186

Judd took out his pocket knife and began to unfold it.

"Oh, no! Not your first blooms."

He cut them off. "Firstfruits are the best offerings."

"Since they're cut, I won't refuse them. Thank you, Judd."

She rushed them home and into water and held the blossoms between her hands and smelled. She didn't know if her exaltation welled out of the springtime or her absurd infatuation.

She knew what the infatuation would be, what it always had been. For two weeks she would feel wonderful, excited, ecstatic— above herself, not merely beside herself with joy. She clasped the knowledge that when she had thought she could never love another man, she did. Then in swift succession would come the anxiety, the humiliating knowledge that she had given herself to empty dreams, the dread of reality, and the taste of the ashes of her flames.

She sought the control in her profession that she lacked in her personal life. Her office offered a more manageable space than her cavernous house and its grounds, although she had Lucy to clean the house once a week and had replaced Mark Stamps with a younger neighborhood boy for the yard work. In the office she rearranged her furniture to give herself a full view of the door as well as the window, and she brightened it with new pictures. It seemed a complete little world, adequate to hold her life at the moment. Sometimes she hated to leave it to go home.

But the next year would be a different matter. Her sabbatical would be the first one she would control. During her only former one, she had stayed at Harper with her family for her professional development project on Wallace Stevens, using Vanderbilt's library when necessary. But this time she could propose something involving travel. She thought of Judd's command to go somewhere she had never been before and seriously considered Robinson Jeffers's California. Certainly that would be a treat, to see the Pacific Ocean and the whole Carmel area.

But that would commit her to leave Meadorsville. And she might not want to leave. She didn't want to think about the reason. But she wrote her sabbatical proposal to study Jeffers's poetry and to submit her own poetry for publication; she had published thirty or so poems in journals and little literary magazines through the years, and it was perhaps not unrealistic to think of collecting and submitting a volume. Where the sabbatical application asked whether travel would be involved, she penciled in "Possibly." *I can't hedge my bets any better than that.* She set the application aside; in the two weeks until the deadline, she might think of something else she wanted to do.

Classes were under control. In the poetry class, she built on the earlier discussions about contrasts in "St. Agnes" and "La Belle Dame" in analyzing "Ode on a Grecian Urn." She wanted to elicit the contrasts between life and art from someone besides Katy Cohen, and finally she pulled them out of square-jawed, practical Jack Brown with as much tugging as Grandad might have used in getting a big-boned half-Hereford calf out of an undersized Black Angus cow. She felt exhausted but good.

The committee for the sophomore literature textbooks met again that afternoon. Evelyn came in late again and purposely didn't sit by Rob. But she could see him, and she thought that he avoided looking at her. She felt rejected.

At the end of the meeting, however, he waited for her at the door. "Evelyn, do you have a copy of *The Tale of Genji?* I've never read it, so I scarcely feel competent to vote for or against it for the Asian lit component."

"Yes, in my office. Are you going back to yours now?"

"Yes."

"I'll get it for you now then."

They talked on their walk about some of the alternatives the committee was considering. She was acutely conscious of him walking beside her.

When they reached their offices, they found a reporter-photographer from the school newspaper waiting there. Rob said, "Hello, Sally."

The girl, pert and pretty, announced her mission: "I'm photographing faculty and interviewing them about their political views before the election, and I was hoping to capture you, Dr. McFergus." She smiled.

Evelyn thought, *Be careful what you try to capture; you may succeed.*

Rob smiled back. "I'll be with you in a minute, Sally; I just need to get a book from Mrs. Knight."

Evelyn found a copy of the first volume of *Genji* among the books she had been reviewing after the last committee meeting. "This first volume is all we'd teach, Rob. It's kind of a shame; the sixth book is the one really justifying the claim that Lady Murasaki was the first novelist. But obviously we can't ask sophomores to read all six."

"Maybe the Chinese poetry anthology would be better."

"That's what we have to decide. But *Genji* does show very different values from those in most Western literature. Cultural diversity appears more directly in narratives than in poetry, I think."

"Maybe this'll work then. I'll return it to you soon."

"There's no hurry."

Sue Hart married Jeff Fisher in Nashville at her parents' house that Friday night. Evelyn was the only person from Harper College there; Sue was evidently serious about her Victorian plan of concealment. She looked the way a bride should, excited and happy, in an azalea-pink dress that emphasized her brown eyes and short, soft-curled brown hair. Her older sister was her only attendant. She wore a lighter pink dress. Their parents looked rather bewildered; Mrs. Hart wore an indefinite beige-pink. Jeff's parents seemed stiff. Perhaps they disapproved, felt that Sue had entrapped their son. But he looked happy too, boyish and eager. His new brother-in-law, who was balding in front, stood up with him. A few other friends were present. The couple were going to the Smoky Mountains for the weekend and would be back in their separate classrooms on Monday.

Sue and Jeff had written their own vows, leaving out the traditional *obey* for the bride but including *love, honor, and cherish.* They didn't mention death or undying love.

Evelyn planned a bridal shower at Harper for the next week. She issued oral invitations, and when people asked about the wedding, she blatantly lied that Sue and Jeff had been married the fall before. It was, after all, no one's business but their own.

When she went to Curtis Hall to invite a friend of Sue's who taught chemistry, the young woman was out of her office, which was next to Ward's. Seeing that she was due back soon, Evelyn read the notices on her bulletin board, then moved to Ward's. A yellowing cartoon there seemed vaguely familiar: it showed a frog joyously playing leapfrog. Then she remembered that it was an S. Gross cartoon from *The New Yorker* that she had cut out and given Ward several years before. It was the only cartoon there.

Lucy helped her with refreshments for the shower. Most of those invited came, and Sue was happy that they seemed to accept her. When someone asked why she was making the marriage public just then, she answered quite readily that she and Jeff were going to have a baby, and the congratulations increased.

Marcia Lee commented to Evelyn that they could have announced the wedding in the fall, "when it happened, of course." Her eyebrows asked her question.

Evelyn shrugged. "I guess they didn't want to then."

A few nights later, Evelyn and Judd were both running late and ate out together before walking. Over dinner she told him about the difficulty choosing the Asian literature for the sophomore course, and he confessed to a long-term desire to learn Chinese.

"They say the best way to learn a foreign language is to sleep with a native speaker," she volunteered.

"The only foreign language I'm fluent in is Latin," he responded.

She laughed, but he seemed preoccupied.

On their walk, too, he was quiet. She looked around for a subject. "Isn't that jimsonweed, Judd? Granny always despised it, but its bloom is rather pretty."

"Yes. It's datura, you know: quite a powerful plant. It's been used as an hallucinogen, and its berries are poisonous."

"Quite treacherous for a simple weed!"

"Yes."

She couldn't think of much else to talk about, and he didn't respond much when she tried. When they reached his corner, he told her good night and left right away.

She sat down in the library with a stack of research-paper drafts and did a few, but her mind wasn't on it. Feeling restless, she scanned the titles on the nearby shelves and pulled down the *I Ching*, then fished three dimes out of her desk drawer and cast the coins.

She got Lake over Water, whose character, a stick figure boxed in with openings scarcely big enough to breathe through, represented Trapped. The advice was to strike out boldly to free oneself.

She eyed the stack of unexamined papers. *I could have tried the Tarot*, she thought. *Maybe it would give a more nearly possible answer than the Chinese.*

She began grading again, but her mind wandered into the wintery feeling the spring day had given her, and she started writing stray words on a grade sheet. She got out clean paper and began writing; the images came readily, but the words were slower.

> Minutes fall like snow
> On the peony buds
> On the tulips
>
> Oat-mites swarm their blizzard
>
> Insects stipple my windshield
> Blurt like sleet
>
> This forty-fifth spring

What is this about? Aging and being trapped and seeing death in flowers when they're just blooming. Time. Maybe that's the title. No, "Times." Not all the time. But now. Please let now *pass. But when it passes, what times then? Will other times be better? Is time running out?*

The next night, Judd was delayed at the hospital with an emergency, and they began their walk late again. Dusk was becoming darkness

as they neared home, and the fireflies were coming out. Evelyn remembered that Granny always called them lightning bugs. "We
used to catch as many as we could to put in a jar. I always wanted to
catch enough to make a flashlight so I could read under the covers."

"Did you ever?"

"No, I don't think so. The poor things would probably have suf-
focated anyhow. Look, Judd, how many there are in the field ahead!
I never saw so many!"

They walked silently, watching the fireflies rise from the tall
grasses, what must have been thousands bright against the dark
slope of the hill. "Come on," he said, and stepped over the ditch,
offering his hand to help her. They leaned against the rail fence.

In both directions the fireflies lit and went out, lit and went out
like pale Christmas lights. Watching them and taking them in, Evelyn felt their peace. She was content just to watch the lights in the
growing darkness. She hesitated before speaking because she didn't
want to interrupt the moment. "Do you think it's like the turtles
coming up onto the beach in the spring to lay their eggs, that we
happened to come here just on the one night of the year when the
fireflies light up the earth like stars?"

"No. I think this probably happens every night at this time for a
while every spring. We just never saw it before." His voice sounded
hesitant; she could see the shadow that he was but not his face.

A car sped down the little lane; they heard its tires squeal as it
braked around the curve, slowing for the intersection with Franklin
Pike. It broke the wonder of the scene, and she sighed and turned
back toward the road.

He stepped back over the ditch and held his hand out again. "Are
you tired, Eva?"

"Not really, Judd. Just tired of myself." She stepped over and let
go. "I'm not very happy with myself these days."

"Do you want to talk about it?"

"No, I . . . well, I don't know. Maybe I do." She couldn't see him at
all by then, and he seemed a disembodied voice, someone she perhaps could talk to. *Maybe that's what it's like to confess to a priest in the
box, when he's hidden, when he's like God Himself.*

"If you do, then go ahead."

"I've let myself fall in love with a married man."

The only sound was their footsteps, rubber soles thubbing on the
asphalt.

192

She said, "I'm sorry. I shouldn't have broadcast my folly."

"No, I'm not judging you. I'm just trying to remember my bit of Browning. I think he's the one who said this: 'How is it under our control/To love, or not to love?' "

"You shouldn't encourage me."

"I'm not trying to encourage or discourage you. Maybe I'm just looking for forgiveness." He sounded halting again, tired himself.

She looked at his shadow but found no clue to his meaning. "You mean absolution?"

"Can you absolve me?"

"Oh, no, that's not what I meant, Judd. *You* don't need it. I meant for myself."

"We all need it."

"Thank you for trying to comfort me, but I need it more than most."

"Don't take too much pride in your sin, Eva. You really aren't the first. Or the worst."

She felt strained but tried to lighten the tone. "Thank you, Father Adivino."

"*Pax vobiscum.*"

"And with you. Fine pair we are, a lapsed Methodist-Presbyterian with a Jewish confessor."

"Also lapsed, I fear. Good night, Eva."

She had meant to ask him in again to share her dinner, but his farewell sounded so final that she didn't. "Good night, Judd."

The sophomores were reading Chekhov's stories. Evelyn had focused on the theme of freedom. In the stories assigned, Chekhov developed freedom as a lack of hypocrisy, a finding of oneself beneath the veneer of social custom. The theme reminded her of the battles of the sixties about racism, Vietnam, and materialism. Usually Chekhov's characters lacked freedom because they couldn't escape from hypocrisy. Often the theme centered on women trapped in meaningless marriages: "A Calamity," "At Home," "Anna on the Neck," "About Love," and, of course, "The Lady with the Pet Dog."

She asked the students to cite examples from the stories of hypocritical behavior, and unbidden the scene of Gurov eating watermelon after seducing Anna rose in her mind. It came so bright and clear that she wanted to save it, with the red of the watermelon and of Gurov's mouth dominating the foreground and Anna's anguish reduced in the shadowy blues of the background. Evelyn's gaze rested on Rebecca Cane, the art major, and she realized that she wanted to paint the scene. She called on Rebecca for an example of hypocrisy.

Rebecca answered, "When the man in 'Lady with the Pet Dog' sits and eats as if nothing has happened when the lady has just slept with him. She's sincere, not hypocritical: she's upset by her sin."

"Yes." Evelyn was able to go on with the discussion, but the fact that Rebecca's thoughts had run with her own claimed part of her attention. She felt as though Rebecca had given her a confirmation of something, a sign. *Maybe it means I'm supposed to paint that picture. I could audit studio classes under Nina Wilton next year.*

The idea of taking courses in art excited her. It would be like writing poems, but she knew the medium of words so well that she could manipulate it to say what she wanted. Perhaps in painting, where she didn't control the medium, it would tell her things she didn't know. She always told her composition students about the use of the right brain in creation; maybe she could practice it in a new medium herself. Maybe she could quiet Virginia Woolf's Angel in the House, Auden's Watcher at the Gate. Maybe she could paint what she couldn't say. She could still add the plan to audit Nina's class to her sabbatical proposal.

Rob brought back her copy of *Genji*. He asked, "Did you know you had a poem in here?" He kept back a folded paper as he gave her the book.

"No." She held out her hand.

But he still kept it. "I like it, but it's different from your usual Imagist or Dickinsonian poems. You didn't use caps or punctuation, and I haven't the faintest idea what you mean, but you make me feel—well, conspiratorial." He handed it to her, his expression questioning, almost accusing.

It was the poem about private shadows. She must have stuck it into the book after rewriting it. She looked at him, and he was still watching her. It was almost as though he could see into her mind. Hiding, she looked down, then turned away to lay the poem on her desk. "Thank you, Rob."

"You're welcome, I'm sure." He reached out and ran his fingers down the back of her neck below her upswept hair, squeezed her neck, and left, closing her door.

She fell into her desk chair; her knees were water.

That night Evelyn made two lists of possibilities, one for Rob and one for Marcia Lee. Maybe she was what she seemed to be, unbearably temperamental and domineering, the mother in his novel, and he didn't like her possessiveness and was trying to break away from her; that was what the novel seemed to say. Evelyn called that the Trapped scenario.

Maybe Marcia Lee was strong and he was weak, and she mothered him and he needed her so he could let himself remain a child. That was Sons and Lovers.

Maybe she was weak—mad or a drunkard or on drugs or chronically ill—and he was trapped into the responsibility of preserving her and Trey while seeming to be dominated. Evelyn labeled that Jane Eyre.

Or maybe Rob and Marcia Lee were incredibly in love with each other and her dominance expressed an affection that he fully shared. But his hand on Evelyn's neck didn't indicate that. She didn't label it.

Or maybe he was already promiscuous, laying half the women he met, and Marcia Lee kept tight reins on him because she had to. Evelyn remembered his smile at the pretty reporter for the school paper. That was Don Juan.

And how should I label myself?

The last of the fruit-tree blossoms had fallen long before, but the yellow poplars were bearing the gold-and-orange cups that earned them the name of tulip trees. Or was it their large-notched leaves? A strange tree was blooming in a yard she and Judd passed each evening; she would have asked Ward what it was had they still been married. It bore white blooms like fringes, with four long, drooping petals on green stems. About a week after the fireflies, she asked Judd what it was, but he didn't know either.

In his black polo shirt and shorts, he looked spare, pared down to muscle and bones. The planes of his face had always been carved smooth, but now even his lips were drawn tight. He was very quiet, and she felt that he was separated from her. She regretted all over again saying anything to him about her guilty infatuation; it had distanced him from her, and she realized that she had no other close friend.

That night she dreamed that she went wading waist-deep into a pond to smell the flowers. But she found only two clumps, both white. One was a water lily with petals twisted like a chrysanthemum's around its hidden heart. The other was a datura plant, cut off and submerged, its leaves bruised, floating beneath the surface like a ghost. She didn't know which to try to smell. She entreated someone she couldn't see: "I can't even feel wet."

Evelyn cursed under her breath when she looked through the windows in Will Hall at the end of her sophomore class. It had started raining, she hadn't brought an umbrella, and she had to go to the Center for a meeting. She waited at the door a minute, hoping faintly that the rain would stop, but she knew that it wouldn't. Finally she put her class folder over her head, clutched the student folders against her chest, and dashed out into the weather.

It was not a gentle, well-behaved rain; tumultuous and malicious, it gusted from unexpected directions into her face, lashing her eyes and soaking her hair. Except for the lines of the sidewalk, she couldn't see where she was going.

When she reached the Center, the door opened for her. She blinked her water-blinded eyes to see Rob holding it, and the irrational thought came, *He's been waiting here for me for years.* "Thank you," she said.

"You're welcome. If you'd called me, I'd have brought my umbrella to shelter you." He brandished it and smiled.

"That's surely more than I deserve."

"But not more than I'd do for you." His eyes seemed dark. He opened his umbrella. Then he was gone into the downpour.

By the time her meeting was over, the sun had come out. She noticed the watercolor blue of the petunias in the flower beds along the walk.

His office door was closed.

That afternoon, in her faculty mailbox she found a gray linen-weave page, folded like a business letter and sealed with embossed red wax. Inside was a poem, a haiku. There was no signature, but she recognized Rob's hand, disconnected black letters totally unslanted:

> even in sunlight
> i remember you running
> shining through gray rain

Evelyn thought, *The biologists have our anatomy wrong. Emotions aren't in the brain, or just in the pounding of the heart; they're in the lungs right here in the middle of my chest where it's tight and in my throat where the larynx is swollen up.*

She put the note in her jacket pocket and walked home, analyzing the poem. Its context, of course, was *The Tale of Genji*, with its use of poetry to convey emotions between lovers. And although not insistent, this poem demanded a response. Of course, one response—the only right one, Mother would have said, if Mother could be imagined in such a situation—would be nothing. That would answer the only question the poem raised with *No*. Were there any other answers except *Yes* or *Maybe?*

She couldn't think of any. And she rejected *Maybe*. Ambiguity has its place, but she was past the age for coyness.

Past the age. Well past Rob's age. Nine years past. Past the age for foolishness, one would think. Not just foolishness—folly. Wicked folly, hurting others and risking self.

Well, I'm tired of protecting self. What do I have that's so precious to protect? Is feeling pain worse than feeling nothing?

But the others, his wife and innocent child. She had no right to bring them pain.

She telephoned Judd and canceled their walk and sat down at the library table. If she did answer, of course it must be with a poem; anything else would be unworthy of Rob's message. What would she say—if she did answer?

A half hour produced a response, another haiku:

> Garden waits for rain
> Longing to end this parching
> Even with a storm.

That should be unequivocal enough. Brazen enough. All the earth-and-rain symbolism, and to hell with the consequences.

Then she realized that she ought not write a haiku but a unit of *renga*, linked verse, two seven-syllable lines added to his haiku to complete a *tanka*. So she played with her haiku, keeping rain as the link to his:

> Though rain has watered the earth,
> My lone garden still lies parched.

She decided that the new lines were more brazen than her haiku; she had dropped the image of the storm, perhaps trying to ignore the consequences, but she had claimed the garden, made it personal.

And she couldn't decide if she would send it—could send it.

But she took a sheet of white paper with a red border down its deckle edge and wrote the poem in black ink. Her handwriting looked strange to her—irregular, with disproportionately large capitals. She had no sealing wax. She found a narrow red satin ribbon in Elaine's outgrown hair-trim collection, rolled the sheet, tied it, and tucked it inside the key compartment of her purse.

The next morning she took the note out and started to tear it up. But she didn't. She replaced it. And when she picked up her mail, after looking to make sure no one would see, she put the rolled page in Rob's box. *I've cast the die, thrown my hat in the ring, crossed the Rubicon—all those irrevocable things.*

She almost walked back to the box and took the poem out. But she didn't.

She stopped in the bookstore after her morning class. Rice wrapping paper was in stock, and she bought a large sheet in which pressed plum blossoms had been embedded. There was no sealing wax, but she bought a wine-colored beeswax candle.

Rob's door was closed again, although she knew that he usually left it open for office hours. When she opened her own office door, a blue watermarked note lay inside. She stepped over it and put down her books. With racing heart she picked it up.

> waiting clouds gather
> rain would quench lone garden's thirst
> if it lay ready

Not yet! This is going too fast. I need time. I haven't thought it through; I shouldn't rush into something like this.

I shouldn't do something like this. It's madness to do this, madness.

She folded the note again and put it inside her roll book.

Judd called her that afternoon. "I wondered if you plan to walk today."

"Yes, I need to, especially since I missed yesterday."

"You're all right, aren't you?"

"Yes, thanks. I just had some things to do yesterday."

"I'll look forward to seeing you then."

"Me too. Bye." *That makes no sense at all. I can't even carry on a normal conversation.*

Practice had made the act of walking easier. Her muscles usually did their job now without thought, but missing a day made a difference. She felt the effort of moving.

She also found it hard to concentrate on what Judd was saying. She caught her mind repeating in time to the steps, "Robert, Robert, Robert, Robert, Robert." She never called him that, but the rhythm of the walk required it. And there had to be five repetitions in a series. Iambic pentameter, of course. No, the feet were trochees.

She realized that Judd was silent. She didn't know how long he had been; she had been walking in a daze. "I'm sorry, Judd. I'm not very good company this evening."

"That's all right." They walked in silence a minute more before he added, "Want to talk about it?"

"No—just some things at school I have to work out."

"Let me know if I can help."

"Thanks. I will." *That'll be the day!*

That night she composed her next poem.

> All day I shall watch for clouds.
> Fallow earth awaits the rain.

It took her quite a while to decide on the best place to copy the poem onto the rice paper. Then she cut it out, wrote the poem, and folded it. The wax from the candle made a satisfactory seal, and she impressed it with a small gold monogram pin bearing her maiden initials; she didn't know why she had never had it restyled, but now she was glad that she could call herself something bearing no claim of Ward Knight's.

As if that made you a virgin again, she scoffed, *even if you haven't slept with Ward in almost a year and a half.*

Of course, the wax letters were backward.

His answer, written on red paper as smooth and thick as parchment, linked the series to its beginning, and she admired his skill:

rain will fall at dusk
no need for garden lanterns
you will light the way

She closed her eyes, the page between her hands. *Japanese paper lanterns. Paper love.*

Book Three

Summer

Already with thee! tender is the night.

—John Keats, *"Ode to a Nightingale"*

XII. Evelyn

A Secret Passage

*E*velyn left campus as soon as her posted office hours ended at three. By the time she got home, her clothes were sticking to her skin from the heat and humidity.

The first thing she did was cancel her walk with Judd. He wasn't in, but she left the message with Angela, his receptionist. Then she went to the door of her bedroom. She rejected the bold, harsh rust-and-navy graphic designs of the room. *No. Not here where I've slept with Ward thousands of nights.*

The only other bedroom on the main floor had been the nursery first, then a guest room when the children moved upstairs, then Granny's room when she became too feeble to live alone. In its recent redecoration, Mother had made it English country, old-fashioned. The wallpaper bore pink and raspberry roses between wide pink stripes, and the rug was pink. The white bedspread Granny had crocheted for Evelyn and Ward topped a raspberry comforter on the cherry double bed from the suite Evelyn had asked for from Lanier Bluffs. White eyelet embroidered lawn for the dust ruffle and curtains, the white dart-and-egg ceiling molding, and Battenberg lace softened the flower colors, which were picked up in upholstery and a table skirt.

205

Not smart, but feminine. A bower. That's all right. Evelyn plumped and rearranged a few pillows, opened a window on each side, and lit a lamp. *I'll have to draw the shades on the north toward Judd's house; we couldn't be seen from the west unless someone climbed a tree!*

Next she bathed and shaved her legs. She was still ten pounds overweight, but the walking had firmed and toned her. At least her breasts weren't big enough to droop. But she could offer Rob no young, virginal body. Nor was she an experienced seductress, mistress of the arts of love. What could she offer him? She washed her hair; she would leave it down to dry but would probably have to use the blow-dryer.

She dried herself and did the whole scent routine: perfume in the rinse water for her hair, body lotion, splashes of cologne, bath powder, perfume on her pulse spots, and cream sachet. *It smells like a whorehouse in here.*

Well, isn't that the plan?

She turned on the exhaust fan while she put on her makeup.

The white streaks at her temples showed particularly stark against her dark hair in the fluorescent lights of the bathroom mirror. *Maybe I should have dyed it. It's too late now.* She felt regret, then scoffed at herself. *Silly! He's seen you every workday for six years. Do you think he never noticed your gray hair? He said you're nine years older. He knows.*

He knows, and he doesn't care. He still wants you. Happiness welled up in her again.

But her practical white terry robe seemed impossible. After some rummaging through drawers, she found a cranberry negligee and gown. She held them up against her and looked in the bedroom mirror.

So what do you think you're going to do? Greet him at the door dressed for bed?

Why not?

Because it's silly. Because it's brazen. Because you can't do it.

So you wear street clothes, something you wouldn't be scandalized to be seen in if the tax assessor dropped by. She picked out a white silk shirt with a lace collar, an emerald-green skirt with a wide belt, and green pumps. She thought of the old English custom of brides under twenty-six wearing green, women older wearing brown. *So my green's for hope, not youth.*

Now, what are you going to wear underneath?

She thought of Elaine's bodysuits and teddies. She certainly couldn't wear black lace with red hearts, not under her white blouse. Why not leather and chains! But she could find something white and lacy that Elaine had left. Elaine had offered!

She went to Elaine's room and searched the drawers of her lingerie chest until she found some satin-and-lace bodysuits. There was a white one, and she took off her terry robe and tried it on and looked in the mirror.

This is absurd. I might as well wear nothing. She didn't look at herself while she took it off. She went downstairs and put on her comfortable cotton briefs, a well-constructed bra, and a tailored slip. She dried her hair and dressed, then put her hair up, using no spray.

And it was only five o'clock, three hours until dark.

She wasn't hungry. She thought food might even make her sick; she felt fevered.

She had papers to grade, of course, but knew she couldn't concentrate on them.

She went upstairs to the library and sat on the couch and read Keats and thought about how tuberculosis had cheated Keats and Lawrence and Mansfield and Chekhov and Kafka of their lives and about how Mozart had died filled with unplayed melodies and about how Chekhov's world could be bleaker than Kafka's because Chekhov did fill his with real things, things that could be delights but weren't and things that people prized more than real delights. Then she got up and searched until she found Richard Wilbur's "Love Calls Us to the Things of This World" and read it and felt better, thinking of the possibility of balance.

She took the volume of poetry downstairs with her, mixed a pitcher of fruit tea, and took a glassful and the book to the front-porch swing, seldom used since air-conditioning. She sat there reading until it grew too dark on the porch, where screens and wisteria vines and shrubs shaded her. Then she sat and looked at the dogwood trees, Carolina hemlocks, and rhododendron that Ward and she had planted under the tall trees to hide the lawn from the road.

He won't come, she thought. She was close to tears.

But as soon as she saw a figure step through the foliage at the cemetery end of the yard, she knew that it was Rob. Her heart pounded. She watched him all the way, and when he approached the porch, she got up and held the screen door open for him and said, "Hello." Her voice sounded strange to her, high and thin.

"Hello." He came through the door and put his arms around her and pulled her against him and kissed her. "I've wanted to do that for a long time," he said as he smoothed the hair back all around her face.

"Why?" she asked.

He laughed. "That's a funny thing to ask. Just because I wanted to, because I want you." He began kissing her again.

She accepted it: *To want to is its own reason.*

His lips moved down her chin and throat, and she said, "Come inside," and led him into the house. She closed the front door and locked it.

As it turned out, she needn't have worried about the bedrooms. Kissing, they sat on the couch in the last light from the sunroom windows; he began taking down her hair and undressed her and she him, and then they made love in the dusk on the carpet in the middle of the living-room floor.

She reached the still point that is like dying, and he held her and whispered endearments until she came back to life enough to stroke him, his body now miraculously hers too.

He kissed her. "You make it hard to leave you."

"Do you have to so soon?"

"Yes; Marcia Lee thinks I'm doing research for my novel tonight; I'll have to leave soon to produce something to show. She won't put up with too much of that."

He bent his head and began kissing her breasts again. She closed her eyes, her fingers in his hair.

Finally he kissed her lips, then pulled away. "I have to go now. Thank you, my love, my lovely."

"Thank you, my love." Her fingertips gave his face a last caress. She helped him sort out his clothes to put on.

Still naked, she went with him to the front door, but not across the porch, even in the dark. He kissed her again, said, "Good-bye," and left. She watched him disappear; the house loomed empty behind her.

She put on the white terry robe after all. She had to sponge the carpet with cold water. She hoped it wouldn't stain; that might be hard to explain.

She slept in her rose bower by herself.

The next morning, his office door was closed, but there was a manila folder on her floor containing more than ten typed pages and a note:

Dearest Evelyn,

I know I should produce a morning-after poem like Prince Genji or at least an aubade like the troubadors, but I'm really a novelist, not a poet. Please accept my inferior offering.

Yours,
Rob

The manuscript was a photocopy. *He probably had to show his excuse when he got home. But what a lot he wrote! I wonder what time he did get home. Maybe she waited up for him. Maybe then they made love. What do they call it on the sports news, a ''twi-night double header''?*

She put the images out of her mind and shamed herself and read the manuscript. It was a continuation of his novel; Keith, the son, had taken out the girl he was attracted to, Valerie, and gone to bed with her. Although Rob had made Valerie a blonde, there were enough details to show that he had Evelyn in mind. *He wasn't lying to Marcia Lee; he was doing research last night.* She debated the ethics of the situation. Was he just using her for the sensations and ideas of his writing? Or was he using the writing to further the affair? There was no doubt that she found it enormously flattering and moving to read Keith's view of the encounter, his uncertainty and happiness. It was a sharing of feelings she had never had with Ward.

She tried to separate her emotion from her judgment and write a dispassionate critique. But she caught herself in continual *double entendre:*

Dear Rob,

I find nothing to criticize. The passage reads smoothly and advances characterization and plot. The dialogue and internal monologue are moving, especially Keith's joy. The pace may be a little fast at first.

Yours,
Evelyn

Well, I might do better in a poem. But not yet. She replaced Rob's note with her own and slid the manila folder under his door and turned to her class work.

Their schedules were almost opposites that term, she having only morning classes and he only afternoon. She had a committee meeting at the long lunch break. Between his two classes that afternoon, he poked his head through her open door.

"Thanks for the kind words, but I'll quibble about your one criticism. The pace is not too fast; it's too slow, years too slow."

He smiled, and she smiled back. She felt happy: peaceful and excited at the same time.

He looked down the hall both ways. Then he stepped inside. But he still spoke quietly. "I won't be able to get away this weekend. Can we meet tomorrow at noon?"

She spoke the answer her look gave. "I'd like to. How?"

"We could drive. Separately, of course. You have trees all around your house and enough garage space for a stable of studs."

She wrinkled her nose. "I never thought of you that way. My stud. So the only time we risk getting caught is turning into and out of my drive."

"Yes, and if there's traffic then, I'll drive past and turn around somewhere and hope for less when I come back. Are your neighbors nosy?"

"Not especially, I think. The only ones likely to notice are Judd and Mrs. Tibbets across the street, and she eats early and naps, and Earline usually feeds Judd lunch in the library, on the far side of his house from me; don't turn around in the lane there. My neighbors on the other side are silent as the grave." She paused, then added, "Mrs. Tibbets is a gossip; she has nothing else to do."

"Then we'll have to be careful." He grinned. "Here's to our first nooner, Evelyn."

She grimaced again, then smiled. "Let me give you a key into the house from the basement garage." She gave him hers; she would park at the side and go in the main-floor door. She would have to remember to open the garage door.

210

She drove to classes Friday for the first time since Judd had started her on her walking program and left from her eleven-o'clock class without going back to her office. That morning she had mixed chicken salad and stuffed tomatoes; no reason they should go without lunch.

But Rob wanted to make love first. This time they used her new bedroom, and the day was cool enough that she opened the windows and let the sweet early-summer air in.

Ward had been her only other lover, and he had been less tender, less slow, less aware of the feast of the senses they could be to each other, smell and sight and taste as well as touch. And sound: their voices and their words. Rob knew the words. *He would bind me forever with his words alone. It's not fair that he can move me so with his words.*

While they were eating, she said, "How long did you stay up writing Wednesday night? You wrote so much."

"It was after two before I quit. I could have gone on and on. I feel as if I could write the whole thing if I could spend a week with you, Evelyn. With time-outs for research, of course." He grinned.

She didn't want him to think she was fishing for a compliment, but as a writer herself, she wanted to know. "Why's it so different from your ordinary writing pace?"

"You've never written fiction, have you?"

"Nothing except one short story I wrote in college for a contest. I didn't win. Is it so different from writing poems?"

"I think it is, at least for long fiction. You see, you can carry a poem in your head and bring it out and fiddle with a line and put it back. But when you write a novel, it holds you; you have to travel into its world and stay there. And if something makes you come out, back to the real world, it's a struggle, not to mention an irritation. I think you're part of the world of my novel, not my real world."

"Then I'm really just your fantasy." His idea didn't make her feel fantastic in the current sense.

"You're really my world the way I'd make it if I could. And if I could, I'd make it again right now." He leered.

She laughed. "That's the best offer I've had today."

"I thought what we just did was all right."

"That was the sweet fruit of the best offer I had yesterday. Unfortunately, even Harper's leisurely lunch break doesn't allow time for enough sin."

"That's the hell of it, you know. Only the good get eternity, and they don't have anything to do during it."

"I'm not complaining. Men are like jewelry: if a woman gets a few good pieces, that should be enough."

"Lady, you have a wicked mind."

"And here I was trying to pay you a compliment."

He got up and mock-bowed. "Good intentions duly noted. They lead the same place sin does, though."

"Then I'll take the low road." She stood and kissed him good-bye.

"And I'll be at Harper before ye."

All afternoon, she caught herself humming "Loch Lomond."

The weekend stretched long ahead of her, her aloneness broken only by her walks with Judd, which were both a relief and an interruption of her memories. She kept replaying her meetings with Rob, the way he looked, what he said, the feel of his flesh under her fingers, his fingers on her flesh. She wanted to stop time at moments in her memory like pausing a videocassette. Indeed, she wanted to stop the whole season just where it was with the full leaves and grass blowing in the summer wind. To stop time at hazy summer forever.

Partly she feared how she herself might change. She had thought she loved Ward, even through her terrible need for Greg. But her love for Ward had died and left her empty. If it could die, so could this.

Or Rob's love for her could die. She wasn't even sure she should call it love; maybe he just had an itch, a desire for variety, changing flavors from burnt almond caramel to mocha almond fudge. A few more licks, and he would crave cherry.

Certainly she was not sure why he was attracted to her. She could see why he might want to escape Marcia Lee, his intellectual inferior and a termagant besides. But he could have found younger women.

But he chose me. And then she would feel full again, bubbling over with joy, wanting to stop time.

Saturday morning she baked cookies to mail to the children, packed them, and got them to the post office before it closed. *You're bargaining,* she accused herself. *You think if you're a good mother, the fates will let you have Rob.*

The coming week was the last week of classes, so she had to bring classwork together in the last meetings and prepare for final exams. She also had to finish grading over the weekend: all the late submissions and rewrites. She could face only a few at a time. Then she would put Edith Piaf or Sarah Vaughan or *Porgy and Bess* on the stereo for a while and hum or sing with the records. Sometimes she even improvised a dance, secure in the privacy of her own foolishness.

Town was very different from the mile of country road she and Judd walked, even in its vegetation. In town the magnolias and crape myrtles had begun blooming, and beds of red begonias ringed with dusty miller brightened the lawns and campus. But along the road were fields of tobacco or corn or hay separated from each other by dense fencerow growth. The scattered houses sat far back from the road with fields, not lawns, in front. Honeysuckle clambered over bushes and fences, and trumpet vine climbed even the telephone poles. There were also uncultivated fields, grown up in Queen Anne's lace, chicory, milkweed, rabbit tobacco, and thistles. Steam rose between the ranks of trees on the hills as the evening chilled the moisture in the air.

In town, the ubiquitous mockingbirds staked out their territories and defended them fiercely with their songs. Robins hopped on the lawns, and occasionally a thrush sang from a hedge. But in the country, meadowlarks and red-winged blackbirds dotted the fields, and swallows dipped after insects at dusk.

She saw a flash of blue among the thistles Sunday and thought it was a bluebird, but Judd said, "No, I think it's too slim; it may be an indigo bunting."

They watched, and when it flew up again, they could see clearly that it was. Although lighter, the blue was more like a peacock's head than the clear blue of a bluebird. The bunting made a cheeping sound, not very musical. But the beauty of its back and wings was enough. A similar brown-and-white bird answered and flew too.

"Is that the female?"

"Probably. I thought I glimpsed some blue on her too. I'll look them up when I get home."

"I never saw one before," she said.

"I've seen them farther out on this road," he said, "but never this close to town."

She remembered then that he had changed his walks for her, shortened them. "You don't walk as far as you used to, do you? I could go farther with you now."

"Do you want to? We're walking about two miles a day now, not bad, particularly in this heat."

"But I'd like to go on. We haven't seen what's past the curve." They always stopped at a bridge before a bend.

"Good. We'll go around the curve today."

They didn't say anything else for a while. Then he said, "You've . . . seemed happier lately."

"Yes. I am."

He didn't ask why, and she knew he wouldn't. She felt awkward not explaining but knew doing so would have been even more awkward. *What could I say? ''I'm having an affair with the married man I told you about''? And what could he reply?*

He said, "I'm glad for you." But he wasn't looking at her.

"Thank you. Oh, look, Judd; there's the bunting again."

The bird flew toward them, landed on a thistle only six or seven feet ahead, and stayed until they came even closer. Then it flew away like a rock skipped across a pond, skimming the weed tops, landing on a thistle, then flying still farther across the long field until they lost it.

Around the curve were more fields like the ones they had been going past. They didn't see any more buntings.

Monday afternoon was the last committee meeting for selection of the sophomore texts. Evelyn deliberately didn't sit near Rob and avoided looking at him; she wasn't sure that she could control her expression. She felt divided into a public and a private self and felt the breach like a chasm opened in her chest. *That's my guilt. I know I deserve punishment. Whatever innocence I have had before was not my resisting evil; it was the absence of temptation, my naiveté.*

She also feared losing him. Each morning she took a longer time to choose her clothes. Nothing she had seemed right: it was all too familiar to him or too out of date or so plain that it was dowdy. And she seemed too old or plain herself. She wondered why he paid her any notice at all and knew that sooner or later he would find someone younger and prettier or would just realize himself how ordinary she was.

And she was jealous. Every night when she went to bed, she thought, *Marcia Lee has him now. She lies beside him every night, all night long. She has him in ways I can never have him.*

But Evelyn had him again at noon on Tuesday. They didn't take time to eat.

That night, Jessica called from Houston to say that she was coming to Tennessee for a visit and to ask when the best time to see Evelyn would be. Glad at the prospect of seeing her but realizing the problems of seeing Rob then, Evelyn said, "It would be best if you would visit Jonathan or one of the others until after graduation. That's June eighth. Then I'll be able to spend more time with you."

"That sounds good. I'll be there around the eleventh, then."

"That's great." *And not so great.*

Then Evelyn realized that the children would be home even sooner. She felt guilty all over again; she had forgotten her own children in thinking about her lover.

Wednesday night, Rob came to her after telling Marcia Lee he would be writing. And he was; again he left Evelyn for his office, where he produced a section of his novel about Keith's growing involvement with Valerie. The next morning Evelyn read her copy carefully for signs of disenchantment, but she found none.

She wrote for him too, a poem.

I feared that symbol's cracked
Communication
Heard awry would fracture
Comprehension.
But your ears translate symbol's
Tinkling soleness:
Hear the octave tremble
Into wholeness.

The wrenched rhythm and rhyme in the third and fourth lines seemed appropriate, and *tremble* seemed *le mot juste*. Wondering if he would get the allusion to I Corinthians 13—he didn't pick up biblical references, she had noticed—she entitled it "Your Charity" and left it under his office door.

The upper-division students were knowing enough to ask rather specific questions about the final exam in poetry; she had encouraged them to make their own list of possible questions, and she was pleased that their priorities accorded with her own. Almost all of them had listed the literary subjects of diction and imagination and the philosophical subjects of death, sex, duty, and faith. Not only Katy Cohen but also Jack Brown and a couple of the others anticipated the relative value of art and life as the question she was most likely to ask about Keats.

They were too shrewd to believe her, though, when she said she didn't have a preconceived answer that she expected for the questions. She reminded them of the concepts of ambiguity and Keats's Negative Capability, saying that these applied to criticism as well as literature. But they still were hung up on the idea that a work of art had a single, definite meaning and that she was expecting them to parrot an interpretation given in class or written in some of the criticism in the bibliography (not all of which, of course, they had read). She tried to convince them that she was more interested in their ability to conceive a possible reading of their own and to support it with logic. She even sacrificed a perfectly good potential question and showed how it could be answered either positively or negatively. When she had finished, Anne Harvey, one of the most avid grade-grubbers in the class, asked, "But which is the *right* answer?"

"Both of them," she said.

Anne looked unbelievingly at her. "Which will you give better credit for?"

"The one with the better support."

"Then it's really a test of writing."

"It's really a test of thinking. To the extent that thinking has to depend on communication for evaluation, you're right. But in a greater sense, it's a test of the way you as students have learned to think not just about literature, but about life. If you don't think about people and events in the larger context of their interrelations and your whole life, you will have learned nothing from your education, even if you can recite every one of Keats's odes and all the criticism ever written about them."

Anne shook her head.

Walking home in the oppressive heat, Evelyn realized that like a child she was avoiding stepping on cracks, even where the frequent maple roots had raised the sidewalk and fractured it like a spider's web. She remembered the childhood rhyme, "Step on a crack,/ Break your mother's back." *A venial sin, I'd think; what do I deserve then? "Sleep with your lover,/Pay with tears forever."* And having thought it, she had to live with that rhyme all the way home. Even after she quit walking, it echoed in her mind intermittently through her dinner.

It came again as she walked with Judd. She tried to exorcise it by talking, as they usually did, about their surroundings. "I haven't seen many songbirds today," she complained.

He sighed. "All the ones I've noticed have been dead: a meadowlark and a cardinal and two brown undistinguishable ones so far. All flattened onto the pavement."

"Oh! I didn't see them. I always hate to see the pretty ones killed."

"What about the homely ones?"

She suddenly felt flip. "God mourns over the sparrow, so I don't have to."

After a pause, he said, "I'm going to Baltimore for a while."

"Are you going to visit Rachel?"

"Yes, I'll stay with her. But I'll visit other relatives too; I have an uncle and two aunts still living there. And I'll go by Johns Hopkins to see a few old friends."

"How long will you be gone?"

"I . . . don't know. I've asked Jim Bonnette and Avery West to handle any emergencies, and of course the office staff can handle routine things, inoculations and such."

"My sister Jessica is coming here from Texas right after graduation. I don't think you've ever met her, have you? She's the beautiful one."

He looked at her then. "My dear, you're no sparrow. And while I regret not meeting your beautiful sister, it's you I'll miss."

"I'll miss you too, Judd." She realized that it was true. Whom would she walk with? "When are you leaving?"

"As soon as one of my patients has her baby, probably about this time next week." He added, "I hope you'll continue to walk without me."

"I will. But I won't enjoy it so much."

"I'm selfish enough to be glad that you think so." He was looking at the blacktop again.

On Friday, the last day for her other two classes, she felt almost wistful. She had not applied for one of the few summer-school classes Harper offered, and in the fall, the sabbatical would free her from teaching responsibilities. So she would not have a class again until fall of 1981, more than a year away. The rhythm of the academic year normally governed her life so much that she felt awash, deprived of an anchor. Her freedom stretched as a void.

Yet the value of freedom was the whole point of her last discussion of Russian literature with the sophomores. The Chekhov stories and Tolstoy's *Death of Ivan Illich* showed that it was costly. But she strove to show them that life without freedom was meaningless too. They saw that Ivan's tragedy was giving up his freedom, trying to be like everyone else, merely to violate no rule of decorum. It was harder to get them to see that his salvation came when he understood that he still had the freedom to love, that he could be like his compassionate servant Gerasim instead of like his businesslike, unfeeling doctors. Freedom was necessary if not sufficient to make his life worthwhile.

Despite the difficulty, some students did see. And maybe some of the others would learn. And maybe some—maybe she—would occasionally be able to apply what they knew in their own lives.

She felt that she was moving between the public world lit with the scorching sun or harsh fluorescents and the private world of fog and shadows concealing her and Rob. She grew impatient with the public world and longed for the shadows. The weekends, when Marcia Lee claimed Rob so totally that Evelyn didn't see him at all, had become hardest of all. The weekend before exams, she and Judd walked, but he refused her invitations to eat with her. She felt a little angry with him for not helping her get through the long days.

She busied herself with preparations for exams and the children's return and Jessica's visit. She moved all her personal things into her bower out of the master bedroom, where she would put Jessica. She considered taking apart the dual-king bed and having two twin beds in the room; that would give more flexibility for guests. But although she felt that her own life was new, she wasn't ready to start another redecorating project to change her external world, especially without Mother. Maybe there would be time to get some more advice before Mother and Father left again for their interrupted Grand Tour.

Beginning on Monday, the exam schedule destroyed normal routine. She wondered if she would see Rob at the office. She didn't before she gave her poetry exam, but his door was open when she came back. She looked in and said, "Hello."

He looked up from his desk and smiled. "Hi. Got a minute?"

"Sure."

"Close the door."

He got up and kissed her. "I have a surprise. Marcia Lee's leaving Friday to go see her folks. She won't be back till Sunday night, after graduation. Am I invited to come over to your house to play?" His

219

fingers moved up and down on the vertebrae at the small of her back, his thumb hooked around the curve of her waist.

"Anytime," she said. His touch was enough to make her want him, and she had learned him well enough to know that he wanted her too. "The weekend seems a long time away, though."

"Too long. But I have to give an exam now. And I won't be able to get away at night till exams are done."

They both knew the rush of getting senior grades in. "I'll look for any signals then," she said, "lanterns in the tower of the Old North Church or what you will."

"What's your schedule tomorrow?"

They compared and concluded that they really wouldn't be able to meet before Friday. And he wasn't sure what time Marcia Lee would be leaving that day.

She asked, "What's your favorite food?"

He grinned. "Fried chicken—breast."

"I'll batter it in buttermilk the way Granny used to."

"Sounds great."

Then, just as she put her hand on the doorknob, Evelyn remembered. "Oh, Rob! Ted and Elaine are both supposed to come home sometime Saturday."

His face fell like a child's whose birthday has been canceled. "Can we still have Friday night at least?"

"Yes, as far as I know. Yes. We won't have to give that up. Come Friday as soon as you can."

"You bet."

Judd telephoned her at the office Wednesday. "Eva, I have to cancel our walk tonight; I'm leaving this afternoon."

"Oh, I didn't think you'd go so soon." *I sound as if I'm complaining; I've no right to do that.*

"Well, Lacie Edwards had her baby early this morning, and they're both doing fine, so it's a good time. I'm driving the Blue Ridge Parkway part of the way, so it'll take longer, and I thought I might as well leave today instead of in the morning."

"Of course; I understand. When will I see you again?"

"I don't know. Good-bye, Eva."
"Good-bye, Judd. I'll miss you."

Evelyn didn't feel like taking her and Judd's usual walking route that afternoon. It wasn't just that she felt unprotected without Judd, although even in rural Meadorsville a woman walking alone was not as safe as she used to be. She just didn't feel like seeing the things they had looked at together without him.

Walking up and down the streets in town was quite safe, of course, even after dark. But she opted instead for a walk through the cemetery. There was no fence between it and her property, just a line of trees, so she left her house by the recreation-room door in the basement, followed the line of apple trees between her house and Judd's office back to the ravine, walked along the mixed trees bordering it, jumped its summer-trickling branch, and cut through the pines along the southern boundary into the cemetery. The trees held in the day's heat and kept out any breeze. She followed the roads through the stones marking the Meadors and Harpers, the Thorndikes, Curtises, and all the Macs and Mcs.

In an older part of the cemetery, she was surprised to see her own middle name, Montgomery. There were three gravestones together, two much older than the third, which read, "Cyrus Montgomery/Beloved Husband and Father/1853–1928." Beside him was "Marie Montgomery/Beloved Wife and Mother/1865–1887," and at their feet was "Infant Son/1885." The older stones were not the polished granite of Cyrus's; they were pitted and moss-grown.

But of course. I carry Nana's maiden name. And Jourden Marie was named for her mother. And I knew that Nana grew up near Harper; I had just forgotten. It never occurred to me all these years that I lived so close to them that I could have seen their graves every day. My great-grandparents.

Nana was born in 1887. So her mother must have died in childbirth or shortly after. Poor motherless child. And the empty space here by Infant Son. That must have been for Nana. But she lies in Cedar Springs next to Grandfather Lanier.

Where will I lie? She shook off the morbid thought. *I'm supposed to be walking for my health, not gandering and maundering. But I'll come back sometime and put flowers here. Every life ought to be remembered.*

Friday before graduation was traditionally Illumination Night at Harper: the campus would be strung with electric lines like Christmas lights, and colored Japanese lanterns would be put over each bulb. Around the lake the effect was always especially striking, with the colored lights reflected in the water. The maintenance crew were stringing the lights up when Evelyn took her freshman grades, the last ones, to campus that morning. Haze hung in the air like fog.

There was a note from Rob under her door; he thought Marcia Lee would leave with Trey around ten, and he would call her at home. She knocked on his office door, but there was no answer. It was eight-thirty, so she filed her own grade records, watered her office plants, and left for home.

She changed into the red silk shantung draped dress that she had worn when Jessie had married Sterling Wilson; she knew she was overdressed, but it was the most becoming thing she had. She felt as nervous as she had when preparing for Rob's first visit, but there was little to do. On Thursday, Lucy had cleaned the house as usual, and Evelyn had made desserts, a chocolate cake for lunch because she knew it was Rob's favorite and a citrus snow with Grand Marnier sauce to go with the chicken for dinner, which was marinating in buttermilk. She had made French bread for both meals and shrimp gumbo to warm up for lunch; it was always better the second day anyhow. So now all she had to do was straighten a few pillows, set the table for lunch, and start the first of a stack of Mozart sonatas on the stereo. She sat down with *Newsweek* and tried to concentrate.

Although she was waiting for its ring, the phone startled her at eleven. Rob said, "I'm free at last. I'll be there in ten minutes."

"I can't wait."

"When will you evict me for your cruel children?"

"Elaine won't be here until one or two Saturday, and Ted will be later. Stay through lunch if you can. I got steaks to broil."

"Marcia Lee's going to call at noon Saturday. She would have called tonight, but I told her I was going to a movie."

"She won't try to call you late tonight?"

"I don't think so. If she does, I'll just say I had a headache and turned the telephone volume down and didn't hear it. If she doesn't believe me, that's tough."

His rebellious tone agitated her; she felt guilt at causing a breach with his wife. "If you think it's all right . . ."

"My dearest Evelyn, I wouldn't give up the next twenty-four hours for anything I can think of, Faust's bargain included."

"Then don't spend any more of it talking on the telephone."

"No, I won't. But I did pick up a movie for us to watch tonight. You have a VCR, don't you?"

"Yes, VHS, not Betamax. What is it?"

"Let's let that be my surprise."

"Don't knock—just come in."

She had put the garage door up and heard him drive in and lower it again as she put the fruit salads, bread, and gumbo on the table. He brought an armload, a florist's box as well as the videocassette, his briefcase, and a shaving kit. He put them down on the table and looked; she could feel his eyes like hands stroking her body.

"Well! You look gorgeous!"

She colored. "Thank you."

"Open the box."

It contained a half-dozen red roses.

"I would have gotten you the full dozen, but Marcia Lee watches my money like a hawk."

"I love them." She cut the stems, put them in a vase, and tried to smell the blooms, but of course they had only the muted odor of commercial flowers grown for durability and looks. She substituted them for Granny's blooming African violets ranged down the center of the table.

"I have a schedule for today," he announced. "We can't spend the whole twenty-four hours making love, at least I can't, much as I'd like to. And I want to have ordinary time with you anyhow. So I brought my manuscript to go through with you this afternoon. After dark we'll drive around campus to see the lights. I'll wear a hat and glasses, and we'll use your car; you can tell anyone who sees you I'm your cousin from Opelousas. Then we'll watch the movie, and by that time I won't be able to keep my hands off you. Tomorrow we'll begin to face reality again.''

They followed his schedule except for a few stolen kisses. During lunch she asked him something she'd wondered about, whether or not he had had affairs with other women.

''I had a pretty checkered past, but after I married Marcia Lee, there was only one—a girl in grad school. She was in my Modern British Fiction class, and then we took a seminar together.''

''What was she like?''

''Not like you. She had long brown hair like a mermaid's that she wore in a ponytail, and she used to pull it over her shoulder and play with it in class, and she sang folk songs, so I called her Lorelei. She was just . . . someone to get away from Marcia Lee with, someone to go to art-movie matinees and talk about freedom in John Fowles with. Marcia Lee's idea of culture was *The Sound of Music*. Lorelei had a tiny room a hundred blocks from campus. Used to wear miniskirts and a long, fringed, embroidered vest.''

''How . . . was she different from me?''

''She didn't make me love her. It was all pretty cool, dearest worrywart. She just caught my eye one day and hung around after class waiting for me to proposition her, and when I did, she accepted, and when the year was over, she left grad school to travel—hitchhiking was her plan—through Europe. And I never heard from her again. Or wondered about her till now. Maybe that's the root of my philandering with you: unresolved longing for a girl I haven't thought about for ten years. Obviously repression.''

He grinned, and she was ashamed of her questions. But she was glad that he had answered them.

He spread his manuscript on her desk in the library and sat in her desk chair and read it from the beginning while she lay on the couch, listened, and commented. Past his head she saw Cressida. But the lines of flame around her had changed; what Evelyn traced now was wings. *Maybe since she has wings, she doesn't need feet. Except for landing gear, of course.*

When she awoke, it was light, but before sunrise. His arm lay across her waist, and she thought his turning might have awakened her. His shoulder was bare and cold to her touch from the air-conditioning, so she carefully worked it under the covers. Then she rested her palm against his warm ribs. He sighed in his sleep, and she studied the tousles of his hair, the fine lines across his forehead and around his eyes and mouth, the straight, long lashes, the dear lips. She closed her eyes and felt his warmth next to her and the weight of his arm claiming her. *I have this. Whatever happens now, I have had this.* Fulfillment settled around her like a blanket, and she went back to sleep.

The next thing she was aware of was his lips nuzzling into her neck. She clasped his head and kissed it through the hair. "Rob, my love."

"Evelyn, my own." He moved down her body, kissing and caressing her, uncovering her, then covering her with his own body, folding her in his arms while she enfolded him.

Again she felt as if she had died, and the death was the sweetest life she had ever had.

She cooked a country breakfast of biscuits, sausage, eggs, and tomatoes, and they talked about the movie, *Apocalypse Now,* of which they had slighted the ending the night before, and how it related to Conrad's *Heart of Darkness.*

She said, "Eliot refers to Conrad too in the epigraph to 'The Hollow Men': 'Mistah Kurtz—he dead.' "

"I thought of that poem this morning when I woke up with you beside me, the second stanza of Part III, where Eliot talks about meaningless ritual instead of love because we wake alone."

She couldn't speak, and she knew he could see the tears ready to spill. Finally she touched her eyes with her finger and mastered her voice. "My waking this morning was not alone." The words were like a song in her own ears.

"But it's not enough, Evelyn. I want a life with you, not stolen moments. What I have except you is worse than being alone."

She reached across the table toward him, and he took her hand and went on. "I have to ask Marcia Lee to free me."

XIII. Jessica

The Longest Way 'Round

*J*essica knew that Evelyn was different somehow. "You're looking great, Evie. Haven't you lost weight?"

"Yes, around fifteen pounds since Christmas."

"Dinner was great, too."

"Did you notice the incest of the menu? The crookneck squash, the cucumbers in the sauce, and the honeydew are all members of the same vegetable family."

"Sounds like you lived with a botanist too long. I'd think for vegetables, even incest must be an improvement. Or are you anti-sex since your divorce?"

Evie blushed. "Actually, I'm pretty pro-sex these days."

"Well! Want to tell me about it?"

She looked around. "Where are the children?"

"I don't know, but I don't think they're within earshot."

"Let's go into the sunroom to be sure. We can see anyone coming from there. Close that door, will you?"

"Why all the secrecy?"

"I've . . . been sleeping with someone."

"Are you enjoying it? You look either miserable or guilty."

"Certainly guilty. He's married."

"That doesn't answer my question. Is he a good lay?"

"Jessie!"

"Well, you've spent most of your life with good reads instead. They're not the same, sister."

"I . . . love him. The way I . . . loved Greg."

She looked at Evie. *This may be serious.* "You know that he's dead?"

"Yes. In Vietnam. How did you know?"

"Well, aside from the alumni bulletin, where you probably saw it too, Marshall told me."

"You've seen Marshall?"

Guess it's confession time for me now. "Yes. Several times in the last year. He's in Dallas now. He started a security business there when he retired from the army. It's doing quite well. He looked me up."

"How did he know about Greg?"

Saved by her own self-absorption. Well, it's not the first time. "They saw each other in Nam—ran into each other by accident first, then kept up with each other."

"What did he tell you about Greg?"

"He became a psychologist. I knew that from college, but I don't remember ever telling you anything about him after you married Ward. He became a psychoanalyst even. You can probably credit yourself with that—his profession, I mean; if anybody ever needed therapy, he did, after you." *She's not going to say anything to that.* "Anyhow, he worked in the inner city with abused children. Was practically some sort of miracle worker, I guess. But his number came up in the draft, and he didn't ask for deferment. So he wound up in Nam and got himself killed saving a buddy. Marshall heard about it from the buddy."

Evie was crying.

Jessica put her arms around her. *I didn't have to be so hard on her. She never willed any of it. She was just too busy doing what she was supposed to do to be human or kind.*

After a while Evie pulled away and took out a handkerchief. "Did he ever marry?"

"No."

Evie cried a little more, then wiped her eyes and blew her nose. "Tell me about Marshall."

"What do you want to know?"

"What I did to him. I know what I did to you. I drove you into marriage with Brad Cunningham, a perfect cipher, bland enough that even Father accepted him—after all, he was no rival—and into a divorce as predictable as sunset and into marriage with Sterling Wilson, who at least isn't a cipher but . . . well, I overstepped my bounds before and have no right to now."

"You're apologizing! You're actually admitting you were wrong about something!"

"Yes. I should have long ago. I knew at the time that I had no right to come between you and Marshall. Greg told me then that I didn't, and I wouldn't listen to him. Jessie, I am sorry. I messed up your life and mine and Greg's and Marshall's and Ward's."

"And Brad's and Sterling's. Though I have to take blame for caving in to you. That's what I've finally realized, that no matter what you did, I could have acted differently too. And now I don't have to stay a fool."

"So you're going to make a change too?"

Here goes. "I've told Sterling I'm leaving him. I won't take his money, not even what the prenuptial agreement gives me. I've seen too much how he gets it. And I could do perfectly well on the income from what Mother and Father gave me when they divided up the money among us. Mine's just been drawing interest all these years. And if Marshall will have me, I'll marry him now."

"Jessie, did you ever sleep with Marshall? Back then, I mean."

"Of course I did. I wasn't a complete fool."

"Has he never married?"

"He's married right now. For the third time—he's beat my record. But they're breaking up; she wants out as much as he does. He'll divorce her whether he marries me or not."

"He'll marry you."

"Yes. He will." *He will. Thank goodness for great favors, he will.* "So what about your new love?"

"Jessie, his marriage wasn't breaking up—until he got involved with me."

"Well, well, Evelyn Lanier the homewrecker."

"He has a five-year-old son. And he's nine years younger than I."

"Congratulations! Somebody here at the college?"

"Yes. Another English teacher. His name's Rob—Robert Gordon McFergus, Jr. His son's named for him, so they call him Trey."

"The wonder is you both put your books down long enough to do anything. Are you really smitten? You don't have to answer that. You've just opened up to me about yourself and apologized after over twenty years—something's obviously changed you."

"But it's wrong, Jessie."

Here come the waterworks again. "Is his marriage right except for you?"

"No."

"Then you can't hog all the blame, can you?"

"I feel I'm to blame either way. If I marry Rob, we're tearing up his marriage. And if I don't, maybe I'm wrecking his life."

"Like with Greg." *It probably never occurred to her that after Marshall I might have saved Greg myself if it hadn't been for hurting her. If anybody can save anybody.*

"Yes. Just like. There's a poem by Keats, presumably to Fanny Brawne, that I keep thinking of."

"Trot it out. I know by now I might as well listen when you get a poem on your mind, or you'll work it in some other way."

"Not long before he died, Keats wrote this on the edge of a manuscript he never finished." She recited as if she were staring at a dying man:

> This living hand, now warm and capable
> Of earnest grasping, would, if it were cold
> And in the icy silence of the tomb,
> So haunt thy days and chill thy dreaming nights
> That thou wouldst wish thine own heart dry of blood
> So in my veins red life might stream again,
> And thou be conscience-calm'd—see here it is—
> I hold it towards you.

"And every time I read that, I think of Greg. And if I held back from Rob, I'd be doing the same thing to him."

"Good Lord! Why can't you just be simple, Evie, and love somebody easy?"

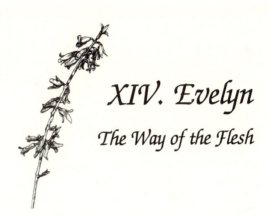

XIV. Evelyn
The Way of the Flesh

*E*laine and Ted had brought their own heartaches home. Elaine was fighting against attachment to Bill but had already asked him to come for a visit as soon as he could. She was tied down to her usual summer job at Joe Hillson's law office; Bill worked for his father during the summer and had more flexibility. She talked to him on the telephone at least every other day and in general seemed only half present in Meadorsville.

Ted, on the other hand, had lost Melissa near the end of the term to a student her own age. She was the first girl to dump him, and his pride as well as his heart was wounded. He began healing himself by asking out a series of girls he had known in high school, and Evelyn was reminded of Ward when Rose Muir had started dating Reaves Thompson. Or, for that matter, when she had asked for the divorce and he had started seeing Mary Will right away. Ted's current head-long career from one girl to another was one of the few times she had seen her son behave like his father, and she wondered if masculine pride was universally the same. Except for Greg.

Everyone had assumed that during the summer the children would live at their mother's and visit Ward and Mary Will only

231

occasionally. Ted worked at the local computer shop, and both children sometimes came home for lunch or just dropped by to pick something up. Evelyn was happy to have them, but their presence ended her freedom to see Rob at home and his to call her there. The nearest safe trysting place was Franklin, too far for their brief opportunities. She filled her time with study of Robinson Jeffers's poetry and review of her own poems. But she felt as if the real part of her life had been suspended. She didn't dare call Rob at his home, and she didn't see him at school the few times she went to her own dark office, ostensibly to pick up mail and water plants. After summer school started, she called him at his office when she thought he might be there but didn't reach him for several days.

When she did, they arranged to meet at school during his office hours. She propped a chair back under the knob of her locked door, and they turned out the light and drew the blinds and made love on the carpet in the shadows of the bright day.

The bookshelves rose around them, and she said, "Think of all the sympathetic witnesses we have, Rob: Anna and Vronsky, Emma Bovary and Léon, Edna Pontellier and her Robert."

"You chose all unhappy ones, Evelyn. Are you unhappy?"

"No, my love." She tried to convince him with her kiss. "I just can't think of any loves like ours that end happily."

"There are other witnesses too, you know—Rosamond Lydgate and May Archer and all those unpleasant, right women who hold their men."

She looked at his leg and ran her hand over it; the hairs were lighter than his black crown and shaven beard. "I don't ask to hold you, Rob. You don't owe me anything, and if you don't want to see me ever again, I can go somewhere else."

He held out his hands and pulled her up into his arms. "That's not what I meant; losing you is the furthest thing from what I want. I want to be able to see you without having to make an appointment, to have you with me anytime, to hold you as often as I think about you. But to have that, I have to talk to Marcia Lee. And so far, I haven't been brave enough. I'm too big a coward."

"It's not cowardice to avoid hurting someone. Heaven knows, if anybody understands that, it ought to be me; I stayed married to Ward Knight twenty years rather than tell him sooner that I didn't love him. Rather than face it myself."

He was running his hand over her hair and down her back, and she closed her eyes and rested against him. He said, "Did you ever love him . . . like this?"

"I loved him, although not the way I love you. But I always had to protect myself from him. There's something in Ward that would have killed what I am."

"What do you mean?"

She moved back from him then, fastened her bra and blouse, and pulled her denim skirt down against the onslaught of the air-conditioning while she tried to move from the sweet fog of their lovemaking to form her thesis. "I don't know exactly what I mean, but he's a scientist, and the scientist has to order everything, measure it, find out the common essence that makes it what it is and label it by that and have it fit into the limits of everything like it. The humanist wants variety, every leaf different, every life different. And variety is chaos, not order. I don't mean that the artist doesn't seek order, but he wants order in variety, not conformity."

"Marcia Lee wants to own me. She's always used her sex like money: she gave me her virginity, so I owe her my body and soul. But I won't be owned. You don't try to own me, so I want to give myself to you, let you do what you will with me. There's a paradox for you!"

She debated with herself but asked anyhow. "I do want something from you, Rob, unless it's too painful: tell me about your mother dying."

He shifted away from facing her directly. "God, you go for the jugular, don't you? You make me wish I hadn't quit smoking or had some whiskey."

"Forget it; I don't want to hurt you. I just wanted to know all I can about you."

"No; that's all right. I'll try to tell you. But first I have to tell you what I remember about my mother before." He sat with his eyes closed. "I remember being little sitting on her lap while she read me a story. I was very tired from playing outside, and it had been hot, but she had bathed me and put cool pajamas on me. Her voice was sweet and high, and she was soft, and she smelled good. Her hair was like yours, dark and long and soft, and it came down like the rain and . . . sheltered me." He opened his eyes and looked at her. "All this must be like what thousands of other people remember about their mothers."

She stroked his hand.

His mouth twisted. "Then she was sick, and there were bad smells, medicine and death, and I couldn't see her much or touch her, and she was lying there talking to me in a voice that was a long way away. She wasn't mine anymore, and she didn't care. She was sick a long time, and I got along without her. My father took care of me when he was home, and I learned to take care of myself when he wasn't, and sometimes she was at home, and someone, her aunts or her sisters, would come and stay with us, but I always had to stay outside her room except that sometimes she'd call for me to come in when I got home from school, and she'd ask me what I'd learned that day, and I always told her, planned on the way home what I could tell her if she asked me. Or she'd be in the hospital, and I'd sit in the waiting room downstairs and do my homework or color in my coloring book while my father sat with her. Then when I was nine, she died, and they said she wanted to go to heaven to be with Jesus. They put her in the ground, and she was gone."

Evelyn had continued to stroke his hands while he talked. When he finished, she held his face on both sides and kissed him on the forehead, each eyelid, then the nose, the chin, and finally the mouth. *Forehead bender,/Eye winker,/Tom Tinker,/Nose dropper,/Chin chopper,/Mouth eater.* "She cared. She never wanted to leave you, Rob."

He held her again. "I'd like to think that."

"What did she die of?"

"I don't know—probably cancer."

"Didn't your father ever tell you?"

"We didn't talk much. He wasn't much to me. He was always working or tired or—remote. He joked with other people, but he never did with me. When he died, it was like losing a stranger."

She squeezed him. "That's why Trey means so much to you."

"Yes. I don't want to be the kind of father mine was."

"And that's another reason you can't confront Marcia Lee."

"Yes. All during her pregnancy and delivery, she made it clear I owe her for having him too. If I asked for a divorce, she'd never let me see him if she could prevent it. And the courts might let her."

"I don't ask you to do that."

"Can you keep me from asking myself?"

They held each other.

She wasn't sure that she wanted him to ask Marcia Lee for a divorce. If her love for Ward had died, mightn't her love for Rob? And mightn't his for her? But she would not decide for him.

He had never asked her if she would take care of Trey; he had just assumed that she would. And she would. That she was sure about.

Rob and Evelyn left notes for each other under their office doors, sealing them against the custodial staff. Evelyn's personal notes to him were all emotion. She wrote frequent poems to him too. *As mushy as an adolescent's,* she thought. She would have been ashamed for him to know she was capable of some of them and didn't even make fair copies, much less give them to him. But she kept them. And she gave him the better ones. She wondered if she should include some of these in the stack of her poems that she was considering for publication. But most of them would have to be altered if she did; they revealed too much.

One night, Evelyn awoke in the dark from a rare nightmare. She didn't remember the earlier part of the dream, but just before she awoke, she had been biting Marcia Lee above her left elbow, scraping to the bone with her teeth. The ferocity frightened her; she had not known that she could hate someone that much.

She lay awake until it was time to get up. She could not think or plan; she only lay in the dark and waited for whatever disaster was to come.

Jeff and Sue Fisher had bought one of the Victorian houses on Curtis Street and were repairing and remodeling it; they planned to live on the first floor only and rent out the bedrooms on the second floor to students as a means of supplementing Sue's income. Jeff had passed his comprehensive exams and started his dissertation; he wouldn't be working, but he wouldn't have to commute to Nashville either.

They invited Evelyn to a housewarming, and she accepted gladly. She assumed that Rob and Marcia Lee would be there too, and she would rather see him publicly, even with Marcia Lee, than not at all.

But the McFerguses didn't come. Evelyn first watched anxiously to see them, then, when she was sure they weren't coming, went through the rest of the evening disappointed, empty. Nothing mattered since Rob wasn't there. She tried to be a good guest, attentive to the conversation, complimentary to Sue on her refreshments and to her and Jeff on the attractiveness of their thrift-store decorating. But she really felt nothing about anything present; her feelings were all absorbed in Rob's absence, which was like a black hole, sucking in everything, making it all nothing.

She did come out of her absorption when, as she was making her thanks, Sue asked, "Are you going to be around tomorrow?"

Evelyn knew from Sue's expression that she had something serious to talk over again. "Yes. Why don't you come to the house for coffee?"

"I'd like that. What would be a good time?"

"Is ten all right?"

"Fine."

"I'll expect you then."

"Thanks, Evie."

"You're welcome." *Just what I'm fit to do—serve as Mother Confessor again.*

Evelyn went home feeling empty and dreading the uncertainty of her emptiness. *If only I knew when I could see him next. If only I were sure I would see him again. What if he dies before we can see each other again? What if he decides to break with me instead of Marcia Lee? What if I never see him again? What good would anything be without him?*

236

She cried awhile, then got out pen and paper to try to catch her feelings, hold them so she could look at them as an object, study them and see what they were and what she was. Her resulting poem showed her lack of confidence in the permanence of any happiness; she entitled it "Thrown."

> Surprised at the lift
> from the saddle
>
> the sudden flight
> the golden dandelion's shine below
>
> she screams inside
>
> but knows
> no sound
> foretells the shock
> of wide-spread ground
> at end of this high ride.

And this may be the only sound I can ever make about it.

Before she finished her first cup of coffee, Sue was crying. She explained that she felt that Jeff was unhappy.

"Have you asked him how he feels?"

"No. I can't talk to him anymore."

"Why? Did you already quarrel and hurt each other?"

"No. It's just that I can't tell him how I feel."

"How do you feel?"

"Ugly. Selfish. Mean."

"You aren't ugly, Sue; you're a vivacious, pretty girl. Is it the weight that bothers you?"

Sue nodded. "And my skin; it's as bad as when I was thirteen."

"Does Jeff . . . still want to make love?"

"Yes."

"Then he must not find you totally repulsive. Why do you feel selfish?"

"For making him marry me."

"I thought he wanted to marry you."

"He did. But maybe he regrets it now."

"Maybe. Has he *said* anything about wishing he hadn't?"

"He couldn't tell me that. He wouldn't be that cruel."

"All right, then, has he said or done anything to show that he's excited about having the baby, that he wants it?"

"Yes, he talks about it all the time, and he's been working on the nursery when he ought to be working on his dissertation."

"Then maybe instead of being selfish, you're sharing something with him that means a great deal to him."

Sue blew her nose. After a while, she said, "Maybe I am. But I still feel mean. Evie, the truth is I'm not sure I want this baby myself. Or maybe even Jeff. Everything's changed. I had my life all to myself before, and I could do whatever I wanted to. And now I always have to consider what Jeff wants. And when the baby comes, there'll be sleepless nights and croup and temper tantrums and not much money, and I won't be free at all anymore. And I feel mean to think about all that."

"Did you ever read Erasmus's *The Praise of Folly*?"

Sue shook her head.

"It says that no sensible person would become a parent because of the pain and anxiety. But it also says that no sensible person would continue to live because of the same problems. The point is that living involves pain and anxiety, but without them, we can't have joy and growth. Having a baby and bringing it up is one of the greatest joys I know. And living involves relations with other people; to avoid close relations with others is to avoid life."

"I guess that's what bothers me the most. I don't feel close to Jeff anymore; I felt closer before we married."

Evelyn felt her own chest tighten. "You can't let that happen. But keeping close doesn't mean not having any disagreements. Believe me, I know. Ward and I didn't quarrel. And we never even talked about the big disagreements. But that doesn't make them go away; it just makes them grow in the dark like a fungus in the cellar until it swells and takes up the whole space and spreads through the house, and there's no air to breathe anymore."

They sat silent until Sue covered Evelyn's hand with her own. "Thank you. You help; you always help me. But I have to ask for more help. How do I talk about this with Jeff?"

Evelyn smiled wryly at herself. "I just told you I failed at that. But you and Jeff don't have the accumulation of hidden antagonisms that Ward and I built up." She saw a heap of bones lying beside them in the middle of the sunroom floor, some dry with age, some moldy, some still bloody. "You have to tell him how you feel. If you don't, he may think your unhappiness comes from something he's done, and then things get worse. Don't let that happen."

"I won't. And thank you again. I'm going to have to pay you for therapy."

"Oh, I'm no expert, Sue. Just the opposite."

They were quiet again for a moment, and Evelyn debated asking about Rob. It would be natural; they needed a change of conversation. "I wondered why Rob and Marcia Lee weren't at your housewarming last night."

"Marcia Lee had bridge club, and Rob couldn't get a baby-sitter for Trey."

He didn't even call Elaine or Ted. He could have come without Marcia Lee, and he didn't. He knew I'd be there, but he didn't want to see me. The pain twisted. She almost felt physically ill; a heaviness weighted her chest and abdomen. She tried to concentrate on the conversation. But all the time, she was thinking, *He didn't want to see me.* When Sue left, she went into her bedroom and had herself another cry.

A couple of days later, Evelyn went to her office to care for the flowers and found photocopies of a new chapter of Rob's novel. It depicted a quarrel between Keith and his mother after he tells her that he wants to marry Valerie, and it culminated in Keith's stabbing the mother. A note paper-clipped to the last page said,

> Dearest,
>   I probably can't use this; it leads nowhere and just destroys Keith's chances for Valerie. But it expresses Keith's rage and frustration.
>
> Yours,
Rob

So he hasn't rejected me. But he doesn't know what to do.

He's even considered murdering Marcia Lee. And that makes me happy. What kind of person have I become?

At home Lucy was cleaning; she gave Evelyn another note and said, "Dr. Adivino left you this."

"Oh, he's come back! Thank you, Lucy."

She put down the mail and books she had brought from the office and read the note:

> Dear Eva,
>   I'm back. Call me if you want to walk today.
>   Always,
>   Judd

Men all sign the same: "Always" or "Yours" or something noncommittal. Always what? Your what? Women are ready to commit at once: "Love" is what I'd sign to Rob or Judd at this point.

But the word wouldn't mean the same thing to both. She telephoned Judd at once and asked him to dinner before their constitutional, and he accepted.

Dinner was lively. Elaine had gotten a call from Bill to tell her that he could come for a visit the next week, and she was overflowing with happiness. Ted had decided that Hailey Branham, one of his former girlfriends, had become much more interesting since high school, and he had been spending most of his time after work with her. Elaine suggested that when Bill came, the four of them could go together Sunday afternoon to the Volunteer Firemen's Ice Cream Social, an annual fund-raiser in Meadorsville.

Ted agreed and said, "Why don't you come too, Mom?"

"I don't really want to be a fifth wheel."

Ted said, "Dr. Adivino could come too."

240

She wished he hadn't said anything; it placed Judd in an awkward position.

But Judd said, "That sounds good. Will you go with me, Eva?"

"I'd like to. Thank you."

When she and Judd walked, she confessed that she had missed her exercise three days while he was gone.

"You did better than I, I'm afraid. Except for a couple of short hikes on the drive up, I didn't walk for the first week. And I missed several times the next two."

"Doctor! I'm shocked!"

"You should know that doctors take notoriously poor care of themselves."

Evelyn told him about walking in the cemetery and finding her great-grandparents' graves.

"I visited the Jewish cemetery in Baltimore while I was there too. My Uncle Judah died last year, and I took Aunt Leah to visit the grave."

"He's the one you're named for?"

"Yes, Judah's my full name. We were both named for Judah Halevi, a Sephardic poet. Funny—he was a physician too."

"That's somehow right: a poet ought to be able to heal the spirit. And maybe a physician has to heal the spirit too."

"I don't feel able to heal anyone, body or spirit, right now."

She looked at him; he did seem stooped and gray. "You're supposed to come back from a vacation feeling renewed."

"The way I feel, I should be named Methuselah."

"Oh, Judd! You're not old! You just need some exercise. That's what you get for not following your own orders. The poet will have to heal the physician."

"I may be a hopeless case, but I appreciate the effort, Eva."

"Speaking of names, why have you always called me Eva? Is that the Hebrew for Evelyn?"

"The Hebrew for Eve is Hava or Hawah. So, yes, when I call you Eva, I'm making you a little closer to . . . my experiences." He still looked at the road. "There are so many differences between us. Is it all right for me to call you Eva?"

"Why, of course; since you want to, I wouldn't have you call me anything else."

"Thank you."

"You're welcome, I'm sure." His gravity troubled her, and she began questioning him about his sister and family. But they all seemed to be doing well. She wondered if the visit to their hometown had made him miss Anna more; she remembered that Anna had been buried in Baltimore. Maybe he had been to her grave too. She considered asking, but turned the conversation to the scenery instead.

He seemed to lighten, and at the end of the walk, he said, "I'm glad I have my walking partner back."

She said, "Me too. Any more walks through the cemetery, and I'd probably become a ghoul."

"Better to walk with the living than the dead."

She agreed and thought, *Yes, he's been thinking of Anna. She was such a sweet, lovely woman; no wonder he misses her.*

Bill Jackson arrived from Knoxville early Saturday afternoon. He was medium, Evelyn decided: medium height, medium coloring, medium handsome. He brought a kitten for Elaine, an elegant puss with gray stripes over a beige undercoat. Elaine christened her Wilhelmina and began spoiling and terrorizing her at once, cradling her and whirling her madly through the air. Bill watched Elaine, and Evelyn watched Bill. He seemed all right, but she withheld judgment. At least he watched Elaine. Elaine seemed to try to avoid watching him. Maybe that was because Ted and she were there.

At dinner, Elaine said they were going to visit her father and his new wife that evening.

Evelyn said, "Poor Bill. You're subjecting him to all of us at once."

Bill said, "I don't mind. I tried to get her to come meet my family last fall."

Elaine looked down. "Well, I will one of these days. I just don't want them to know what a crazy woman their son's taken up with."

"They'll love you the same way I do." He smiled and was handsomer than medium. "And if they didn't, it wouldn't matter anyhow." He didn't look worried.

Elaine blushed.

Why can't she just accept the fact that he loves her?

Oh, sure, and you're so good at just accepting things, Evelyn.

For the Firemen's Ice Cream Social Sunday, the playgrounds at the elementary and junior high schools were encircled with booths, and the street between them was roped off. Loudspeakers broadcast calliope tunes. Despite the sultry day, everyone in town already seemed to be there when the Knights and their friends arrived. Getting through the crowds as a group of six was impossible, but the children and their dates still waited to include Judd and Evelyn in their fun. They ate barbecue, coleslaw, and corn on the cob and sampled every flavor of ice cream available, judging the fresh peach the star of the day. Bill and Ted showed off their muscles and aim at the dunking machine, and the boys became friendly rivals at the game booths while Elaine and Hailey enjoyed their attention.

Bill attempted to win a large teddy bear for Elaine by knocking empty drink bottles over. He spent more on tickets than he would have spent to buy the toy at a store. Ted jeered him, and Elaine urged him on.

Evelyn was laughing with Judd at his efforts when she saw Marcia Lee coming through the crowd toward them. When Marcia Lee recognized her, she looked around as if to turn aside, but there was no other way to go. So she headed toward them, but her face was red, and her eyes darted hate at Evelyn.

She knows. He's told her, or she's found out. Evelyn felt sick.

Rob was behind Marcia Lee, hidden by her and Trey, whom he was carrying. Then he saw Evelyn, and his face went askew, like a Picasso portrait, his eyes out of focus. The carnival music blasted on derisively.

Evelyn said, "Hello, Marcia Lee. Hello, Rob."

Marcia Lee said nothing. Rob said, "Hello, Evelyn. Hello, Judd."

His face still seemed twisted. Then he was past them.

She knows. And he's wrenched. What have I done to him? She put her hand to her head and swayed, and Judd whispered, "Steady!" and put his arm behind her and his other hand at her waist. She concentrated on keeping her balance.

Judd kept his voice low. "Do you want to go home?"

"Yes. Please."

He touched Ted's arm. "Ted, your mother's not feeling well. I'll take her home."

"What's wrong, Mom?"

Judd said, "Probably something she ate. Don't worry; I'll take care of her."

Ted said, "You're the doctor; we can't ask for better than that."

Judd guided her through the crowd around the elementary school. As they passed the deserted front steps, she said, "Wait a minute," and sat down in the dusky light and tried to stop the world from whirling. But then she felt hot and cold at the same time and knew she was going to vomit, and she stood up and walked into the grass and leaned over and lost her meal.

Judd supported her again and wiped her face with his handkerchief. "It's all right; you're all right," he said over and over, crooning it like a mother to a child.

"I'm not all right. I'm all wrong."

He led her back to the steps and said, "Sit down."

She did and began crying, hopeless.

He pulled her head onto his shoulder and held her, saying, "Eva, Eva, Eva."

Ashamed of her weakness, she stopped crying and pulled away. "I'll . . . I'm all right."

"Do you think you can walk home, or should I get my car?" They had all walked to the festival.

"I can walk. It's only four blocks."

"All right." He helped her up.

She was dizzy for a moment and felt the sweat break out on her forehead again, but he offered his arm, and she steadied herself. He led her around the school and up the empty street next to it.

They walked in silence. Evelyn tried not to think of Rob's face, just to walk and breathe in the cooling night air. *Step, breathe in. Step, breathe out. Step, breathe in.*

She unlocked her front door and went through. Judd didn't follow, and she turned around.

"If you're all right, I'll not come in. Are you?"

She nodded. "Except . . ." *Except my heart, my soul. That's warped, wrenched like Rob's face.*

"Rob McFergus is your . . . young man, isn't he?" His voice was low.

She nodded.

"Oh, Eva, Eva. Poor Eva." He stood a moment looking at her, then turned and walked fast over the porch. The screen door banged behind him.

She didn't get up the next morning, and each of the children came in before they left for work to see how she was. She didn't tell either of them that she had lain awake all night, watching the shadows of the leaves move in their rectangles of moonlight over the walls.

But she had decided. She couldn't do this to Rob. She couldn't tear him away from his child and burden him with guilt. She couldn't ask him to choose between her and his family.

She would use the sabbatical to make plans to leave Harper, then pay back the sabbatical money so that she wasn't obligated to stay the required year afterward. That should give enough time, too, to sell her big, mathematically exact, crazy, empty house. She would try to find a job close enough that the children could see her and Ward too without a lot of travel; maybe she could work in Nashville or get a job at one of the state schools. There were laws against discriminating because of age, and affirmative action favored women in higher education. Though heaven knows, men were a minority in English. She might not get the salary she had now, and she'd be leaving the only home she'd ever known except Lanier Bluffs. But she would do what she had to.

She had to set Rob free. She turned her face into the pillow and cried.

She called Judd to cancel their walk, citing the mugginess, but he said, "No, Eva, you have to heal your physician. Remember that I won't get my exercise if you don't."

She paused. Of course, he was just saying that to make her walk, manipulating her for her own good as he did everyone; he had walked alone for months before she started too. But his insistence also told her that even though he knew about her and Rob, he still accepted her. And his forgiveness was very important to her, she realized; had he condemned her, she would have felt cut off from the whole human race.

She said, "All right. But you're a hard taskmaster."

"I won't ask you to make bricks without straw."

"I'll remember that when our next contract talks begin."

He said, "By the way, if you're worried about psychosomatic illness, I've had seven people contact me today to find out whether they had a virus or the firemen's coleslaw was spoiled."

"Thanks for coddling me."

On their walk he kept their talk on a book he had been reading, Tom Wolfe's *The Right Stuff*, and on the birds and plants that they saw. At the end she said, "Thank you for making me walk tonight."

"You're welcome, Eva. Always."

Bill announced happily at dinner Wednesday night that Elaine had finally agreed to marry him after they both graduated. Elaine blushed like a stoplight but smiled. They had arranged for her to visit his family in three weeks. He and she were together all the time after that until he left the next Sunday; he even went to the law office Thursday and Friday, reading books for his seminar in the fall while she worked.

Evelyn was concerned for Elaine. Bill seemed to love her. Certainly he focused on her whenever they were together, and he had a sense of humor strong enough to rein in her more outrageous flights. But Evelyn asked Elaine if she was sure she loved him.

"I think so, Momma. How can anybody be sure?"

Evelyn shook her head. "I don't know, dear. I do know you need to be completely selfish about deciding to marry anyone; be sure you're doing it for yourself, not him."

"Oh, I want him, all right. I'm not always sure I'm best for him."

"That's up to him." She felt that she needed to say more but didn't know what.

Evelyn continued in her resolve to cut off her ties with Rob. She left no more notes for him. He left a couple, one trying to set up a meeting; she didn't answer them. She started going to her office only in the afternoon when classes were all over and the building was deserted. She would unlock the mail room to check her box and get water for her flowers from the kitchenette. Even his closed office door reminded her of him, and she felt his absence as a continual ache.

The third time she went to the office late, she heard someone shouting outside and went to the window. On the quadrangle, Rob was throwing a Frisbee to Trey. She turned out her office light and stood back from the window a little so she could watch them unobserved. Anyone would have known it was a father–son game. Both were wearing white shorts and bright T-shirts, and their tanned legs and black hair showed clear-edged against the grass in the summer sun. They ran and shouted and laughed.

I would take that away from him. I can never give him that. Even without my ''surgical castration,'' I'm too old to give him a child. And if I could, it would never take the place of this one.

Evelyn went to see Miss Pangburn, a retired English teacher under whom she had studied. It was a duty call, for it hurt Evelyn to see the old lady, who had been a perceptive, stimulating, caring teacher, now in her dotage. Evelyn recognized that she was going out of guilt over Rob, just as she had hounded both children lately about things they wanted her to cook until they had told her to find something else to do. *Penance*, she thought. *Well, at least, it fills my time. Nothing but Rob can fill my life.*

Miss Pangburn was happy that she came. The housekeeper-yardman, Gabe, who had grown old watching over her, opened the draperies in the parlor and took the sheets off the furniture and went to the kitchen assuring them that he would be back with tea, which he accompanied with Ritz crackers.

The old house sat around them in silence, offended at their invasion. Evelyn imagined the ghosts of former residents, momentarily routed, conspiring to oust them.

Miss Pangburn showed Evelyn the cards from students she had gotten all the way back to Christmas and the gifts from her nieces and nephews for Christmas and her birthday, mostly embroidered handkerchiefs still in their boxes, scented soap and toilet water, and guest towels. One niece had sent a box of floral stationery with stamped envelopes, and Miss Pangburn apologized because some designs had been used up and she couldn't show them.

"She sent it to you to use, Miss Pangburn. And I'm sure the people you wrote were glad to hear from you."

"Oh, I write everyone who corresponds with me. I have quite a few correspondents, you know."

"Yes, I can see that. And how are your cats?"

There were three prowling the room, and Miss Pangburn told her of the others who lived outside, in the sheds, stables, and old barn. She detailed how every morning Gabe cooked oatmeal for them in a cold-pack canner and ladled it into dishpans on the back porch and they came out from everywhere. "There were thirty-three the last time we counted," she said.

As Evelyn left, she thought, *This is where I'll be in thirty years.*

Evelyn went to the office to water her plants after several days' neglect and found a manuscript in its usual folder. When she picked it up, she saw a sealed envelope under it, "Mrs. Knight" written on it in Rob's unslanted, separated, curious, dear hand. Inside was a note dated three days before:

> Why haven't you gotten in touch with me? You know I can't reach you except this way. I have to see you. I feel abandoned. Are you trying to kill me? Leave me some word. Please. I'll check every day.
>
> Yours, always,
> Rob

Then he doesn't want to be free of me. She held the note to her heart. And "Yours, always," was certainly better than either word alone.

But he doesn't know what's best for him. This doesn't give me any right to hurt him.

She opened the folder then. There was no note in it, but the manuscript was dated the day before, two days after the note.

In the new chapter, Valerie had broken with Keith and started going out with someone else because Keith hadn't asserted his independence from his mother, and he was contemplating suicide.

Evelyn dialed Rob's number. *Please, let it not be Marcia Lee who answers. I'll just hang up if it is. But I have to reach him. I can't not answer this.*

It wasn't Marcia Lee. Rob said, "Hello."

"Rob, this is Evelyn. I'm at the office; I just got your note and read your manuscript. When can you come here to meet me?"

There was a moment's silence. "The earliest that we could talk about the paper is tomorrow morning. Would eight o'clock be all right?"

"Anytime—eight is fine. You can't talk now?"

"That's right. I'll see you then."

"Rob? Wait."

"Yes?"

"It wasn't because you wouldn't break with Marcia Lee. It was because I couldn't bear to tear you apart between us."

"I'll think about that before we meet."

"Good-bye, my love."

"Good-bye."

She replaced the receiver. *So much for my noble attempt to give him up.*

❧

Evelyn checked Rob's schedule before she unlocked her office the next morning: he had his only class at ten and no office hours before class. Sue's schedule was identical, and it was not likely she would be in early. The other members of the department weren't teaching in summer school or had early afternoon classes. So the office wing would likely be hers and Rob's for two hours.

When he knocked and she let him in, neither said anything before they kissed. When they stopped, she said, "I never meant to hurt you, love. I just wanted to protect you from having to choose between me and your family."

He gripped her arms above the elbow and drew his mouth together. "I'm a big boy now, Evelyn. I have to decide for myself what I can take and what I can't. And I can take the consequences of my choice. But I can't take your choosing for me."

He let her go and walked to the window. "I told Marcia Lee I'm in love with you and want a divorce the week before we saw you at the firemen's festival. I thought I'd be able to tell you the first of the next week, by note if no other way. I never thought of seeing you before then. Certainly not of you and Marcia Lee seeing each other. Or of seeing you with another man."

"Oh, Rob! There's nothing between Judd and me except a long friendship. You know we've lived next door to each other forever."

"Since long before you ever met me."

"And I never wanted him the way I want you."

He turned toward her again. "Is that true?"

He had that in the manuscript too—Valerie seeing another man. "It's true. I've loved one other man the way I love you, a boy I knew in college. But I never made love with him. He died in Vietnam. And there's no one else I want like you."

He held out his arms to her then, and they began kissing. They made love, and it was not slow and tender but intense, almost violent. Then they were tender with each other, expressing their love with their lips and bodies, not words. Finally they lay still together, pressed against each other.

She felt a deep peace. *We've loved each other without holding anything back, body or soul.*

"My one love," he said.

"My one love," she echoed.

Finally he looked at his watch, sighed, and pulled away from her. She sat up too, and they dressed.

She sat in her desk chair and said, "Do you want to tell me what Marcia Lee's been like?"

"No. I wouldn't expose you to her bedlam. But I'll tell you the upshot. No pun intended. I thought enough about buying a gun for self-defense that I went down and talked with the village constable about the best kind to get. And then I was afraid I might use it on her . . . not in self-defense."

250

"You wrote . . . something like that earlier in the novel."

"I've felt it more than once. She says if I leave her—move out to start divorce proceedings or not—she'll take Trey to Memphis and I'll never see him again. And I know she'd poison him against me. I could fight for custody, but I don't know how much of a chance I'd have. Mothers usually have to be obviously unfit, and I can't say that she doesn't love Trey, but I don't think he'd have any kind of a chance at a normal life if she brought him up without me."

"So what her stance gives you is alternatives of losing your son—throwing him away, to put it in the bluntest terms—or giving me up. I've said before in every way I know that I won't ever blame you if you choose him. Or her."

"But I'll blame me. For the rest of my life. What kind of life do you think I'll have if I stay with Marcia Lee?"

"Maybe she'll change."

"What could change her?"

"I don't know; I don't know her. I don't know what she was like when you married her." *If she's changed since then, if you've changed her. Or, if not, why you married her the way she is.* She felt that her thought was cold, but she didn't voice it. She considered another possibility. Was compromise possible? "What would happen if . . . you didn't leave her, and we kept on seeing each other?"

He looked at the print of Morris Graves's gouache *Wounded Gull* above her computer. "Then I think . . . one of us would buy a gun."

"But that's what we're doing right now."

"Yes. Except that I have to leave you right now and talk with thirty sophomores about Andrew Marvell's wooing his coy mistress." He stood up and held out his arms, and she gave him a long good-bye kiss.

She said, "At least, I won't be coy."

"Don't. Until further notice, consider yourself as vital to me as air."

"I'll be here anytime you ask."

"Monday morning?"

"At eight?"

"At eight."

Nina Wilton called her that noon and asked if she knew how to play bridge. "I know you're not an addict, Evelyn, but I'm hosting my group tonight, and two people have canceled. I've gotten someone to agree to fill in for one, but I can't think of anyone else to ask but you."

"I'm not very good, Nina, but I'm willing to hold a hand. I'll review my Goren. Maybe I can be dummy most of the time."

"I'm sure you'll do well. I'll be glad to have you for my partner. We usually start around seven and play a couple of rubbers, then have some refreshments. Things break up around ten-thirty. Is that all right?"

That would rush her with Ted's dinner and her walk with Judd, but she'd try to get Judd to walk before dinnertime and send out for pizza; Ted never complained about that. Elaine was going shopping with Amy right after work and would eat out. It had been oppressively hot for a week, and walking early would expose Judd and her to greater discomfort. But going to Nina's would be something to do to get away from thinking about Rob. "Fine. I'll see you then."

Evelyn spent a while finding and then studying the copy of Goren that she had bought for the brief period when Ward had wanted her to play with him. He played for blood, and her attitude that cards were an occupation for one's hands while talking with friends was incomprehensible to him. He soon found a group of men with real interest in the game and left her with Thursday nights free to grade papers. She ruefully figured that Nina would understand his attitude all too soon. But she did review points and bidding strategy and hoped she'd remember some of it.

She arrived early and settled into the far reaches of Nina's great room. She stayed there, hoping not to be noticed, when Marcia Lee came in. There was no point trying to appear polite; the best she could hope for was not to play with Marcia Lee that night. There were three tables, and Nina had said they usually played only a couple of rubbers, so maybe Marcia Lee and she wouldn't have to see each other.

They didn't for the first rubber. Evelyn made some strategic mistakes but didn't revoke or do anything else totally embarrassing. Nina didn't seem upset, and Evelyn relaxed a little. They lost the rubber. Nina complimented her on some plays and told her what she should have done on some others, but it was as a teacher, not an irate partner.

Nina said, "Now I think our next table's ready."

Evelyn turned in the direction in which Nina was looking and saw Marcia Lee glaring at her. So there was no avoiding contact. Marcia Lee's partner was Annice Strother, whose husband taught political science.

Evelyn greeted both women, and Annice replied and asked about Elaine and Ted, but Marcia Lee didn't say anything to her at all. Evelyn hoped they could get through the rubber without open conflict.

For the first game, Nina got the bid and won. For the second, Evelyn held strength in both hearts and diamonds, but only five cards in each. Her other three cards were all small, two clubs and a singleton in spades. Nina opened the bid with one club. Annice passed. Evelyn answered with one heart. Marcia Lee bid one spade. Nina answered Evelyn with two hearts, and Annice bid two spades. Evelyn bid three hearts. She hoped Marcia Lee wouldn't go three spades, and she didn't; she passed, and Nina and Annice made the second and third byes. So Evelyn was to play in hearts.

When Nina spread her hand, Evelyn realized that they could probably have made at least a small slam. Nina had five hearts too and the four high cards in clubs. The only high heart they didn't have was the jack. And Nina had only two spades.

That means Marcia Lee would have killed us in spades; they have as many as we have hearts. And we would have gone down in no-trump too. But now I can draw off their trumps, lead clubs from Nina's hand, use my strong diamonds, and take all their spades with trumps.

She did it. Marcia Lee, who had only the jack of hearts and the trey, practically wept as she lost the jack to Evelyn's queen. But it wasn't flawless play; she lost two tricks, and she shouldn't have. *So I would have lost a small slam. Thank God I didn't play this with Ward and lose a bid. He would have cut my throat.*

But of course she and Nina won the game and the rubber. Marcia Lee turned away from the table before the others got the cards straightened. Nina seemed happy enough. When they stood up, she hugged Evelyn and praised her play. Evelyn pointed out her own mistakes, and Nina said, "So? You're not ready for the tournaments yet. But it was fun to watch you, and I hope you enjoyed playing."

"I did. I really did. Now can I help you do anything?"

"Yes, thanks. You can help me serve. The dining table is ready, but I have to finish the punch and cut the cake."

"I'll be glad to do whatever."

Nina decided to cut the cake at the dining table in the great room and gave Evelyn instructions to add the gin and raspberry sherbet to the punch. She gave Evelyn the ice-cream scoop, and Evelyn got the punch out of the refrigerator and set it on the countertop, poured in the gin, and got the sherbet out of the freezer and began scooping it out to float on the gin.

Nina, carrying the cake and cake breaker, said, "I'll take the cake on in; you bring the punch."

Evelyn knew Nina's gin-sherbet punch, a concoction that seemed ladylike but wasn't, from other parties; it was just as well she hadn't drunk any before she played cards, she thought. She had just picked up the punch bowl and was carrying it in when Marcia Lee came in.

Marcia Lee said, "So! This is where you went. You can't hide in here from me."

Evelyn said, "I wouldn't—"

But Marcia Lee said, "Oh, yes, you would. You'd sneak around just the way you've been doing with my husband. But you won't get away with it."

"I don't want to hurt you."

"Oh, no! Of course not! You're so kind! Well, I want to hurt you. I want you to pay for what you've done to me!"

She snatched a meat cleaver from Nina's knife rack and rushed toward Evelyn, who screamed, dropped the punch bowl, flooding the floor, and ran. But Marcia Lee was between her and the door, so she dodged behind the table. Marcia Lee, lunging with the cleaver, chased her this way, then that, screaming, "You can't have him! I'll kill you first! I'll kill you!"

Nina came through the door just as Marcia Lee slipped on the wet floor and slid down. The knife flew through the air and stuck upright in the kitchen flooring and vibrated back and forth. Evelyn, petrified, stared at it. Marcia Lee, her dress stained with punch and smeared with sherbet, was crying and beating the floor with her fists.

The cardplayers rapidly filled the doorway behind Nina, who went to Marcia Lee and tried to get her to stand up. "It's all right. Just get up, Marcia Lee, and we'll get you cleaned up. Rayna, will you please call Rob and ask him to come get her."

Evelyn slipped from behind the table past Marcia Lee and Nina, keeping Marcia Lee in view as she backed toward the door. Eileen Chandler tried to stop her. "What happened, Evelyn? What's going on?"

The other women turned toward her, the same questions in their faces. Someone said, "Good Lord, it's just a card game."

Evelyn shook her head and went out Nina's back door and found her car and pulled across Andy and Nina's lawn to extricate it from the other cars parked behind her and drove home. Seeing Rob come to get Marcia Lee was the last thing she wanted to do.

XV. Rob

A Dead-end Street

*R*ob couldn't recall the first time he met Evelyn Knight. It was probably when he came to Harper College for his job interview. Since they had adjacent offices, she answered many of his first-year questions, and he came to respect her mind. Trained in New Criticism, she analyzed literature perceptively, sometimes originally, if not always with extensive scholarship; she almost always saw the main things about a work as he did. They weighted the elements of composition about the same too. She synthesized different works well and applied the lessons of literature to current topics.

In faculty meetings she could be merciless in opposing those who failed to match her ideals, and he knew that the students judged her interesting and fair but hard. The best students sought her out, and the lazy and weak avoided her.

As a poet, she had greater sensibility and powers of observation, particularly of nature, than originality. Her lyrics were almost all subjective, and her persona seemed herself; she used poetry to conceal and reveal. Once in a while, she created an image or twisted a phrase that sliced to the bone.

He often saw her children at the office. They would stop after their school, or she would bring them there as she stopped on the way to Elaine's art lesson or Ted's basketball practice. That was why he thought of asking Elaine and later Ted to sit with Trey.

But he had never thought of Evelyn as anything except a colleague until one Saturday morning when he stopped at her house to get some books she had promised him about Dante. Ward let him in and directed him to the sunroom, where she and Ted sat going over the draft of a composition he had written, just as Rob had seen her conferring with many students. But her relation with her son was different. Her fingers were curved around Ted's arm, and they were laughing together at something. She looked up from the paper at Rob and smiled, and her eyes were happy. He wished that he had made her look like that.

She would have gotten up and looked for his books right away, but he insisted that she finish talking about the paper first. He sat down and watched her and Ted.

Soon after Marcia Lee left for her bridge party, Rob put Trey to bed. He was marking the first drafts of his last summer-school assignment when Rayna Hull's phone call interrupted him. She said, "Rob? You have to come to Nina's and get Marcia Lee. I don't know what's happened, but I think . . . anyhow, she's hysterical and doesn't need to be here and ought not drive herself home."

"I'll be right there. Nina Wilton's?" *Of course; there's no other Nina in town.*

"Yes."

"All right. Thank you. Good-bye."

He hung up and just stood, dazed, for a moment. Then he began thinking. *Can I leave Trey? I'll have to. What if she's . . . totally out of her mind? Will she come with me? Is it about Evelyn? What did she say? I can't just stand here; better get going.*

He checked to be sure Trey was asleep and left. The same questions kept going through his mind on the drive to Nina's, although he knew there could be no answers until he got there.

Some of the women were leaving when he arrived. One or two greeted him and looked at him curiously; others averted their gaze.

He didn't see Evelyn; he didn't think she was part of Marcia Lee's bridge group.

Rayna, not Nina, answered the bell. "She's in the bathroom with Nina. She fell down and got punch all over her dress."

"Is she hurt? Do we need a doctor?"

"No, I don't think so. You might want to call Oliver." Oliver Johnson, Rayna's second husband, taught psychology.

"What happened, Rayna?"

"Nobody really knows, Rob. She and Annice played Nina and Evelyn and lost. Evelyn was in the kitchen getting the punch, and Marcia Lee went in there. There was a lot of yelling and running, and Marcia Lee fell down and cried, and punch was all over everywhere, and Evelyn left."

Rob felt the questions in Rayna's eyes. He looked away. "What were they yelling?"

"It was just Marcia Lee, and she kept saying she was going to kill Evelyn." She paused a moment. "A knife was stuck in the floor."

Three blind mice. "Do you have any idea what she wanted to kill her for?" He still didn't look.

"No. Marcia Lee takes her cards seriously, but I never saw her try to kill anyone before for beating her." Rayna's laugh was like a hiccup.

He couldn't think of anything to say, and the silence stretched out until they heard Nina's voice coming through the next room: ". . . be all right now, and Rob will be here soon— He's here already."

Marcia Lee didn't look at him. Her clothes were a mess, and her hair had obviously been rearranged by someone else. Her face was clean of makeup.

He walked to them and took her bare arm. They had not touched each other except by accident since he had told her about Evelyn, and he was afraid she would flinch. But her flesh was still as death.

He said, "Come on, Marcia Lee, I'll take you home now." He wanted to ask Nina what had happened, but this was clearly not the time. Besides, Trey was at home by himself. So he just thanked Nina and Rayna and left.

Marcia Lee walked with him like a sleepwalker, and he helped her into the car and drove her home in silence. He led her inside and put the car up.

Then he went into their house to face her. She was still standing in the living room, dazed, so he led her to a chair.

She collapsed into it and covered her eyes with one hand and began crying. She was shaking.

He hated to watch her cry, knowing that he was the cause of her grief. He wanted to walk out, go to the bedroom and pack his clothes and leave her and never see her again. But he knelt by the chair and put his arms around her, held her until she quieted. And he felt sorry for her; she felt weak in his arms.

"I tried to kill that . . . that whore. I would if I could. But I couldn't, and I made a fool of myself, and now everybody'll know, and I won't dare show my face. And it's all your fault."

His jaw tightened again, and he got up and went to the front door to lock it and go to bed.

"Are you leaving?" she said.

"No, but God only knows why I don't." He went down the hall to the tiny office–guest room behind the living room; he had been sleeping there since he had told Marcia Lee he wanted a divorce.

He heard her go up the steps soon after. He listened to know if she looked in on Trey, but he couldn't tell. He lay awake awhile, then finally slipped up the steps himself, trying to keep her from hearing him. The boy was all right; he lay asleep in the shadows from his night-light. Rob straightened the covers and kissed him on the forehead before he slipped back down the steps.

Saturday morning he called Brandon to cancel their tennis match. When Brandon asked if he was all right, he just said that Marcia Lee wasn't well.

When he went into the kitchen to start the coffee, she was there cooking bacon.

"Will you eat?" she said.

"I'm not hungry. I'll just get some coffee and walk over to Nina's to get your car if she or Andy's going to be home."

Marcia Lee looked red-eyed. He supposed he was himself. He hadn't slept, and he felt both tired and restless, as if he could run a hundred miles.

"You're not going to Nina's; you're going to see that—that slut again."

"I only wish I could. But I can't see her till Monday. Marcia Lee, you can't want me like this. All we do is fight, and you'd be happier without me, too."

"I won't let her take you if I can stop you. And even if she has you, she can't have Trey too. If you divorce me, I'll never let you see him again." She looked as wild as one of the Furies.

Rob unfolded his newspaper and pretended to read it while he drank his coffee. He wondered if her mad behavior had given him an out; maybe now he could win a judgment that she was psychologically unfit to rear Trey.

When he saw Nina, she asked him in for coffee, and he questioned her about Marcia Lee's behavior. She told him all she knew. When she told about the knife, she pointed out the scar in the soft vinyl of the kitchen floor.

She didn't speculate about the cause, so he asked her.

"Well, I don't think the cards were anything more than a final straw. I saw that she . . . had something against Evelyn when we sat down at her table. But you must have a better idea about that than I do, I'm sure."

He paused, debating how much to tell Nina. "Yes. I asked Marcia Lee for a divorce so I can marry Evelyn."

"I thought it must be something like that. Are you sure that's what you want?"

"Sure as breathing." He set his mouth and looked straight at her.

"And Evelyn?"

"I think—I *believe* she wants me too." He meant the word as a confession of faith, like the witnessing in Marcia Lee's church. "But Marcia Lee's using Trey to try to keep me. And I want him too. Nina, would you be willing to help me?"

"How? What could I do?"

He explained his plan, ending with what he thought was his strongest argument: "I wouldn't try to keep him just for myself, but I can't think he'd have a decent life if she brought him up by herself. And I can't see a decent life for any of us if Marcia Lee and I stay together."

Nina had been drawing lines on the table with her finger. He wished she had had a pencil so he could see what she was thinking.

The movements were straight, with abrupt changes, not at all like the round shapes in her watercolors of fruit and vegetables, witty personifications, that hung over the table.

She said, "Is Evelyn willing to bring Trey up? Taking on a child is no small task for a woman her age."

Rob didn't know why, but he felt sure. "I never asked her, but I know she would. Not just for me."

Nina looked at him and smiled for the first time that morning. It was a rueful smile. "Yes, you're probably right. And yes, I'd be willing at least to testify about what happened. I wouldn't want to have to decide myself, but I'd give the information I have to a judge to help him decide."

"Thank you. You've given me the best hope I've had in months." He got up and made his farewells.

The day seemed brighter; driving home, he noticed the mimosa and magnolia blooms and the beds of red cannas all over the campus. He felt that he could even face Marcia Lee again.

They ate lunch in silence except for Marcia Lee's nagging Trey and the boy's prattle. That afternoon Rob took him and a neighbor girl to the park to swing and slide and play on the seesaw. After dinner, he gave Trey his bath and put him to bed. Then he went into his office–bedroom to finish marking the student drafts he had started.

He slept better that night. Sunday morning he ate cereal with Trey and Marcia Lee. She looked pale and tired, and he felt sorry for her. He could do that if he could get Trey away from her, he realized; if he didn't have to hate her, he could pity her. Even be ashamed for hurting her.

She came to the door of his room after she had dressed for church. Her dress was white. "I don't suppose you'd go to church with Trey and me today."

He looked up from the essay he was reading. "The roof'd probably fall in. Why do you ask?"

"It's just—after the other night, Annice and Melie and some of the others who probably heard about it will be looking. And it'd be easier—if you went with me."

He stood up. "Sure. I understand. I'll get ready."

"Thank you." She turned to leave.

"Wait. Won't they wonder more if I do show up?"

Her head and shoulders were bowed. "I don't know. I just don't know if I could go without you."

He saw her hands trembling. "All right. I'll go. Give me ten minutes."

He avoided touching her, and he kept Trey between them during the service. The preacher kept saying that once a man was saved, he was always saved. Presumably he meant a woman too, but he wasn't strong on avoiding gender discrimination. Rob kept wondering what one was saved from. And for what? He remembered the preacher at his mother's funeral saying that she had left this life to go be happy with Jesus.

On the way out, Rob nodded and spoke to Marcia Lee's friends and the college employees he knew. The preacher shook his hand at the door and said, "We're glad to see you here today; we hope you'll come be with us regular."

Rob said, "Thank you." He couldn't think of a worse fate.

That afternoon he tried to work on his novel while Marcia Lee played with Trey. He had thought of having the mother be ill; that would be a bond to keep Keith from leaving her for Valerie, his having to care for her. But he couldn't think of any scenes to show it. He might have to begin at the beginning of the book again and build everything around the illness. Or would it be a sudden illness that came up after the affair with Valerie began?

He thought of the cancer that had threatened Evelyn, of the scar, the thin welt that ran through the top of her pubic hair, of the curves of her flesh over her hipbones and around her navel. His palms felt empty, and he wanted to fill them with her hipbones. But he would have to wait to meet her. *Monday*, he told himself. *I can wait until tomorrow morning.*

Marcia Lee and Trey were sitting at the coffee table, drawing. They didn't have wax crayons like the ones of his own childhood; they used felt-tipped acrylic markers in colors that reminded him of shopping malls and Saturday-morning cartoons on television. Trey was drawing a construction machine like one in his favorite Richard Scarry book. Marcia Lee had drawn a house and, beyond it, a garden. It was a primitive like Grandma Moses's. Or like one of Marcia Lee's third-graders' when she had taught in Germantown. She was putting plants in the garden; she drew rows of bilious green dots on the paper—angry dots chasing someone out, driving him past the edges where he could hide, beyond the edges of the paper, where no one could see him. Or her. Marcia Lee rubbed her chin across the marker handle as though it were a knife to cut her throat.

He was at the office by seven-thirty Monday morning. He closed his door and leaned against it, waiting, listening. When he heard steps coming down the hall and the jingle of keys, he opened his door and was about to extend his arms when he recognized the custodian, who was emptying wastebaskets. He greeted her and turned and sat down at his desk as though he had been working there before. When she closed the door, he resumed his listening.

At ten till eight he heard steps and keys again, but he waited until the keys clicked in Evelyn's lock before he opened his door again and stepped out. Then he just stood and looked at her. After Friday, she might not want to see him again.

But her face showed him that she did. He felt the balm of knowing fully, surely, that she wanted him. He reached for her, and she came and kissed him there in the hall.

In her office they hurried through their usual precautions against discovery and made love. They hadn't said a word. Then, while he caressed and kissed her hipbones and stomach and she stroked his hair, she told him everything that had happened Friday night. He sat up and told her about his talks with Marcia Lee and Nina and his hope of getting Trey.

She rumpled, then smoothed his hair. "If we tell about all that, everyone'll know about—this." She kissed his forehead as if to soften her implied shame.

"Dearest, they'll know anyhow. Marcia Lee won't hesitate to accuse me of adultery. And after Friday night, half the town probably suspects anyhow. Besides, divorce hearings don't have to be public. But I don't care; I'd claim you before the whole world today if it wouldn't hurt my chances of getting Trey."

"The judge would probably still think our adultery justified her actions."

"Maybe. It's risky. But it's a chance I have to take. I can't live with her like this. That's the only other way I'd have of keeping Trey."

"Have you thought—that she might really be insane?"

"The idea has crossed my mind."

"What if—she were to do something to Trey?"

He hadn't thought about that. The idea crusted around his heart like ice. "Good God." He covered his eyes with his hands and thought. "I have to finish classes this week. Then we have a while before fall term begins. I'll have to trust getting through classes: I can't stay home with her all the time or stay awake all the time I'm home. But after this week, I swear I'll take him somewhere she can't get him—ask for an injunction to keep her away from him. Nina's testimony ought to help me get that, at least. I'll talk to a lawyer right away and take the boy and leave Saturday after I turn grades in."

"Elaine works for Joe Hillson; he's the smartest lawyer around that I know of."

"But she might find out about us then."

"I have to clear the air with my family too. It's high time I owned up to my wrongs since I don't intend to repent of them. And if Elaine and Ted reject me, well, that's the price I pay for you. I've given them what I can, and I don't ask them for their lives."

Knowing the cost of her choice, he kissed her. "Thank you."

She began dressing again. "We'd better not meet for a while; you need to be free to plan and watch . . . things. I'll tell Elaine and Ted the first chance I get and leave you notes. As soon as you know I've told them, you can telephone me again."

"That'll make things easier."

"It'll be a relief to me, Rob. I hate living with deceit."

"Maybe we won't have to much longer."

"Oh, I hope so, my love. I hope so."

That night at dinner, Marcia Lee accused him. "You've been with her."

"I told you I'd see her today."

"You're happy." She was bitter.

"Yes. She makes me happy." He didn't feel bitter. He wanted her to understand. "I don't hate you. I just want to be with her because she makes me happy." He looked at her, pleading.

She burst into tears and left the table.

Trey looked at him. "Daddy, what's wrong with Mommy?"

"She doesn't feel well, Trey. It's like when your stomach hurts." *Only it's her heart. And I'm the one that hurts her.* His own heart felt heavy. But he wanted all the more to get away from her.

Then he felt anxious about Trey. "Has Mommy been hurting a lot lately?"

"She's been mean. She won't let me go out and play with Leanne. She just wants me to stay in here with her and read or watch Big Bird."

All the more reason to get him away from her. She'll hold him the way she tries to hold me.

Tuesday morning he found a note from Evelyn saying that she had talked with both of her children, so he called Joe Hillson and made an appointment; the earliest he could see him was Thursday morning. He wrote an answering note to Evelyn and left it under her door. After class, he posted a notice that he was ill and went home before office hours. He had talked with each student during the long class and knew that no one was likely to come looking for him anyhow.

At home, he made a point of staying near Trey and Marcia Lee while he marked the second drafts of the last paper, even though their presence—and his thoughts about them—distracted him. He didn't finish until after Marcia Lee had gone to bed. The last drafts would come in Thursday, and unless someone still had trouble and had to do a fourth draft, he'd really be through before the last class meeting and would just give out grades then. That would free him to come home early Friday and prepare to leave.

At their Thursday meeting, Joe Hillson advised caution. He warned against Rob's giving the appearance of kidnapping Trey; he immediately began proceedings for an injunction against Marcia Lee and records of Rob's concern for the boy's welfare and Nina's and Evelyn's accounts of Marcia Lee's actions the week before. He warned Rob that the case was not strong and he might well lose Trey anyhow.

Rob had not seen Elaine on the way in, but she was talking with the receptionist as he left. He greeted her.

She looked at him appraisingly. "Hello, Dr. McFergus." She didn't ask about Trey as she usually did and made no other effort to continue a conversation. Rob thought how much more she looked like Ward than like Evelyn. But she didn't close him out. Not yet, anyhow.

He found another note from Evelyn at his office; it said only that she loved him. He called her and told her about the conference with Hillson, and she said the words again, loud and open. They sounded good.

Then he told her about seeing Elaine, and she said that she couldn't really tell how Elaine had taken the news: she seemed to be withholding judgment. Ted had been noncommittal too. "I—didn't tell them we've already slept together, though they probably guessed. But I don't pry into their lives, and they'll have to give me the same courtesy."

"I don't think you have to ask their permission."

She laughed wryly. "No. But it's a strange position to be in, confessing to my children."

Friday he dismissed class after only a quarter of an hour, left his grades at the registrar's office, and walked home.

The front door was locked, although he could see Marcia Lee's car in the garage. He went in and called, "Marcia Lee? You here?"

The house was quiet, so he went into the kitchen and began making himself a peanut-butter sandwich. But he felt uneasy; Marcia Lee hadn't cleared away the breakfast dishes. Also, she usually did any visiting with neighbors in the afternoon. So he started looking through the house.

Marcia Lee's bedroom door was closed, but from the hall Rob could see Trey sleeping on his bed, although he had almost given up naps. Rob knocked on Marcia Lee's door, calling her. Then he tried the knob. It was locked. "Marcia Lee!" he called. "Open the door!" His heart was pounding. He tried to open the door again. Then he backed up and tried to knock it down. But it wasn't so easy as it seemed in the movies; the oak had the solidity of old houses.

He turned to the other room. Despite his noise, Trey lay unmoving. Kneeling by the youth bed, he touched Trey's shoulder first, then shook him, calling his name. There was no response. The boy lay pale and still, like one dead. *No! He can't be!*

And he wasn't. Rob could feel the pulse in the wrist. But the breathing was slow.

The upstairs phone was in their bedroom. He ran downstairs and looked up Dr. Bonnette's number. His hands were shaking so that he couldn't dial the 0 straight through and had to push down the phone hook and start again. And then all he got was a busy signal.

He called Evelyn. When she answered, he couldn't speak at first. "Hello?" she repeated.

"Evelyn, it's me, Rob. Trey's asleep and I can't wake him up, and Marcia Lee's locked herself in our bedroom, and I can't get Dr. Bonnette."

"I'll call Judd, and I'll be there as soon as I can."

"Maybe—you'd better not come."

"I'll stay in the car. But you may need me."

"All right. Come. It can't be any worse."

When Adivino's car turned into the driveway, Rob was raising the ladder to the bedroom window. He saw Evelyn in the car. Adivino jumped out of the car and ran toward him. He took off his suit coat and threw it on the grass and put his hand on Rob's arm. "Better let me go up. She may need me, and anyhow . . . that way I can see how things are." Then he called to Evelyn. "Eva! You'd better go inside and see about the boy."

She got out of the car and said, looking at Rob, "Upstairs?" Her face was tense with fright.

Rob said, "Yes—to the right." Then he turned toward Adivino again and held the ladder.

He wanted to believe in someone to bargain with then, someone to listen to him while he kept saying in his mind, *Please let him be all right, let them be all right. If they're all right, I'll do whatever I have to, but please, please let them be all right.* But while he said it, he couldn't think that he was talking to anyone but himself.

Adivino climbed quickly despite his leather-soled shoes and the doctor's bag he carried. At the top, he yelled down, "Turn away to protect your face. I have to smash the window."

After the crash, Rob looked back at Adivino, who knocked the remaining glass inward and disappeared into the room. It seemed a lifetime until he reappeared. "Come up the stairs. She's alive. I'll unlock the door and see about the boy." He disappeared again.

He met Rob on the landing, Trey in his arms, Evelyn following. She looked white as a ghost. Rob turned to let them come down.

Adivino said, "Eva will take the boy to the hospital. Eva, my car keys are in my right coat pocket. Drive safely, but go as fast as you can. Here, take him."

Evelyn took the boy out of his arms as he continued. "Tell them to pump his stomach at once. I'll phone as soon as I can. Rob, maybe you should go with her."

"No. Marcia Lee . . ." He couldn't say any more, but drew back to let Evelyn pass.

"We'll take her after some first aid."

Rob said, "What has she done?"

"Slit her wrists. Probably taken something too, although I didn't see a bottle. But she'll be all right. Eva! Go on! The boy's small; it wouldn't take as much to . . . affect him."

On the way back upstairs, he questioned Rob about medications in the house. Rob didn't really know.

Adivino opened the bedroom door; his body blocked the view as he went through, and then Rob saw. Marcia Lee lay on top of the bedspread, her face white and pinched. Blood smeared the bed and her dress.

"Did Evelyn see this?" Rob's voice was hoarse.

Adivino nodded his head. "I closed the door, but she went in when I went to see the boy."

There were small cuts around the slashes across Marcia Lee's wrists. Rob asked, "What are all the scratches?"

Adivino said, "Most people don't quite know how hard to cut. They're called hesitation marks."

Rob imagined Marcia Lee sitting on the side of the bed, getting up enough nerve to cut deep.

Adivino directed Rob in helping to tape Marcia Lee's wrists. Then the two men carried her down the steps and out to Rob's car. Adivino talked the whole time. "I want you to drive her to the hospital and have them pump her stomach too. I'll phone in directions, but first I'm going to look for any pill bottles or anything that might show what she used. I think they're both going to be all right. From the condition of her wrists, it couldn't have been too long since she cut them. Do you think she planned to have you find her?"

Rob had trouble speaking. "No. I didn't tell her I'd be home early today. As far as she knew, I'd be in class for more than another hour and have two office hours after that."

"Then she probably meant to succeed."

"Yes." His mouth was dry.

The car was small, so they put her in the passenger seat, and Adivino fastened the safety harness. "I'll be at the hospital as soon as I can, and I'll call sooner. Just think about driving to get both of you there safely." He slammed the door, and Rob backed down the drive.

Evelyn was watching through the emergency-room door when Rob drove up. She turned and evidently signaled to someone, for two young men in gray coats rolled out a gurney and helped him unload Marcia Lee. They told him to go to the desk and rolled her down the hall and through two metal-clad swinging doors.

He went to the desk and began answering questions about Trey and Marcia Lee and the college group insurance plan while a young woman filled in forms on a typewriter. In the middle of a question, she stopped to answer the telephone.

When she hung up, she said, "That was Dr. Adivino. He says the medication was most likely just a painkiller for cramps. If that's the case, you probably don't have anything to worry about, Mr. McFergus."

Nothing but guilt, and fear that she'll try again, and maybe some hate thrown in, plus whatever this does to Evelyn.

He looked at her sitting in a gray vinyl-covered chair, her eyes on the floor. Then she looked up at him. He was glad that she could still look at him with love in her face like that. And glad that the typist was looking at her forms again. But there were other people in the room too, leafing through magazines or staring at the droning television set. He looked away from Evelyn so that she would look away.

He wished she hadn't seen Marcia Lee on the bed.

When the clerk was through, he went and sat opposite Evelyn. She looked up from her lap, and he whispered, "Adivino says he thinks they'll both be all right."

Her eyes filled with tears, and she looked down again.

He moved to the chair beside her and took her hand, despite the witnesses. She squeezed his. But then she took hers back and drew into herself.

He remembered the hospital waiting rooms where he had sat when his mother was ill.

Then all he could think about was Trey, his face, his smile, his grubby hands raised to Daddy when he came home, his voice, his small bones and fine hair, his body, so sturdy yet so vulnerable. Rob put his head on his hand. He was responsible for that body, and he had risked it for his own pleasure.

He felt Evelyn's fingers on his free hand, and he seized them and looked at her. Whatever his anguish, he had to have her to hold on to.

She shivered, and he realized that the waiting room was cold.

He said, "I have a jacket in my car. I'll get it."

When he came back, Adivino was there, talking to Evelyn. She saw him and said, "Here he is."

Adivino held his hand out to Rob. "They're both all right. The boy's semiconscious. Your . . . his mother isn't, but she's breathing more normally."

"Can I see them?"

"Why don't you see the boy first? I'll see about her. You can probably take the boy home tomorrow. She should probably stay here awhile."

"Is she still in danger?"

"Her physical condition is improving. I'll talk with you after you've seen your son."

"What should I tell him?"

"He probably won't be awake enough to ask questions or even respond much. Rob, I'll have to fill out a report for the constable about this, and I'll need some information from you."

Rob nodded. "I just want to see him. Can't I see him first?"

"Of course."

The boy still looked white and half asleep. His face looked heavy, as if his skin were falling down, and his eyes drooped. But he did ask when he could go home. He didn't seem scared to be in the hospital.

Rob said, "A little later, after you've rested. Your stomach may still make you sick. But I'll take you home as soon as I can." He wished he had asked Adivino when.

The boy nodded. He lay down again, and Rob could see the drowsiness in his eyes.

"Why don't you just sleep some now, and I'll come back and get you soon."

"Okay," Trey said. His eyes were closed again.

Then Rob worried that maybe he ought not sleep again. He wished he'd asked about that too. He asked the nurse at the desk, and she said it was all right.

Adivino was with Evelyn again when Rob went down. He was holding her hand, and Rob felt his jealousy return. Then he shoved it into the back of his mind.

Adivino stood up, beckoned Rob to follow him, and led him to a door labeled FAMILY CONFERENCE ROOM. He reassured him about Trey's condition and told him to treat the boy normally when they went home, probably the next day. He said, "I need to check him over after we finish talking, and then if he's all right, you can go out to lunch or go home and finish that peanut-butter sandwich you were making."

Rob resented the invasion of his privacy. "You looked in more than my medicine cabinet."

Adivino's look was direct, almost admonishing. "I thought I might need to tell someone what had happened."

Rob realized that Adivino meant he was gathering facts for testimony in case there was an investigation. He wondered if Adivino had even suspected him of staging the whole thing, of risking his child and attempting to murder his wife. He felt the anger run through him like whiskey. "You said you need to ask me about something for the report to the constable."

"Yes. But first, I need to find out all I can about the medication. In the bathroom I found two glasses and an empty bottle. It had held a palliative for menstrual cramps, very common, but with a potential hidden danger: one of the ingredients in sufficient dosage can cause liver damage or even necrosis. The patient can seem to be all right after the stomach's pumped, and then four days later, the liver dies."

"And the patient too?"

"Yes, after pain. Necrosis of the liver is fatal. I've sent blood samples to the researcher at Vanderbilt to try to ascertain dosage for both Marcia Lee and Trey. He's good, but it'll take a while. And I've sent for the antidote, methionine, just in case. If I knew how much she had, I could get a pretty good estimate of how much she could have taken and given the boy. The prescription was refilled three weeks ago, and there was no old bottle in evidence anywhere. Do you know whether she's had menses since then?"

Rob hadn't slept with Marcia Lee for months. He shook his head.

"Then we don't know until the report on the blood analysis how much she took. I don't want to wait for that. So I'll order the methionine administered to both of them as soon as possible. Then they should be all right—physically. I've already ordered a blood transfusion for her."

Rob cleared his throat. "And mentally?"

"Well, that's a whole new problem. People who attempt suicide often try again. And the boy . . . you'll have to decide how much she should be with the boy."

"You mentioned a transfusion. How much blood has she lost?"

"Oh, probably less than a pint."

"But it was all over her and the bed."

"Yes. Well, a little goes a long way. But there's something else. I need to give you this. It may explain some things." He handed Rob an envelope. "Is that your wife's handwriting?"

All that the round letters said was "Rob." "Yes. That's Marcia Lee's writing."

"Open it, and show it to me. You may need me for a witness."

Inside, a single line was written across a notepad page: "Now you can be happy with her." As he absorbed the irony, Rob thought, *The sole literary achievement of her life.* He handed the sheet to Adivino.

Adivino read it and said, "This clarifies things. I have to report the incident as an attempted suicide. I don't know about Trey; he told me when I asked him that his mother made him take some pills. He said three, but he held up four fingers, so I can't go by that. Nevertheless, the fact that he's even semiconscious indicates that the dosage she gave him was probably too small to cause death, and we don't know if that was by intent or not. I'll talk with the sheriff before he even gets the constable's report; I think he'll agree that there's no reason any of this should be made public. But he'll probably want a deposition from each of us."

Rob nodded. He hadn't thought of the legal problems. What if Marcia Lee was accused of murder?

And wasn't that what she had tried?

Surely that was the best evidence he could have for his injunction against her. It was probably strong enough to win a custody battle, even. He'd call Hillson as soon as he could. Maybe he could win.

He said, "Maybe . . . you should tell the sheriff everything, report what Trey said too."

Adivino studied him again. "Yes, it might suit your purposes better if everything was known, at least to the police."

So Adivino agreed. But Rob still didn't feel triumphant. "What about Marcia Lee? After . . . after she's physically all right?"

"Well, what I'd advise for the moment is that she stay here, and I'll contact some psychiatrists I know in Nashville about the best treatment for her. Right now, and probably in the near future, I don't think . . . seeing you will help her."

Rob nodded. Whatever she needed, he would have to give her. Short of his body and soul. Or Trey's.

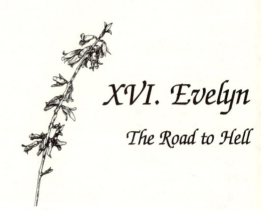

XVI. Evelyn

The Road to Hell

*E*velyn could have walked home, but Judd insisted that she wait until he had talked to Rob. She sat and watched for them to come back.

When Judd came from the elevator, he was alone.

She walked to meet him and asked, "Where's Rob?"

"He's with Trey. The boy's all right; tomorrow he can probably go home."

"I could help him take care of Trey."

He shook his head. "No, Eva."

She knew that of course he was right. She dropped her head, and she could feel the guilt rising in her. And the grief, grief for all of them, Rob and Trey and even Marcia Lee, Elaine and Ted and herself all. She tried to control it; she didn't want to break down there in the hospital waiting room.

Judd led her to the chairs again. "I have to give some instructions. I won't be but a few minutes; I'll be right back."

When he returned and asked for his car keys, she couldn't find them in her pockets. Then she looked in her purse and handed them to him. She didn't talk; she felt too tired to speak. He said nothing either, but offered his arm.

274

On the drive home, he didn't speak until they were almost there. Then he told her that he would get whatever Earline had cooked for lunch and bring it to her house.

"I can't eat," she said.

"You have to eat. Making your body suffer won't help your mind. It's after three o'clock, and none of us has had any lunch."

She didn't object further.

She had left the side door unlocked. From the car, he watched while she entered, then called that he would be back in a few minutes and pulled out.

She forced herself to set the table and brew tea and put ice in the glasses. By that time, he was back. He tried to carry on a normal conversation, but she couldn't keep her mind on what he was saying. All she could think about was the two faces, so like each other, the boy's, looking as though he could be dead, and Rob's, looking tortured. And the bloody figure on the bed. The food stuck in her throat.

"Eva, do you want to talk about this?"

She shook her head. "I can't. What is there to say?"

"You asked me for absolution once, and I gave it. I give it again now. You never wanted to hurt Trey. Or his mother. You are not responsible for what she did."

She started crying then. He didn't try to stop her, and he didn't move from his seat across the table. He did reach over and cover her hand with his and squeeze her palm with his thumb.

Judd didn't leave after lunch. He helped Evelyn clear the table, and he put the dishes in the dishwasher while she put up the food, and she expected him to leave her alone then. But he followed her into the living room, where, not knowing what else to do, she invited him to sit down. He said that he had to make some calls about a patient and asked to use her telephone. She suggested that he use the one in the library, and he went upstairs.

She sat down on the couch. She curled up into a ball, thinking, *I shall be round, with no corners, nothing to reach out or break off.* She tried to empty her mind, but every ten or fifteen minutes, he would come down again—asking her for a notepad, getting a glass of water, asking her about a teacher who had left the college. His persistent presence seemed so strange that she wondered if he was actually calling anyone and went to the foot of the stairs to listen. But he was; it was evidently long distance, for she heard him giving his credit-card number. Why didn't he just go home and call from his own phone? She resented his being there; why wouldn't he leave her alone?

The ring of the telephone at her elbow startled her, and then the sound of Rob's voice was even more of a shock. "Evelyn?"

Maybe Judd can hear me from upstairs. "Yes. Let me change to another extension."

She picked up the phone in the bedroom and said, "I want to hang up the phone in the living room."

She closed the bedroom door when she got back. The extension was on Ward's side of the bed, so she sat there and stared at the picture of her mother and father while they talked; she had hung it to replace one showing the four of them, Ward and her and the children. "I'm back, Rob. Judd is upstairs, and I thought he might be able to hear me from the living room."

"What's he doing there still?" Rob sounded angry.

"I don't know. He's been calling people."

"That's why the line's been busy. I've been trying off and on for almost an hour to get you!"

"I'm sorry. I don't know why he's still here. I wish he'd go away and leave me alone!"

"Dearest, I'm sorry for all this, for bringing all this down on you."

She said, "It's not your fault. It's my fault. I should have known better. I should never have begun this with you."

"Don't say that. If I didn't have you, I couldn't go on." He was quiet, and she couldn't say anything either. Then he continued, "But awful as this is, it may be the solution to our problems. Now I have proof that Marcia Lee's not a fit mother for Trey."

The enormity of Marcia Lee's acts hit Evelyn only with his words. *She tried to kill her own child!*

But I drove her to that. I made her want to lose her own life and take her child with her. How could I hurt anyone so much?

"Evelyn? Dearest?"

"I . . . I don't know what to say, Rob. I've never hurt anyone so much as I've hurt her."

He was quiet too for a moment. "You'll hurt me more if . . ."

She felt his need as though it throbbed into her ear through the telephone lines. "I don't know. I don't know anything, Rob. But I love you. I do know I love you."

"Then I can bear . . . whatever I have to. But dearest, you may have to tell the police what happened. Did Adivino tell you that?"

"No. That is, I don't think so; I don't remember his saying anything about it."

"Well, all you have to tell them is what you saw. I talked to Joe Hillson, and he thinks we have a good case now. In fact, he thinks Marcia Lee might not contest my request for custody."

"What's to happen to her now?"

"I don't know. Your doctor friend is supposed to be arranging things for her. That may be what he's been telephoning about. Now I'd better check on Trey; Adivino and the nurse both said he'll be all right, but I still don't want to leave him alone for long."

"Of course. How has he been?"

"All right, but sleepy. He's playing with a toy car I got him in the gift shop here."

"Let me know as soon as you know anything."

"I will, dearest. I love you."

"I love you."

When she hung up, she went into the hallway. Judd was sitting in the living room in a chair with its back to the sunroom, so the afternoon light coming through the sunroom windows and the glass wall turned him into a dark shadow. She couldn't see his eyes. She thought, *This is intolerable. I'll ask him to leave me alone.*

As she was trying to shape her words, she heard a car door slam and the front door open. Elaine came in calling, "Mother! Where are you?"

"Right here." She moved into the living room.

Elaine's face showed her anger. "How can you just stand there after all you've done?"

"How do you know?"

"How do I know? The whole town knows. You've lived in Meadorsville more than I have; ten minutes after something happens, everybody knows it. Now they know that Dr. McFergus had to climb a ladder to break into his own bedroom because Mrs. McFergus tried to kill herself and Trey because you've been carrying on with her husband.''

Evelyn felt unbearably tired, almost too tired to speak. But she did. ''So what can I do?''

''You can do something besides stand there and say 'What can I do?' as if none of this was your fault.''

''I know it's my fault. All of it's my fault, and I knew from the beginning that it was wrong. I'm not trying to excuse myself; I really want to know. Tell me what to do, and I'll do it. I'll do anything I can. Just tell me what.'' Tears choked her.

''I don't know. Maybe you're right. Maybe there's nothing you can do. You've already messed everything up.'' Elaine was crying too. She turned away and ran up the stairs.

Evelyn turned to go into her bedroom. *Bower.* The word tasted bitter in her mind. *Brothel. I can't stay there, lie on the bed where . . . Nor Ward's room.* She went into the bathroom and closed the door and cried.

When she came out, she was startled to see Judd sitting in the same chair looking toward her, evidently waiting for her. He had heard Elaine, heard everything between them. Her resentment swelled. *Why doesn't he go away and leave me alone? This is none of his business.*

''Judd, go home. Please. Thank you for your concern, but . . .''

''But you'd rather I left you alone. I will, Eva, as soon as I'm sure you're all right. I'll—''

''Mother.''

Evelyn had not heard Elaine coming down the stairs. She stood at the foot and set down a suitcase. Wilhelmina was in the crook of her arm. ''I'm going to Dad and Mary Will's. I called, and it's all right with them. I'll come back later and pack my other things. I have to go back to Danville pretty soon anyhow, and I can't stand it here any longer.''

Evelyn felt as though the words hit her in the chest. She pressed her hand against the bones under her collarbone. ''I . . . Will you see me again?''

''I don't know. I called Ted, and he may come too.'' Elaine's eyes and mouth showed her enmity and her victory.

"Oh! Don't . . ." Evelyn turned away. *I can't bear it! My punishment is more than I can bear! Oh, let me die and be done with it. Not to have Elaine or Ted or Rob. No one. No one.*

She began laughing then, laughing at this stupid woman who was beating her hands on the wall, falling to the floor, dissolving in salt tears like Lot's wife in a rainstorm, this stupid, silly woman who had messed everything up.

Waking from the dream was a struggle like trying to swim up to the surface of the water when something was pulling her down into the mud at the bottom. Then she was fully awake and felt the cold sweat.

She had been in the world of the dream before, the world of the *podpolya*, the crawl space with its slime and vermin and the death-stench of bones, but she had not known it then. Now she recognized it and knew it for her own.

She opened her eyes and didn't know where she was. Then she realized that she was in Ted's bed, and she remembered her waking life, remembered fighting against Judd until he had splashed her with cold water and made her take something, remembered fighting when he tried to make her lie down in her own stained bed, remembered fighting when he carried her up the stairs to Ted's.

And she remembered the dream. It spread out like the ink from a squid and darkened the light of the early morning.

Then she knew what she must do. She must get up and find a razor blade and cut her wrists. She must do it better than Marcia Lee. The cuts must be clean and deep. It was what she must do now.

Book Four

Autumn

Ay, in the very temple of Delight
    Veiled Melancholy has her sovran shrine,
        Though seen of none save him whose strenuous tongue
Can burst Joy's grape against his palate fine.

                —John Keats, *"Ode on Melancholy"*

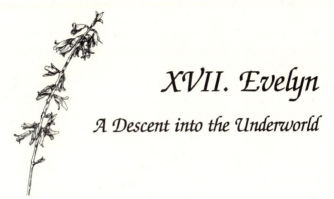

XVII. Evelyn

A Descent into the Underworld

*T*he only razors Evelyn could find in the bathroom were one-piece disposables. She didn't think their blades would work; they were dull as well as sheathed in plastic. She knocked a bottle of aspirin out of the medicine chest. It made a fearsome clatter on the tile floor, but it was plastic too and didn't break. If it had been glass, she would have used a sliver of it. Of course, she could break one of the glass bottles, but that seemed wasteful, and it would make a dangerous mess. Before she did that, she would go down to the basement to Ted's airplane supplies; he probably had razor blades for the balsa. Or at least a utility knife.

Then she remembered that Ward had always kept a package of single-edged razor blades in the library desk to cut items from magazines. Maybe he hadn't taken those.

She left the bathroom light on; she would come back there and cut her wrists over the tub so the mess would be easier to clean up. Maybe she'd sit in the tub—get a pillow and lean back against the cold enameled cast iron and go to sleep forever with no dreams.

She found Ward's razor blades. She took the paper sheath off one and looked at her wrists. The blue veins were apparent. The artery,

283

she thought, was deeper. That might be too hard to cut to. But it would probably work faster. She'd see.

"Eva! What are you doing?"

Judd stood at the top of the steps, disheveled, with his shirt unbuttoned at the top, his clothes wrinkled and no shoes over his socks. His chin was covered with stubble.

I could lend him a razor, she thought, and almost giggled. He walked toward her. Then she knew he was a threat. "Don't stop me, Judd. I have to do this."

"Why?" He was still walking.

She backed away. "Because of the dream I just had." She felt the file cabinets behind her, blocking her way.

"Tell me." He stopped about a foot and a half in front of her.

She looked down. "I can't tell you; it's too terrible."

"My poor Eva." He extended his open palms toward her, and when she made no move, he took her left hand and reached for her right. Then he looked at the razor blade in it. "Put that down; you don't want to cut me, do you?"

"Oh, no!" She put the blade down on the desktop, and he swapped her left hand into his left, reached around her back to take her right, and guided her to the couch, his arm behind her. She felt weak and leaned against it.

"Sit down, Eva."

She shivered in her nightgown.

"You're cold; let me get you something." He brought an afghan from Ted's room and wrapped it around her, sat beside her, and held it around her shoulders with one arm. "Now tell me what you dreamed."

Sitting on the edge of the couch, she looked at the dream while she told him. "I was slaughtering the innocents. I slit their throats and watched the bloodstains spread down over their bodies. Rachel was crying for her children. But I hid them in the earth: I was pushing everyone into a void, all the people of the earth, tucking them under the edge of the earth like a rug. I twisted them up and bent them to bury them. They were small and weak, and I controlled them.

"But there were too many for me, and I was afraid they would find my plans, which were written down, a thick sheaf of papers, and they were my poems. Someone found them, and then everyone

284

caught me, hands everywhere clutching me, and they were going to destroy me. And all the imaginings of my heart were wholly wicked." Her words sounded strange in her own ears, but they were the language of the dream. She felt again the icy hardness of her dream and awakening and tried to shrivel herself to nothing.

He pulled her against him then and held her, and she cried, all her strength draining out with her tears until she felt as if she would fall over without him. But he went on holding her. "Eva, dear, you never wanted to kill anyone. The worst thing you could do now would be to kill yourself. Then you would hurt . . . many people beyond repair, Rob and Marcia Lee and Trey as well as Elaine and Ted and your parents."

She started crying again. "But I can't bear to live with myself."

She cried on his shoulder, and he stroked her hair.

"Of course you can. You're a strong woman, and you can bear whatever you have to. And you have to get through this. For . . . everyone who loves you."

He held her until she grew quiet again. Then he leaned back and looked at her. "I could give you another sedative, but I'd rather not. It might just make it harder when you have to do without them. Can you go back to sleep?"

His eyes were a light that penetrated. She felt cold, but she was out of the inky fog of her dream. "I don't have the energy to do anything now."

"Good. Then you need to go back to bed and rest." He went to the desk and began picking up the blades.

Watching him, she realized how strange his very presence there was. "Judd?"

"Yes?" He turned to look at her again.

"Why are you still here tonight?"

He looked down at the desktop. "I'm sorry. I didn't go home after you told me to. I slept downstairs on your couch. I didn't want to leave you here alone."

"You knew?"

"No. I thought . . . I just wanted to be here."

Then she knew the worst thing that she had done, done to him for months. She had used this kind, dear, understanding man, keeping him without taking him, hurting him, although she had half known that he loved her.

Had known. Of course she had known. But she hadn't wanted to know fully. She had chosen to disregard him, twist him up and shove him under the rug.

Involuntarily she sobbed. "Thank you," she said, her voice choked. It was all that she could say. She couldn't love him back; he wasn't Rob.

"You're welcome, Eva."

He was looking at her, but she looked away, ashamed. *Keeping without taking, just as I always used Greg Beall. Better not to keep, to let go.*

But I can't let go now. I have to have someone. If I have to go on, I have to keep him. She looked at him again.

He smiled. "It's all right, Eva. It's all right. Go to bed now. I'll be downstairs."

She wondered if he really did understand.

The front door awakened her, and she heard Judd's and Elaine's voices. She was surprised to realize that she had been sleeping. *Without a dream,* she thought with relief. *Maybe I won't have to dream again. Ever.*

But I'll have to think. Oh, I can't bear to think. And remember.

Then she remembered that Elaine had left her, gone to Ward. And Ted. Ted must have gone too. She was still in Ted's bed.

She closed her eyes. If only she could sleep again. If only she could sleep forever.

She heard steps coming up the stairs and recognized them as Elaine's. *Maybe she's come back to forgive me.* She sat up in bed and listened, hoping. But the steps turned in at Elaine's door, and then she heard the sound of drawers being opened and closed.

She's come back to move all her things to Ward's. Evelyn closed her eyes and lay down again and wished for oblivion. *"Easeful Death."* She recited the stanza to herself as she translated each sound Elaine made: the opening of the closet doors, the retrieval of suitcases from the eaves closet off the library. She didn't call Elaine's name. She had no right to summon her.

She counted the trips up and down the stairs: three. Then Elaine was talking with Judd again. No; it was Ted. He must have come to pack too. And she was in his room. She had to get out of his way.

She got up. The air-conditioning was cold. She had no robe there, so she wrapped the afghan around herself again and went downstairs. Ted was helping Elaine take her suitcases out.

Evelyn said, "Ted? I came out of your room so you could get your things."

"Why, Mom? Are you kicking me out?" He set down a suitcase and crossed to her, and she knew in a flood of joy and tears that he at least still loved her. They held each other, and he went on, "Bad enough that you booted me out of my bed last night."

"Where were you?"

"I slept in your old bedroom. I'll stay there if you want."

"No, no. I'll be all right tonight in my own bed." She thought of all the things Elaine could say about that.

But she didn't. She hadn't spoken since Evelyn came downstairs. She had set her suitcases down, but now she picked them up again and started outside.

Ted went back to the heap by the front door to help her. Evelyn held the door open for both of them, then went around them to open the porch door. Ted thanked her.

None of them spoke after that until Elaine and Ted were taking out the last load. Then Evelyn said, "Good-bye, Elaine." She wanted to say, "I love you." But she felt that she didn't have the right; Elaine didn't want her love.

Elaine said nothing but kept walking toward her car.

Ted was looking at Evelyn. "I'll be right back, Mom."

Her throat was too full for her to say anything to him.

When he came back from loading the car, she said, "Where's Judd?"

"He's gone to the hospital. He said he'll expect you to walk with him tonight, since you both missed your exercise yesterday."

She closed her eyes. *That's what I can't do. I can't go on living as though nothing has happened. I can't pretend to myself that I have anything left to live for.*

Ted said, "Aren't you going to fix lunch? It's nearly eleven-thirty, and I'm starved."

She opened her eyes. "What would you like to have?"

Ted talked about his plans for the new year at Duke, his courses and friends. After lunch, he insisted that she drive with him and Kevin to a marina on the Duck River to watch them fly airplanes. She washed her face and dressed in culottes and tennies, thinking, *I won't have to change for walking.*

Then she realized that for an hour she had not thought of Rob or Trey or Marcia Lee. *I can forget them. As long as I have even one that I love, I can live without even Rob. I can live in the world of routines and escape the underworld at least. I can learn to live without the sunlight.* Relief and guilt mixed in her reflection.

The day was cooler than the scorching dog days they had been having, but the sun shone through the tenacious haze, and the water sparkled against the deep green of late summer. There were other Saturday lawn pilots already flying their craft, and the tiny planes looked like bees as they zoomed and looped, soared and sailed across the sky.

Ted had packed a lawn chair for her, and she sat in the shade at the edge of the field and watched the boys. Although many of the modelers used plastic, both Ted and Kevin still preferred balsa, silk span, and coat after patiently sanded coat of airplane dope. Ted had brought two planes, an F-15 and one of the newer SR-71s, a Blackbird, and Kevin had his tried-and-true F-4 Phantom. Evelyn teased Ted that he had brought her only to use her big car because his wouldn't hold all their planes.

"No, I have to show off for my mommy," he said and smiled.

She wanted to hug him, but she just smiled back and said, "Then show me."

He flew the F-15, a favorite, first. She watched it rise and swirl above the green peaks of the trees and wished that she could rise up like that into the air, above the trees and their shadows and the earth itself. Somewhere there lay the light. *Shadows lie on the earth and bury the wheat seed, but birds can rise and fly.*

After a while with the F-15, Ted got out his newly finished Blackbird. It sailed up and leveled out and cruised just as it should. But then it started dipping toward the left, and the flight was erratic, not smooth anymore. Kevin shouted advice, and Ted shouted back, but before Kevin could reply, the Blackbird dipped, nosed up, dipped, plunged, and crashed into the ground.

Some of the other fliers brought in their planes and went to survey the crash. They stood around and looked at the plane. Ted took out the engine, and they all huddled over it. Then, shrugging and talking and joking, they scattered over the field again and began their own flights once more.

Evelyn wanted to go to Ted when he lost his plane, but she sat still. She watched him come across the field toward her, the remnants of the Blackbird in his hand.

When he was in earshot, she said, "Can it be fixed?"

"No. I think it's a lost cause. Something went wrong with the engine; that's why it couldn't respond when I tried to right it. And the fuselage and wings are all pretty well destroyed." He showed her the broken wood and torn covering.

"All your work gone."

He shrugged. "I do it for the work. And the risk. It'd be nice if they never cracked up, but then I'd probably lose interest."

She thought of the night-blooming cereus and nodded. "It's like flowers; they wouldn't be so precious if they lasted forever."

"Yes, like that. I'll make another one like this sometime. And if I don't, I'll remember this one."

She dreaded seeing Judd for their walk that evening. But he said nothing about Friday's events. They talked of the things they saw along the road, and he asked about what she had done that day, the children's plans for school, and her own plans for the sabbatical. She started telling him about selecting poems for submission to editors. "I'm not sure my poems have any interest for anyone except me." She felt ashamed of the time she had spent on them. What were they except another form of self-centeredness? She felt like disclaiming them; if she published them, maybe she should use her old pseudonym, Vivian Bond.

"Several of them have been published in journals and little literary magazines, haven't they? And didn't the woman at that writers' conference, the one who ran her own press, want to publish a chapbook of your poems? They must have interested her and the editors who've already published some."

"But my poetry tends to be so personal."

"Isn't the best poetry personal? Would you like Keats's poems so much if he hadn't written about his fear of death and his love for that young girl?"

The answer was obvious. "No, probably not."

"Is that your real worry, or are you afraid that people will read your poems and know too much about you?"

"Maybe that too."

"Well, that's something only you can decide—how much of yourself you want to reveal to anyone with the price of your book."

"It's not just how much I reveal; it's how much they understand."

"Ah—that's the risk that we all, poets or not, have to decide whether we'll take or not. Whether we can let others see how we feel, not knowing if they'll understand."

Do you wish you hadn't let me see how you feel? She couldn't ask that question. She tried to frame a kind answer to what he hadn't asked. "If our feelings are given as a gift, they're valuable even if they aren't understood."

But he applied her words to her book. "Then so are your poems."

Then she wondered, *Do you not know how much you've let me see of how you feel? Or did I misunderstand you? Or am I misunderstanding you now?* She decided, not for the first time, that she was an epistemological skeptic. *So why do I spend so much time teaching the value of knowing and communicating? Why teach at all? Why write?*

Judd interrupted her speculations. "I'd be honored if you'd let me read your poems, at least any that you'd consider for a general audience."

She knew that he read all kinds of things, poetry, fiction, and plays as well as referential writing. "Would you? I'll be glad to have an informal, friendly editor before I submit my writing to a stranger."

"I'll look forward to reading them."

Ted and Hailey were in the living room when Evelyn got home after walking, although she remembered that earlier in the week, Ted had said they planned to go to Nashville to a rock concert Saturday. That made her realize that he and Judd must have planned for one of them to stay with her all the time.

The realization embarrassed her: she had to be watched over like a child. She felt the blood in her face as she returned the couple's greetings and declined their insistence that she watch the latest Monty Python videotape. "No, I'm going upstairs to do some . . . writing." *The one time I need grading, as an excuse, and I don't have any.*

"Okay, Mom. But you'll be sorry you missed this; it's hilarious."

She went upstairs and got out the folders in which she'd been keeping her poems. But she kept thinking of the conversation with Judd, of the futility of knowledge and communication, of Keats and his death and his poems.

She started doodling the Grecian urn as she saw it in her mind. But the shapes weren't enough; she needed color. She realized how acutely aware of color she was. She closed her eyes and saw the vase in terra cotta and black, the colors of the Greek vases she had seen in museums. And then the image cracked and fell.

She saw herself broken into the pieces of colored glass in a kaleidoscope, trapped in a box, falling. But she made no pattern.

She didn't know how long it lasted, but she realized that her mind had gone as blank as a television screen when the set was turned off. She came to consciousness looking at Cressida trapped in her door. The ring on the prisoner's left hand began to swirl, the whorls of the wood moving faster, and it glowed red. It moved so fast that it turned into a ruby. The eyes were rubies too, the right one in its proper place and the left one at the top of the headdress. They were glowing and turning and growing. Then they were spatters of blood. They split apart. They were wounds, red, bleeding, writhing wounds.

She stood up and pulled her eyes away, looking at the room filled with books, her life. But they had failed her; she couldn't sit all night and read. Or write.

Judd had told her she was strong, that she could bear what she had to bear.

But not alone. I can't bear it alone.

She dialed Rob's number. The rings went on and on, and there was no answer.

So I have to bear it alone.

She thought of calling Judd but didn't—and didn't know if that was for his sake or her own.

So she sat down again at the desk. The sketch of the vase caught her eye, and she began writing words about it.

Several sheets of scribbled, crossed-out, interlined paper later, Ted called up the stairwell and asked if she wanted popcorn.

"No—yes, I think I do. I'll come down." She closed the folder and put it back in the short file cabinet beside the desk. She went downstairs and talked with Hailey and opened soft drinks while Ted popped the corn. Things seemed normal, and that was the strangest part of the evening.

When they had finished the popcorn, she excused herself and changed the sheets on Ted's bed and went back downstairs to her new bedroom. *You made your bed. Now you'd better learn to lie in it.*

She didn't sleep in it. About midnight, she heard Ted's car pull out of the drive to take Hailey home, and she heard him come back after a fairly long interval and go upstairs to bed.

She kept going over what-ifs. First they were What if *this* hadn't happened? What if I had done *this*? What if *this* had happened? She stopped when she asked, What if Marcia Lee had succeeded in killing herself and Trey?

Then she began thinking, What if I do *this* now? *What if I help Rob get Trey from Marcia Lee and marry him? Then do we live happily ever after? Not likely. Not unless we could forget all the grief of these days.*

But what if I don't marry him? What if Marcia Lee recovers and they try to live together? That doesn't promise to be any fairy tale either. And what if she so sick she can't recover?

That for the moment seemed the happiest possible outcome: if Marcia Lee was incurably insane, they could have each other with a clear conscience. *That's a consummation devoutly to be wished. Second only to her really having killed herself, of course. The Jane Eyre ending.*

She turned her face into her pillow and cried until she seemed to have no mind left.

As daybreak lighted the windows, she remembered awakening in that same bed with Rob beside her. She got up then; neither her body nor her mind could stay there any longer. She stood at the window and looked outside, but the August fog isolated her from the world. Everything was a pale gray blindness.

She went into her old bedroom and dialed Rob's number again. Again the rings sounded on and on into a void.

Ted's arrangements to fill the house with his friends and her own resolution to live in the routine world got her through the next day. She floated downstream, sitting and watching the volleyball games and horseplay, keeping a book or newspaper in her lap to help her through any times that one of Ted's friends wasn't talking with her. But she had trouble concentrating on her reading; she felt numb, and the loss of feeling itself was a pain, a loss of self. So she welcomed the distraction of Ted's friends. Hailey especially sat with her, and Evelyn asked about her plans and family and got to know her a little better as a person, not just as Lou and Sid Branham's little girl or Ted's date. Judd came by and sat down to talk with her but was paged after a few minutes and had to leave for the hospital. She asked him to come back and have supper with Hailey, Ted, and her, and he did, although he was late.

Afterward when they walked, she asked about Rob and Marcia Lee, and he told her that Marcia Lee was in a Nashville hospital and Rob and Trey were staying with friends in Nashville. He said he hadn't talked with Rob or the doctors since Saturday. She tried but couldn't picture Rob there; she didn't know the friends or their home.

She watched some mindless comedy on the VCR with Ted and Hailey. She almost nodded off twice during it, and when it ended, she excused herself, took a warm bath, and went to bed, hoping to be able to sleep.

And she did. But it was not sound sleep; she would doze off and dream and wake up. The dreams were confused, crowded scenes; she was with strangers or people she barely knew in some vast, impersonal place, a hotel or department store or office building. Once she was lost in the La Salle Street Station in Chicago, and she was trying to go somewhere, but she didn't know where. Each time she woke up, she would tell herself to go back to sleep, and she would, but she didn't feel rested in the morning.

She heard Ted's clock radio cut on and send out the cheerful tones of his favorite Nashville disc jockey, then the blast of Led Zeppelin. He would be at work all week, and she would be home alone. She thought of Elaine and wondered if she would see her before she left for school again. At any rate, when Ted and Elaine both went back to college, she would be alone all the time. And she would not be teaching. What routines could she live by then?

She wondered if Elaine had taken everything from her room. She decided to check as soon as Ted left.

The morning fog, typical for August, persisted. She turned a chair toward the blankness of the window and sat down to wait for the sound of his car leaving.

Soon he knocked lightly on her bedroom door. "Mom? You awake?"

"Yes, Ted. Come in." She got up and turned the chair again.

"I wonder if you'd do me a favor. Do you have time to go through my clothes? I've got some I need to wash, some to take to the cleaners, and some that need mending or buttons or whatever. I thought you might have time to sort them."

"I do." For the last two days, she had seemed to have all the time in the world with nothing to fill it. "Will you be home for lunch?"

"No. The staff's going to River Inn today to celebrate Win's birthday."

So they're really going to trust me without a baby-sitter? Fancy that! "I'll see you this afternoon then. Do you want to ask Hailey over for dinner?"

"Yeah, that'd be great. I'll call and let you know by noon whether she's coming."

"That's fine."

She dressed and went to the kitchen to eat breakfast. Between them, Ted and she had managed to fill her day. She wished for something to fill the nights.

She forcibly turned off most of her mind while she sorted and mended. At ten-thirty Judd called her. "I wondered if you'd leave the boy to fend for himself today and have lunch with me at the tearoom. Earline's brother's been ill, and I told her to take the day off."

No, the baby-sitting service is still operating. She accused Judd: "You knew before I did that Ted won't be home for lunch today."

"Ye-es, I did. But that doesn't mean I don't want your company for its own sake."

"Why don't you come here? I don't mind cooking."

"It'll be good for you to get out."

Might as well call a spade a spade. "I don't know if I'm up to all your plans to save me from myself."

He didn't answer at once. "I had hoped I was a little subtler than I've evidently been."

"Subtle or not, you've been kind, and I appreciate it."

"Then save me from a lonely lunch."

She knew it for another of his manipulations, but she was too tired to resist. Besides, she didn't really want to be by herself. "All right."

Haze still hung in the air at noon. The tearoom was crowded with people they knew, and Judd and Evelyn talked with most of them before the meal was finished. Rayna Hull was the first to come over and ask about Rob. "I heard that Marcia Lee's sick in a hospital in Nashville."

Judd answered, "Yes, she's there for a few days for some tests."

Rayna looked at Evelyn. "Is Rob with her?"

"I heard so. I haven't seen him for several days." The evasion came out more easily than she expected; she had mustered her forces against attack.

Judd answered too. "I think he and the boy are staying in Nashville with friends."

Evelyn kept her face as straight as her father had taught her to do when she played cards. Not that she held any aces.

On the way home, she asked, "Have you heard how Marcia Lee is?"

"Physically, she's all right. She didn't lose much blood, and the effects of the drugs are pretty much out of her system by now. Emotionally, she's torn up. All three of you have been through a great deal. I wasn't lying to Rayna and Jim and the others; the doctors are giving her all sorts of tests."

"Will she—be all right?"

"I'm not qualified to answer that question."

She didn't say anything.

He went on, "I'm more concerned with you. Are you all right?"

"I'm all right now in the daytime with you. Even with those people we've just been grilled by. Nights—well, nights are a different matter."

He looked at her. "That's how it was for me after Anna died. Ted and I agreed to keep you busy in the daytime; you've figured that out by now. But no one can fill the nights."

"No." She remembered Cressida's wounds and shivered in the August heat. Then she remembered the poem. "Last night I wrote something."

"A poem?"

"Yes. Wordsworth wouldn't approve; it certainly wasn't recollected in tranquillity."

"What was it about?"

"I can't even remember now. When we get home, I'll show it to you."

"Thank you."

"You're welcome, I'm sure. It's no great favor."

He didn't say any more.

When they pulled into her drive, she said, "Come in, and I'll get the poem. I'm curious myself now."

She led him up to the library and handed him the paper without reading it herself. He looked through it and handed it back without comment. She read silently too:

> vases tumble
> down my mind
> terra cotta
> marked with black
> rows of archaic
> skysigns

at any moment
they will break

When she looked up, he said, "But they didn't. They didn't, and they haven't, and they won't."

His eyes held her, and she nodded. She felt all the weariness of the restless nights.

Then past him she saw Cressida in her door, normal, without rubies, without wounds. But she felt afraid again. "Judd, I know I'm being silly, but please do me one more favor: look at the closet door. Do you see anything there in the central panel?"

He walked to the door and traced its grain lines with his fingers as he talked. "Here there was a large limb coming out of the trunk, pulling it out so that the saw cut across its layers and made all these pointed lines centered around it, and here there was a small branch, and here was another, and here and here and here there were twigs." He looked at her, questioning.

And the lines resolved themselves into what he had called them, the cross section of a tree. *He sees what made them, what their reality is.* She could still see Cressida there if she looked, but a casual glance revealed only an oak panel, not a woman trapped in wood. Not Cressida punished for her infidelity to her lover, not Viviane bound as punishment for her enchantments.

"Thank you," she said. She had never felt such gratitude to someone before; it drowned her, and she looked down. She was afraid she was going to cry again, and she didn't want him to see her.

"You're welcome, I'm sure." He touched her shoulder and turned and went down the stairs. She heard him close the front door, the porch door, and his car door and start the engine. When the sound of the car disappeared, she turned back to Ted's jeans and tops. She would have to cook dinner when she finished. Such boring work had become her escape.

The telephone rang at ten o'clock that night. "Evie? This is Sue Hart Fisher. Sorry to call so late, but I . . . I think I may be beginning labor. But it's almost a month early."

"What does it feel like?"

Sue described, and Evelyn remembered. "I think you'd better call your doctor. Who is it?"

"Your neighbor, Judd Adivino. Evie, would you mind terribly . . . I mean, I know it's late and all, but . . ."

"Do you want me to come to the hospital? I'd be happy to, if Jeff won't think I'm in the way."

"Oh, no. He's at the point where he wants to call my folks to come, even. Uh, oh! There it goes again!"

"You'd better hang up and call Judd. I'll meet you at the hospital. Do you have your bag packed yet?"

"Oh, yes—for the last month."

"I'll see you there. Sue?"

"Yes."

"Call me back if Judd says it's not time."

"Sure. Bye."

Judd called five minutes later and said he would drive her to the hospital.

The baby was born a little after midnight. He weighed only five and a half pounds, but Judd said he was fine otherwise. Evelyn got to hold him when they brought him to the nursery after Sue and Jeff had met him. She had forgotten what it was like to hold a baby, a tiny, living human, helpless, totally dependent on those around it. Jeff came looking for his son again as soon as the nurse shooed him out of the recovery room.

On the drive home, Judd said, "This is the part of being a doctor that I like best. So much of my work is unhappy. But most of the time with a delivery, there are at least two happy people."

"I'm happy too." She meant it. Holding the child had bound her to her mother again and to Granny and to her own children. *A baby binds us to it by its need. But the need is living, filled with hope. And satisfying the need gives us life. Even if Elaine never speaks to me again, I'm still happy in her. And I have Ted too.*

Judd looked at her. "I see that you are. Do you think you'll sleep tonight?"

"I think so."

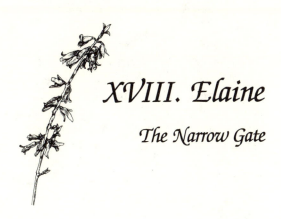

XVIII. Elaine

The Narrow Gate

*W*hen Elaine came into the foyer, she could see a man lying on the couch in the living room. He sat up, and she recognized Dr. Adivino. Then he stood and walked toward her. He looked as if he hadn't slept all night.

"Elaine?" His voice was almost a whisper.

"Yes. I've come to get the rest of my things." She stopped, then asked, "How is she?"

He shook his head. "If you see her, please . . . don't say anything else to upset her."

Oh, by all means, don't upset her. "Did anything happen after I left?"

"She woke up when the sedative wore off. She . . . was going to kill herself."

"Oh!" She sat down. *She has no right to do that. She's hurt me too much already. And he didn't have to tell me.* "Does Ted know?"

"No. I don't think he heard us."

"Don't worry; I don't want to talk to her."

"Elaine, please don't tell your father either. I think it would bother her for him to know."

"You can be sure I won't tell anyone any more about her than I have to."

He nodded. "Thank you."

Well, she has another man to take care of her again.

She had planned to strip her room, take everything personal and never have to come back to that house again. By the time she packed her clothes and the books and things she wanted for school, she knew her car would be full. Besides, she wanted to get out before her mother got up. She didn't want to feel cold and shaky the way she had the night before when Momma had gotten hysterical and it had taken Dr. Adivino and her both just to hold her and Dr. Adivino and Ted to make her take the sedative and get her to bed. Momma had never acted like that before.

Elaine kept thinking about Bill. She had thought about calling him the night before, but it had been too late. Now she was glad she hadn't; maybe she wouldn't have to tell him about it at all. She could just say she had quarreled with her mother and moved in with her father and stepmother.

Thank goodness she didn't have to stay with Momma. Dad was the same as he'd always been. The way a father should be, of course: teaching his children justice, as Fromm said. Of course, he'd been harder on Ted. A mother was supposed to teach unconditional love. And, to give her her due, Momma had. Elaine had always been sure she loved her and Ted.

But this last was too much. She couldn't stand this. Momma had loved Rob McFergus more than her own children, or she couldn't have done this to them, exposed them to public humiliation this way. Ted might forgive her, but she never could. She closed the last suitcase and carried it downstairs.

Dr. Adivino had evidently gone, but Ted was up. He must have slept downstairs, for she hadn't heard him while she was upstairs.

He said, "Have you seen her?"

"No, and I don't want to."

"Aw, Elaine, have a heart. You know she loves you more than anything."

"Not more than that man, evidently."

"You're just jealous."

"No. I'm ashamed of her. I don't even like her."

"Hush! She's coming down."

Momma's appearance was a shock. Her hair was uncombed, and her makeup was smeared all over. She was all huddled up in the afghan Granny had made Ted. But it was her expression that was so awful. Elaine couldn't have said anything even if Dr. Adivino hadn't told her not to. She got away as quickly as she could.

In a worried voice, Mary Will wondered where in the world they were going to put all Elaine's things, and Elaine assured her that she would take most of them to college soon. She had learned early that Mary Will hadn't expected the quiet of Twin Elms to be assaulted when she married. Dad had done little to alter the house; he seemed happy that it had remained basically unchanged since before the war, as Mary Will was always saying, meaning not Vietnam or even World War II, as Granny and Grandmother and Grandfather meant, but the Civil War.

She and her stepmother had already been through one war themselves. Wilhelmina had been a real trial for Mary Will. She was afraid the kitten would break something or scratch the furniture, and she knew it would leave hair everywhere. She couldn't bear for it to be around food, and of course it could leap anywhere, onto the dining table or even the kitchen counters. Finally Mary Will and Elaine had worked out a truce: Wilhelmina could stay in Elaine's room or the cellar, but nowhere else in the house. Elaine learned to close doors rapidly, and it was a pain to carry the litter box in and out from the cellar or her bedroom upstairs. But Mary Will placed no other limits on Elaine's freedom.

Right after she and Dad got the car unloaded, she called Bill. She had told him the week before about her mother's confession that she loved Dr. McFergus, and he had not been scandalized. She knew that his parents were very conservative, so she had been relieved. Now she told him that Mrs. McFergus had tried to commit suicide and kill her son because of the affair.

"Well, that's pretty extreme. Is she . . . deranged? I mean, trying to kill the kid is just too much."

"But don't you see? It never would have happened if Momma hadn't . . . carried on with her husband."

"Don't be too hard on your mother, Elaine."

So he was going to side with Momma too. He and Ted and Dr. Adivino. Were women the only ones who could see how wrong Momma had been? She bet if her stepmother knew all that Momma had done, Mary Will would side with her for once.

Bill went on, "Love makes people do dumb things sometimes, honey. Do you think your mother would approve of everything we've done?"

She remembered her mother's warnings, given before she ever had started dating, about hurting herself or others by premarital sex. "No. Probably not. That's different. We're going to get married."

"And she planned to marry this guy too. You told me before: she told you and Ted because he was asking his wife for a divorce so he could marry her. And that's what made his wife do what she did."

"It's still different. I didn't take you away from somebody else you were married to."

"No. You made me break up with the girl I'd been dating for two years. What if Lynne had tried to kill herself over losing me? Would it be your fault? Anyhow, do you think your mother would throw you out if she knew we've slept together?"

She wouldn't answer him. "You and Lynne didn't have a child."

"Just don't be so hard on your mother, honey. She loves you."

"I'm not so sure of that."

"Do you want me to drive over for the weekend?"

She thought about having him; she needed someone of her own now, and his words had reminded her of how much she missed him physically. But then she remembered her mother's suicide attempt. No telling what kind of mess he might get in the middle of if he came. And Mary Will wouldn't be any too happy to have another of her empty rooms disturbed. "No. But maybe we can both return to Danville early?"

"I've been thinking about more than that. Maybe we could meet at some JP's and get married before this school year instead of afterward. I mean, what difference would it make, besides our not having to be so careful?"

Not so soon; it's too soon. I'm not sure anymore. "I don't know, Bill. I—I'll have to think about it."

302

After she hung up, she looked at the phone. She felt like a little girl again. But she couldn't run to her mommy. That's whose fault it all was.

She called Amy. She remembered as soon as she heard Amy's drowsy "Hello?" that Amy had late shift on weekends at the motel restaurant where she worked. She usually didn't get home till one or two in the morning, and sometimes then she was too wound up to go to sleep right away.

"I'm sorry, Amy. I forgot your schedule."

"That's all right. Just let me know sometime when you've pulled an all-nighter to get a paper in, and I'll return the favor."

"I am sorry. And I would've remembered, but I've been upset."

"I heard something at the restaurant—about Mrs. McFergus and Trey."

"And my mother?"

"Yes. I'm sorry, Elaine. If anybody knows how you feel, it's me."

Elaine remembered when Amy's mother had run off with a married man the first time, when Amy was thirteen. Amy and her sisters had stayed with the Knights while her father had followed the couple and persuaded Mrs. Lund to come back. Amy had slept in her room, and Elaine had pretended to go to sleep so Amy could cry. So far as Elaine knew, Amy hadn't cried when her mother left for good with another man a year later. *What Momma did wasn't that bad*, Elaine thought.

She said, "I've left home and come to stay with Dad and Mary Will till school starts."

"Don't cut all your ties, Elaine. You might want your mother back again."

"After what she's done? Not till hell freezes over!"

"That's what I thought at first too."

Amy never talked about her mother, so Elaine hesitated. But she had brought it up. "And have you changed your mind?"

"Yeah. Yeah, I've changed my mind. I've thought about why she did it, Dad's drinking and all. And I miss her."

"I'm sorry."

"Me too. For both of us. But you can still do something about it."

"I don't know. I don't think so, Amy."

"Well, just don't burn your bridges while they're still standing."

Elaine stayed out of Mary Will's way as much as she could all that weekend. She was glad when Monday morning took her back to the office. She thought she recognized Dr. McFergus's voice once calling for Mr. Hillson, who asked Cindy to do some typing for him after that, although Cindy usually did only Mr. Leek's work. But she didn't ask Cindy anything about it. She just wanted to forget the whole ugly mess.

Life with Dad and Mary Will settled into a routine. She ate dinner with them but stayed in her room and read the rest of the time or watched television if they left for the evening. She called Bill when she got too lonesome but wouldn't talk with him about her mother. She truthfully told him she hadn't seen her. She still didn't tell him about Momma's suicide attempt.

She felt sorry for Wilhelmina in her cramped quarters and began taking her outside awhile each day after work. The kitten hadn't been spayed and had been a housecat all her short life, so Elaine watched her all the time. She aped the mannerisms of predatory cats even though she couldn't have observed them. She stalked bugs and watched the flights of flies and even bees and tried to pounce on them.

One afternoon when it was almost too hot to bear outside, just as Elaine was thinking of going back into the air-conditioning, Wilhelmina stiffened in front of a spirea bush and began a sound Elaine hadn't heard from her before, a kind of vibrating whine. The cat looked almost like a hunting dog on a point except that her tail twitched back and forth. Her hair was raised and her eyes were fixed on something inside the bush.

Lifting her, Elaine bent to peer into the bush. At first she saw nothing in the shadows. Then she saw a small mass, something spherical about the size of a plum, at the heart of the arching branches. It was a nest.

Late for hatchlings, she thought. *And so small. It must be a hummingbird's nest. Like the one Momma showed me.*

She rustled the branches a foot away from the nest, watching for bead eyes or sudden flight. But there was nothing. She knelt down and reached into the bush and pulled out the nest.

It looked just like the one that she remembered, made of fine, tightly woven brown fibers like roots. Momma had called her that day and shown her the nest in the bushes beside the detached garage. They could see a single pea-sized egg in its downy lining. They had gone looking for the parent birds, stealing to the bright trumpet vine on the back fence of the garden, then to the althea bushes along the ravine. There they had seen a male, ruby throat bright between a blur of wings, hovering, moving to another bloom, hovering again. Momma, eyes shining, had squeezed her shoulders. "It's a gift, Elaine."

If I find a hummingbird . . . She tried to remember where there were deep-throated flowers at Twin Elms. Then she thought, *This is silly. I saw the nest. That's enough.* She raised Wilhelmina into the air. "You've done all the prowling you can do today, little lion. Let's go inside."

She carried the hall telephone into her room and dialed home before she could change her mind. Ted answered.

"Ted? This is Elaine. I want to talk to Momma."

"You're not going to upset her again, are you?"

"Edward Knight, I've got enough sense to know what to do. And what's between us is none of your business anyhow."

"Well, I'll call her, but if you get her all torn up again, you'll have me to answer to."

The receiver tapped the table. It was a minute before her mother said, "Elaine?"

"Yes, Momma. I wondered if I could come over and talk with you sometime."

"Yes." Her voice sounded tight. "Of course. Come now if you want."

"I'll be there in a few minutes then."

By the time she reached home, Elaine had decided it was a mistake to come. She didn't open the door but rang the bell, and Momma came to the door. She looked thinner. And she had on no makeup, not even lipstick. Her hair, though clean, hung down straight, not even caught in a queue. But she didn't look wild. Instead, she seemed almost inert. She let Elaine in and said, "Let's go into the sunroom."

Elaine closed the glass door between the sunroom and living room. She hadn't seen Ted, but she was willing to bet he was close enough to hear.

They were both still standing. "Momma, I can't go back to school without talking to you."

"I've hoped that you would forgive me."

"Well, I haven't. I still don't know how you could have done this to us. I understood when you and Dad separated; I've always known you all have struggled against each other. But now for you to take up with Dr. McFergus— He's just not suitable in any way. Even if he weren't married, he's years younger than you are. It's ridiculous."

"I know it. But I love him. And he loves—loved, anyhow—me."

"Is that all it is, just lust, like two teenagers in heat?"

Her mother looked at her, the tears spilling but her voice full-volume. "No. I did say love, not lust. Rob and I loved each other. Though as for that, yes, I still need someone to love with my body. It's still alive."

Elaine thought of her own desire for Bill. She turned toward the table and sat down. Then, knowing there were tears in her eyes, she looked back at Momma. "All right. So why don't you marry somebody like Dr. Adivino, somebody at least as old as you are, somebody not married already?"

Her mother's jaws tightened, and her lips trembled. She sat down across the table and shook her head. "I didn't fall in love with Judd."

"Falling in love. Isn't that just a foolish explanation for letting your emotions get in the way of common sense?"

306

"Of course it is. Elaine, all my life I've tried to control my emotions with my common sense. All it's ever brought me is emptiness."

Elaine reached across the table and gripped her hand. "Oh, Momma, I don't want to blame you; I want you to be happy too. But I don't know how you can be, how we can be. Sometimes I think I'll never be happy again."

Momma put her head on the table and sobbed. Elaine came around the table and hugged her mother and cried too.

Momma stopped before she did, and they looked at each other. Then Momma asked, "Do you think sometime you might be able to forgive me?"

"I forgive you, Momma. I never should have blamed you."

"You had the right. I'll understand if you go away and never see me again."

"Momma, would you throw me away if I had done some horrible thing? Murdered someone?"

Her mother shook her head.

"Well, I couldn't throw you away either, even if you'd done a lot worse than you have."

She called Mary Will and said that she wouldn't be home for dinner. Then she joined Momma in the kitchen to prepare their food. They agreed that it didn't make sense for Elaine to move back home for the brief time until she had to leave for school. But Momma asked her to come home for dinner every night. "At least, I can cook for you then. You don't have to spend the evening, of course."

"But you hate to cook." She began peeling potatoes.

"Oh, yes and no. Sometimes I enjoy cooking, giving it as a gift to someone. I hate *having* to cook—being expected to do it as my duty because I'm a woman. You know how it used to irk me that your father and I could go through the same kind of day teaching and come home, and he would read his journals while I had to cook dinner."

"Why did you do it? Why didn't you tell him he had to do it some of the time?"

She shrugged. "Pavlovian conditioning, I suppose. I assume that psych classes still teach about that. I was brought up to expect to cook, just like my mother, and he was brought up to expect me to. Mary Will and I are almost the same age, you know. I imagine he'll get along fine with her for the rest of their lives. It's the tension between what I was expected to do as a wife and my role as a so-called liberated woman that helped separate us. If I had never learned to think, we'd still be together."

"But you depend on men for their traditional roles too. Now you ask Ted to check your car when there's something wrong. Or you ask Dr. Adivino for advice if the gutters leak or something. Why, you won't even drive your own car if there's a man around to do it for you."

Momma looked at her. "I don't, do I?"

"Let's face it, Mom, as a liberated woman, you're only half done."

"Well, I've not been liberated very long. Maybe your generation will get the hang of it."

"Not likely, as long as you sew all Ted's buttons on."

Her mother sighed. "I haven't done a very good job about a lot of things, I know."

Elaine washed the potatoes. "You have done a good job at a lot of things. That's what bothers me, I guess. Mom, you've really been a great mother. And from all accounts, you're a great teacher. So if you've messed up your life like this, what kind of a chance do I have?"

Her mother was mixing a vinaigrette. She put in ground mustard and mashed out the lumps, then reached for pepper. "Your own chance; all we each have is our own life. And I know I've been a fool about lots of things, but I still hope that I haven't irrevocably messed up mine. Can you see the pin oak?"

Elaine leaned a little sideways from her post at the sink and looked at the thirty-foot pyramid, alone in the center of the side front lawn. "Yes. What about it?"

"I look at that sometimes and think, *I can be that if I have to. I can be a freestanding tree.* That's not what I want most; I'd rather be part of the woods bordering the ravine, rustle my leaves there with the others. But if I can't have you or Ted or Rob or—or even Jessie or Mother or Father or Granny—if I can't have anyone else, I know I *can* stand alone. I've learned that these last days. Though even now, Judd and Ted prop me."

"Isn't standing alone the best? The safest at least? As long as you lean on someone else, you can be left to fall." She didn't look at her mother.

"No. That's not the best. It's better to love than not to love. Being afraid of being hurt means being afraid to live." She poured in the vinegar and oil and shook it. "Standing alone is second best; it's better than clinging. I don't want to cling to you or Ted, and I don't want you to change your lives to keep me company. I even told Ted the other day he was going to drive me crazy if he didn't start running around again with his friends as he always has and leave me alone some. Thank goodness he has. And that's the chief thing I have against a marriage like my mother and father's, for their sakes. or like your father and Mary Will's; she's spent her life so far waiting for marriage, and now she does nothing but cling to Ward, and if he dies first, she'll do nothing but look back on what they had. That seems like a waste of a lot of time that could be spent doing other things too. Being something herself."

"Dad seems to like it."

"I've no doubt. Maybe it's good for him. But the only thing a goose is good for if you feed it all the time is killing for pâté. And the average fat goose liver isn't any more worthless than the average fat human ego."

"I see you can be your old self again."

"Yes. If I know I have my daughter's love as well as my son's, that's enough to secure me. Even enough for me to tempt the fates and be catty."

Elaine put the kettle of potatoes on the rangetop and turned on the burner. "Mom, what would you say if Bill and I decided to get married right away instead of waiting till next June?"

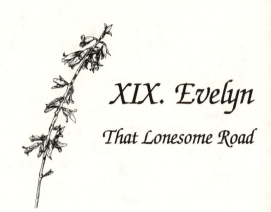

XIX. Evelyn

That Lonesome Road

*W*hen Elaine told her father that she and Bill planned to marry right away, Ward wasn't happy about the whole idea. When he did bow to the inevitable, he vetoed the idea of a justice of the peace; he insisted that the couple marry at Twin Elms, where he and Mary Will had been married.

Bill drove down from Knoxville for the weekend to make arrangements. He stayed with Evelyn. The family except Ted all met in the library at Twin Elms on Saturday afternoon to discuss plans; Mary Will had invited Evelyn and Ted for dinner as well as Bill, and Ted would come after work. The meeting was almost like in-laws-to-be conferring about their children's wedding.

Evelyn was amused to note how similar Ward's wedding plans for their daughter were to their own wedding at Lanier Bluffs, and she made a note to ask Elaine if they were like his own second wedding to Mary Will. Of course, Mary Will had not worn Evelyn's wedding dress as Elaine intended to do, despite her threat to wear her "slut dress," a red satin one-shouldered draped sheath with a slit to bikini height that she had bought primarily to torment her father and secondarily to shock her friends. Evelyn would have to make some al-

310

terations in her wedding dress; Elaine was a little taller and fuller, especially in the bust, than she had been.

The meeting with Ward and Mary Will went well. Actually, Mary Will said almost nothing once she was assured that the small guest list would not threaten the peace of her house. Evelyn offered to put up all the out-of-town family, Bill's as well as her own, except Ward's mother; Mary Will could shoulder that cross at least now. But Evelyn would ask Judd for the use of some of his empty bedrooms or rent motel rooms rather than have Bill's family suffer Mary Will's anxiety. She was glad Elaine had evidently made up her quarrel with Judd; he was one of the few people outside the family that Elaine wanted to invite.

Bill and Elaine agreed to most of Ward's suggestions. Evelyn thought they probably would have agreed to almost anything that didn't delay their being alone together; as soon as the major plans were made, they excused themselves "to look around the garden," which Mary Will's gardener did keep in superb shape.

Mary Will excused herself too to check on the progress of dinner.

When everyone had left Ward and Evelyn alone, she felt crowded in the spacious library. *We're filling it with our memories. How do we get through a whole evening in company together? Worse, how do we get through these next few minutes alone?*

He was sitting in a wing chair beside the empty fireplace, looking at his hand on his leg. She wondered if he was thinking about his new wedding ring, and she broke the silence with a peace offering. "You look as though this is where you belong."

He looked up. "Yes. I think I do."

"I'm glad. I hope you've gotten something good out of the hurt I caused you."

"You didn't hurt me." His eyes, hard, looked past her.

No, I should have known better than to say that. "Good. I never wanted to hurt you."

"I do need to know one thing." He still wasn't looking at her. "I want to know if McFergus was the reason you . . . we broke up."

"No. I swear that to you, Ward; there was nothing between Rob and me—nothing at all—until this spring. I never even thought of there being before then."

"Was it Adivino then? I know you've been seeing him all the time since I left. I'd rather it was him than McFergus."

She grimaced. "No. Judd's just a friend. I tell you, there was no one else. It was just that we . . . didn't belong together."

He looked at her then, and she saw the cords tighten in his neck. "Why, Evelyn? I've tried to figure it out all these months, and I still don't know. I always provided for you; I couldn't give you as much as your father, but you seemed happy with what we could afford."

She thought of his mother and was repulsed that he had thought she had the same values. When Ward's father had died and left Mildred a sizable amount in insurance, Evelyn had wished that Webb could have seen Mildred's happiness; at last he had done something to please her. Evelyn said, "Oh, Ward, it was never that. Money was the least of it; that's never what I've wanted."

"What was it then? Maybe I wasn't such a good lover. . . . But Mary Will seems to think . . ." His face turned red.

She hurt for him so that her voice was hoarse. "You were a good lover."

He stood up and held his hands out in front of himself and shook them. "Then what was it? What did you want that I didn't give you?"

She shook her head. "I don't know. If we had talked like this before . . . if even once, you had told me how you felt . . . or asked me . . ."

"Did *you* talk with *me?* I didn't have a clue. I didn't know you were even thinking about leaving me until you told me that night."

She bent her head. "I didn't know either. I didn't know till I told you."

"You didn't even think it out?"

"If I'd thought it out, I never would have done it."

He laughed and settled into his chair again. "It's a little late to be sorry."

She realized that he had misunderstood. And she had misspoken: she meant that she *couldn't* have broken with him, not that she wouldn't, if she had taken the time to think about it, to let herself be paralyzed as usual by thought. But maybe his misunderstanding was better. Sitting back, hands on the chair arms, he seemed to have regained his self-possession. After all, what had his questions been but an attempt to free himself of blame? Maybe it was better for him to think she regretted breaking up with him. It cost her nothing but some pride, and that didn't matter.

Not much mattered. She wondered herself now: What mattered enough for her to want? Just tenderness? Was that what she had found and wanted in Greg and Rob that Ward had not given her? Was that enough to make such a difference?

The silence stretched out. She couldn't honestly say or imply to Ward that she did regret breaking with him; even without Rob, she was happier without Ward. Being with him all the time, feeling that he didn't really love her, didn't value her love except as a possession, didn't really value *her*, had been a constant pain, a constant rejection. Without him, she could stand alone like the pin oak.

Maybe she could have done something earlier to save their marriage. Maybe she could have talked with him, told him how she felt, how she needed his tenderness. Maybe they both could have changed. Now Mary Will made that an academic question.

But the immediate problem was that neither of them seemed able to think of anything to say. And the silence became unbearable.

Finally, she came back to her original offering to him. "I'm glad that you seem to be happier now with Mary Will."

"She's a great girl. Old-fashioned and sweet."

Neither of which I am, by his standards. She smiled. "Then I haven't done you irreparable harm?"

"No. Maybe you did me a favor. Thank you."

She laughed outright then. "You're welcome, I'm sure." But something echoed from a long way away: "If that's how you feel, you're not doing Ward Knight any favors marrying him." Greg's dead words silenced her laughter.

Just then Mary Will came in, and Ward stood up. She said, "You two seem to be having a good time."

She's been listening. The way an old-fashioned girl keeps on top of things. Evelyn wasn't sure how she knew, but she knew. "Yes. I was just saying I'm happy that Ward's second marriage agrees with him so well. And what a lovely house you have, Mary Will."

"I'll have to show you around sometime." But instead of offering to at once, she hooked her arm through Ward's. "Dear, would you mind coming with me to check the sauce for the roast? Something doesn't seem quite right. Evelyn, I'm sure you can find something to read in here."

"Oh, yes, I'm sure I can." *Something long. I think I'll have time.*

When Evelyn called her in Houston, Jessie asked to bring Marshall to the wedding. "It'll be a good way for Mother and Father to see that we're really going to get married. But we'll stay in a motel. I don't want to scandalize Mother and Father by sleeping with him under their noses."

"But they'll know."

"What they surmise isn't my business. And don't worry, Evie; I'll tell Marshall not to answer the phone in our room. I don't want to kill our parents with shame any more than you do. But I won't pretend that we don't sleep together. And we are going to be married just as soon as Sterling and I get uncoupled."

"I haven't any right to judge, Jessie."

"How are things going for you and your young Lochinvar?"

"I'll talk about it when you get here."

"I'll hold you to that."

On the Monday before the wedding on Friday, Rob called Evelyn. "I've heard about Elaine's wedding, and I know this is a busy time for you, but I need to talk."

Her heart pounded. "Oh, Rob. I couldn't ever be too busy to see you. Can you come over?"

"You don't fear for your reputation?"

"Hunh! What reputation? Come."

"I'll be there in five minutes."

She hung up the receiver carefully. *Oh, Lord. If I could pray now, I'd pray for strength. Help me through this.*

He parked in the driveway and came to the side door. He looked five years older, his eyes tight and his smile brief. "Hello."

"Hello." She didn't hold out her hand but turned to lead him through the dining room, and he followed her into the living room. Then she turned toward him and opened her arms. "Rob. Rob." It sounded in her own ears like a cry of pain.

He caught her and held her to him so hard that her ribs hurt.

Then he loosed his arms and stepped back. "Whatever happens, I want you to know I have loved you and love you more than any other woman."

He didn't say "shall love." "That sounds like a farewell."

314

He nodded and looked down. "All I've done for days now is think, think, think about us, all four of us. And I can't come to any other conclusion. But you have to know why. And I have to tell you. For myself, not just you."

She nodded and gestured toward a chair; she didn't trust her voice. Rob sat there, and she sat opposite him.

Her eyes felt dry. There was a fire inside her, under her collarbone, burning all the air out of her lungs, pushing up something heavy and hot to sear her throat and larynx and consciousness.

He began, and she knew he had thought through it all and planned what he would say. "At first, Marcia Lee wouldn't see me. I would go to the hospital and ask the nurse, and she would say the doctor said I couldn't go in unless Marcia Lee said I could, and she didn't want me to. And I didn't want to either. Not really. I hated her, Evelyn. She kept me from you. She had taken you away from me whether she lived or died. Then finally after three days, the nurse said the doctor—the psychiatrist, Dr. Garrison, not the medical doctor—wanted to talk to me. So we talked. Or I talked, and he listened for about two hours. I told him what had happened this last—God, it's just four months. It seems like a whole lifetime. Anyhow, he listened to it all, up to bringing Marcia Lee to Nashville, when he saw for himself."

He paused, but she didn't interrupt him. She nodded for him to go on.

"I told him—things about us. He asked why I loved you more than Marcia Lee, and I told him you took me as I am and Marcia Lee tried to make me hers, to own me. And he asked me what I wanted to do, if I wanted to be free of Marcia Lee to go to you or if I wanted to try to mend things."

He stopped then, and she controlled her voice and said what she had to say, the massive heat swelling her chest more all the time. Molten lava. "And you said you wanted . . . to mend things."

He shook his head. "No. I told him I hated her. I said that I would put up with her for Trey's sake if I had to, that I wanted most of all for him to be safe and happy, but I didn't think that could happen if he lived with his mother."

"And what did he say?"

"He said, 'That's what your wife thinks too. She wants to give the boy to you.' "

Then Evelyn knew that the lava inside her was building, getting ready to erupt, to parch through her ribs and skin and escape her, break out of her body to pour over Marcia Lee. "And what would she do to herself . . . if you took him?" She couldn't say, "If you left her for me?" She couldn't go that far. Not after her dream of the underworld. But that was what she meant. What she wanted.

"That's what I asked. And he said, 'I think she'd do a better job than she did this time with the razor.' And I knew I couldn't let that happen."

She nodded and said the words, tasting their bitterness. "She's changed."

"Yes. She doesn't blame me now. It'd be easier if she did." He got up and walked to the glass wall between the sunroom and the living room and looked out. "When I first went in to see her, she cried and hid her face and said she had ruined my life."

Evelyn forced herself to look at that, to see Rob's guilt and guess his tenderness. But she didn't want to hear any more of what she knew he was going to say about Marcia Lee. She didn't want to have to feel for her rival. She saw Marcia Lee again lying on her bed, the bloody bed she had lain on with Rob, insisting on being seen with her bloody arms and dress.

He went on, "I think she'd changed before. I think she really meant what she wrote."

"Wrote? When?"

He turned back toward her. "She left a note. Didn't Adivino tell you?"

"No." She forced herself to ask. "What did it say?"

"She wrote, 'Now you can be happy with her.' I thought at first she was being sarcastic. But now I think maybe she really meant it."

Evelyn felt herself growing hard, charred where the molten stone had surged through her. "Why did she drug the boy then?"

He ran his fingers through his hair. "I . . . don't know. But I don't think she did it to hurt me."

Now you've made him defend her. Poor tactics if you're fighting for him. And you ought not be. You ought to be gracious at least; you're going to lose him anyhow. You've lost him. "No, I don't think she was trying to hurt you. And from what you say, she's not now."

"No." He raised his brows, pleading with her to understand. "Evelyn, she *is* changed. And she needs me."

She saw then that his aging was more than guilt and grief. He

316

shone with a certainty that he hadn't had before. *He's all grown up now. Maybe it took this.*

He added, "I guess I finally noticed that she's . . . a person." His look was half irony, half plea.

But she still felt hard. And cold now, burnt-out. Hollow. The shell of a blasted tree. She forced on to the end. "So what do you plan to do?"

He sat down again, this time on the couch perpendicular to her chair. "Well, faculty retreat starts next week, and I certainly can't find another job for this year. You won't be on campus much now anyhow with your sabbatical. But I'll look now for a job somewhere else and go next year. I don't think I could stay here and see you every day, knowing . . ."

"I could leave instead of you, resign now before my sabbatical so I didn't owe Harper next year. Or pay my sabbatical money back."

He shook his head. "That's pointless. Marcia Lee can't go on living here; we have to go somewhere she can have a new start anyhow. And I can leave more easily than you; I don't have your exalted rank. Wyatt'll write me a bang-up recommendation just to get rid of me without a fuss. You know how he is about not rocking the boat. And I think I can finish my novel now, so that should help my mobility."

"Has this made a difference in the novel?"

"Yes. Before, I thought it was all about you and me and Marcia Lee; you were Valerie from the start, you know, long before you thought of me—as a lover. But the mother really isn't Marcia Lee. Keith can't relate to any woman until he gets something straight about his mother. And it's not that she's possessive; it's that he thinks she's never really loved him. He can't really love any woman until he works that out." He was tracing the lines of the couch upholstery with his fingers.

She was silent a moment, her mind running through the parallels, feeling old. "All your mothers have loved you, Rob."

He looked at her then. "Thank you. But Adivino's the one you ought to marry. He loves you, you know."

She stood up and walked away from him then. If there had been anything close at hand, she would have thrown it. At Rob, at Judd, at the universe. "Yes. I know. But I don't love him. Not the way I love you."

He came to her then and took her in his arms and turned her face up and kissed her, and she knew it was the last time. She closed her eyes and willed him never to stop. But he did.

Evelyn forced herself to go through the rest of her day's tasks. But she felt numb, burnt out, dead. She phoned the florist, photographer, and caterer for last-minute arrangements, finished the alterations on Elaine's dress, and pressed everything the two of them and Ted would wear during the festivities before she began preparations for dinner. Nothing seemed to go smoothly.

She was grateful that Bill's family was following the Southern custom of hosting the rehearsal dinner Thursday night in Nashville; that was one less thing to arrange. As usual, Ward had made the grand plans and left her to implement them. And as usual, she thought that she had to do everything herself to see that it was done well. But she felt like an automaton; nothing she did really mattered. The rest of her life didn't matter.

Just at dusk, the phone rang. Ted had come home from work and leaped to answer it; at this time of day, it was usually Hailey. But he called her: "It's old Dr. Adivino."

She had forgotten their walk. And Judd was the last person she wanted to see just then. Or even talk to. "Tell him I can't—oh, never mind, I'll tell him."

When she greeted him, he said, "I wonder if you're deserting me tonight."

"I'm afraid so, Judd. There's just too much to do with the wedding Friday. I'd better cancel for the rest of the week." *I'll decide then if it's worth the effort to resume.*

There was a heartbeat's pause. "Does this have anything to do with your visitor today?"

He has no right to ask me that. No right to spy on me, see Rob's car. "I don't know. I'll call you. Good-bye." *Damn! I'll have to see him at the rehearsal dinner and wedding. But I won't have him forced on me. I don't owe him that.*

When she lay in bed that night, she felt closed off from everyone by her own hardness. She had no natural love toward anyone; all the good she had ever done was because others expected her to do it or because it suited her own pride and selfishness.

And now even the year was dying. The leaves were drying on the hackberry trees, always the last to leaf out and the first to shed. Then the rest of the leaves would fall and the bleak winter would come, and there would never be another spring. Not for her.

She awoke remembering that Rob had been in her dream, but she couldn't remember what he had said or done. She resented having to awaken when she couldn't remember.

Wednesday the guests began arriving. Evelyn's parents had delayed their return to Europe until after the wedding. Her house was filled with relatives. She had forgotten what menageries of small children were like; she began feeling less like a travel agent and more like a wild-animal trainer. For once, she delegated a task by appointing Ted, whose last day at work had been Wednesday, to domesticate his cousins.

By the time of the rehearsal Thursday night, everyone was in place except Jessie and Marshall, who were flying into Nashville just before the dinner. With Elaine's approval, Evelyn had bought a new blue mother-of-the-bride dress for Friday, but Thursday she wore the red silk dress that Rob had caressed with his eyes.

The rehearsal went smoothly. Amy was Elaine's maid of honor, and a friend from college was the bridesmaid. Bill's brother Tom was his best man; Ted was the groomsman. Evelyn realized with relief that most of what she could do had been done and that there was little she could do if a catastrophe arose now anyhow. She began to feel more like a spectator than a participant and to breathe more easily.

Elaine had depicted Bill's parents as so conservative, religiously and financially, that Evelyn was surprised to see wineglasses and champagne flutes in the banquet setup for Thursday night. But she wouldn't have objected to something stronger. For once in her life, she could understand wanting to get thoroughly drunk just to escape. Her only happiness was Elaine and Bill's.

Her place card put her between Mr. Jackson—Thomas Sr.—and Ted. Marshall and Jessie hadn't arrived by the time dinner was supposed to begin, but they came in soon after. Evelyn felt the pride and envy she always had for her beautiful sister; Jessie would look wonderful to the grave. Marshall didn't seem so handsome now. His hair had grayed, and his football muscles had become flab. He looked like a typical businessman, one who wouldn't stand out in a crowd. But he smiled at Jessie, and Evelyn saw again what her sister had seen in him all those years.

Jessie led him straight to Mother and Father, who were talking to Ward and his mother. Evelyn watched for Father's eyes to go hard when he saw Marshall. But if they did, she couldn't tell. His smile was even straight, not the ironic pull to the left, as he shook Marshall's hand. *Was I wrong about that too? Well, why not? I have been about everything else.*

She turned her head and saw Judd looking at her. She hardened her heart and turned back to Mr. Jackson and began asking him about his business.

She drank more than she should but not so much that she didn't remember to focus on building relations with the Jacksons. After all, if she expected Elaine to stay part of her life, they would be part of it too. They seemed to be good people, like her parents and most of the people in Cedar Springs she had grown up with, more like small-town people than city dwellers. But of course Knoxville wasn't even as big as Nashville.

She danced with Ted, then Mr. Jackson, then Bill. Ward was waiting when she and Bill stopped, and he held out his hands. She assumed the partner's place without saying anything either, and they were silent for most of the dance. She thought, *There's not a thing about him that's not as familiar as my own skin. But we're still strangers.*

She said, "Ward, you asked the other day what went wrong between us. I don't know all of it, but I think a good part was just that we never really saw each other. I don't think I really know you, even now." Then she was almost frightened; for Elaine's and Ted's sake as well as her own, she didn't want to make him angry. But she'd had too much wine.

He seemed almost amused, as much as he was ever amused, and she was relieved that her words hadn't upset him. He shook his head. "I sure as hell don't know you, lady."

"Then we're lucky our daughter knows us both." She slid away from her insight.

"Yes. I'm glad the children were almost grown before . . . before we s-split up." His lisp indicated that he was a little drunk too.

"I'm sorry for the pain I've cost you."

"Apology ac-accepted."

She decided then that he was drunker than she was. The dance ended, and he bowed and left. The dance had been like their marriage, touching without knowing.

It was just always him being him and me being me and neither of us ever seeing the other truly as we are. Ted's wedding . . . grandchildren . . . there'll be other times. But he'll never see me now. And there's no point now in my really looking for him.

She headed for a group of her family and laid her hand on Marshall's arm and said, "May I have the pleasure of this dance?"

He looked at her so blankly that she thought he had forgotten her and said, "I'm Evelyn—Jessie's sister."

"Oh, yes. I know *you*. I'd *never* forget who *you* are. And you're welcome to the—pleasure." There was more irony—not just sarcasm—in his voice than she would have expected.

She lowered her eyes as she moved into his arms. "I've started apologizing this evening, and you're next on my list."

"Lucky me."

"Yes, you are lucky—lucky to have Jessie, not me. And she's lucky to have you. I apologized to her earlier, but I owe you too. I've known for years—knew at the time, even, in a crazy way—that I had no right to stop you and Jessie. And I want you to know now that I wish you every happiness."

"Thank you. Jess is happiness to me."

"I hope it stays that way."

"After all these years, it will."

She envied his certainty.

Marshall took her back to Jessie, announcing that he was expecting to be elected President any day since Evelyn had just given him her blessing. She blushed as Jessie hugged her. They sat and talked awhile about life in Houston and Jessie and Marshall's plans, and then the women went together to find a rest room.

While they were redoing makeup, Jessie said, "Now I want to hear about Lochinvar."

"At this point, he's ridden off alone."

Jessie squeezed her arm. "Oh, I'm sorry, Evie. What happened?"

Evelyn motioned toward the sofas, all mauve and celadon. They sat down, and she told Jessie everything, up through Rob's farewell. Unhappy as she was, it was good to tell Jessie; no one else that she could tell knew her so well, not even Judd.

"I'm sorry. What are you going to do now?"

Evelyn shrugged. "Get through each day as it comes. Grade papers, wait for grandchildren, and knit afghans." *Grow fat and old, ugly and mean.*

"Sounds like a living hell to me. You know, when I saw you last spring, you really seemed alive. Isn't there anything else you can do to live? Anybody else to love?"

"Would there be anybody else for you without Marshall?"

"Nobody else as good—as good for me, I mean. But yes, there'd be somebody. Or something. I don't intend to shrivel up and die till I have to. And you ought not either."

"I don't have much choice."

"You don't have any choice over what happens to you. You have a choice about what you do about it."

"Thank you, Reverend Wilson—if Wilson's what you're still going by. Now we'd better get back before someone thinks I've really gotten polluted tonight. Or Marshall comes looking for you." *No one will be looking for me.*

But Judd was. He was standing at the edge of the dance floor searching the crowd until he saw them, and then he moved toward her at their brisk walking gait.

"I wonder if you'll dance with me."

She still felt hard toward him. But his phrasing touched her. She raised her arms to him to show her acceptance. "That's about as tentative an invitation as I've gotten tonight."

"At least I'm aware of the thin ice I'm treading after overstepping when I called you the other day. But I wanted to see you to apologize for that. I know I had no right to ask you . . . anything. And I'm sorry."

"Your kindness has earned . . . rights. One of them is . . . closure on my confessions and release from the role of my confessor. Rob came by Monday to tell me that he's going to try to mend his marriage."

"I'm sorry for . . . the pain that must cause you. It's a brave thing for him to do; he won't have an easy time."

"No."

"As for closure and release, I've never assumed my role unwillingly. I'm available for rehire if you want."

"Thank you. I'll keep that in mind. But I don't intend to need a confessor again."

He didn't answer, and they danced in silence until the music stopped.

When the minister asked, "Who gives this woman to be wed?" Ward said, "Her mother and I do," and Evelyn thought, *That may be our last concerted act. Certainly publicly.* And the vows themselves reminded her of standing beside Ward in the same dress Elaine was wearing, swearing even to obey him until death. It had been a long time ago. Elaine and Bill both promised to love and cherish but not

323

to obey; they did say, "Till death do us part." The old words that Cranmer had translated for the Book of Common Prayer from the Use of Sarum reverberated like Shakespeare's words in her mind; the language was a comfort, but the substance pricked her. She had violated Rob and Marcia Lee's as well as her own vows, and the centuries of traditional marriages rolled in to crush her.

After the early supper at the college commons and the departure of the bride and groom, most of the out-of-town guests left too. Evelyn's bulging house emptied except for her parents, Ted, and herself. Her father and son went into the basement to talk planes; Ted was his grandfather's best audience for war stories.

Evelyn and her mother settled into the sunroom with coffee and orange juice respectively to watch the sunset and unwind.

Mother said, "What are you going to do now, Evelyn?"

"Clean up just enough to get through the weekend. Lucy's coming Monday instead of Thursday, bless her. Then maybe I'll make applesauce and freeze some apples for pies; the trees are loaded. I gave all the early apples away."

"No, I mean for the rest of your life."

"Have you been talking with Jessie?"

"No. Why?"

"Because she's been pestering me too."

"I don't think it's pestering to worry about my own daughter."

"Why are you worried about me? It's Elaine that's gotten married. My life will just go on the way it has."

"I'm worried because you look unhappy. Hurt. Drawn into your shell. Don't tell me you don't have a shell; you've always had one, and now you seem to be hiding there most of the time."

"I'm all right; I just need a routine to settle into. It's not a good time for me to have a sabbatical; I'd be better off knowing what I had to do now."

"You mean you don't want that free will you were touting in your version of solitaire."

"Free will's vastly overrated. You know somebody said we just want kind masters."

"Maybe what you need is a kind companion. It frightens me just to think about having to live without your father."

"Not everyone can have a storybook romance like yours."

"No, not everyone can have a love like mine. It's something that takes luck. And a lot of work—on both sides. But you could have someone. You must know Judd Adivino's just waiting for you to see him."

"If one more person throws Judd Adivino at me, I'm going to . . . to shut myself up in my room and never come out!"

Her mother fingered the juice glass. "I'm sorry, Evelyn. It just seems so . . . reasonable."

"I'm sick to death of being reasonable. I've been reasonable all my life. Most of it, anyhow."

"I'm sorry."

They sat in silence a moment, then her mother said, "You asked me about redecorating your old bedroom. Maybe we can make some plans about that before we leave tomorrow."

Evelyn accepted the truce. "Yes. Let's go look at it."

After her parents had left Saturday afternoon, Ted suggested that they both drive to the mountains the next day, Hailey with him, and Monday he would drive on to Durham while she and Hailey drove back to Meadorsville. "It'd be a real favor to me, Mom."

She said, "I see Judd's taught you how to manipulate people."

He grinned. "It was my idea. I'll get to see my two best girls a little longer."

"It sounds good to me. Are your things in good enough shape to pack and leave in the morning?"

"Absolutely. I just have to run a couple of tubs of laundry tonight."

"All right. I don't have to do much to get ready."

She made motel reservations in Gatlinburg for Sunday night and called Lucy to tell her where her check for cleaning the house would be and called Judd and told him both that she needed her exercise again and that she was going partway to Durham with Ted. She told herself that Judd had never in the slightest way forced himself on her, and he couldn't help it if everyone else seemed to be doing it for him. And she didn't know what she would do without him after Ted was gone. She worried about not being able to let Elaine know where she was. But then it wasn't likely that Elaine would be trying to get in touch with anyone before Wednesday, when she and Bill had to be back at Centre.

They reached Gatlinburg in plenty of time for a hike before dark. In one of the trips they had made with Ward during his studies of conifers, they had picked a favorite overlook with a pleasant walk down to a mountain creek, so she and Ted had no debate about where to go. They had visited and photographed the spot in all seasons, with dogwood blooms and trilliums, with summer weeds and swarms of insects, with blazing color, with fallen leaves and snow. Going there was almost like returning home.

As soon as she got out of the car, the chill reminded her that it was September in the mountains, and she got a sweater. Their breaths fogged in the air. *This is the death of the summer,* she thought.

They scrambled down the path between the tall skinny trees, the sun spotting the trunks and the plant-mottled ground. These were mixed deciduous—maple, locust, oak, ash, elm, hickory, sycamore, and tulip poplar—with patches of rhododendron and a scattering of hemlock.

The stream of clear water foamed white around the boulders strewn down its course and lay green in the still pools. Lichens, white on the gray granite, and mosses, chartreuse to forest black, had established their living invasions of the lifeless rocks. The chill air was empty of the clatter and buzz of civilization.

While Ted took Hailey upstream to show her the next waterscape, Evelyn sat on a dry rock at the side and watched the water. A rock shaped like a sarcophagus had caught a mass of driftwood that broke up the rushing water into spume and spray. The curves that the water had carved into the stone pleased Evelyn; she clambered down and felt them, then looked in the eddies for pretty rocks and picked up a few pieces of sand-pitted quartz.

Upstream where the banks pressed in, one huge boulder bore the flood. A profusion of water always cascaded over its jutting top. At the moment, sunlight was hitting the water and spray at the bottom of the falls.

Evelyn looked at the trillium leaves at her feet and remembered seeing their white and pink and waxy yellow blooms when snow-melt swelled the stream to a torrent. But even in a dry summer, water always poured over the boulder here.

She looked at the water and the sunlight and waited for Ted and Hailey, peace in her heart. When they came, she called them to her station and pointed out the landmarks, then said, "Ted, I have a request to make of you, and Hailey, you can witness. When I die, please cremate me and scatter my ashes on the bank here."

"You'll probably outlive us both, Mom."

"Well, I'm not planning on dying soon, but I certainly hope you outlive me. And I think being here will be a good end for me."

"It's probably illegal, Mom. This is a national park, you know."

"Yes, I know. But what I want is a lot more natural than being locked up in a metal box in ground made useless for anything else. The worst my ashes will do is make the soil a little more alkaline here."

Ted didn't say anything, but he reached for her and hugged her hard.

When they were saying good-bye the next morning, Ted told her, "Be nice to old Dr. Adivino, Mom. He's done a lot for you."

She nodded. *One more endorsement for the reasonable.* She turned to her car to leave him and Hailey to their farewells.

On the drive back with Hailey, she kept thinking, *He'll soon be gone too. He's a man already.*

After leaving Hailey at her home, Evelyn stopped by the near-deserted supermarket to replenish her bare larder. She rounded a corner and almost ran into Rob, who stood reading the label on a box. His startled expression brought back their meeting at the Firemen's Ice Cream Social, and she wheeled her cart around and pushed it to the checkout and left without even getting milk.

She lay on her bed that night picturing Rob as she had glimpsed him. She remembered every hair, every wrinkle in his unironed shirt. She wished that she could divorce herself from her traitorous body still wanting Rob. She wished that she could resign from living. *I'll just say, "No, I've had enough, thank you. Count me out." I can't bear seeing him again. I have to leave town, get away so there's no chance of running into him. I can't bear to live without him, and I can't bear to see him and know he'll never be mine again. I can't bear all the empty hours I'll have to spend without him.*

The next morning, Judd called her. "I'm going to a medical conference in Seattle next week. I was going to fly, but I'd rather drive if you'd go with me to keep me company and take turns at the wheel."

She thought a moment. "Yes. I'll go. I have to get away." *Well, why not? Whyever not? Anything to get away from here, so I never have to see Rob again.*

XX. Judd
The Going-to-the-Sun Road

*J*oe Carduci's owlish glasses and twitching mustache brought back memories of medical school exams and Anna, memories smelling of flowers and wine but also of formaldehyde and death. And Judd's frustration at being unable to help Anna. What good was it to be a doctor if he couldn't even save the woman he loved?

But he found nothing about Joe or Baltimore to remind him of Eva. That was what he had come for. He wanted to get away from her, from the love and pity and anger that seeing her filled him with. He couldn't go on loving her and seeing her, knowing that she loved Rob McFergus. It wasn't humanly possible to endure. Since the night of the fireflies he had wanted to get away from her almost as much as he wanted her.

So Joe's letter had seemed providential, and he had come to Baltimore as soon as he could to investigate the possibilities of joining Joe's practice there. It would be easy professionally; the two men had kept in touch through the years, seeing each other every time Anna's illness required her return to Hopkins, and Judd knew that Joe hadn't changed in values from the wisecracking Italian kid he'd met in his first college class. It was mostly their friendship that had made Joe decide to go into medicine in the first place. They had joked about the Catholic and the Jew keeping each other in line.

Spending some time at Hopkins again, he caught up on old friendships and new medicine. And Rachel and her family were there; they'd always been close, and there was no one like family, after all. They knew him best; they were most like him. Why not move back?

Leaving Meadorsville would be hard, though, aside from Eva. He had chosen a rural practice because of the close associations with his patients; he derived satisfaction from knowing two or three generations of the same family, knowing that relief of Mrs. Malvin's asthma depended on her getting out from under her mother-in-law's domination. And he himself was rooted in the life of the town; he would have to tear himself out of it at an age when he just wanted his life to be familiar. He would have to rebuild all his associations except those with Rachel and her family, his few cousins and remaining aunts and uncle, and Joe. And of course there would be pain as well as its alleviation in leaving Eva. But he wanted to quit even thinking about her.

He mentioned her to no one, not even Rachel, who had met her long before on some visit to Meadorsville. He visited all his relatives and Joe and Vickie and their children, who were all grown and some married like his niece and nephews. They stayed up late talking about old times. But the old jokes between them, the private meanings that kept friendship alive, popped up like faces he couldn't find the names for at first. The years were like a darkness that he had to feel his way through. Almost every morning he indulged himself by staying late in bed whether or not he could sleep. And he couldn't help thinking about Eva, wondering what she was doing, whether she missed him.

Although he didn't tell any of the other relatives about his possible relocation, he told Rachel, and she urged him to come, even offered him Josh's old room for as long as he wanted to stay with her and Sam.

Finally he decided that he didn't want to come. Being in the places he had been with Anna made him think of Eva almost as much as being at home. Since Anna was gone, Eva was all he had left. Being near her was better than being alone, even though she loved another man. And she might need him. So he thanked Joe, declined, said his good-byes, and went home.

From the time that Eva called him when Marcia Lee McFergus attempted suicide, he seesawed a thousand times, feeling for Eva and even for Rob McFergus, hoping for himself and not daring to hope. Her recognition that night of his love brought him a bitter peace: he knew that at last she knew and that she could not love him. He could live with that. At least she knew. And if she needed him, used him even, well, that was something. He told himself it was a kind of calm to know there was no more hope. He still loved her. He was the way he was.

Most of all, his hope dead, he felt alone. There was no one he could talk with, no one to share his life as Anna had shared it as long as he could remember until she died. Sharing their lives was what he wanted from Eva. But now his life was cut off from hers.

He knew he had been lying to himself when he saw McFergus's car at her house. He felt the old, painful, foolish hope rise; it had never died. Of course, he knew too that he shouldn't say anything to her: if she and McFergus had agreed to be lovers again, knowing would bring only pain, and if they had definitely parted, his best policy was patience, letting her wound heal. Nevertheless, he had to ask her. Her rebuff let him know at least that the meeting had hurt her. But that knowledge brought him no happiness. Then at the rehearsal dinner he felt dismissed: Eva was through with him, even if she didn't have McFergus.

When she called to tell him about her trip with Ted, he felt forgiven, needed, almost encouraged. The two days that she was gone, he debated about asking her to go with him to Seattle. He knew that he was taking advantage of an ebb in her resistance because both Ted and Elaine were gone. And the whole scheme was shaky, especially the route through Waterton-Glacier. He had been there with Anna, and he wanted to go with Eva. He wanted that much at least. And he had fought fair long enough. When she accepted, he knew that his happiness and its price were the same: being with her, knowing she didn't love him. He would pay.

He spent the rest of Tuesday morning arranging about his practice. Avery and Jim agreed to take care of his patients again, and Angela and Martha could handle the routine at the office.

He hurried through Earline's lunch and spent the afternoon lining up motel rooms. Eva had insisted from the first that she would pay part of the gas as well as all her own expenses, and of course he had known that she wouldn't share his room. But it wasn't easy to get two rooms at the same place on such short notice. So when he started in the Glacier area, he was surprised that his first call reserved rooms in St. Mary, right at the east entrance to the park. He and Anna had had to stay at Browning, over thirty miles away, even though he had made those reservations more than a month in advance.

The explanation for the easy reservations this time came when he called for rooms on the west side of the park. The clerk took his credit card number, then said, "You know, don't you, that's the last week we're open. You may have some trouble with the snow."

"This early?"

The man laughed. "We ain't in Tennessee, mister. The middle of September can be right nasty here."

Maybe the whole thing was impossible. He should take this as a sign that he ought to give it up. Give Eva up. "That's all right. I want the rooms." *I'll buy tire chains.*

"Okay, they're yours. Just call twenty-four hours in advance if you have to cancel."

The hurried departure limited his talk with Eva to arrangements. He warned her about taking warm clothes for the park, and he was somewhat relieved that she didn't wonder why they were going so far north when the main route to Seattle was farther south. She'd probably wonder when she looked at the map. But he'd cross that bridge when he came to it.

They were both tired after packing the car and didn't talk much the first day. He reflected that they had missed their walking, of course, for several days, and she had just driven back from Gatlinburg on Monday before setting out for the Rockies on Wednesday. *For Seattle. You have to remember that you're supposed to go to Seattle. Remember that you've told her you have to be in Seattle for your conference a week from tomorrow. What you'll do when you get there is your problem, doctor.*

When they did talk, he noticed that there were blank spots they couldn't fill in, like holes in a jigsaw puzzle when pieces were missing. They couldn't mention the McFerguses, and both of them shied away from references to their own relationship, past, present, or future.

They discussed the rapid change of the season from the dense green summer of home to withering yellow-brown, then frost-touched gold and orange as they moved farther north. She told him about a spot in the Smokies that she especially liked. She said she had told Ted she wanted her ashes scattered there, and Judd scanned her face to see what she meant.

But she said, "No, I'm not contemplating anything drastic again. You don't have to worry about my driving us into Puget Sound or something." She laughed, but sounded more rueful than mirthful.

They were rested after a good dinner in Chicago's Chinatown and a good night's sleep, and they agreed to spend the morning at the Art Institute. He enjoyed her enjoyment as well as the paintings themselves. They shared their favorites with each other; some they had both liked before, like a Monet landscape in which sunlight had warmed snow to rose.

The afternoon's drive, through Wisconsin mostly, was pleasant, and it was new territory for Eva. She commented on its similarity to home and was surprised after the flat Indiana and Illinois terrain. But then things leveled off north of Minneapolis, and except for the colorful Badlands, the landscapes for the next days were boring. The leaf color even narrowed to yellow: poplars, aspens, and birch, then just aspens. They stopped and walked for fifteen or twenty minutes several times a day for their circulation rather than taking their usual longer walk.

She talked more when she was driving than when he was. Sometimes she read or worked on the manuscript of her poems while he drove, and he was quiet then so as not to interrupt her. One day while she was driving, she asked him what he knew about the poet he was named for, and he had to confess that he knew very little. "Halevi wrote some religious poems that were used in the liturgy when I was a child, and if he'd been my contemporary, he'd have been called a Zionist: he left his home in Spain, wife, children, and all, to go to the Land of Israel. But he died somewhere in Egypt, so he never got there."

"That's sad. He died unfulfilled."

"Yes." He wasn't inclined to pursue that line; it would stay a blank in their jigsaw picture.

"And he was a physician too?"

"Yes, but my Uncle Judah wasn't; he was named for him more directly than I. There was another Sephardic Jew who combined poetry and medicine, but his name was Moses: Moses Maimonides." He thought of the *Mishneh*, the Book of Ahavah, the Book of Love. Ahavah; Eva. That was as close as he would ever get to poetry.

The afternoon sun shone on her untanned hands. On their backs, red and blue showed under the skin. Where her ringless fingers extended beyond the steering wheel, the sun shone through like a flashlight hidden in the hand. Her nails, never polished, were rosy, and the red-lit flesh itself seemed to give out light. *Flesh. Just flesh. Like Anna's, perishable as the wax of a candle. Not mine to keep. Not even to have.*

She kept her hands at the prescribed ten- and two-o'clock positions. The right hand curved around the wheel, but the left was only hooked over it, stiff-fingered.

"Do the joints of your left hand ache, Eva?"

She looked at them. "Yes . . . I guess they do. How did you know?"

"The way you're holding the wheel, as if it hurt to grip it."

"I hadn't thought about it. But the knuckles and wrists of both hands hurt sometimes. I guess it's arthritis."

He questioned her and advised her about minimizing permanent damage.

334

When he finished, she asked, "How much do I owe you for this consultation, doctor?"

"I'll deduct it from the bill you send for keeping me company."

At Glendive, Montana, they were to leave the interstate and cut up via state roads to US 2. Before dinner, they walked in the park; that day's driving had taken less time than he expected, and he had planned some time for the park. When they first arrived there, some of the cactus blooms were still open.

She had been wearing her hair in a ponytail instead of her usual upsweep, and it was hanging in front alongside her throat. It reminded him of a sable toque and neckpiece that Anna had. But Evelyn's hair was more like something living, like a black squirrel's tail. Maybe that was the difference between Anna and Evelyn: an urban sophistication and a rural naturalness.

He told Evelyn about stopping in that same park with Anna eleven years before.

She said, "I always liked Anna a great deal. She's one of your chief attractions, you know." She smiled, and he permitted himself a small congratulation for the first personal reference. He noticed that she was wearing her old perfume again, not the sharper scent she had started using that year.

She asked when he had met Anna, and he told how they had grown up together, attending the same school and synagogue and playing with and pestering each other while their parents visited. "She was almost like a sister to me. We knew everything about each other. And it was more than just being together; it was that we were alike, as if each was the other's second self."

"I've known two men like that."

He ventured, "Not Ward." *And not me.*

"No, Ward was never like me in most ways. The first was a boy I knew in college, after Ward and I were engaged."

She didn't go on, and he didn't ask who the second was. *Maybe we can never say Rob McFergus's name to each other again. I can't if she doesn't.* He looked at that hole in their puzzle. It seemed to blank out the whole center of the picture.

She shivered. "We'd better go back to the motel and eat."

The next morning was overcast, and it became obvious within their first hour of driving that snow was likely. It began as hard little pellets spitting at them, but as the day advanced and warmed, the flakes grew larger and wetter. The sun struggled with the storm cloud and eventually won. He and Eva congratulated themselves that the slight accumulation would soon melt. But he worried about the mountains ahead; the higher elevations would be colder.

Eva didn't seem worried. She praised the more varied scenery and a good lunch; they had delicious soup at a little log restaurant/gas station at the intersection of the highway and a smaller road, and the view of the mountains ahead was spectacular.

That afternoon she read him some of her poems. He wanted to understand them and asked her about them; he often had to ask her to read them several times. He didn't know whether they moved him because they were good or because they showed him things about her. One she had written when Ward's father had died. She called it "Snowmen," and she didn't have to tell him that she was talking about everyone dying:

> In the winter dawn you lie asleep.
> I think of the whitehaired man
> Who gave to you the form
> He kept himself, but cannot keep
> This snow-chilled morn.
>
> The warm white bedspread falls and lifts
> As you sleep formless now
> Beside me. Form is I know
> The strongest, shortest of our gifts
> While earth bears snow.

He told her he liked that poem best, and she asked why.

"Probably because it's so close to what I see every day. Form is, I take it, the body, life, and I work to try to hold that. But I see it lost every day too, claimed by snow, melting like snow, so I know how short it lasts. How strong its . . . gifts can be. Snow has its own form, its own beauty too."

"Yes." She was silent, then added, "You make a pretty good explicator of poems, doctor."

"Thank you." He prized the praise.

They couldn't reach St. Mary by dinnertime, so they stopped at Shelby, and over dinner she asked why they had taken the northern route. He had his answer ready; the truth, he had decided, would serve best. "I wanted to show you Glacier Park. There's time to go through it tomorrow, and we'll go back the faster way. No point retracing our steps exactly."

"No, no point at all."

He relaxed. However, he was still worried about the drive to St. Mary. He shouldn't have planned to cover so much in one day.

Although they arrived late, it was all right. They didn't run into snow, the car continued to take the grades well, and US 89 was a decent highway. Eva seemed relaxed; indeed, she fell asleep before they reached the motel. His luck was holding.

That night he dreamed about Anna. She was helping him pack for a trip, her small, deft hands folding his shirts. When he kissed her good-bye, he said, "I'll see you tomorrow."

She said, "Maybe I'll leave before then." She was laughing.

He laughed too. "I'll follow you, you know." He could feel her ribs as she lifted her arms to him again.

His first thought the next morning was that he had overslept; light filled the room, although its window faced the west. When he looked at his watch, it was not late. Then he realized with a sinking feeling that the light must be reflected off snow.

The unblemished expanse outside, as blank as the holes in their jigsaw picture, confirmed his fears. At worst, they wouldn't be able to get through the park on the Going-to-the-Sun Road. At best, they wouldn't be able to see some of the places he had wanted to show her.

"I'm sorry I've gotten you into this mess," he said when she opened her door.

She smiled. "So now you're causing the weather as well as prognosticating it."

"What do you mean?"

"Your name, oh thou diviner of things to come. Have you forgotten our talking about the fogs of August and the caterpillars last summer?"

Her smile and tone reassured him. Perhaps there was hope for the day after all. "Do you have warm clothes?"

"Yes, even boots. How are your tires?"

"Good. Radials new last month. And I have chains."

"Well, then, what's the problem? It's not a mess; it's an adventure. Let's get started! Not without breakfast, though—I'm starved to death. Must be the mountain air."

Despite her cheerfulness, his anxiety didn't lift until the rangers at the St. Mary Visitor Center reassured him that the Going-to-the-Sun Road was passable unless it snowed more. Even then he noticed the qualification. And they warned that the western side of the mountains always got more snow than the eastern. His guilt over the whole scheme nagged him; he really didn't deserve success.

As he drove up the mountains with Eva, his spirits rose too. He had forgotten the marvel of the road, how it climbed steadily through the granite and gneiss, raising them almost effortlessly up among the stark peaks. These mountains were not so tall as Colorado's Fourteeners nor so ruggedly jagged as the Tetons, but their unbroken, treeless slopes were as uncompromisingly solid as the Pyramids. He had forgotten their names; Eva tried to distinguish

them by examining the map. She was fascinated by the words themselves, particularly those translated from the Blackfeet names: Bird
Woman Falls and mountains named Rising Wolf, Little Chief, and
Going to the Sun. She wondered what Appekunny and Kootenai
and Kintla meant. Redgap Pass reminded her of the Redhorn, a
mountain in a story she said she'd liked as a child, and she asserted
that the names of Singleshot Mountain and Two Medicine Lake had
to refer to stories.

"Maybe you'll write a poem about the names."

"Oh, yes. I'll take notes. You were right, Judd; I've gotten too ingrown living in my own little world. I should have left Meadorsville
sooner." She looked down, and the light went out of her face. He
knew she was thinking of the summer's catastrophes.

He pulled off the road at the first turnout, and they got out to walk
along the stone guard wall. She walked ahead, and he watched her;
she seemed small against the looming mountains. At the guard wall
she turned and called, "Come look!" Her voice too seemed small,
lost in the vastness. He walked toward her.

One advantage of the snow was that they had seen only two other
cars except for a ranger vehicle, and they were alone at the turnout. He enjoyed the silence, deeper than any he could remember.
There was no electrical hum of fluorescent lights or murmur of air-
conditioning fans. No power lines or advertisements broke the view.
The unmarred snow stretched as far as they could see; it was only a
couple of inches deep on the road, but he knew it must be deeper on
the peaks. They were alone in a silent, beautiful world.

He wanted to reach for her, put his arms around her. But he didn't
dare. He couldn't assume that she felt any of what he felt. Not since
the night of the fireflies.

She turned the dark blanks of her sunglasses toward him and said,
"Judd—"

"What?" He looked into the valley, not wanting her to see his
thoughts.

"Nothing. Oh, look! What are they?"

He turned toward the direction of her gesture. "Mountain goats."

They were bounding down the slope above them, stopping on the highway to sniff the air and examine the temporary invaders of their habitual world. Evidently reassured by Judd and Eva's stillness, a few wandered around; some stood like heavy-coated statues, and one sprang onto the top of the stone wall, gave them a sardonic look, and plummeted down the mountainside, landing on a ledge dizzyingly far below them.

"Oh! How can he do that?" Her whisper was awed.

"He trusts . . . his own powers and his world." Something ached inside him, but he knew he couldn't call it his heart. Maybe it was just another blank spot. He turned toward the car without looking at her again.

From his trip with Anna he remembered the tundra exhibit, the wonderful, intensely colored flowers he had seen there with her. Smaller than the blatant penstemon, lupines, monkey flowers, paintbrushes, and shooting stars that they had seen at lower altitudes on that trip, these alpine flowers clung to the earth, hoarding their energy to explode in the burst of their blooms. Even blue burned when it was mountain forget-me-nots.

But he would not be able to see these with Eva. Their brief season must be over. It was, after all, fall. September. How had he thought that flowers could bloom in September?

Still, he parked the car near the Garden Wall, and they got out to walk on the fenced path lined with sterner commands than the KEEP OFF THE GRASS signs in the usual park, signs telling of the struggle for life on solid rock at eight thousand feet above sea level on the forty-ninth parallel. Eva walked silently ahead of him, her arms crossed in front of her jacket, a red scarf and her sunglasses hiding her. She slowed or stopped to read the posted lessons, mostly warning that careless steps could crush twenty years' growth.

And there were no flowers. The wind and sun had removed most of the snow; all they could see was the scrubby, woody plants, pale green and small-leaved. He looked at them and voiced his reflection. "It makes you wonder what's the use."

"What do you mean?"

340

"Why bother? They grow for twenty years, and this is all they are. And we could kill them with a few careless strides. Or the goats or sheep may eat them tomorrow." He felt empty.

"Ward said once that the purpose of life is to perpetuate life. I hated that; it seems so pointless. Now I think it all depends on what you mean. If it's just to go on replicating what's there because it has existed, there's no point. To grow, to change, to be part of a variety— that's a point, though. The lichens come first on the rock, and then mosses, and then little creeping things like these—Ward would be able to name them; I can't—and sometime maybe there are flowers and someday even trees. Remember, I was just in the Smokies. They're old mountains, worn down and not so dramatic, but full of life."

"These plants bloom."

"Well, there you are then. There's a point."

They were walking back along the narrow path when she stopped and turned toward him. "How do you know they bloom?"

"Anna and I saw them eleven years ago."

"And now you brought me here. You're taking me all the places you went with her."

He knew it had been a mistake, and he was afraid she knew it too. He braced himself. "Yes. I brought you here too."

She looked at him a moment, her eyes behind the mirrors of the glasses, then turned and resumed walking.

He held one of the missing puzzle pieces; there was no place to fit it in.

Before they ate lunch in the Logan Pass Visitor Center, Judd had to check with the rangers about the road to the west. When they said it was clear and no more snow was expected, his spirits lifted. They still had half a day.

Eva said she wanted a souvenir and bought a sweatshirt showing evergreens in front of the peaks at the pass. Keeping to her passion for words, she chose one that labeled each mountain and had the park name emblazoned on the back.

She spread it over her chest and told him, "Elaine would say I was

341

guilty of false advertising. When her friends began going through puberty, she and Ted used to rank them on a scale from the Grand Tetons to the Great Plains." She laughed.

He thought of her small, shapely breasts and looked away. It wasn't very sensitive of her to make that joke to him.

The hot lunch fortified them, and they got into the car again. He asked if she would like to hike a little around Lake McDonald before they left the park. He had originally planned to go with her to Grinnell Glacier and its little emerald lakes, Grinnell, Josephine, and something, as he and Anna had. He had given that up in the morning; it would have required their taking another road altogether, a risky side road. And since seeing the bloomless tundra flowers, he realized that what he had really wanted was to find at the edge of the ice the pure yellow glacier lilies, like spring's trout lilies at home, to see them with Eva as he had with Anna. He should have known better. Flowers that were gone couldn't be found again. They were lost, like other pieces of the picture he had wanted to make.

The afternoon's drive took them down the west side of the Continental Divide after the morning's east. There were more trees on the west, mostly evergreens. Lake McDonald was much less exposed than St. Mary Lake at the east because of the surrounding trees.

The snow was gone—had melted or had never fallen on this side. The air was still chill when they got out and began walking around the lake, and it was windy. Eva kept her arms clasped in front of her body, coiled into herself.

They rounded a wooded bend and saw a black long-haired, long-legged dog playing at the edge of the lake. He was running into the water and snapping at the waves.

"Do you think he's trying to catch a fish?" Eva asked.

"I don't know."

They stood and watched him awhile. He would chase along the

342

length of a wave and try to bite it, then run back to his starting point.

Eva said, "Maybe he's a retriever—part water spaniel or some such."

"Looks like useless activity to me," Judd said.

"Maybe it's just a game. Maybe being here in the sunlight trying to hold on to the sparkle of the water is enough."

He thought about the alpine flowers. He kicked the pebbles in the moraine at his feet, then squatted to look at them. They were sedimentary, layers of green, red, and gray, flat, with edges rounded by the water and worn smooth. He picked out a wedge-shaped one, stood up, handed it to her, and began walking again.

As they walked, she continued to look at it and rub it between her thumb and fingers. She put her hand on his arm to stop him, held it out, and said, "Look at how smooth it is, how wonderful. It's lain here forever with no one to pay any attention to it. It's been beautiful just the same." She took off her glasses and looked up at him waiting for . . . he didn't know what.

He didn't dare to think that she meant anything personal. Then he knew he had to find out. He couldn't let the chance go by, even if he lost . . . everything. "It doesn't matter to the stone whether you see it or not."

She took up his meaning. "It matters to you though."

His heart thumped. "Yes. It has mattered for a long time."

"And for a long time I didn't see you. But I'm looking now." She was, her eyes as blue as the flowers he and Anna had seen in the tundra.

He stepped ahead and turned to face her, framing his next question in his mind. Then as he pivoted on his left foot, the heavy sole of his hiking boot caught on the side of a rock and he felt himself losing his balance. *Some mountain goat you'd make.* A pain shot through his leg, and he came down on his arm. He thought, *Old fool!* Then there was nothing.

XXI. Evelyn
The Miraculous Staircase

*W*hen Judd first went down, he lay so still that she thought he was dead, and her feelings poured over her like a waterfall—fear and guilt and anguish and frustration. *He can't be dead; he has to know that I've changed my mind!* Then she found his pulse. Though relieved, she realized the problem of getting help for him. Even if she could have carried him, she would have been afraid of injuring him more. She couldn't bear to leave him there alone while she tried to get help. Maybe a ranger would see their car pulled off the road. No one might come looking for hours, maybe even days.

She wondered if the dog they had watched by the lake had an owner nearby. Retracing her steps, she saw him and whistled, and he trotted up, tongue lolling, tail wagging. She let him sniff her, then felt for a collar. There was one. It said CHARLIE and gave a telephone number. *A lot of good that is! Though it means his owner has a phone.* She didn't know whether or not it was a local exchange.

And what could she do next? The dog couldn't tell her where to go.

She stood up and called, "Hello! Is anybody there?" Her voice lost itself among the trees, but she called again anyhow, and again. The

344

dog rested on his haunches and watched her, friendly. Maybe he could show her the way. "Charlie! Go home! Go home, boy!"

He got up and came over and nuzzled her hand, and she repeated, "Go home, boy! Go home!"

He turned and began to trot off into the trees. *What if I get lost? Then there'd be no help for Judd.* Her heart pounded as she followed him. She stopped and noted the position of the sun. *I'll follow him for ten minutes.* She looked at her watch. He waited for her to catch up.

Although the route he took wasn't a path, at least the forest floor was clearer than in the tangled Southern woods she knew. And she was wearing hiking boots. She checked the sun every few minutes, and he seemed to be going in a straight line.

When they came out of the trees and she saw the house and gravel road, she said, "Oh, Charlie! You're a good boy, such a good boy." She would have hugged him had he not danced on ahead of her, danced toward the wonderful, beautiful house.

In the small hospital in West Glacier, scarcely more than a clinic, Evelyn watched Judd through the anxious first hours. He had a concussion as well as a break in the left forearm and strained tendons in that leg. She kept the pebble he had given her in her pocket and rubbed it; at least he had provided her with a worry stone. She didn't really believe the doctors' assurances that he would be all right; she didn't deserve for him to be.

Miraculously, he seemed fine. He had fallen on Monday afternoon, and on Tuesday morning not long after she awoke in the chair by his bed, he stirred, yawned, and opened his eyes as though nothing had happened. Then he blinked and said, "Where am I?"

Her relief lifted her heart. "That's a clichéd line if I ever heard one."

"What happened?"

"If this is the best you can do, I might as well go talk to somebody else. You're in the hospital, doctor, taking some of your own medicine. As for what happened, you tumbled down and hit your head and broke your arm."

He couldn't remember falling or even stopping at the lake.

345

However, he could remember, and told her, that that was frequently the result of a fall: "The patient may never remember the trauma itself or events preceding the trauma."

"Maybe in this case that's just as well."

"What does that mean?"

She smiled. "Oh, nothing. Maybe it'll keep you humble. Now I'd better call the nurse. All this talk may not be good for you."

He ate a small breakfast and kept it down, a good sign as both he and the nurse told her. Evelyn judged that he was rational and began asking him about their reservations for the trip. "We paid for two unused motel rooms last night, and we don't want to do that for the rest."

He didn't make the expected joke about thrifty Scots; he did tell her where the list of reservations was. He also asked her to telephone Avery West and Jim Bonnette and tell them what had happened. "They're taking care of my patients."

"And what about your conference? Do I need to notify anyone that you won't be there?"

He looked at her as if resigned to the guillotine. "I guess it's time to pay the piper. I lied to you, Eva. There's no conference. I just thought you needed to get away, and I . . . wanted to be with you."

She laid her hand on his for a moment but spoke accusingly. "Well, we'll settle that score one of these days. You lied!"

"I'm sorry, Eva. I know I had no right to." He was looking down.

"Of all the people in the world, I would have thought you would be the last. It's a great reassurance to know you're human, you know. Now I'll have to think about what your lie deserves."

"I'm sorry I've spoiled your trip. You should go on without me. It was really California you wanted to see anyhow, wasn't it?"

"We'll talk about that when you're better. Just rest now." She considered kissing him good-bye but only smiled and squeezed his hand.

Dr. Carpenter wanted to keep Judd in the hospital for observation another day, so that night Evelyn slept in her previously unused room at the West Glacier motel. She canceled all their other reservations, the ones for the trip back too, since she didn't know when he'd be able to go.

She called Angela at Judd's office and told her, then asked her to tell Dr. West and Dr. Bonnette.

Angela asked, "Is there anything else, Mrs. Knight?"

Evelyn hesitated. She didn't want all her bridges burned. "Angela, I'd appreciate it if you didn't mention to anyone that I'm with Dr. Adivino. You know how people gossip." *Angela's not a gossip herself; still, it's not likely this will stay secret, anyhow.*

"Of course, Mrs. Knight."

Now I've set her mind wondering at least. Oh, well. The whole town probably knows about me and Rob anyhow. This is far less harmful. Truth is, it's perfectly upright, though scarcely circumspect.

And he made up the whole conference! The sly old fox!

Because of Judd's concussion, Dr. Carpenter warned him to delay traveling for a few more days. Evelyn couldn't get a second room at their motel, her room had only one bed, and that motel was closing for the winter after the weekend anyhow; if they had to stay longer, she would have to move them sooner or later. So she found another motel and reserved a large room with kitchenette and two beds for Judd's release from the hospital. *The worst that could happen is that I'll be embarrassed,* she thought. She told him that she hadn't been able to get two rooms. One lie deserved another.

His face was expressionless. "That's all right."

Like many of the motel rooms and cabins they had stayed at in the West, this one had no television set. Before, neither had regarded that as a drawback; the first night Judd was out of the hospital, though, she wished for a diversion. The arrangement was somewhat awkward; she told herself that it would be all right as soon as they

347

got things straight between them anyhow. He seemed strong enough to deal with a little stress.

She was the one who wasn't ready just yet. She needed some time or some sign or something. Maybe she had misread him entirely; he had kept looking off into the distance all during the trip, maybe wishing she were Anna, realizing she was a mistake. She said, "Do you suppose they have some games in the motel office? Maybe I should check."

"That sounds good. Or maybe there's something in a drawer."

She had unpacked their clothes and put them into the dresser, but she hadn't looked in the other storage places. In one of the kitchen cabinets she found a box containing an assortment of dirty plastic poker chips, a deck of cards, and a small, strange-looking walnut board with holes in rows and three pegs.

"Do you know what this is, Judd?"

His face lit up as he reached for it. "It's a cribbage board. I haven't played for years, but when I was growing up, I used to go down to the fire station close to my house and play cribbage with one of the firemen almost every afternoon."

"How do you play? Is it like Chinese checkers, so you jump the pegs?"

"No, the board is just for scoring; it's a card game. You probably wouldn't like it; Anna never did."

Much as she had liked Anna, she was tired of comparison. "But I'm not she."

"No." He looked at her soberly. "Do you want to learn? It's a good two-person game."

"Yes. Let's try it."

"All right. First, we'll need another peg. You look through the box, and I'll see if I can find one in the cabinet or a wooden matchstick to make one out of."

She thought about taking over his task herself; it cost him such effort to move or bend his left leg. He had insisted earlier, when they were moving in, that he had to work the soreness out. So she concurred: "And I'll count the cards to be sure there's a full deck."

They sat at the small table, the board between them, and he explained the game to her. It was about seeing relationships, putting things together to make them count for something. And the counting itself was elaborate; on each play, they could count values or matches or runs with each other's cards, and after the hand was played, they counted again the original cards they had held. And there were scores for things like playing the last card, the opponent's having to say *go*, and turning up the right starting card.

He said, "You'll have to do all the dealing, though I think I can hold my cards in my left hand. Show me your cards this hand, and we'll practice before we really play."

She dealt the six cards and discarded two into the crib as he advised her. He tried to explain why they were the best to discard since as the dealer, she would get the crib. Then he turned up the top card from the stack, which he called the stock. "This card is called the starter," he said.

"Like yeast for sourdough." She liked the analogy.

As he continued to explain and they played, she began to catch on. The words interested her as much as the game. "Why do they call the jack *his nobs* or *his heels* in those situations? Do you know the origin of the terms?"

He shook his head. "There are other unusual terms I haven't told you about, too. If you win—peg scores all around the board—before I get halfway, I'm *lurched.*"

"We don't want that to happen; you've lurched already, and look where it's landed you." She laughed cheekily.

"Very funny. Something else undesirable is muggins. If I overlook a possible score in my play and you see it, you can say 'Muggins!' and claim it for yourself."

She said, "That sounds all right to me. But you're less likely to overlook a score than I am."

"No, I couldn't claim it. At least, while you're still learning. The rules specify mercy for inexperienced players."

"Well, that's very kind of the rules. I need all the mercy I can get."

"Also, if you have a hand and there's nothing you can count, you say, 'I have nineteen,' which means no score, because nineteen is the first possible total that won't count anything."

Maybe that's what I've been holding, she thought. *Or is it just that I've deserved muggins all this time for not seeing what I held?* She deliberately slowed her words; she couldn't slow the pounding of her heart. "I don't think I want to play after all."

"Of course. I'm sorry I've kept you up." He didn't look at her but started gathering his cards by pushing them against the edge of the board.

Her hand over his stopped him. "I don't want to quit because I'm tired; there's something else I want to play." She stroked his hand, tracing the raised veins along its back, then looked at him, questioning. His expression hurt her heart; it showed the anguish she must have cost him. She got up and went around the table to him. He stood up, and she put her arms around his neck and kissed him.

"Oh, Eva. Oh, my Eva. My Eva." His good arm clasped her, and his fingers cupped her hip as they kissed again.

When they broke apart, he said, "Now you'll never know if you'd have won."

"I don't care about a game; I'm winning what I want."

"Maybe not. I don't know if I can oblige you in my crippled condition."

"You just keep your arm out of the way, and I'll do the work tonight. You'll have time later to do your share."

Both were happy with her labor. As they lay together afterward, he asked, "What made you—turn to me?"

"I'd have to be a stone-hearted woman to resist you after you literally threw yourself at my feet."

"Then it's because you feel sorry for me."

"No, actually I realized several days ago that I want you. It was after one of those interminable drives across the flatlands, and I dreamed I was falling through the air carrying a suitcase that held all I owned, all my books and clothes as well as several paychecks I hadn't yet cashed. And all at once the suitcase was gone. I had lost everything. I thought, *I'm wearing my good gray suit.* You know the one—Pendleton, classic, wool; you've seen it a thousand times. And everything was all right. I was fine as long as I had my good gray suit. And when I woke up, I knew that suit was you."

He didn't say anything, and she said, "Don't you believe me?"

"Oh, yes. I believe you. If you'd made it up, you could have made it more flattering, I guess."

She smoothed her hand across his chest. "I finally realized that the only thing wrong with you is that everyone else saw that you were right for me before I did." *Reasonable. That's what Mother said.*

He took his good arm from under her and propped up his head. "So—you decided this was the best thing for you to do."

"Yes. I'd been trying to let you know several times before you fell, but whenever I started to say something, you got a sort of determined look—set your mouth—and stared off into nowhere. Till what I said made you turn and fall."

"I still can't remember that."

She began with the pebble from the moraine and told him, ending, "What were you going to say when I told you I was looking at you then?"

"I don't remember. What I want to ask now is, Since you *have* looked at me, what do you see?"

"I see the kindest man I know. I see that you ought to be called Job. You've been more patient with me than is human."

"There was nothing for me to do except be patient; I love you."

"I know. You've known the worst about me, and you still love me."

"I thought you'd never notice."

He's teasing, but he's accusing and telling me his pain too. That's the price of my selfishness—my taking from him regardless of his feelings. I would have lost his love if it weren't uncommon. I deserved to lose it.

In the morning he was awake and looking at her when she opened her eyes, and he persuaded her to work for them again. Then he began learning her body with his fingers and lips.

When he was kissing her breast, she said, "I don't have much there to offer you."

"You're just right. Women always think they're too little or too big. Men always think they're too little."

"You aren't."

He lay back on his pillow. "I'm jealous of . . . your young man's body, you know. You've had better."

The irony of the phrase hurt her. "Call him Rob. He's not my young man."

"I suppose I don't want to call his name because it might . . . invoke him, conjure him up. I want to blot him out."

She sat up and began caressing him then. "Your body pleases mine. For several days, you've been making me feel the way nice girls aren't supposed to. Actually, my body seems the easiest part of me to please. Any number of mindless louts could probably satisfy it." She laughed.

"I'm glad I'm one of the crowd at least."

She looked at him; his eyes were closed. *So what does this make me? I've slept with three men, two in the past few months. Would have slept with Greg too. Just a slut! But it doesn't mean the same thing, loving Rob and loving Judd. And if I could have Rob back? If things worked out somehow? How can I love two men at once?*

She kissed his cheek and got up.

She had boundless vitality. She got books for them both at the library, read, worked on her manuscript, wrote new poems, wrote letters to Ted and Elaine. She didn't tell them about her changed relationship to Judd. The poems were about breaking with Rob, about the trip, mostly about Judd. She wrote one about cribbage that she gave him; she knew she never would submit it for publication anywhere. He looked at her when he had read it, and his eyes told her that he understood.

He didn't mention marriage. And she didn't open the subject either. Perhaps he would have to wait. She had hurt him long and deeply, first without knowing, then even after she knew. It was her turn to be patient.

And perhaps marriage wasn't the answer. Perhaps she should plan a life without marriage. Certainly they could go on being lovers for as long as they wanted to, living in their separate houses, conveniently close. Having their separate lives. Their freedom.

As long as we want to. Meaning there might be an end. Love isn't undying. I loved Ward once. I know my love isn't strong enough that it can't die.

Judd isn't Ward. He will help me keep on loving him. He's loved me in spite of myself.

Real love ought to be independent of its object. Like his for me.

You're not that good, Evelyn. Judd may have been. You're not. That's what you call God.

Because she had to do all the driving on the way back, it took longer than the drive west. They stopped earlier every day too since they had not made advance reservations. She didn't mind; she lived in the moment, taking each day's pleasures as they came. She found those days full of ordinary pleasures, talking with Judd, learning about his years before Meadorsville, learning about his work and people he knew that she hadn't seen him with, learning about him. She realized that, as well as she had known him for years, she hadn't really seen him until she recognized him as part of her own life. Now she felt at rest in him, like water that has run downhill and found its own level in a quiet lake.

There was still a reserve in him, a barrier. She saw him sometimes draw into himself, studying something. She blamed herself; steadfast though he had been and still was, she had hurt him, and she would have to prove herself now to win his trust. *Going to bed together didn't solve everything. So when did it ever?*

She drove long after dark the last night to reach home, and she unloaded his luggage, unpacked what he had to have right away, helped him into his pajamas, and kissed him good night before she went home, tired but content. When she unloaded her own things from his car, she noticed that the night seemed strangely warm. Then she remembered that they had driven five hundred miles south that day; it was still the first half of October, and it wouldn't even have frosted yet. She'd have to see in the morning what it was like. The night smelled cidery from the apples that must have fallen, unworked and ungiven. It was a shame that they had gone to waste.

The air was clear of the fogs of August and September. The morning was not hot. Trees were as green as when they had left; the dahlias and gladioli were still blooming. She cut some and filled vases for the living room and sunroom. She called Judd and asked him to join her for lunch; he pled pressing work but invited himself to dinner. *So he*

feels at ease with me. And still wants to see me. She was surprised that evidently some part of her had doubted.

She watered the houseplants; she had brought home the ones from the office after Rob's last visit to her, and Lucky had cared for them all while she was gone. She was glad that they seemed to have recovered from their malaise after Granny's death, even the spathiphyllum on which she had done radical surgery. Then she called Nina Wilton to make an appointment to talk about art lessons.

In the afternoon she drove to the grocery to restock perishables and get something for dinner. Planning to tease Judd about the spurious trip to Seattle, she chose Pacific salmon despite the out-of-season price.

Then she walked to the college. She had no idea of Rob's hours but avoided Will Hall, especially her office; she could go there some evening or weekend. Her first destination was the library. She looked for books on Judaism and Sephardic culture. She found several: some on ritual and theology, a translation of Judah Halevi's poetry, and a cookbook.

Her second purpose was to talk with Nina. She had missed the chance to enroll in studio art classes for fall semester, but she still envisioned the illustration of Anna and Gurov for the Chekhov story, and other images crowded her mind, memories of childhood scenes and figures and objects that she could take only as symbols that she wanted to paint.

Nina worked out a plan with her. She could attend sessions of Nina's first drawing course at once, catching up on what she had missed as best she could with reading and Nina's help. She would be spending six hours a week in the studio, plus the time it took for her to make up the work already covered. For Design and Color, Nina recommended reading the text whenever she had time now and waiting to audit the course along with Drawing II spring semester.

After they had finished their plans, Nina asked her, "Why all this interest in visual arts? You have your poetry for expression, and you control it well."

"That's just the problem; I control it. I use words to do what I tell them to; I manipulate them. I want a medium I can't control to tell me what I don't consciously know already. Does that make any sense?"

"Yes, it sounds like another way of trying to know oneself."

354

"Exactly. I have to know what I am in order to become whatever I'm to be. And I've been too good at deceiving myself into thinking I know what I am already when I don't have the faintest idea."

"Sounds like the normal human condition to me. I hope that art can help tell you."

"There's something else about art too. Keats's odes deal with the distance that it puts between the artist and the natural world—the alienation of Ruth from her surroundings when she listens to the bird, the frozen objects on the Grecian urn. My words all carry other art with them, in them, other poems and stories and plays. Dealing with an unfamiliar medium will force me to look again at reality itself, not something derived through the art of words. I need that."

Clear as the morning had been, it had rained while she was in Nina's office. Now the air was warm, humid, like summer again.

As they walked that night, she told Judd about her conversation with Nina.

He said, "Anna was interested in painting before—her illness."

"I've been thinking of her a great deal lately. Probably . . . I'm jealous. You've shared more with her than we'll ever have together."

"Then I should be jealous of Ward."

"No. You and Anna *shared*. And I'm jealous of Anna's . . . soul, spirit, whatever. I want to know what made you love her."

"My history has repeated itself. I got to know her over the years, and when we were old enough, I realized I loved her. The same with you."

"Well, we're certainly old enough."

"That's not what I meant. I see I'll have to be more careful with my words with you."

She reached out to touch his arm. "No, dear one. I'm the one who needs to change. I knew what you meant. But it touched me so much that I had to make light of it. I've grown . . . afraid to accept tenderness. I need to be able to take it so I can give it back without masking it in humor."

He caught her hand.

She went on, "What touches me is that you know the very worst about me, my selfishness and thoughtlessness, and you still love me."

"Yes. I love you."

His quiet tone and the very simplicity of the words pleased her. She absorbed them.

He let go her hand and said, "Eva, do you love me?"

"Why, of course. Why else would I have gone to bed with you?"

He shook his head.

She thought, *I could just say it. "I love you." But it's not necessary.*

They walked a minute or two in silence. Then he said, "You don't have to be jealous of Anna. I let go of her before I realized I loved you. I think in some ways I let go of her before she was gone, during those long years I knew she was going. Sometimes I even blamed her for going, I think."

Like Rob's mother. Well, if I have to profit from Anna's death, I'll take that. I bear no responsibility for it, at least. She caught his hand again. "I won't go unless I have to. I'll do whatever the doctor orders to prevent ever having to leave you." She smiled at him, and he squeezed her hand.

She thought about Rob that night after Judd fell asleep on her pillow, thought of Rob's loneliness and guilt. *At least I have to make sure he doesn't feel guilty about leaving me. I need to tell him . . . what? That I'm free of him? That I've replaced him? That doesn't seem kind. Is it even true?* She lay awake a long time trying to decide what she had to tell him and fell asleep before she succeeded.

The next morning she telephoned his office. She heard the altered ring that meant the call would roll over to the department secretary the next time, and she hung up; Wilda would of course recognize her voice. But then she thought, *Maybe a student assistant will answer. If not, then I can hang up.* She felt the old cloak of deception fold around her like fog as she listened to the regular rings and the rollover signal and two rings in the department office before an unfamiliar masculine voice said, "Hello, English Department."

"I was trying to reach Dr. McFergus. Would you please tell me a good time to call him."

"Just a minute; I'll look up his schedule."

She wrote it down as the student read it aloud, and she thanked him. She didn't know whether she was frustrated or relieved that she wouldn't be able to reach Rob till the afternoon.

He answered: "Hello; Rob McFergus here."

She thought, *I can be calm. It's just Rob; whatever has happened these past months is over.* Then she felt the agitation of her heart. *Oh, no, Evelyn; you don't get off so easily as that. The body's ties are stronger. And the heart's.*

Rob spoke again. "Hello? Is anyone there?"

"Rob, it's Evelyn. Are you free to talk a few minutes?"

"Hold on just a minute."

She heard the receiver put down, and it was a moment before he returned.

"I'm here alone, and I closed the office door. What do you want? Is something wrong?"

"No. That's why I called. I wanted to tell you that things are all right for me."

There was a pause. "That's good."

"But you don't see why I had to call to tell you that."

"No. I can't say I don't give a damn, but I can say I don't know what good that does me."

"Are things . . . worse?"

"No. Things are just going on and on and on the same. Every day I struggle through the same things, guilt and anger."

"Judd said it would be hard for you."

"Judd. I hear you've been with him all the time lately. It's amazing how many people find it necessary to tell me that."

"Rob, that's one of the reasons I had to call you. You need to know two things about Judd and me. One is that I'll always love you, whether I love someone else or not. The other is that you have no reason to feel guilty . . . about me. I'll always remember what we had and prize it. Still, I'll go on living without you; you aren't responsible for me."

"Well, I guess that's good to know. Sometimes just being responsible for myself is too much, let alone for Trey and Marcia Lee."

"How are they?"

"Trey's all right. He's pretty normal, I think; at this point he just knows his mother's sick. I remember what that's like and try to let him know he's loved anyhow. He goes to nursery school while I teach. Marcia Lee's in a convalescent center. I go to see her every weekend, and Trey can see her too. We're trying . . . to work through things. I don't expect us to be like one of the families on TV where everything is great; maybe we can be some sort of family."

Something he and I can never be. "I hope it all works out. And if I can do anything for you, call me."

"Thank you."

The irony in his voice kept her from saying anything for a moment. Then all she dared was "You're welcome. Good-bye."

She was crying. She went into her bedroom and flung herself across the bed they had shared and would never share again. After a while she realized that that wasn't why she was crying; she was crying for the grief and pain he had and must continue to endure. She wanted him to be happy, and there was nothing she would ever be able to do to make him happy.

It would be all right if he could find happiness without her. And maybe that was what was happening. Hadn't Marcia Lee loved him enough to let him go, even to go to her, Evelyn?

And that was what she wanted to do now too: to let Rob be free of her love so he could love his wife. She felt the emotion wash through her like a cleansing flood: she wanted Rob to be happy, even without her.

That didn't mean she didn't love him. It meant that finally she really did love him, love him enough to want his happiness, not her own.

What did that mean about Judd? What about this reasonable love she had decided to have? Other women had accommodated themselves with reasonable loves; not many had known grand passions, she guessed. So she was lucky; at least she had had Rob. She could be satisfied with a reasonable love now, satisfied with companionship.

What about Judd? Was it fair to give him only the embers of her fire? Maybe she wasn't doing any favors for him either. But breaking with him didn't seem right for him or her. Maybe she never should have started this.

For the present, she could decide only not to tell Judd about the call; there was no need to hurt him with more references to Rob. She got up and went to look for facial tissues.

Since Evelyn wanted to learn about herself, Nina assigned a self-portrait for her first drawing. Sitting in front of the bathroom mirror dressed for the street or classroom, she tried to objectify herself. She wasn't happy with the resultant drawing.

She showed it to Judd, and he said, "You're posed for it; it's how you want to show yourself to others. Look in the mirror now; you don't look stiff like that."

She looked. Her hair fell loose over a satin nightgown with dropped shoulders and a ruffle of sleeve but deep, wide décolletage. And her face was different, open, not wary. She resolved to draw herself like that the next day.

The work went more smoothly. She forgot that it was herself she was drawing; she lost track of the time as she copied the lines. She liked the arch of the throat, so she echoed it in the drape of the satin and the fall of the hair. She named the drawing "Eva." Only "Mrs. Knight" would have fit the first.

The next day, she showed Nina both drawings, and Nina commented on the greater fluency and appeal of the second. "You've caught something about yourself here that the other drawing wouldn't suggest to anyone."

"Maybe I don't want anyone to see it. Or only a few, at least."

"Somewhere along the way, Evelyn, you'll have to decide whether you want to know yourself enough to risk letting others know you too."

"You know quite a bit about me—more than most people."

"Yes. Still, it isn't as if you'd chosen to show me what I know, is it?"

Evelyn didn't answer. For the next drawing she selected a dress that reminded her of a maternity dress she had worn with both pregnancies, and she drew herself cradling a child. *What I need is to be able to put all these into one picture, these and Evelyn playing a blue guitar and Evelyn dancing and Cressida and Jessie and Elaine and Mother and Granny and all the other women I am. And the things—a mockingbird, a pin oak, a*

moth—who knows what? Portrait of the Artist as a Middle-Aged Woman,
1980. More crowded than angels on the head of a pin. Could anyone make
sense of such a hodgepodge? Could even Judd find me, all of me?

And what a selfish pursuit anyhow—to spend my time trying to know
myself. Or to show others.

Judd too liked the second and third drawings better, although he
said, "Those still aren't what I see when I look at you, Eva. Maybe
when you're looking at yourself, you don't look the way you do
when you're looking at something else."

"Maybe I have to draw what I look at. Will you pose for me?"

He surprised her by shaking his head. "I don't think I want to risk
your looking at me that much."

"You're a handsome man, mysterious and intriguing. What do
you have to lose?" She smiled as she caressed his face.

Refusing to answer, he shook his head again. She let it drop.

The days had slowed as she filled them with Judd and the drawing
and her poems. Hurry was gone. She savored the clarity of the late-
October air, the lavender wild asters and blue ageratum and cerise
buckbush berries and scattered lingering honeysuckle, the turning
leaves and darkening cedars. Even the gray rain beautified the earth.
As she walked under her umbrella from Nina's class one afternoon,
she noticed how the tennis courts glistened like an enormous aqua
pool with a freestanding maple flaming behind it.

I could be like that. Why do I need Judd?

She didn't know the answer. Maybe it was like what she had told
Elaine, that she had to relate closely to some other person. Or maybe
it was just her upbringing, her generation. Maybe younger women
like Elaine could like the tree stand free, without men, without marriage. There was no intellectual reason they couldn't. At least as
much as men could stand free of women.

Could men?

Judd helped her select poems for her manuscript. Diffident at first, he gave perceptive if unacademic reasons for his choices. She mailed the manuscript to the first editor who had agreed to see it. She limited it to poems written before Rob; she felt that she needed more perspective on the last year before submitting its poems anywhere. She did notice as she went through those poems that imagery of rain, fog, and haze pervaded them.

When she passed the manuscript package to the postal clerk, she felt a loss. This fixed what she had been when she had written those poems; she could not change them any more than she could change the self she had been then.

She studied Jewish commentators on the story of the Fall in the Garden of Eden, and she wondered for the millionth time why Eve hadn't taken the fruit of the Tree of Life instead of the Tree of Knowledge. *What is life without knowledge? How can life be meaningful without choice, without the chance of evil as well as good? Aren't the two trees the same—living is knowing? Or learning, anyhow? Learning evil as well as good?*

The next morning she dreamed that she was driving up the snow-covered Going-to-the-Sun Road. It was schematized into a spiral around a single mountain, whose top was beyond her sight. It was almost like the frosting on a cake, with the snow spread evenly over the curving plane of the road in unbroken whiteness. There were no guard walls, but she was not afraid. The dream had no plot; she was just following the road upward, rising, seeing the same vistas from different levels.

Awake, she looked out her window into the November fog and thought of the construct for life that she had arrived at when she had begun teaching world literature: the Greek justification of suffering by learning, Milton's justification of free will and concomitant evil in the world by grace, and Goethe's justification of sin by growth. Did she still see them? Yes. But now she saw them in new ways, with new understandings and nuances. Her free will and suffering and sin had taken her to another level, and the vista was changed.

There are different answers for different people. And for the same person at different times. Keats was right for himself at his moment. Had he lived longer, he might have found something more beautiful than Fanny Brawne's uneven brows and crooked nose, something better to do than to burst Joy's grape. I wonder what answers I need to learn next.

Evelyn noticed scanty blooms on some of the shrubs when she went to class: viburnums and a snowball bush seemed to feel the continuing warm weather as a second spring. She resolved to check Judd's lilac bushes when she got home.

Her search was rewarded. She found three or four blooming limbs on his lilacs and some sparse forsythia blossoms. A look in the garage showed his car gone, so she couldn't ask permission; she took the flowers anyhow. She put them in her crystal vase and set them on the sunroom table; they caught the afternoon light, and the crystal shone like bright water.

Looking at them, she remembered Judd's face above the forsythia he had brought her in the spring. She thought of his eyes reflecting the gold of the blooms and giving light themselves. Something inside her unfolded; it was first a bursting, then a blossoming. *He knows me, and he loves me. And I know him and love him too. Loving Rob doesn't keep me from loving him too. I love Judd.* Light flooded through her.

She wanted to see him. She studied herself as she applied lip liner. She wanted to be beautiful for him, to give him something precious. She wished that she could bear her head to him like a flower poised on the living stem of her body.

She and Judd had developed a pattern for most of the nights since they had returned from their trip. Unless he had a night meeting, they ate dinner together: she cooked for him and they slept at her house, or he cooked for her or took her out and they slept at his. That afternoon she was in the kitchen when she heard him come in after his hospital rounds.

When they had kissed, she held him a moment longer to look at him and stroke his cheek.

Then he looked away, and she let go and turned to her dinner preparations again.

He said, "I saw your—Rob McFergus today."

She stopped rubbing garlic over the lamb roast. "Oh? Did you talk?"

"Just a greeting. He gave me a . . . strange look, though. He must know about us."

"Yes. I called and told him myself a while back." She looked for a reaction.

At least he didn't focus on empty space. But all that his face revealed was an intensity. "Does that . . . what does that mean?"

"It means I wanted to let him know that I'm happy with you so he wouldn't worry about me."

His brow puckered. "Are you happy . . . with me?"

It was another of those things that she had thought she didn't need to say, but obviously she did. She said, "You make me happy." The words might be inadequate; they were necessary.

He kissed her. When she leaned back from him, he took a long, deep breath, then let it out. His face looked naked, vulnerable, and she saw that she had gone on hurting him even after she had given herself to him. She had given her body and kept back what was really herself. Her own lip trembled. She said, "I love you, Judd."

He clasped her again, and she wished that she had given him the bald words sooner. She would have to continue reminding herself to nourish him as he did her.

When he returned to the kitchen after setting the table in the sunroom, he said, "However did you spirit the lilacs back from April?"

She smiled and said, "Actually, I stole them from my neighbor when he wasn't home this afternoon."

"You mean they were blooming there in my own yard?"

"Yes. I saw some other shrubs blooming on campus today, so I went looking for lilacs."

"That's why I love you—because you bring me lilacs in November."

"Another way of looking at it is that I take them from you, you know."

He shook his head. "No—they would have wasted their fragrance in the desert air before I found them."

"Then my theft is forgiven."

"I think I'll still collect my fine. Speaking of wasting, there's a perfectly gorgeous sunset being staged for our benefit out there, and we're ignoring it." Gripping her shoulders, he moved her, floury hands and all, into the sunroom.

A low bank of gray clouds was turning plum. Sunlight like liquid gold flowed through the veins of the clouds as their edges darkened into grape.

She said, "It's sundown on Friday; doesn't that signal the beginning of the Sabbath?"

"Yes . . . for those who keep the Sabbath. How do you know about that?"

"I do know the Old Testament at least . . . except whatever books are in your canon but not ours. And I've also been reading about Judaism. You don't celebrate . . . I probably don't say it right even . . . kiddush then?"

"No. Anna and I did sometimes, as a sort of memorial to our childhood. Giving thanks to . . . whatever gives us this." He gestured toward the sky, which had become a gray pearl with only a little blush at the horizon.

"Then you aren't Orthodox?"

"No, Eva. I—believe in something that gives life and wills our growth. But I can't limit that to a god who would choose me and my people and deny you and yours. Or anyone else."

"And I can't consider you damned forever unless you follow the rules I was brought up with."

"Do you believe in anything now?"

"Yes—I believe there is love in the universe."

"What makes you believe that?"

"You, dear one." She kissed his cheek. "And living. Just—creation. Now have I passed my catechism, Father?"

"Not quite. I still want to know why you read about kiddush."

She felt shy and ran her finger down a stripe in his shirt before she answered. "I want to know as much as I can about you. Although we're different, I want to understand you as well as I can. I'm glad you're different."

"The French had something to say along those lines: *Vive la différence*, I think?"

"I mean more than biology. I've been . . . very ingrown, with all those Hendersons and Laniers and Cutterfields and Montgomerys. It's time I recognized Adivinos and Changs and Radovskys."

He kissed her.

She went on. "I've been reading poems by your Sephardic bard too: he wrote some pretty passionate love lyrics as well as religious verse."

"They wouldn't have taught us those in Hebrew school."

"And I've been studying Sephardic cooking too. Actually, it's a lot like Southern cooking, especially Creole."

"Well, that's the Mediterranean influence for you. Maybe you can cook honey almond cake for me sometime; I remember my mother's. With all this study of my heritage, have you run across the marriage laws?"

She didn't look at him. "No."

"Then you don't know the implications of that last game you played in West Glacier."

She shook her head.

"Well, aside from a few technicalities like your being a godless Christian instead of a true daughter of Israel, one valid contract of marriage under Judaic law is the cohabitation of consenting adults. I wouldn't have pressed my legal point if you hadn't shown me your eagerness to accept my cuisine, literature, and rituals."

She stroked his familiar, alien face. It pleased her that her fingers marked him with flour. "So you've manipulated me into something else for my own good. Well, I suppose it's too late to regret what can't be remedied." She sighed histrionically.

After that kiss he said, "I don't suppose you'd oppose a marriage legal by the laws of the land too."

She smiled. "You know me—always following the rules."

"Except for flower theft and a few others."

"I knew you wouldn't let me get away with a couple of lilacs. I suppose I'll have to marry you to get any more."

"Yes indeed. I recognize my forsythia too."

"Well, it's a heavy price for a handful of blooms. On the other hand, Persephone ate only a few pomegranate seeds, so I suppose I'll have to pay too. If you don't let me get back to my bread, it's going to be a long time till it rises and I can feed you."

"I think we could fill the time profitably," he said. He did let go and followed her back into the kitchen.

She shaped the long loaf and stretched it diagonally across the baking sheet, which was greased and sprinkled with cornmeal. Then she took her sharpest knife, an ugly, rusty iron one that always took a good edge, and slashed the top at two-and-a-half-inch intervals. She looked sideways at him and grinned. "Doesn't this scare you?"

"You always scare me to death."

"You're pretty brave to say so. You scare me too, you know."

"If I ever stop, you'll probably leave me. That's why I asked you to marry me legally too."

"You've decided to make an honest woman out of me."

"It'll take more than a marriage license to do that, my dear. You have more layers than an onion, and I doubt if you know yourself what's at the core." He was smiling, but she knew he meant it.

"So that's why you asked me—so you can go on exploring?"

He smoothed the hair away from her temples. "Yes. That's why I ask you. Because I want to explore you for the rest of my life."

"You know that I'm not convinced there's anything here for you to find."

"And if there is, I couldn't find it. And if I could, I couldn't communicate it. Yes, I know all that. But I also know there's everything there, and I can find it, and we can communicate it to each other."

His hands were already telling her things she wanted to know, and she decided it would take a good forty-five minutes before the bread or anything else required her attention. "Like the fireflies." She closed her eyes and seemed to see them. "Everything's already here, and we just have to look."

"But we may not see the same things, Eva. And what I see today may not be what I see tomorrow."

"I know. Isn't it wonderful? We'll always be able to go on asking questions and finding answers, even if they change." She paused. "And the wonder is the change."

"That's a good thing to know."

"It *is* a good thing. To know. And to feel."

Acknowledgments

I thank all of you, relatives, students, colleagues, friends, and strangers, who have read my earlier books, especially those who have told me that you enjoyed them. I continue writing for you.

My editor, Sandra McCormack, and I have now worked together for more than seven years. I depend upon her tuned judgment and prize her friendship as well as her faith, patience, perseverance, and skill in helping me bring this series to completion. Her perception of what should be added has always been invaluable, and on this book she has also helped immensely in seeing what to cut and how to organize. Cal Morgan and Greg Cohn have always cheerfully aided me in business matters. I thank Joan Higgins and Lori Rick, hard-working publicists. The St. Martin's Press art and production departments have handled my work well. Sabrina Soares and Ted Johnson have been helpful copy editors.

I am, as always, grateful to my family for their support and help. Some of my husband's and children's college experiences and some altered conversations with my children appear in this book. My mother, the bridge player, checked my action about Evelyn's winning hand. Carol Kyle again graciously contributed to as well as tempered the book. Deborah Arfken, Tamara Baxter, Janet Blecha, Louise Clara, Bené Scanlon Cox, Neva Ferguson Friedenn, Susan Goodin, Jim Hiett, Dan and Joyce Jewell, Al Lawler, Mandy McDougal, Ruth Falk Redel, Virginia Thigpen, Phyllis Tickle, and Carolyn Wilson have been very supportive in many ways. I owe a belated thanks to Ron Watson for support of my first novel. My writers' group for this novel has been Janet Blecha, David Flynn, Mickey Hall, Jim Hiett, Jeanne Ireland, Dan Jewell, Al Lawler, Edmon Thomas, and Roland Whitsell. I value their many perceptive suggestions and their encouragement; this was an especially difficult novel for me, and they have given special assistance.

I have used information and/or anecdotes from David Black, Nancy Blomgren, Fred Blumberg, Louise Clara, Clement Dasch, David Flynn, Richard Harville, Jean E. Hardy, Hal Hooper, Allen Haynes, Carol Kyle, Janice Slaughter, Carl Spragg, Virginia Thigpen, and Angela Elliott Vallandingham. I am grateful to all these.

Before thanking my graduate school professors, I want to thank the academic dean of my undergraduate college, Howard Evans, without whom I would perhaps never have gone to graduate school and taught college. That I took no courses from him or his beautiful, intelligent wife Charlotte is one of the regrets of my Muskingum student career. I also have used the Muskingum world much more than that of Volunteer State Community College for the Harper College setting, and Davidson College, Belmont College, and Vanderbilt University have contributed bits and pieces, including sources for artwork. Except for a few minor references, I have not based characters on actual people from any of these schools. As always, I am grateful to the faculty, administration, staff, and students of Volunteer State Community College.

My best teacher ever was Merritt Yerkes Hughes, consummate scholar and gentleman. Other professors at the University of Wisconsin whom I remember fondly are Frederic B. Cassidy, Mark Eccles, John O. Lyons, Walter B. Rideout, Ricardo B. Quintana, and Alfred S. David, a charming summer visitor from Indiana.

Since I am writing mostly about the time of my own adulthood, I have few sources to cite other than those referred to in the text. *The Jewish Encyclopedia,* Faye Levy's cookbooks, and Abraham Millgram's *Jewish Worship* gave me wide-ranging information I needed. As in all my books set after 1919, *American Chronicle* by Lois and Alan Gordon helped immensely.

I read a condensation of *The Three Faces of Eve* when I was a teenager and knew as I wrote this book that the two had some relation. I reread the full version after the second draft of my novel (which already included references to the movie) was finished and realized that the structure (my Evelyn's three men, counting Greg and Rob as composite) and characterization both relate to the true account. The name Evelyn, committed to in my first sentence of *Private Knowledge,* may well be a subconscious reflection of that. Especially interesting to me was the discussion of intimacy at the end of the full version of *The Three Faces of Eve* (not, I think, part of the condensation I had read before), which reflects much of the difference between my Evelyn's relations to Ward and to Judd.

I am grateful to the following authors or publishers for permission to use quotations from the works cited:

Excerpt from "Animula" in *Collected Poems 1909–1962* by T. S. Eliot. Copyright 1936 by Harcourt Brace & Company. Copyright © 1964 by T. S. Eliot. Reprinted by permission of the publisher and Faber and Faber Limited.

Excerpt from *Woman in Love* by D. H. Lawrence. Copyright 1920, 1922 by D. H. Lawrence, renewed 1948, 1950 by Frieda Lawrence. Used by permission of Viking Penguin, a division of Penguin Books USA Inc.

Excerpt from *Mysticism* by Evelyn Underhill. Copyright © 1961 by E. P. Dutton. Used by permission of Dutton Signet, a division of Penguin Books USA Inc.

Some of Evelyn's poems are written especially for this book, and some have appeared under my own name in *Number One, The Hieroglyphic, Bubblework,* and *Southeastern Miscellany.* I am grateful to the editors of all these.